POR VIDA

POR VIDA

DANIEL VERASTIQUI

CHANNEL 8 PRESS
Austin, Texas

Cover design by Lauren Ellis

"There is no upgrade path for the soul."

- *From The Reflections of Noetica, Volume VII*

ONE

You never really stop being a soldier.

Even after you come home and take the uniform off, even as your memories of the war turn to nightmares, you never give up on the principles that define a warrior.

Courage. Commitment. Self-sacrifice.

Every man or woman who ever picked up a gun to defend this country knows that coming home can be the hardest part. Home is a paradise compared to Syria, Iran, or Afghanistan, but it's unfamiliar. Here, nothing is expected of us, and yet we're still the same people who ran head-first into the hail of bullets, the same people who dragged brothers and sisters, their legs or arms destroyed by IEDs, out of harm's way.

We never really stop fighting—whether that's against the dreams that come every night or the regrets we carry with us from our failures.

Failure to live up to the code.

Country. Corp. Family. Self.

A month ago, I managed to let all of them down in less than twenty-four hours. We knew the Máquinas were coming, and yet I made no effort to reenlist. When the machines crossed the border, the country fell, and I did nothing except focus on my family. All I could think about was getting them to safety, and I couldn't even do that.

The least of my commitments is to myself, but it's enough to keep me from putting a gun to my head. There is nothing left for me in this world, and yet I can't seem to leave it. That's not what warriors do. They don't run from the fight.

We are the fight.

In the few books I've read about PTSD, I've come across the theme of redemption a few times. Now I wonder how a man can truly serve himself after the apocalypse. Is it enough to merely stay alive, or is there a higher purpose? I don't mean any religious bullshit or spiritual destiny. When you get right down to it, *why* am I still here?

The country and the Corp are gone. Angie and Gretta are gone. It's just me and the bunker—my home at the end of the world.

But it's not all hopeless. I stocked the bunker in the hopes of bringing my future sons up for sleepovers and weekend-long games of *Aftermath:America*. I've got plenty of food, some weapons for hunting, and more movies and TV shows than a man could watch in two lifetimes. I'm sure there are bunkers out there better equipped for what's coming, all filled to the brim with MREs and faded copies of *Guns & Ammo*.

I was never a hardline prepper like those Lost Pines nutjobs from the '10s. Though we operated in the same circles, I didn't share the same worry that Iran was getting ready to invade and that we'd all be screwed because our own government was trying to disarm us. And no one truly believed the stories about domestic terrorists programming a MESH-transmitted virus that would turn everyone's brain into pudding.

Honestly, this was all supposed to be for fun. These walls protecting me from the elements and the synthetic killing machines were just an expensive goof. None of this was supposed to be real.

And for a while there, it didn't feel real.

After the war broke, after I lost my family, I stayed holed up in the bunker for two weeks straight, slowly losing my mind, coming ever closer to just shutting down and taking the easy way out. Later, when I finally did venture outside, it only reinforced what I already knew.

I was alone.

The first thing I noticed was the lack of MESH traffic. Despite being a peer-to-peer network, the MESH repeaters in Billings and Park City should have been casting a wide enough net to be heard up here in the mountains. With the MESH silent, that meant either there was no one left alive to transmit or they were too far away to be useful.

My only human contact at the time consisted of watching old videos of Angie and Gretta. Despite the pain of seeing them alive and happy, I kept watching, going all the way back to when Angie and I first met, our first trip to Vegas, to Big Sur, all of it. Sometimes I put them on a loop while I slept so I could dream of them.

Sure, I'd wake up crying, but you don't avoid drinking just because there's a hangover at the end.

The day I came out of the bunker, I'd told myself I couldn't keep hiding from the world—whatever state it happened to be in now. If my life meant nothing, then the only thing left was to give it to someone else. I tempted the fates making the trip to Billings, searching for other survivors, but only because I wanted to serve. I wanted to protect someone.

Maybe it's true that warriors need wars.

Or maybe it was selfish to want someone to take care of because it would make me feel okay about my continued existence.

For two weeks, I searched the mountains, avoiding predators both natural and unnatural. Máquinas, for all their killing prowess, have no gift for stealth. Stomping through the trees the way they do, they kick up a lot of noise, and that brings out the bears and the big cats and other beasts with sharp teeth. Even with training and a good weapon, I'm nowhere near the top of the food chain anymore.

I know for a fact that my Admiral 640-series Survival Bunker is not the only safe haven in the mountains. But either the owners of those bunkers never made it out of the city, or they were too scared to poke their heads out and greet me.

No other humans crossed my path. I went out twice a day and never met anyone.

Today was different though. Today my entire future coalesced into a single adrenaline-soaked moment. Meaning has returned to my life, and it feels like the bunker has pushed through to the surface and the walls have come down and I can breathe fresh air.

Angie, you would have been so proud of me.

I saved a life today.

It, too, doesn't feel real. Every time I get up to piss, I peek into Gretta's room just to make sure there's still a woman sleeping in there, tucked in under those princess pink sheets Gretta picked out herself.

You won't believe how she got here either. All this time I'd been searching under rocks for survivors. I should have been looking to the sky.

I was on my second trip out for the day when it all happened. I'd gone an hour up-mountain, but didn't stay long. The wind had come up and flakes were already starting to fall, so I headed back to the clearing when the sun was still a fist above the horizon. I'd seen some deer tracks on the way up, so I kept my Dragunov rifle at the ready in case some foolish buck wanted to be my dinner.

When I got back to the clearing, I found a Máquina waiting for me. That wasn't out of the ordinary; there were always one or two coming or going, usually the same synthetics operating on set patrols. By the askew beret, I knew it was my friend Mac. Normally, he just passed through, head not moving but eyes and ears taking in every piece of data available. Today, however, he stood rigid about two meters from the hidden bunker entrance, as if he were looking for patterns in the seemingly random arrangement of rocks and tree branches.

I had the drop on him, but the Dragunov is a firecracker of a weapon. I'd gotten the Vietnam-era rifle off a darknet trade some years back, and though I'd fired it at the range, I wasn't prepared for the noise it made the first time I fired it amongst the trees. The echoes lasted forever.

It was one thing to take down a deer and drag it back to the bunker before anyone came to investigate, but killing a Máquina? It was like the feeds always said: *where there's one synthetic killing machine, there's always another.* Somewhere in the forest around us, Mac's partner was stalking through the trees, maybe circling around me for an easy kill.

Whatever list of pros and cons I was building in my head was made moot by the distant sound of an engine. Mac and I both turned to the west and saw a single-prop Cessna fly low out of the setting sun. Mac broke off his investigation and moved to the center of the clearing.

Every last part of me wanted to signal the plane, to tell it *hey, I'm down here, and I'm fucking lonely,* but there was no time. It was too close, nearly overhead. What could I have done? Shot at it?

That's a stupid idea for a human, but evidently it was S.O.P. for a synthetic. Mac ripped off a dozen rounds from his FX-05 as the plane passed overhead. He went to a knee, pressed the short scope to his eye, and put the tap on full open. Distant pings echoed back. The engine began to labor, letting out a *chug-chug-chug* that reminded me of ancient cars on their last drop of gasoline. Black smoke trailed through the shimmering sky as the plane disappeared beyond the pines.

Mac stood and took off after it, and for a moment I thought the danger had passed. There was a clear path between me and the bunker, just a few meters to safety.

But that's not who I am, is it, Angie?

I'm the motherfucking fight.

I shadowed Mac from a safe distance, not wanting to let him know I was creeping up from behind. Each time his head turned, I stopped and took cover. This put me a hundred meters behind by the time we got to the crash site.

Once I could see the plane, I set up behind a tree and scoped the area with the Dragunov. Smoke drifted into the sky in thick, black clumps. Trees popped and crackled as their trunks burned. The plane had come to rest right-side-up, but its wings had come off and the tail was missing.

Downwind of the crash, I was treated to a sickening bouquet of smells: burning rubber, aviation fuel, and melting flesh.

I crawled on my stomach to a dense thicket about twenty meters from the left side of the plane. The blue and white paint job on the hull was marred with streaks of ash and soot. Wires and tubes hung from oblong holes where the wings had once attached.

The impact had busted every window.

Flames ate at the human silhouettes inside.

My heart sank. All dead. No survivors. Just me and Mac and a giant fucking beacon for all the drones to see.

Mac stood on the other side of the wreckage, the back of his head appearing hazy through the heat. He surveyed the crash with his rifle poised, ready to kill anything that might have survived.

As if anyone could be that lucky.

I was ready to pack it in when I heard it.

Heard *her*.

She was face-down on the loose pine needles, half-hidden by a smoldering wing.

Mac heard her too and moved into position behind her. I saw his black caterpillar of a finger inch its way onto the trigger.

She wasn't me, nor my family, nor the Corp, but in a plane that small, she had to be country. I knew right then what I had to do. And yet I hesitated.

Just a second. Just a brief, human moment.

And then she lifted her head, looked at me.

She was the first human I'd seen in a month, and suddenly it didn't matter if she died from her injuries right there in the dirt or on the way back to the bunker—I was *not* going to let Mac kill her. Even if it gave away my position.

Even if this was all for nothing.

I flipped the safety off and pushed the Dragunov's long barrel through the thicket.

"Hey, Mac," I said.

TWO

And I'll be dancing in the pain.

The altered JellyStar lyric repeated in Vida's brain as memories of flame burned through her synapses. Yellow and orange ghosts wavered all around her when she closed her eyes. They pulsed with an unbearable heat, as if some demon were breathing in the substance of her being and exhaling nothing but pain.

She was on her stomach. That much she knew.

Below the smell of smoke and ash, there was a pleasant aroma of pine. She felt the needles press into her cheeks, digging and relenting as she struggled to lift her head. Her splayed arms contracted, raising her shoulders from the dirt. Blood and tears obscured the world, but through the veil, she made out shapes of trees and undergrowth.

In front of her, something moved.

A long, black barrel pushed through a thicket, glinting in the golden flames she felt at her back.

She looked deeper, finally saw a lean face framed by a camouflage hoodie. He had pale skin and wide eyes that were as surprised to see her as she was to see him.

The barrel flashed. Something whizzed by above.

From behind, Vida heard the plink of metal hitting metal. Looking over her shoulder, she watched a headless man stumble in place, his arms flailing, before falling backwards into the fire.

Her vision snapped into focus.

The plane. The shapes in the windows.

Mouths open, screaming silently.

She tried to connect the shapes to her memories, but couldn't remember being on the plane, couldn't remember whether she knew the people who were now nothing more than ash.

"Can you move?"

Vida dug shaky fingers into the soft dirt and tried to drag herself away from the broken wing. Everything hurt, her legs barely responded, and above it all, a dull hum blanketed the world.

Her arms buckled. She fell into the dirt, picked herself up again, and stared at the pool of blood she had left behind.

The man eased through the thicket with the rifle pressed to his shoulder and the scope scanning the woods behind her.

"We don't have much time," he said. "They're coming."

Her fingers went numb, then her arms. She was six feet away from the man and yet it felt like a chasm separated them.

He paused, pressed the scope to his eye, and fired two shots into the trees.

"Now we really have to go," he said.

Vida lifted a hand to the stranger, not knowing if he was better or worse than the unknown danger closing in behind her. All she knew was overwhelming pain, and no good decision would come out of it. She felt her body withdrawing from the world.

Her senses dulled.

Her hand fell.

Flames turned to ash.

Ash turned to darkness.

* * *

I've come to believe the pain will never stop; the storm rages on.

A full minute went by before Vida realized she was awake, that the colorful mural on the ceiling above her wasn't a product of her dreams. The relative calmness of the small room made her wonder if perhaps the plane crash had been part of some nightmare, though it wouldn't explain why she was in an unfamiliar bed under unfamiliar sheets.

She took in the room, which was no bigger than a jail cell, rectangular, with one wall dedicated to closet space, and the other taken up by the bed. A fold-down desk hung on the wall near the foot of the bed. An LED strip and mirror filled in the space above it.

Vida pulled the sheets to her chin as a knock sounded at the door.

Her eyes jumped to the hangers on the closet door where her jacket, shirt, and pants hung, charred and streaked with dirt.

The door inched open, revealing the man who had saved her life. He was dressed in a faded Blake Shelton t-shirt and blue jeans, and if the dampness of his light brown hair were any indication, he had recently bathed. Gone was the fear in his eyes. Instead, he sipped casually from a thermos—the rich aroma of coffee wafted towards the bed. In his other hand, he held a glass of water.

"How are you feeling?" he asked. "I brought you some pills for the pain."

He held out the glass, but Vida didn't move to take it.

"It's okay," he said, "you're safe now." He flipped the desk down with his elbow and placed the water on it. Three blue pills dropped from his palm.

"Who are you?" Vida asked. "Where are we?"

"Two very good questions. I'm sorry I didn't have time to introduce myself earlier. My name is Doyle, and this is my bunker. I call her the Admiral. She's twenty feet below the Montana dirt, so you don't have to worry about any Máquinas getting in here."

Máquinas.

Vida tried to find meaning for the word, but nothing came. Panic welled in her chest. She felt exposed, naked, with nothing to protect her except a few blankets and her underwear.

"And what should I call you, ma'am?"

A spectral hand grasped her heart and squeezed in a slow, sickly rhythm. She saw Doyle's lips continue to move but heard nothing. A process had spun off from her internal programming, and it was racing between the infinite rows of her memory banks, looking for the answer to what should have been a simple question.

What is my name?

Vida began to shake.

As the question repeated, other questions joined it. *Where am I from? What came before the crash? Who am I?* The more the questions repeated, the louder they got, until the words themselves degenerated into clanging and crashing.

The tears came, warm and wet.

"Hey," said Doyle, kneeling next to the bed. "It's okay if you don't remember. Here, give me your hand." He took it without waiting for a response and guided it to the side of her head.

She felt damp gauze.

"You hit your head. You probably have a concussion. I tried not to let you fall asleep, but we had to double-time from the crash site before the Máquinas got to us. I'm sure your memories will come back to you. You just gotta give it time."

Vida thought about her family, saw the blurry faces of mom and dad. Everything else was shadow. She turned away from Doyle, shut her eyes, and cried.

After some time, Doyle spoke again, but his voice had lost its jubilance.

"My next words," he began, pausing to take a sip of coffee, "were going to be *nice to meet you.* Usually when people say that, they're just being polite. But now… you really don't know how happy I am that you came along. I've really been waiting for some sign of life from the world, and now you're here. The circumstances could be better, but the net-net is that you survived. You made it through the first month of the invasion, fell out of the sky without breaking any bones, and wound up safe here in the Admiral. Either you're the luckiest woman I've ever met, or God has a plan for you."

"I have no idea what you're talking about," said Vida, wiping her eyes.

"Don't worry," he replied. "All you need to know is that you're alive and safe. Something bad happened up there on the surface, but you'll remember soon enough. And if you don't, I'll fill you in. I almost envy you, not knowing what went down. I can't stop wondering how we're going to get past it. *If* we're going to get past it."

A mechanical hum filled the lull in conversation.

Vida stared blankly at the wall, tried to breathe despite the crushing pressure in her chest.

"You're probably hungry. I'll make us some dinner."

"What time is it?" she asked.

"1935 hours, um, seven thirty-five."

The next words caught in her throat.

"What day?

"November 7th, 2045. It's a Tuesday."

Vida shook her head. The date meant nothing to her.

"Do you like Mexican? I make a mean burrito."

"I don't know."

"Well," he said, groaning as he stood, "maybe it'll trigger a memory, verdad? There are some fresh clothes in the closet. They should fit. You look about the same size as…" He drifted off, unable to finish the sentence. "Well, when you're ready, join me in the solarium. Bathroom is out here to the right if you need it."

"Thanks."

"De nada, Vida."

She turned to face him, asked, "Huh?"

"That's what I'm gonna call you until you remember your name. It's nice, right? Spanish for *life*. Do you mind?"

Vida shook her throbbing head.

"The wife and I were learning Spanish before everything went to shit. I'm trying to keep it up in case a Máquina ever wants to have a conversation."

"Your wife?" asked Vida. "Is she here?"

Doyle bit his lip, shook his head. "I'll see you at dinner, Vida."

He pulled the door shut, leaving the room still and quiet. No cars driving by outside, no birds chirping beyond windows. It was almost as if the world outside didn't exist anymore.

Twenty feet under the dirt, she thought.

Buried in silence.

Vida pulled the covers back and swung her aching legs over the side of the bed. Despite the pain from before, they were largely unscathed. Her knees were red, skinned in a few places, but nothing was broken, no gashes oozed blood. She wore simple black underwear, lined at the edges with only a small amount of lace. Similar bra. She bristled at the idea of Doyle seeing her in such a state.

A scream rose in her throat, but she pulled it back. She wanted to cry for help, to beg her friends and family to rescue her.

I just can't see their faces through the pain.

Vida took a deep breath, decided there was no way to deal with the memory loss head-on. If Doyle was right, and she prayed (to whom?) he was, then all she needed to do was wait for the answers to come to her. In the meantime, her stomach rumbled.

She dressed in the clothes she found in the closet. The shirt was a little too big and much too flannel for her taste, but the sweatpants were warm and comfortable.

At the desk, she downed the three blue pills and chased them with the entire glass of water. In the mirror, she caught the slight edge of her reflection—just an ear poking through a wave of long, brown hair. Five little dots spoke to jewelry once worn but now missing.

Vida struggled to bring herself closer to the mirror.

Buzzing. Humming.

Something beyond the borders of her perception, waiting for her.

Was it a person? A husband? A child?

Maybe it was just the sum feeling of her previous life.

That was where she would be truly safe, not here with Doyle, not buried underground. Remembering home was only the first step of a much larger goal: getting there.

That was worth surviving for.

Vida opened the door and stepped out into the corridor.

From around the corner, she could hear Doyle singing in Spanish.

"Me enamoré, la primera vez, que te vi…"

She wondered what the words meant.

THREE

Construction advisory for U.S. Route 101 until January 10, 2035. Multiple accidents have been reported. Would you like to re-route?

Kagan looked up from his palette and squinted at the dashboard. The minimap showed the 101 outlined in crimson streaks. Surrounding arteries were a rosy shade, but at least they were moving. Orange and yellow icons showed three wrecks ahead, all before his exit to Santa Monica Boulevard.

"Re-route through Wilshire," said Kagan, his eyes lingering on the vidscreen to confirm Priya had heard him.

A tiny gear icon turned. The blue navigation line shifted.

Kagan returned to his palette.

There was an all-hands meeting at 9:30, and he was going to be late. That was sure to piss off his boss, Wayne, but it couldn't be helped. Los Angeles traffic wasn't about wondering if there would be a delay, but rather, how long the delay would be. Worst case scenario, Kagan could just join the meeting through the MESH.

He cleared the reminder for the meeting when it popped up. As the car turned onto Wilshire, he swiped aimlessly at the third and fourth pages of his news feed. They contained mostly ads and gossip pieces. VFeed was supposed to be tuned to his interests, but lately it seemed to be adjusting based on his demographics.

White male. Thirty-five years old. Single and looking.

Eastern European women in sheer black robes waved from tiny portals in his feed.

Hot Ukrainian Women Looking for Man Sex 24/7.

Even the spam was carefully tailored to his proclivities.

His finger traced over the vidscreen and tapped on a still frame from *Lost in Your Eyes*, a new drama starring Persian (read Iranian) actress Sepideh Ahmadi. The video played, showing a large fountain under a starry sky. Sepideh faded in, twirling in the darkness in a long, emerald gown. A voiceover about love. A flash of other characters.

Kagan focused on Sepideh's eyes.

How dark. How piercing.

Priya brought the car to a stop at Highland, and Kagan dragged the video into his *Watch Later* list. As he did, the advertisements on the page shifted to offers from Rakuten—other movies and TV shows starring Sepideh for only $29.99 each.

Outside, Wilshire bustled with early morning joggers and teenagers on hoverboards walking dogs. One woman's bright pink leggings and white sports bra caught Kagan's eye. Her ponytail swung from shoulder to shoulder as she ran. At the Highland light, she paused at the curb and ran in place. She checked her heart rate on her sliver.

Kagan saw the disheveled man in green fatigues before the jogger did. He held a cardboard sign in front of his ratty beard.

Veteran of the MX. Anything helps. God bless.

The vet approached the jogger from behind, his hand slightly outstretched as if to tap her on the elbow.

When she noticed him, she darted in front of a black sedan to cross the street.

Priya guided the car around the corner, and the homeless man stared inside. Something about his eyes and the curve of his nose struck Kagan as familiar.

"Do I…" he asked.

Sorry. I didn't catch that.

"Pull over."

The next available parking space is in two hundred and fifty-seven feet.

Kagan groaned and smacked the large red button on the vidscreen, enabling manual drive. He spotted a private driveway off to the right and pulled in.

The cool January morning kept him from overheating as he jogged back down Highland to Wilshire. The vet was still at the corner, though he had shuffled back to his regular position beneath the window of a Starbucks. Kagan patted his pockets as he got closer, found a folded twenty sticking out of his wallet.

"Here you go, bro," he said, holding out the cash.

The vet looked up, gave a weak smile, and reached for the offering.

His hand stopped in mid-air. Hard eyes softened, reddened.

"It *is* you, motherfucker," said Kagan.

The vet withdrew his hand, looked away.

"No speak English," he mumbled.

"Bullshit," said Kagan. He grabbed the man's wrist, flipped it over before he could pull it away. Faded, but still visible under the dirt was a small, black triangle, shaded thicker on one side.

"That was a long time ago," said the vet, snatching his arm back.

"No shit. What the hell happened to you, Raf?" He tapped the cardboard sign. "Is this true? Did you really end up in the MX?"

Rafael Orozco nodded weakly. He looked everywhere except Kagan's face. Finally, his eyes settled on the twenty.

"Can you spare that?" he asked.

"Fuck," said Kagan. He pulled out his wallet and emptied the cash. "Do you know the Plummer Tower at Fountain and Gardner?"

Rafael nodded as Kagan deposited the money in his hand.

"I've got a customer demo at eleven, but I should be able to bail at lunch. Get yourself a lift and meet me there at noon. Vitra Synth offices on forty. Can you remember that?"

"Yeah, I can remember that," said Raf, shoving the bills into his jacket. "Maybe I'll be there."

"No fucking maybe. You *will* be there. Delts por vida? Recuerdas?"

Wayne's voice pushed through the MESH.

Where are you, Kagan?

He checked his sliver. It was already nine forty-five.

"Gotta run," he said. "Plummer Tower. Fortieth floor. Noon. Don't make me come find you."

"Delts por vida," said Raf.

Kagan hurried back to his car, relieved to find it unmolested. The doors unlocked at his approach, and he eased into the driver's seat.

"Get me to work, fast."

I can get you to work safely, if that's what you're asking.

"Just go."

Priya coordinated with the traffic on Highland to open a hole large enough for her to back Kagan's Maserati into. He watched until they had rejoined the flow and then grabbed his palette from the passenger seat.

He searched through his email, dialing back the years until he found the last message from Rafael Orozco. It was dated October 5, 2024, and contained a picture of Raf in San Diego. Dressed in battle fatigues. Ready to ship out. Some kind of covert mission he wasn't allowed to talk about.

The message read:

Oye hermano, I'm shipping out today. This will probably be the last message you ever get from me. I've attached a picture for you to use in my obituary. Please don't touch yourself to it. Or if you do, please make it short. If I don't make it back, tell my mother I love her. Don't forget while you're sitting in your cozy, air-conditioned office that your best friend is out there somewhere in the world kicking ass. How fucking baddass is that? I knew this would happen someday, just like I knew you would pussy out. I don't blame you though. We all gotta play our parts. Cuídate, hermano. Por vida, para siempre. -Raf

Kagan read the email a few times, and when he looked up, the car was pulling into the underground garage at the Plummer Tower. Priya found Kagan's reserved spot next to the elevators and parked. The internal systems shut down as the cabin lights came on.

You have arrived at your destination. Battery is now charging.

Kagan grabbed his bag and headed for the elevator. As he stepped inside, he muttered, "Eleven fucking years."

Destination entered. Eleventh floor. Nixle Chronos, Inc. Offices are currently closed. Hours of operation—

"Cancel," said Kagan. "Take me to forty."

Destination entered. Fortieth floor. Vitra Synth. Offices opened at 7 a.m.

"Thanks."

You're welcome.

It was hard to believe Raf had been out of touch for so long. There was never any report of his death, but when no letters came after a year, then another, and another, Kagan had assumed the worst. The horror stories about Syria, Iraq, and the MX were front page news for years. Unlike news organizations of the previous century, media feeds like Lincoln Continental and VFeed didn't hesitate to post pictures of the casualties.

American soldiers dead. Ripped apart.

Sometimes, there would be a single MX Máquina splayed out over a small mountain of human bodies. Most times, it was just the bodies.

Official stats said that for every Máquina CPU smashed, the U.S. lost sixteen men. Sixteen living, breathing, rightful inhabitants of this earth. Kagan recalled the backlash when the casualties started racking up. The pressure on the government to do something. The flat-out refusal by Perion Synthetics to develop a synthetic soldier that could match a Máquina. If it hadn't been for Vinestead Synthetics stepping in, the human component of the military would have been decimated.

That was six years ago. Since then, the U.S. had replaced most of its fighting force with synthetics.

Soldiers like Raf would have been sent home.

They should have returned as heroes, living a life of government-sponsored, middle-class luxury.

Instead, he was covered in dirt and smelled like shit.

It wasn't right.

The elevator doors opened on the expansive open layout of the Vitra Synth offices. Sharp haircuts peeked over the tops of slate gray cubicle walls. Muted conversations filled the air, drowned out by the noise machines in the false ceiling. Sunlight poured in through floor-to-ceiling windows, bathing everything in a soft, yellow glow.

"Good morning, Mr. Kagan," said Jennavie, the receptionist-slash-actress. Her cobalt hair was up and her breasts were out, but Kagan wasn't in the mood for their typical banter.

He gave her a nod and proceeded down the row to her left.

The meeting room was at the other end of the floor, but even from a distance, Kagan could see Wayne Demeyer, Vitra Synth's Director of Operations, standing in front of a vidscreen wall, pointing enthusiastically at some chart he'd probably slapped together that morning.

The MESH crackled with greetings, some genuine, some more along the lines of *looks like daddy's boy decided to join us.* Earl Glasser poked his head out of the Blender Room to warn him that Wayne was pissed. Kagan merely shrugged.

As he got closer to the meeting room, Wayne's voice pushed through its glass walls.

"You've had three years to work on this, Mark. And every quarter you promise you're right around the corner. What's the hold-up?"

"You say that like the last three years have all been wasted, but our research has revealed more secrets about memory and synaptic storage than anyone else's. Ever. It's true, it's not a marketable product yet, but the building blocks are there."

Wayne put his hands on his hips, glanced at the glass walls, and spied Kagan.

About time, said Wayne, through the MESH.

The rest of the engineers heard the publicly broadcasted remark and turned to look at him.

Kagan paused in front of the door, his thoughts elsewhere.

Well? Are you coming in or not?

Kagan replied publicly. *Sorry, I shit myself.*

Eyes widened. Some of the engineers covered their mouths. Down the hall, Earl's laughter erupted from the Blender Room.

I was going to go shower in the gym, said Kagan, *but I could come in if you really need me.*

The static in the MESH cut out; Wayne had pushed everyone aside.

You're on thin ice, Kagan. Keep messing around and it won't matter who your daddy is. I'll have your ass out on the street.

Speaking of my ass, would you mind if I washed up?

Wayne waved him away, resumed his meeting.

Kagan continued on, taking a few turns until he arrived at his office. He dropped his bag on the desk and walked over to the window. His office faced east, and he could almost make out the buildings lining Wilshire. He wondered if Raf had gotten something to eat and whether he would show up at noon.

A ding sounded from his palette—a text message from Jennavie.

"Did you really poop yourself?" she asked.

"No, sweet cheeks," he wrote back. "Just letting Wayne know where we stand."

"You're so bad."

"Screw him."

"Why not me? Supply closet in ten?"

"Not today. Something's come up. Gonna head out at lunch."

She replied with a frowning emoticon.

Kagan scrolled through his own list of technicolor icons, clicked on a small pile of shit, complete with stink lines.

"Ew," she wrote back, and then went offline.

Wait 'til you smell Raf, he thought, and laughed.

FOUR

"Listen, Martin. We've got a very small window to make this happen," said Jane, "and I don't really see you doing anything to make this a good fit. If your studio wants Sepideh Ahmadi for their picture, then you'll set up a meeting this week. I can't guarantee we'll have any availability after that." She paused, listened for a moment while a tinny voice on the other end of the phone countered. "Oh, I don't know," Jane continued. "Maybe in 2036. I'll see if I can pencil you in then." She examined her gold nails. "No, *you're* out of your league, Martin. Sepideh is a rising star and an award-winning actress, and you're going to respect that if we're going to do business. Okay, fine, if you won't, I'm sure the Sierra Brothers will." A stray cuticle met its end. "Because we're pulling up in front of their building as we speak."

Jane tapped her screen and tossed the phone onto the bench seat next to her. "They'll call back," she said.

Across from her, Sepideh Ahmadi nodded. She'd only caught the tail end of the conversation, but she knew how important it was to keep pokers in every fire in Hollywood. Her agent hadn't been bluffing when she told Martin Dickson of Arvixe Pictures that Sepi had a meeting with the Sierra Brothers, but neither Jane nor Martin was of the belief that a meeting meant a casting or a paycheck. The Sierra Brothers were notoriously fickle, and coming off a string of three number one movies, they were riding high and heady.

The politics of it all made Sepi cringe, but Jane was right at home on a cell phone, yelling and making wild threats at some too-big-for-their-britches (as she put it) director who wanted an up-and-coming actress of Sepi's caliber to audition at an open call like she hadn't just been nominated for a BAFTA for her performance opposite Claire Danes in *The Dark Desert*.

Sepi toyed with the bangles on her wrist and smiled.

"Penny for your thoughts."

Sepi shrugged, turned to look out the tinted windows of the Bourbon Viking cab. The busy streets of Los Angeles scrolled by, held at a safe distance by thick glass.

"I was thinking what I'd do without you," said Sepi. "I wouldn't last a day."

"No, you wouldn't," said Jane, "but don't let that get you down. God gives each of us our own gifts. He gave you beauty and the ability to make people believe you're feeling something you're not. All I got was bad knees and wherewithal. But do you know what wherewithal gets you in this world?"

Sepi shook her head.

"Just about everything there is," said Jane.

Now arriving at Gaudier Plaza. We are third in line for a front-entrance drop-off. Please remain in the vehicle until the doors open.

"Alright, so we've got some time," said Jane, pulling her notebook from her purse. She didn't care much for palettes, instead preferring to keep her thoughts jotted down in flowery handwriting on actual paper. "I spoke to a woman named Esme at reception and she's got a private bathroom you can use to freshen up." She glanced at Sepi. "Not that you need it." Then, noticing Sepi's fingers slipping in and out of her bangles, said, "You're fidgeting. Did you take your meds this morning?"

"Yes…"

"Are you sure?"

Sepi nodded, but in her mind, she imagined the blue pill case on the vanity at home with its unopened *M* tab.

"Are you nervous about meeting the Sierra Brothers?" asked Jane. "These guys are barely old enough to rent a car. Don't let them intimidate you."

"It's not that. I just… I don't know if I want to do a science fiction picture. I want to be a serious actress, not another Elise Portman."

Jane pulled her rosy-framed glasses from her face. "Honey, sometimes we have to do things we're not crazy about. That's just part of being a woman. Dramas and period pieces will only expose you to so many people. We have to grab the bull by both horns and branch out into action, comedy, and yes, even the occasional sci-fi picture. So you play some computer nerd's wet dream. What's the harm? We get exposure. And who knows, maybe the movie will be good."

Sepi narrowed her eyes.

They shared a laugh.

Doors are now opening.

The sidewalk in front of Gaudier Plaza writhed with aggregators. Some wore the press badges of their respective feeds—Sepi spotted Banks Media and VFeed—but most were middle-aged freelancers dressed in khaki shorts and calf-high socks like they were hunting game on the savanna.

"Sepideh, Sepideh, over here!" called a scruffy man with more hair on his chin than his head. He had a dab of white sunblock on the bridge of his nose. "Show us a smile, darling. What are you doing here? Who are you meeting with? Tell us!"

"Does this look like an interview, you vultures?" asked Jane. "Be nice and maybe we'll stop for some pictures on the way out. And you…" She pointed to a short man in too-tight pants. "What was with re-posting those fake nudes? Are your subscribers so desperate?"

The man's smile peeked out from behind his camera.

Sepi shielded her face and made for the front door. It opened at her approach.

"I apologize for the crowd," said a woman from the left. She was dressed in a dark blue blouse and a black skirt. Her eyes had the subtle emptiness of a synthetic human. "I've already informed building security. They should be gone by the time you conclude your business."

"I'll believe it when I see it, Rosie," said Jane, drawing herself up. "Sepideh Ahmadi and Jane Zimmerman for SB Productions. Be a nice robot and get us an elevator, will you?"

"Of course, Ms. Zimmerman. I have one waiting. Please follow me."

Jane rummaged around in her purse for a moment. "And I left my phone in the cab." She sighed, shook her head.

"I'll go with you," said Sepi.

"No, you go upstairs with Rosie—"

"My name is Carmen, madam," said the synthetic.

Jane waved the interruption away. "Esme is waiting for you. She'll show you to the room so you can freshen up. By the time you're done, I'll be back, and we can go land you that lead role in whatever science fiction nonsense these two idiots have cooked up."

"But…"

"You can do this, Sepideh."

Sepi watched Jane disappear through the front doors. Outside, she shook a finger at a nearby aggregator.

"If you will follow me," said Carmen.

The air in the elevator was stale, and the walls appeared to be pushing inward. Each passing second doubled the heat in the car. Sepi held her breath, tried not to let her lungs get out ahead of her. She felt Carmen judging her human frailty.

Finally, the door opened, and Sepi rushed forward, drawing in a deep breath.

"Now that's an entrance," said a male voice.

Sepi looked up and saw it had come from Richard Sierra, one half of the Sierra Brothers. He was tall and angular, with dark brown hair cut close to his head. His suit fit just-so, as if it had been constructed around him. He stood with an elbow on the reception counter and the other hand outstretched towards a young woman in a white cardigan. Her gold name tag read *Esme*.

"Usually people are out of breath when they take the stairs, not the elevator," said another voice. Sepi recognized him as Lawrence Sierra, the younger and shorter of the two. He wore a Los Angeles Rams t-shirt and frayed cargo shorts. His bare feet clashed with the polished hardwood floors.

"Forgive my brother," said Richard. "He's not bright. Have you ever seen that movie *Twins*? It's like that, only with brains."

"Hey, this brain got us *Stavanger Transcending*," said Lawrence. "And that made almost a billion international."

Richard nodded genially at his brother, then asked Sepi, "Can we bring you anything? Water, coffee? Esme can get you whatever you like."

The receptionist came out from behind the desk with her hands folded in front of her.

"Oh," continued Richard, "I promised her she could geek out for twenty seconds. Do you mind?"

Sepi shook her head, wondered what was taking Jane so long.

"It's an honor to meet you, Ms. Ahmadi," said Esme. "I've seen all of your movies and TV shows. I wasn't even a fan of *CSI* until you guest-starred."

Sepi put her hand out and seeing the nervousness in Esme put her at ease. Being an actress didn't just mean performing when the cameras were rolling; there was always a part to play, even when it was just four people standing around a reception area. The public had an image of Sepideh as a confident, serious actress who could conquer the most demanding roles. In the absence of her medication, the only thing that calmed her nerves was playing that character.

I am no longer Sepi, she thought.

I'm award-winning actress Sepideh Ahmadi.

She pulled Esme in for a hug.

"Thank you," she said. "It's always nice to meet someone who enjoys what I do. Would you like a picture together?"

Esme's eyes widened. "Could we?" She pulled out her palette but hesitated to hand it to Richard.

Sepi took it and held it out. "Would you mind, Richard?"

He smirked and got into position to take the picture. "Alright, on three, say *blockbuster*."

"Cheese," said Sepi.

"Thank you, thank you," said Esme. "So what did you say you wanted? Water?"

"I didn't, but a water would be nice."

"Mr. Sierra?"

"Blue Rain," said Richard.

Esme retreated down a hallway to the left.

"Nothing for me, thanks," Lawrence called after her.

Richard gestured to the right. "Let me show you around."

Sepi followed him down a long corridor while Lawrence trailed behind. Spotlights on the walls highlighted movie posters, most of which Sepi didn't recognize. For every tidbit of explanation Richard gave out, Lawrence added something sarcastic.

"This was the first film we did out of high school, *Binary Bastards*."

"It was a B-movie," said Lawrence. "Get it?"

"Fantastic pun," she replied, crinkling her nose at the caustic body spray wafting from the younger brother.

"Not our best idea, I admit," said Richard. He stopped in front of a poster for *Lone Net Ranger: The True Story of Johnny San Vito*. "But here's the one that did it for us. 1.2 billion domestic, 3.5 worldwide. Very popular in China for some reason."

Sepi glanced back at Lawrence for his additional commentary, but he just smiled, looked away.

Richard led her around a corner and then paused to glance at a grid of vidscreens on the wall. Various feeds scrolled, fading pictures in and out before Sepi could really look at them. Richard seemed to absorb it all at once. He reached out and slowed one of the streams.

Twenty-nine dead in Juarez–El Paso incursion. Vinestead synthetics suffer heavy losses.

MESH users complaining of headaches, nosebleeds. CEO Lucas Cotton dismisses claims.

Iranian-American actress Sepideh Ahmadi spotted at Gaudier Plaza. Rumored to be in talks with Sierra Brothers to star in upcoming Kaili Zabora biopic alongside Ever Jovovich.

"Ha," said Sepi. "Is that why you invited me here? You know Kaili Zabora wasn't Persian, right?"

"And John Connor wasn't British," said Lawrence. "People won't know the difference."

"It's just one of the many ideas we're kicking around," said Richard.

"Space operas," said Lawrence.

"Yeah, space operas."

"*Breasts of Betelgeuse*."

"What? No."

"*Jugs of Jupiter*."

Richard closed his heads and sighed.

"*Alpha Centauri… is Full of Tits*." Lawrence laughed to himself.

"Please forgive my brother," said Richard. "Now and in the future."

Esme returned with a small wooden tray containing three drinks. She handed the mildly perspiring glass of water to Sepi.

"Carmen just informed me that Ms. Zimmerman is on her way up."

"Great," said Richard. "Lar, will you please meet her up front? Esme, could you grab the blue palettes from my office?"

"Yes, Mr. Sierra."

"Yes, Mr. Sierra," said Lawrence, throwing up a faux salute.

The smell of AXE receded.

"So," said Richard, stepping closer, "I suppose we only have a few minutes before our respective better halves come back. I'll be blunt, Sepideh. We want to make the most epic movie ever attempted, and we need you to be a part of that. Each of our last movies outearned its predecessor, and your career has followed a similar path. Together, we make a very lucrative combination."

"Why are you telling me this?" asked Sepi, feeling the vidscreen alcove growing smaller.

"Because, you seem like a nice person. Esme is not the only one who's seen all of your work. You were sensational in *Seven Kingdoms*. I think you're an immensely talented actress."

Richard's eyes softened; he slipped his hands into his trousers, drawing Sepi's eyes down involuntarily.

"I feel like there's a *but* coming," she said, looking away.

"It's about Lawrence. He's not exactly the easiest person to work with. Brilliant as a director, I admit, but something's not quite right in his brain. He doesn't see a boundary between professional and personal, especially when it comes to attractive women. I have no doubt a collaboration would make a huge profit, but if you're uncomfortable getting into bed with a man who doesn't know when to keep his mouth shut, well, then..." He seemed to lose his train of thought, searched for more words but found none.

Sepi smiled, put her hand on her chest. She'd played this part in *The Faceless*.

"Are you worried about my virtue, Mr. Sierra? Do you think I can't hold my own against your brother?"

"I think that's exactly what he'd like." A smile. Perfect teeth.

The walls stopped contracting, turned to ether, and melted away.

"You sneaky sneak!" yelled Jane from down the hall. Her body jiggled under her blouse as she trotted down the corridor. "What did he promise you? What did you agree to?"

"Nothing," said Sepi.

"Then why are you smiling?"

"I told a funny joke," said Richard.

"Oh really?" Jane crossed her arms. "Tell me. I love jokes."

"What do you call a woman with two black eyes?" asked Lawrence.

Richard glared at his brother.

"The lounge is ready for you, Mr. Sierra."

"Thank you, Esme," said Richard. "Ladies, shall we?"

FIVE

Doyle's Journal - November 7, 2045

It wasn't supposed to be like this.

War was something that happened across the street, maybe even on our porch, but not in our house. Not to Americans. No country or terrorist organization on earth would have dared to step foot on American soil looking for a fight. The only people we allowed to kill Americans were other Americans: domestic terrorists, eco-warriors, cyber-hacktivists, local police forces, and so on. But those groups were more of a nuisance than anything else, a fabricated threat used by the government to justify domestic surveillance.

We had a delicate balance of bombing distant lands while spilling our own blood on ours.

But then came those damn Máquinas.

Suddenly the war wasn't in some remote desert on the other side of the world; it was in the MX, on our border. The government told us there was nothing to worry about, but the feeds painted a different picture, one about an MX closer to synthetic technology than anyone knew.

When the Máquinas started coming over the border, nobody knew what to do. The media feeds had been right all along, but what did that get us? President Meyer responded with negotiations and diplomatic talks. Even the United Nations got involved.

All the while, the MX government was claiming there was no war. They assured us they had no intention of invading the United States.

Then one day, radio silence.

Then the killing.

Borders fell. People panicked.

I lost everything in the scrum. I watched friends die, watched Máquinas stalk the streets of Billings with impunity. Within hours of the first incursion, VNet went offline, and the MESH turned to static. Slivers went dark. Cell service was nonexistent.

We were all alone.

We.

Angela, my wife of ten years.

Gretta, my daughter of eight.

I don't remember being scared or worried for them when the country got FUBAR'd. All I had to do was get them to the bunker and everything would have been fine.

You might think that after years of preparation and practice that it would have been as easy as a Saturday trip to the lake. Looking back, I see now that those trips we took every few weekends were not good trial runs. They were too peaceful, too lazy in their execution. I never accounted for the clogged roads, the frightened civvies, and hundreds of thousands of Máquinas falling from the goddamn sky like a black rain.

The average person stood no chance against them.

We got within two miles of the bunker and I was running through the trees with Gretta held to my chest when my world truly ended.

I don't know why I ever let Angie get behind me. It only made it easier for the Máquina to sneak up on her.

The scream that came from my wife… I had never heard anything like it.

When I turned to see what had happened, she was already flying through the air. I dropped Gretta without thinking and took the full force of Angie's skull in my chest. The impact fractured my sternum. I fell back, gasped for air, and that's when I saw him.

Six feet tall. Not muscular, but not thin. Nondescript face of muddled MX features.

No glowing red eyes like you see in the movies, no exposed circuitry. Nothing to really separate it from a human except a dull look of disinterest.

That and the careless way it picked Gretta up by the arm, wrenching bone through skin before grabbing her by the throat.

I caught my breath, pulled my gun.

I watched the sights of the Sig Sauer 9mm tremble in my outstretched hand. It was the first time I'd pointed a gun at someone since Syria, if you didn't count the paper targets at Harmony Range. Adrenaline greeted me like an old friend, but its handshake sent tremors through my arms. I dug my back heel into the dirt and put a supporting hand under the gun's grip.

"Let her go," I said, teeth gritted.

The Máquina paused to consider me, but didn't release its hold on Gretta. My brave girl tried to fight back. She clawed at the metal hand around her neck and scraped bits of flesh from the endoskeleton.

There it was: the machine hiding beneath the man.

"I'm not going to ask again."

Eyes as brown as yours or mine flickered left and right, scanning the forest floor, lingering on Angie's motionless body.

Gretta gasped as the Máquina tightened its grip. It held her out to the side and barked at me in Spanish.

"You will not survive what is coming," it said.

"Chinga tu madre," I replied.

I squeezed the trigger, rocked gently through the Sig Sauer's double action, and ripped a ten-centimeter gash in the Máquina's left cheek. The skin fell away, revealing synthetic tendons pushing and pulling through oily sinew.

Fired again.

I grouped three slugs on the MX emblem on the Máquina's chest. You would have thought I lightly coughed on him the way it reacted. It looked skyward to a passing cargo plane as if bored. A string of black specks trailed behind it.

The Máquina threw Gretta to the ground but my sweet girl didn't cry out.

I drained the Sig's clip to the very bottom.

It rushed me, pushing through the hail of bullets as if they were gently falling snowflakes. Metal pinged off hardened chest plates and tore through its lightly armored arms and neck. A russet-black liquid flowed from the many wounds (assuming you can call them that). Once the Máquina got its hands on me, I smelled the liquid's acidic odor.

A metal fist pushed through the loose shards of my sternum.

An exposed tree root took me to the ground. I pulled the Máquina down with me, and we fell onto a blanket of pine needles.

"Die," it said, spitting a sticky oil onto my face.

"Tu primero, pinche tostadora," I replied.

You first, you fucking toaster.

I shoved the Sig into the Máquina's abdomen and pulled the trigger.

Click.

I had forgotten.

Cold, metal fingers closed around my throat. I grabbed its face, tried to bury my thumbs in its eyes. I tore at the gash I had opened with the Sig, pulled on the small tendons, which only made the Máquina open its mouth as if it were yawning.

The world started to darken and it didn't even matter to me.

Or wouldn't have, had I not heard Gretta whimpering.

My hands were covered in its oily blood, but I was able to grab hold of some loose flesh. I tore a line down the Máquina's cheek and exposed the underside of its chin. Inside, the crisscrossing sinew was less dense, and obscured in its shadows, something glowed red. The image of a hamster running in a wheel popped into my head. I don't know why.

Maybe it was the Máquina's grip on my neck cutting off the oxygen to my brain.

The end was coming.

As I began to die, I thought about Gretta, about what the Máquina would do to her with me gone. Would it kill her outright? Or take her prisoner? Or something I couldn't even imagine?

Seconds of my life remained.

I used one of them to draw my knife from my belt.

Another to thread it through the Máquina's arms.

The last to shove it up into its throat.

Razor-like fingernails pierced my neck.

The blade was just long enough to hit something vital. The Máquina went rigid and then fell to the side, taking a good portion of my throat with it.

Blood that should have been returning to my brain now flowed from the left side of my neck. The pain was more intense than anything I'd felt in years. At least when I was enlisted I had a mil-spec Avenging Angel biochip to lock the pain down. The civilian model Guardian Angel they'd replaced it with after my discharge just couldn't handle that level of stress. It churned and burned and turned the sky a million different colors.

I watched the black specks swirl in the technicolor dome.

Reinforcements.

They'd be crash-landing any minute now.

Gretta's cries brought me back, gave me the strength to not slip quietly into the darkness.

With a hand on my throat, I rolled over onto my stomach and pulled myself along the pine needles and dirt until I reached Angie's body.

There was no time to say goodbye. I kissed the blood on her lips and pulled the scarf from her neck to wrap around mine. I tied it, untied it, tied it again. Getting the right balance between stemming the blood and allowing me to breathe took longer than I had hoped.

Overhead, a low-flying drone—a U.S. Jatayu by its markings—made a pass over the forest. A smaller drone—a *Plomo*, the MX version of our Strix Surgical Striker—trailed behind it. Before both disappeared from view, the *Plomo* loosed a pair of rockets at the Jatayu. I didn't see if they hit.

Blood pooled on my chest.

I wouldn't survive another encounter with a Máquina. Hell, at the time, I didn't know if I would survive the current one.

Finally, my Guardian Angel caught up with the incoming pain messages and began running interference. I got up, ran towards Gretta, and scooped her up. We took off deeper into the forest.

I could hear explosions.

Semi-automatic fire.

My boots crunching in the undergrowth.

In my mind, I saw the warm bunks of the Admiral through a rosy filter.

Warmth. Safety. A place to wait out the storm.

God, I loved Gretta. Loved her with everything I had. They say you don't truly know love until you have a child. I never bought into that, at least not until I was staring down at this tiny, scrunched face as it wailed and wailed. She came into the world screaming *I'm here, I'm here, what the fuck is all this?*

She was curiosity on two legs. She kept Angie and me together during the rough times.

We watched her grow together. Watched her eyes widen and soften and narrow and shimmer.

She loved the world with an intensity I had never felt, nor could remember from my own childhood.

Eight years was not enough.

Not enough for anyone, but especially for her.

It's strange now to think of eight years being a short time when the world can change so suddenly. One minute, you're eating breakfast with your wife and daughter. The next, you're covered in blood, racing through the wild from murderous, semi-sentient machines.

It's like every moment, you have to keep saying, "This is how the world is."

You can't get too attached to any one reality.

There's always another one just around the corner.

Or maybe it's already here and you just don't know it yet.

The trees gave way to a circular clearing that backed up to the sheer side of the mountain. Hidden in the rock was a door and behind that door was sanctuary.

I sprinted across the clearing, praying no Máquina was close behind. My heart pounded in my ears. My muscles spasmed. I stumbled twice, finally fell. So close to the entrance I could smell the MREs.

That's when I heard it.

No gunfire. No drones. Just silence.

I didn't want to look down. Couldn't.

Silence.

Silence where there should have been crying.

Silence where there should have been a helpless daughter pleading for her mother.

I rocked Gretta in my arms. She didn't move.

I had another clip for the Sig Sauer in my back pocket; I felt it digging into my leg. Maybe it was time to call it a day. The Machine War wouldn't be decided by me. What could a single, slightly overweight former soldier do about anything anyway?

I'd already failed to protect my family. What hope did I have of protecting the country? Or humanity, for that matter?

Why would I even want to?

Later, after I'd had time to think about it, I would find my own answer, but that first day, I was a bullet's length away from giving up.

It had all gone off the rails. Every last car.

I'd lost Angie, who had held my hand through the PTSD.

I'd lost Gretta, who had shown me there could be a world after all the killing.

I wasn't ready for that.

I had prepared for a different reality, had stocked the bunker for recreation and survival. Even with its moderate number of supplies, it could have supported us for years.

The best laid plans, destroyed by my inability to get my family to the ark in time for the flood.

I hope they can forgive me.

Because I won't.

SIX

The bunker was roomier than she expected.

Though Doyle sounded like he was banging pots and pans just inside Vida's ear canal, he was actually on the far side of an expansive living area. The kitchen was to the left, sectioned off with an island that also served as a dining table. To the right, the living area contained a loveseat and plush chair that formed an *L* in the corner. A wide vidscreen covered most of the wall directly across from her. Dormant, it echoed back a shadowy reflection of the room.

"No puedo vivir con este dolor," sang Doyle.

He poured oil into a small saucepan and dumped in a can of refried beans. When he noticed Vida approaching, he grabbed the bowl of chips he had been snacking on and moved it to the island.

"Thank you," said Vida.

"My pleasure."

"No, I mean, thank you for rescuing me. You didn't have to do that."

He paused, smirked. "I'm just happy to have someone to talk to. Or someone to whom to talk. I don't know." He turned back to the stove, stirred the beans.

"I'm not sure there's much to talk about. I don't even remember being in the plane."

"You'll remember soon enough," said Doyle. "What's going to be fun is seeing how this temporary you matches up with the real you later. Flour or corn?"

"Corn, please."

He pointed a glistening spatula at her. "See? How did you know that?"

Vida cocked her head, tried to recall her last memory of a tortilla. Instead of a hazy flash of lunch with friends, with margaritas and salty chips, all that came out of the gloom was pressure, something invisible pushing hard against her chest, compressing her lungs, squeezing tears from her eyes, twisting—

"Oh, hey, I'm sorry," said Doyle. He came to the other side of the island and put his hands on the steel surface. "I didn't mean to upset you. I can't even imagine what it's like to not remember your life. It's unsettling. I make jokes, bad jokes, when I can't deal with the horror of something. My wife hated it."

Vida wiped the corner of her eye. "I'm sorry about your wife."

Doyle forced a shrug, returned to the stove. "I try not to think about it. Sometimes, I imagine it was just me who left that old world. They're still alive and well, going about their daily routines, maybe a little sad that I'm gone, but they're safe and well-fed and life will go on for them. But me? I transcended some border with an alternate reality and found myself here in this nightmare. Before you came along, it was easier to believe I was the only one left in this reality." He pondered something. "This could have been my personal hell. Which makes you…" Turning, he leveled an accusing finger. "…the devil."

Vida scoffed.

"But," he continued, "company is company, my daddy always used to say." He flipped the corn tortillas on the skillet. "So, is there anything you remember at all?"

Vida searched for answers in the bowl of chips.

"There's nothing there," she said. "It's hard to explain."

"So if I asked you something like… what are three books you'd take with you if you were stuck in a bunker at the end of the world?"

"That's easy. *Letters to Veronica Plath*, the *Witches* series, and…"

Doyle stared at her over his shoulder.

Vida's eyes widened. Where had that information come from?

"Very cool," said Doyle. "See? All that stuff is still locked in there. Getting it out is just muscle memory. Quick, who's the President of the United States? Don't think, just answer."

"Emmett Fitz-Hume? Is that right?"

"No," chuckled Doyle. "Not even close." He turned around and slid a plate across the table.

Two open tacos stared back at her.

"Is this chorizo?" asked Vida.

"Why? Are you a vegetarian?"

"I don't know. Maybe."

Doyle shook the spatula at the plate. "Soy-rizo! Good for vegetarians, Jews, and *moz-lums* alike."

"And what is your faith?" she asked.

"Seventh Day Admiralist," said Doyle. He fixed himself a plate and ate standing at the sink. "I believe in one bunker, the Admiral almighty, protector of Doyle and Vida and the American Way. I give Her thanks and praise." He lifted his plate in offering.

"You're kind of a fool, aren't you?"

"Some women find it endearing."

"What's your wife's name?"

"Angela, Angie for short. She found it endearing enough to marry me. After that, she grew tired of it. Hopefully we'll be out of this bunker before it begins to grate on you."

"Too late," she teased. The taco was warm and soft. It tasted like home.

A minute passed; sounds of chewing filled the bunker.

"Sometimes I feel trapped in here," said Doyle, looking around the room. "I mean, I *wanted* this. I chose this before the war started. The alternative is life out there, waiting to be rescued by a government that may not exist anymore. I can't travel very far, and the MESH is dead quiet everywhere I go, so I have no clue how widespread this is."

"You said we're in Montana?"

He nodded. "Yep. I'm hoping the invasion focused on the western half of the country where we border the MX. D.C. could still be there. East Coast could still be there."

Doyle seemed to deflate, and he grew somber. He quietly finished his meal, took Vida's plate when she was done, and put them in the sink. He paced the small kitchen.

"Is something wrong?" she asked.

"Not really," he replied, "I just… we need to have a conversation."

"I thought we were having one."

"A *real* conversation." His hands were on his hips, but one slipped behind his back. It returned with a black handgun he laid gently on the table in front of him.

Vida held her breath.

"You were out cold for a while. It gave me a lot of time to think about the reality of this situation. My primary goal is survival, and I'm sure you'd like to keep living as well. Problem is, I don't know you, and you don't know me. We have no reason to trust each other."

Vida shifted on the barstool. Her toes wrapped around the footrest.

"But to survive, together, here in this bunker, we have to have that trust." He cleared his throat. "I don't want anything from you in exchange for room and board here in the Admiral. If we can be civil, maybe even friends one day, then that's good enough for me. I stocked this place for two and a half people. It's more than enough for the both of us.

"That said, I consider all of this mine, and I won't let someone take it from me. Happy to share, but I will not relinquish it. I'm a veteran of two foreign occupations. I've gone toe-to-toe with Máquinas and lived to tell the tale." He rubbed the scars on his neck. "You have no idea what I've had to go through to get here, Vida. I'm more than capable of defending myself. Do you understand what I'm saying?"

Vida nodded. "You have the gun. You're in charge." The door was directly behind her. She could throw her water at his face and escape while he was distracted.

"No," he sighed, "that's not it." He picked up the gun, checked the chamber and the safety, and slid it across the table to her. "Sig Sauer P226 9mm handgun. Sixteen in the clip and one in the hole. Safety's on. That's yours now."

An impulse swept through Vida, telling her to grab the gun, point it at Doyle, and force him to open the bunker door so she could leave. Instead, she asked, "What do I need this for?"

"You don't remember what happened when the war started. I have a bad feeling as memories start to come back to you, you're going to want to go outside and see it all for yourself. Worse, you're gonna do it while I'm out scavenging or looking for survivors. Unarmed, you stand zero chance of making it back here safely without anyone—human or Máquina—discovering the location of the Admiral. With the Sig, I'd say that chance jumps to ten percent."

Vida picked up the gun, considered its weight.

"Mostly, I want you to feel safe in here. With me."

She looked up, saw the softness in his eyes.

"I wouldn't want to be in a situation with someone who was stronger than, better trained than, and more willing than me to do whatever it takes to survive. This isn't some gender role bullshit either; it's simple fact. With that gun, you have a much better chance of defending yourself against me. I swear on my Angie's soul that you'll never have reason to, but the thought *will* cross your mind at some point. Can I really trust him? Am I safe here? That there is your piece of mind."

"This doesn't feel right," she said, holding the gun out to her right. "I don't think I've ever fired one of these before."

"Well, we don't have the luxury of target practice, in here or out there. But at these ranges, you don't really need to be a marksman to put me down. Just point and shoot."

Vida nodded. After a moment, she asked, "Will you turn around, please?"

"Um, sure," he replied, facing the sink.

Vida lifted the gun, pointed it at his back, and waited. She eyed her thumb next to the safety. Would it move? Would something inside her tell her to switch it off and fire?

After a while, Doyle asked, "Are we good?"

"Yeah," said Vida. "Just had to be sure."

"Sure of what?"

"That I'm not the kind of woman who can shoot a man in the back, especially one who's just trying to help her. You're right, Doyle. I don't know you. I don't know what kind of man you are except that you put your own life at risk to save mine."

"Yeah, well…"

"And the funny thing is," she continued, "is that neither of us know whether my life was worth saving."

The gloom crept in.

Doyle's voice dimmed to almost a whisper. "All life is precious. The ones I took in Syria and Afghanistan. The ones I'm protecting today. So many people have been slaughtered by the Máquinas. Now is not the time to be worrying about whether we deserve to live. All you need to focus on is *wanting* to live. Do you *want* to live, Vida?"

She nodded, automatically, as she considered the question.

"Things will get better. We will find meaning for our continued existence."

"How can you be so sure?"

"Allah commands it," he said, smirking.

"That's blasphemy."

"Half the people on Earth that we know of don't believe in God. You're not being very tolerant, young lady."

Vida groaned. "I don't even know how old I am."

"She's a young thing, yeah, yeah," sang Doyle.

"What's that from?"

"And she'll always be fi-i-ine," he continued. Then turning, throwing his hands into the air, he belted, "A young thing's got something all the boys crave."

Vida squeezed the gun a little tighter.

SEVEN

Kagan disliked all of his father's friends to varying degrees, but none more than Lucasz Abat. The 95-year-old former CEO, former congressman, and current philanderer was exactly the kind of scumbag you'd expect to find on the Board of Directors at Vinestead International. Although his advanced age had confined him to a wheelchair, his brain was still as spry as ever, no doubt thanks to upper-tier Guardian Angel software. Instead of fading into the periphery of corporate America, perhaps taking up residence at an assisted living center in Irvine, Abat had clawed his way into a position of oversight at one of the most ruthless companies in America. Rumor had it he was second cousin twice removed from current Vinestead CEO P.J. Downing.

Mostly, he was a crotchety old asshole.

And of course, he was late.

Kagan checked the time in the corner of his desktop. The client was forty-five minutes behind schedule, which meant Kagan had been idle for almost an hour. With no other projects to work on or emails to answer or bosses to dodge, he had spent the time staring blankly at his terminal, dragging icons from one side of the desktop to the other, depending on which image of Sepideh Ahmadi faded in. He'd collected so many photos over the years that he hardly knew which one might pop up next. And if the icons were in the wrong place, he might not be able to see her smile, or gander at her legs peeking out through a slit in a long, sparkling dress, or squint at her barely visible nipples through a sheer top.

She was so beautiful.

He knew every picture by heart.

Your eleven o'clock is here.

Jennavie's voice pushed through the MESH, cheery and crackling.

"I'll meet him in demo room seven," said Kagan. He took one last look at Sepideh, gave her a smooch from afar, and then shut down his terminal.

Much of the office had already left for lunch, so the MESH was clean and quiet. Wayne looked up from his desk when Kagan walked by, but he just shook his head and resumed his work.

Jennavie was coming out of the demo room when Kagan arrived. She held a hand to the back of her hip.

"That old man slapped my ass," she said, pausing by the water cooler.

Kagan chuckled. "That's how you tell if it's good or not."

"You're just gonna let him do that to me?" Her eyebrows dipped, mouth settled into a hard line.

"Hey," he said, touching her elbow. "Don't let him get to you. That old coot will be dead soon. Then the female race will be safe."

"No, he won't be, not after you're done with him. He'll be even stronger. And then this shit is really going to hurt."

Kagan ran his fingers through his hair, sighed. "*If* I can close the deal. Abat's got one of those black hole wallets—infinite, but nothing ever escapes it. I'm gonna have to pry the money from his wrinkly old hands." He mimed the action.

"Yeah, sounds real tough," she replied, turning to walk away. "Hey, here's your chance to live forever. No? Okay, bye."

"It's not that simple," he yelled after her.

Demo room seven occupied the northwest corner of the building and had an unobstructed view of the distant Hollywood sign. The designers had left it purposefully sparse, with two facing armchairs and a sofa between them. A coffee table held a tray of water and a perspiring pitcher. In the center of the table, a white doily highlighted an obsidian box. End tables supported half-dome lamps lying dormant in the midday sun.

At the window stood a young woman in a short black skirt. Beside her, Lucasz Abat sat in a wheelchair; a blue afghan covered his legs. His body leaned forward precariously, as if he were preparing to somersault out of the chair. His neck was wrenched backwards, his face doing its best to get a level view of the world. He didn't turn when Kagan entered. His nurse had to tap him on the shoulder.

"Finally," he wheezed. "Is it customary to keep an old man waiting here at…"

"Vitra Synth," said Kagan. He approached, extended his hand.

"Vitra Synth," said Abat, ignoring the greeting. "Sounds like some kind of fertility clinic for robots. I've got no problem with fertility, young man. I could get this girl pregnant with just two pumps. One if she would smile every once in a while."

Kagan traded glances with the nurse, noticed the earrings, the diamonds. Full carats, at least.

"My apologies, Mr. Abat. My father mentioned how important promptness was to you and I failed to prepare for it. I take full responsibility."

"Who else would?" he asked. Then to his nurse, "Gretchen, push me over there by the sofa so Mr. Kagan doesn't have to stand there like an awkward armadillo. Making me nervous, like you might roll into a ball any second."

Look who's talking, thought Kagan.

Gretchen used the controls on the back of the wheelchair to roll the crumbling lump of a man over to the coffee table.

Kagan sat down opposite him on the couch.

"Something to drink?"

"Not unless you want me pissing into a bag during our meeting," said Abat. "Speaking of piss bags, how is your cradle-robbing father?" The wrinkled and spotted skin on his neck pulled taut over his Adam's apple as he turned to Gretchen. "His daddy likes 'em young. Maybe you should send him your resume."

"Dad is doing well. Thank you for asking. He sends his regards."

"He should be sending me checks for that bailout I gave him in '15." He wheezed, coughed. Gretchen patted him on the back. "Ironic. First your father, now you. Twenty years later and the Kagans still want more from me."

"Mr. Abat, you know we don't own Vitra Synth. I have a small amount of stock, but that's it."

"Don't think I don't know what kind of kickback you'll get for signing me up. Some of my money is going to end up in your pocket and don't you try to deny it."

Kagan crossed one leg over the other, looked out over the Hollywood hills.

"What does it matter, ultimately?" he asked. "Money comes in, money goes out, but at the end of the day, worms are eating our brains six feet underground. Sure, you could leave the money to your children, but they might turn out like me. Never worked a real job in their lives. Never learned to live off their own effort. Going through life with one hand firmly grasped on daddy's coattails. What did my kids do to deserve a life of leisure? Just because they're a Kagan? I don't think so. That's how a family becomes weak. You've got a lot of money, Mr. Abat. Why not spend it in pursuit of what you really want? If not, what's the fucking point?"

Abat narrowed his eyes.

"Have you met my son Tomasz?" he asked.

Kagan shook his head.

"He's an asshole. Been waiting for me to die for the last twenty years. Been trying to kill me for the last five. I've been staying alive just to spite him."

"Why stop now? What if you could spite him *indefinitely*?"

Abat licked his chapped lips. "Keep talking."

"How about I show you instead?" Kagan leaned forward and pulled the obsidian box closer. He unfolded the top side and produced two code spheres. He held one up. "Gretchen, would you mind?"

The nurse took the small, sparkling sphere and placed it in Abat's hands.

"A crystal ball," said Abat. "You going to show me my future?"

"Absolutely," said Kagan, running his thumb over the nearly imperceptible bumps on the sphere's surface.

The world shimmered, fell away, as if the Plummer Tower had just launched itself into space. Where there should have been stars, however, there was nothing but black ether. The demo room maintained its shape, weight, and contents, with the exception of Gretchen, who had been sucked through the floor during liftoff.

"One of the hardest decisions about transitioning to synthetic life is figuring out what age you want to be for the rest of eternity. A youthful twenty-five? A stern and imposing forty-five? Somewhere in the middle, with one foot in both worlds? That's not going to be a problem here at Vitra Synth. With our patented RealSkin and TrueAge technologies, we can build your new synthetic body to your exact specifications."

Kagan stood and walked to the window. He leaned his back against it. "Pick a number, Mr. Abat. Any number."

"Thirty-five."

"Thirty-five it is."

A crackling sound filled the air, like the aftershock of a mass message in the MESH.

Abat's body sizzled, glowed. His head bowed as his back straightened. Lines faded out, hair changed color. The skin on his neck, arms, and hands regained its elasticity, hiding the spiderweb of black veins beneath. He groaned, registered the change.

"Please, stand up," said Kagan.

"This isn't my first time in VR," said Abat, kicking the afghan aside. "I hope you don't expect this to impress—" He paused, faltered as he tried to stand.

"Do you feel that? That's the weight of your body. In virtual reality, you're a free-floating avatar with no restrictions, but this simulation is different. This is how your synthetic body will feel once you're in it."

"It feels like my body," said Abat, straining. He raised himself out of the chair, bending slightly at the waist. "My old body at least."

"Vitra Synth chassis have the perfect balance of functionality, weight, and freedom. You regain your mobility without sacrificing the limitations that make you human."

Abat stood up straight, took a few tentative steps.

"Our engineers have worked for decades to ensure our synthetics feel just like the real thing. You'll have all of the advantages and none of the drawbacks of nature's original design."

"What about eating? Drinking? I've seen some synths who just sit there at meals with empty plates."

"You will have no biological need to eat, sleep, drink, or breathe. But, the number of clients who continue to do so, at least around humans, is in the nineties percentage-wise. Some of our competitors push inferior product that mutes biological impulses. We preserve them."

"All of them?"

"*All* of them."

"Don't bullshit me, Kagan." Abat patted his crotch, gave it a hearty squeeze.

Kagan rapped on the window glass with his knuckles.

Out of the ether walked a dozen women of varying design but wearing the same red underwear. They stood on an invisible plane in the unending shadow. Smiling. Beckoning.

Abat approached the wall, still holding himself.

"What's the alternative?" asked Kagan, shouldering up to the thirty-five-year-old Abat. "Pumping your dick full of *iStayHard* for the rest of your life? Watching chicks ride you and stare down at you like they can't believe where their life has taken them, their smiles nothing more than barriers to the vomit they're holding in their mouths?"

"Fuck you. See me again when you're my age."

"Won't happen. I'll be a synthetic long before then."

Abat placed both hands on the glass, struck it softly with his palms.

"You can die without knowing what it's like to be wildly fucked by two teenage girls. That's your choice."

"Who's to say I don't?"

"Point is, Mr. Abat, you're not just buying immortality and the chance to stick it to your ungrateful children. You're buying youth, desirability, and a chance to relive the glory days. Forever."

Abat shook his head; his youthful brown hair swayed.

"I seriously doubt synthetic life feels anything like real life."

"Would you like to speak to some of our previous customers? You and dad attend some of the same functions with them. At least five members of the Kagan Group—"

"Now that's a damn lie. I could spot a synthetic a mile away."

"You've talked to three since walking in the building," said Kagan.

Abat grumbled, folded his arms.

"Tell you what. Why don't you take this demo body for a test drive? See how everything feels."

Kagan gestured to the wall behind them. Four doors appeared; each swung open on its own.

The cries of seagulls spilled in through the first door, as did the aroma of salt water. A snowboard leaned in foot-high powder through the second door. In the third, the sharp lines and pine smell of an outdoor obstacle course appeared. The fourth door led into a cavernous bedroom with high ceilings and walls draped in red velvet. The lights were low and candles burned in the periphery.

Abat grunted as the glass windows disappeared; he stumbled forward. Soft moans filled the room, with vague whispers of lust trailing behind them.

"Take the girls to the beach," said Kagan, "Or take them snowboarding. Or just… take them."

"I just might," said Abat.

"I'll give you the room," said Kagan. "Jack out when you're ready to buy."

He pulled his link, slipped out of virtual reality, and awoke on the couch.

… right fucking now!

The MESH quivered. Jennavie's panicked voice rushed into his head.

What's wrong, asked Kagan.

Someone in the lobby. Says he knows you. The police are coming.

"Fuck," said Kagan.

Gretchen came forward. "Is everything alright? Is Mr. Abat…"

"He's fine, just putting his synth body through its paces. Keep an eye on him, will you? I'll be right back."

He rushed out of the room, screamed into the MESH.

I'm coming for you, Raf.

EIGHT

"Alright," said Jane, "you've got fifteen minutes. Let's hear your pitch." She made a show of checking her watch.

Beside her, Sepi shifted in place on the leather couch, wondering where in the world red cows might roam.

Lawrence had seated himself in the plush chair on the other side of the low coffee table, but Richard stood by the vidscreen on the far wall, either too nervous or too excited to be still.

"So," he said, clearing his throat, "Kaili Zabora. One of the most polarizing figures of the twenty-first century."

"Pass," said Jane. "Zabora's not Persian. You would have known that if you'd lived through her reign of terror."

Richard nodded at Sepi. "Yes, Ms. Ahmadi already informed us of Kaili's ethnicity, but the truth is no one really knows what Kaili Zabora looks like anymore."

"Or if she's even still alive," put in Lawrence.

Jane scoffed. "As if the most wanted domestic terrorist in history would just one day become a beautiful, young Persian." She winked at Sepi.

"Appearances are nothing," said Richard. "We agree that Ms. Ahmadi is a beauty without equal, but we wouldn't be hiring her just for her looks. Kaili Zabora is a complicated woman, and we need an actress who can bring that inner turmoil to the screen. You're right, Ms. Zimmerman. My brother and I came after the Reaping and Calle Cinco de Mayo. But Kaili's story transcends time. It's an eternal struggle that will resonate with audiences today and thirty years from now. But that's only if we can find the right woman to embody that raw passion and maniacal vengeance. We need *Dark Desert* Sepideh Ahmadi."

Jane crossed her arms, sat back on the couch.

"You're unconvinced, okay." Richard tapped the vidscreen, brought up the first slide in his presentation. "For argument's sake, let's just say Lawrence and I have already thought out how we're going to make Ms. Ahmadi look like Kaili Zabora. From the flaming red hair and vaguely Filipino nose to the augmentation scars running the length of her body. If we showed audiences a still image from the movie, they would not know it was Ms. Ahmadi. At all."

Sepi looked over at Jane, who shook her head minutely.

"I wouldn't mind hearing them out," she said.

Jane checked her watch again. "Ten minutes left."

"How much do you know about Kaili Zabora?" asked Richard.

"Not a lot," said Sepi. "I was only three during Calle Cinco de Mayo, and when the whole Perion Synthetics thing happened, I was more into dancing and acting."

"Did you see *Lone Net Ranger*?" asked Lawrence.

"I'm sorry. I didn't."

"We hinted at Kaili Zabora's involvement several times, but we had nothing concrete to go on."

"And now you do?" asked Jane.

"We've been piecing together rumors and gossip for years now." Richard tapped through a few slides, brought up a timeline. "Here's what we think we know. Kaili's sister is killed in 1999. She joins up with Calle Cinco sometime after that. Participates in the Reaping in 2004. Cinco de Mayo in 2009. Goes off the grid for a while until she resurfaces at the center of the Perion Synthetics debacle in 2015. Then the whole Johnny San Vito / Danny Guns Montreal business in 2016. And since then…"

He lifted his hands to the side.

"You don't know?"

"No one really does. Some people think she's hiding out in Columbia. Others say Vinestead has her." Richard moved to a nearby chair and sat on its armrest. "Or maybe she's infiltrated another powerful company and is just waiting for her chance to strike back at Vinestead."

"That's where our movie begins," said Lawrence. He took a sip of his Blue Rain and stood as he set it back down. "Nineteen years," he began. "What has Krazy Kai been up to for *nineteen* years? Like Rich said, nobody really knows. Lots of crazy ideas floating out there. So how do we pick just one? Easy, we don't. The script we've put together features three distinct story lines that all take place in different realities, each revolving around one possible explanation for Kaili's absence.

"Sepideh would need to play the same woman three different ways, look like three different women, and yet find some way to tie them all together with a common emotional playbook. It's the role you were born to play, actually. It's so incredibly demanding the way it is written that we couldn't trust it to anyone else."

Sepi smiled at the intensity in Lawrence's eyes. He might not have been the picture of maturity and professionalism, but there was undeniable passion in the way he spoke about his ideas.

It was almost endearing.

"We had Ever Jovovich read for the part," said Richard, "but it just wasn't right for her. We did offer her the part of Anela Zabora though, so if you sign on, you'll be playing sisters. Would you be interested in that?"

Sepi couldn't prevent herself from nodding, despite Jane nudging her with her knee.

"Ms. Zimmerman, do you think we could get a provisional contract in place so we can release the script to you? You'd have full right of refusal, of course."

"Three things," said Jane. "Sepideh gets first billing. I don't care if you hire a Jovovich or a DiCaprio or what."

"Done," said Lawrence.

"Second, no nudity."

Lawrence groaned. "Then what's the point of making the movie?"

"What my simpleton brother is trying to say," said Richard, "is that Kaili Zabora is a very sexual character. Her exploits in Perion City are well-documented, so there is some basis for nudity."

"Can we at least do CGI sex scenes?" asked Lawrence. "Or would your religion not allow that?"

Richard gave him a sharp look.

"Excuse me?" asked Sepi. "What does my religion have to do with anything?"

"You know," said Lawrence, waving his hand around uncertainly, "your people—"

"*My* people? I happen to be an American, Mr. Sierra. My people are your people."

"Will you shut up, Lar?" Richard took a deep breath. "I'm sorry, Ms. Ahmadi. Our mother gave him a lot of synth when we were young."

Lawrence chuckled to himself.

"What's so funny?" asked Sepi.

"We're going to make a trillion dollars. You *are* Kaili Zabora, except not certifiably insane. You have the passion. You are exactly who we need for this role."

Sepi shook her head. "You two are the strangest people I've ever met. And I've had enough." She stood.

"The lady has spoken." Jane joined her. "We're out of here."

"Wait," said Lawrence.

"That's quite enough out of you," said Jane.

"We'll pay you triple what you made on *Seven Kingdoms*," said Richard.

Sepi and Jane paused at the door.

Jane turned in place. "You don't have the backing."

"We don't need backing," said Richard. "We're the Sierra Brothers. And we're offering nine figures. Plus profit sharing. *If* you sign a provisional agreement today."

"You'd be the highest paid actress in history," said Lawrence.

Sepi considered the paycheck. No more concern about landing parts. No more stressing over auditions. There would only be freedom. Freedom to take on any role, or maybe write and direct something of her own.

"I'm not wearing a green suit," said Sepi. "If you're just going to motion-cap me and CGI Kaili in after the fact, then you can forget it. I don't care how much you're paying."

Richard smiled, turned to his brother. "I think it's time for a demo." Then to Sepi, "If you would be so kind as to follow me."

In the hallway, Esme was standing just outside the door. She panicked when Sepi noticed her, turned around in a circle, and then hurried off to the reception area.

"Big fan," said Richard, leading the way around the corner and into a double-doored conference room.

The room itself was empty except for a cabinet on the wall beside the door. Richard opened it and revealed six pairs of glasses hanging uniformly from six hooks. Below each hook was a small choker of thin black velvet.

"Ms. Ahmadi, are you familiar with Nixle Chronos?"

She shook her head, eyed the empty room. Evercrete floors extended wall to wall; drab white drywall held four large windows that looked out over Los Angeles.

"Well, they've been in the business of augmented reality since before the two of us were born. OcularAR was their first product. Big, bulky, and no one bought it. Over the years, they've refined what started as a headset into these."

He took two pairs of glasses and handed them to Jane and Sepi.

"Put them on. See the world differently."

Sepi slipped the glasses on; soft pads gripped the bridge of her nose.

Reality cut to another channel. Color assaulted her from all angles.

Jane gasped.

The previously empty room was now full of visual stimulation. Hardwood floors supported neo-modern furniture of wood and metal. Artwork—murals really—flowed across corners of the room. Flowers stood in pots and hung from the ceiling. Fans spun overhead, though Sepi could feel no breeze coming from them.

"What is this?" asked Jane.

"Augmented reality," said Richard, donning his own glasses. "A layer of computer-generated imagery overlaid on the real world. Nearly impossible to discern the difference if the graphical resources are high-grade. Right now you're looking at it in read-only mode, but with some downloads to your Guardian Angel chip, you'd be able to rearrange the world to suit you. Don't like the artwork on the wall? Just touch it and imagine something else. It's really neat stuff."

"And it makes movie-making much easier," said Lawrence. He put on glasses as well. "You asked how we're going to make you look like Kaili Zabora? Well how about this?"

He touched Richard's face, causing his features to ripple through skin tones and texture gradients. His black hair turned red. Dimples appeared along his earlobes. Eyebrows thinned. Eyes darkened.

Within seconds, he looked like a vaguely masculine Kaili Zabora.

Richard sighed.

"This wasn't supposed to be the demo," he said. "It will look better on you. I promise."

"You remember the green screen revolution of the late nineties?" asked Lawrence. "Well, we're about to start the augmented reality revolution of the mid-thirties. All the stuff we usually do in post-production can now be done right on set. You won't be acting against a green screen anymore; you'll actually see what the audience will see."

"So," said Sepi, removing her glasses, "I'll have to wear these the whole time?"

"Of course not," said Richard. "Nixle Chronos just came out with a contact lens version. Their CEO, Wade Vunak, he's a fan of our movies—yours too, by the way—so we shouldn't have any trouble getting you in to get fitted this week. Spin up the sets in two. Start shooting in three. And so on."

"We haven't even read the script yet," said Jane.

"The script is fine," said Lawrence, stepping closer to Sepi. "You want to be involved in this, don't you? You understand how this is going to change movies forever."

"A little full of himself," said Jane.

"No lines. No blemishes. A veneer of Kaili Zabora powered by your acting. Pure talent. No tricks." Lawrence raised an eyebrow. "Can you dig it?"

Various threads of doubt and excitement ran through Sepi's head, and somewhere deep down in the cracked center of her self-esteem, a tiny voice asked, "Are we not pretty enough to be in pictures anymore?"

She was not yet thirty, and her looks had so far held up without the need for plastic surgery, and yet here she was being told they would mask her features out completely. What if the next director wanted to do the same? And the next? It would be years before anyone saw Sepi's real face on the screen again, if ever.

Instead, they would see her in public and whisper, "Oh, *that's* why they used augmented reality on her."

It was the digital equivalent of putting a bag over her head.

"I'll sign the provisional," she announced. "Send me the script."

"Excellent, excellent," said Richard.

He collected the glasses and put them back in the case. They followed Sepi down the hall.

As they were about to pass the lounge doors again, Jane asked Richard, "Where do you think you're going?"

Sepi kept on walking, one ear turned to the conversation dimming behind her.

"To grab the contract," said Richard.

"What contract?" asked Jane. "We haven't even started negotiating yet."

Sepi heard the lounge door open, heard Lawrence grumble under his breath. Jane would take care of it, get her the best deal possible.

Sepi paused in front of a mirror just off the reception area. She tried to see Kaili Zabora's features on her own. Could she really play a maniac? A wounded fox hell-bent on killing everything Vinestead? Did Kaili Zabora know Vinestead was now the good guy, that their synthetics were the only things standing between the MX and the American Way?

How would she react if she knew?

How would I, Kaili Zabora, react if I knew, thought Sepi.

NINE

Doyle's Journal - November 12, 2045

I stayed with Vida for several days after I gave her *the speech*. It seemed like the right thing to do. Empathizing with her situation wasn't difficult; though I could remember my life before the *Día de las Máquinas*, it was just as distant and out of reach as Vida's. We are both passengers in the same boat careening down a river that will never run in reverse.

I've given myself over to the current.

Vida still mourns the loss of distant, unremembered shores.

I hear her crying at night, after the lights in the bunker go out. During the day she goes from quiet and withdrawn to social and boisterous at the flip of a switch. I tell her about the world outside and she struggles to accept it. I think it's all just too overwhelming for her.

So I left. Gave her some space. At least for a little while.

I hiked for several kilometers through the foothills, pressing further south than I ever had before. The days were mild but the nights were cold, and I could smell more snow in the air. Trees swayed in gentle breezes. Animals darted through the undergrowth. Birds cried out, sung songs of sorrow or joy or confusion.

Máquina patrols were frequent, but again, not very stealthy. You could hear them coming from a good distance, find some cover, and hole up. I watched more than a dozen kill teams pass by in the same manner: eyes scanning the horizon, guns held firmly to their chests, scowls permanently etched on their faces.

So many. So far from the MX.

I wondered what it was like in the more populated areas: Los Angeles, Houston, New York. Were streets there just filled to the brim with Máquinas?

How did the MX build so many? And so advanced?

I pondered questions like that whenever I had to sit and wait—sometimes up to an hour—while a patrol passed by.

I thought of Angie and Gretta.

I thought of Vida.

I'd be lying if I said she isn't beautiful or that I don't find her attractive. I can't help thinking ahead into the future, wondering whether so much time spent together will cause us to fall in love or murder each other. Both seem unlikely.

The world won't be saved by just two people. If we're going to survive past the stocked provisions in the Admiral, then we need to find other people like us, those who prepared and armed themselves.

That's why I made the trip south in the first place.

Park City is a tiny nothing of a town, but at one time it was a bustling community conveniently situated on the 90 between Billings and Bozeman. Truckers loved it. Tourists found its low hotel rates preferable to the hoity-toity La Quintas and Best Westerns in Billings. The city's anchor business was a sprawling half-acre warehouse named Preparation Inc. It had been featured in several prepper magazines and on feeds as *the* premiere doomsday survivalist supply store this side of the Mississippi. It had everything a nuclear family needed to protect themselves against the coming end times.

That meant supplies.

And possibly, fellow preppers.

I came out of the tree line two kilometers northeast of Park City, closer to the 90 than I had expected. The Máquinas had brought with them lumbering machines as black as coal from the south, including what I had nicknamed a Liftosserato. As the name implies, this modified Mack truck lifts abandoned cars on the highway and tosses them in the median or over guardrails. It looked as if a fleet of Liftosseratos had come through and picked the roads clean.

Travelling parallel to the 90, I made my way into town, keeping to the brambles and brush surrounding the outer streets where abandoned, crumbling houses stood like forlorn gravestones.

Nothing moved. The MESH hissed.

I crept through the streets, past broken stop signs and clogged drain gutters, and never really noticed the green dumpsters until I had to take cover behind one while crossing under the highway.

Looking down Clark Street, I saw dumpsters had been placed at every major intersection. I thought maybe the Máquinas were clean-freaks intent on putting the world back in order. But to what end? So their Máquina families could migrate north? What did a synthetic want for shelter anyway? I'd seen Máquinas stand perfectly still in heavy rain and high winds and think nothing of it.

The longer I waited—a lone Máquina soldier had begun a crisscrossing sweep several blocks down the street—the more I smelled something on the air, the more I noticed flies buzzing around me, circling the dumpster.

I didn't want to look. I had seen enough carnage already. But I had to be sure.

A half-second peek was all I needed.

There were bodies stacked to the rim, and not just thrown in haphazardly, but *compacted*. Torn clothes, soaked in blood, wrapped around the ruined flesh of so many decaying people. They had been there for weeks, rounded up by the Máquinas and put in convenient containers for disposal.

I tried to clear the images, threw up on my boots instead.

The anger that was supposed to overtake me never came. It could have carried me down the street to the Máquina who had done this, could have put my gun to his metal skull.

Sadness instead.

Despair.

There was no undoing the damage. Sacrificing my life now would change nothing.

I crept around the dumpster and took a position on my stomach. The Máquina wavered in the Dragunov's scope, a little out of range, but heading back towards me.

Breathe in. Breathe out. Wait for it to get closer.

Finger on the trigger.

They came from all directions at once, streaming out of boarded windows and broken doors. Ragged, dirty, crouching low and moving quickly, the way no Máquina could have. I counted at least twenty people, mostly men, but a few wavy lengths of long hair streaming in the wind as well, and some small enough they didn't need to crouch.

The Máquina reacted as any cornered animal might; it took a defensive position and began threatening the closest attacker. That happened to be a hulking man in blue overalls. He carried a polished AR-15 at the ready.

He held the Máquina's gaze as a small boy rushed up behind it, carrying what looked like a homemade shotgun, all PVC pipe and gray duct tape. The boy pointed it in the general direction of the Máquina and shot out some kind of netting.

Sizzling. Crackling. Electricity arcing from limb to limb.

The Máquina went into convulsions and dropped its rifle.

Blue Overalls moved in as the boy ran off into a nearby home.

The sparks from the netting started to die down, which gave the Máquina just enough freedom to raise its hand towards Overalls, as if to say *no*.

The command was ignored.

Overalls put two rounds in the Máquina's forehead.

I removed my finger from the Dragunov's trigger.

It was strange to hear hooting and hollering after so many weeks of silence in the bunker. The people of Park City were jubilant, and I couldn't figure out why. The world was still shit. The Máquinas still had the numbers. And yet by taking down *one single machine*, you'd have thought the war was won.

The crowd hoisted the Máquina above their heads and walked off towards the south, filling the air with *fuck yeah* and *that's how we do*. They left nothing behind on the street except a small pool of synthetic blood and two spent shells.

I won't lie. I wanted to be a part of their celebration.

I wanted to stand up and run towards them shouting *I'm here, I'm here!*

But that would have been stupid. Vida was still back at the bunker. What if they weren't taking on new members? What if they wanted the rifle on my back and ammo in my pockets?

It just wasn't the right time. I needed to meet one of them alone or in a pair. If things went south with that many people, there'd be no hope of escape.

I started inching my way backwards, sliding along the blacktop until I was behind the dumpster again.

That's when I felt the cold metal against the nape of my neck, something thick and round.

I froze, thought of the million things I missed about the old world.

"You're not one of us," said a young, male voice.

"Just passing through," I told him. "Saw a Máquina and wanted to take it out, but you guys seem to be doing just fine."

"Yeah, we are."

"Then I'll just be on my way, if you don't mind."

He cleared his throat. "That's up to Harlan. Take your hands off the rifle."

"I'm afraid I can't do that."

The barrel pushed further into my neck.

"I will blow your fucking head off if you don't let go of that weapon."

Younger man, probably not fully grown, voice still breaking. Somewhere between five and six feet tall. Probably leaning over to get the rifle down on my neck. With a quick roll, it could all be over.

"Or I could just kill you now," I said.

His response was a high-pitched whistle that echoed through the abandoned streets. No doubt a call to the others, and since I knew most of them were just a few blocks away, that meant I only had precious seconds to make my move.

I rolled on the street, lifting my arm to push the barrel out of the way with my elbow. Fingers fell on the right spot on the stock and I pulled hard.

The young man, dressed in fatigues a size too big, stumbled towards me, and I used his momentum to pull him face-first into the ground. I heard his nose break, teeth chip. Part of me wanted that to be an appetizer, wanted me to show this fool who really ruled the Wasteland.

Except that he was just a kid, really.

Scared and alone. Driven to horrible things by a harsh world.

People were hard these days, but you couldn't really blame them for it.

That's what the world demanded.

That's what La Guerra Máquina demanded.

I rolled the kid onto his side and made sure the blood from his nose and mouth was flowing harmlessly into the street instead of down his throat. His weapon turned out to be a single barrel, semi-automatic shotgun. I grabbed it by the stock and fished a few shells from his bandolier.

"Sorry," I told the kid, but he was out cold.

I stuffed the shells in my pocket and turned back the way I'd come.

Saw the boy. Saw the wrong end of the PVC pipe.

Something like terror and surprise on the kid's face.

A tiny twitch of his tiny muscles.

Sizzle. Crackle. Electricity arcing in front of my eyes.

The entire world went bright green, filled with exploding stars in all directions. From zero to excruciating pain in the space of a heartbeat. All of my muscles contracted. I lost my balance, fell.

Despite the impact, despite the distant cries of Park City residents, I could only think of two things.

One: was this what the Máquina felt in his last moments?

Two: would Vida be alright without me?

TEN

How do you find meaning in routine?

There was nothing more Vida wanted than to remain in bed all day, bury her head beneath the pillows, and shut out the muted but constant gunfire and distant explosions from beyond the walls of the bunker. The Máquinas were always around, sometimes close enough to hear through the observation ports that led up to the surface. Doyle said they were getting suspicious of the area, which is why he spent so much time scavenging a day or two's walk away.

He had his own routine too, and Vida was sure she'd gotten in the way of it. When he announced he was leaving her alone in the bunker, she understood. It couldn't have been easy to put his new life on hold for her, or to be patient while she tried to process what had happened. He claimed it was just his usual scavenging run and that he'd return soon with exciting stories from the Wasteland.

The date on Vida's palette read November 19, 2045.

Doyle had been gone a week.

In that time, she had clung to routine like a warm blanket.

She woke in the morning when the bunker lights came on. They started soft, cycling through a pleasant yellow hue until they were bright white. Trying to simulate the sun, Doyle claimed. The first order of business was to check the filters in the air recycler. This had to be done every day to keep the bunker from smelling foul. After that, Vida walked the eight paces to the bathroom. She relieved herself and brushed her teeth. Every other day, she got to take a short shower. Once a week, they had agreed, she would be allowed to wash her hair.

Water came from a well just outside the north wall of the bunker. It went down some 120 feet, but so far Doyle had not been able to figure out an automated way to bring water in. He'd discouraged her from going outside to fetch the water herself, so while he was gone, she had to conserve the best she could.

But not today, because today was shower day.

Vida undressed in the tiny bathroom, placing her underwear and t-shirt over the lip of the metal sink. The shower itself was barely large enough to turn around in, but the spray was warm and the steam comforting. Sometimes, if she closed her eyes hard enough, she could catch a glimpse of the time before the bunker, the world she had fallen out of or been rescued from. There was softness there, a gentle blurring of the harsh reality she now found herself in.

The bunker had plenty of food, a well, and electricity that mostly worked, but what it lacked was a reason to persevere.

Doyle had joked about repopulating the world, but Vida hadn't been as excited about the idea as he had.

Who in good conscience could bring a child into the bunker, into this cloistered reality devoid of sunlight and human comforts?

Vida stepped out of the shower and wrapped a towel around herself. She took her dirty clothes to the hamper in her closet. On the shelves were Angela's clothes: underwear, sports bras, t-shirts, and shorts, all in a variety of colors. She dried off and pulled on fresh underwear and a shirt. Angela wasn't much of a pant woman, but she did have a few oversized sweats that didn't fit well but offered more protection against the permeating chill of the bunker than shorts. Before closing the closet door, Vida grabbed the holster hanging from a brass hook.

The gun was the only part of the routine she sometimes ignored. Doyle had told her to wear the holster at all times, but the straps chafed her skin and made sleeping nearly impossible. As a compromise, she hung it in her closet—a mere three feet away from the bed.

Vida wrapped the holster around her waist and threaded the buckle through the makeshift holes Doyle had cut for her. With a practiced hand, she drew the gun, checked the magazine and chamber, and returned it to the holster.

"That's yours now," he had told her, in the midst of some rambling speech about the world not being what it was anymore. She remembered not knowing how to react, whether to be shocked or thankful. Something automatic had taken over, had responded to Doyle's words for her so she could puzzle the situation internally.

And what had that produced? Nothing but a fleeting desire to shoot Doyle in the back, followed by overwhelming guilt.

Vida paused outside of her bedroom.

Put a hand to the side of her head.

She wanted to scream. It wasn't fair to bear this burden all by herself. There had to be people out there who shared—or were sharing—her experience. If only she could reach out to them, find a chatroom in VNet—

Vida stopped, shook her head.

What the hell was VNet?

The answer was there, on the very edge of recall, floating out in some kind of formless ether. She held her breath, reached as far as she could into the darkness.

Once again, her fingers closed around nothing.

Vida shook off the impending breakdown and leaned hard into routine. It was the one constant in her life, and it kept her from trying to solve problems that had no solutions.

If I can just make it another day, she would sometimes think.

More often, it was: *If I can just do the next thing.*

The routine called for a quick breakfast, so Vida shuffled into the main living area intent on taking the slight left into the kitchen. Instead, she stalled in front of the vidscreen that hung on the far wall. How many hours and days had she wasted away watching movies and television shows from Doyle's personal media library? How far back had she gone in the history of sitcoms just to find something entertaining enough to take her mind off the bunker?

The shows all ran together now. All the terrible puns and blunt innuendo. All the canned laughter and pandering.

Movies were better. Watching emotions. Feeling what the actors were feeling. That was humanity.

Now, the vidscreen was dark and just reflective enough to show her a shadowy vision of the bunker. Vida saw herself standing by the table, a young woman in her late twenties or early thirties, thin but not ghastly, tall but not towering. The closer she got to the vidscreen, the more her features pushed through the gloom.

Strong eyebrows that dipped at the center.

Dark eyes. Sharp nose. Thick lips.

Her irises were black. They stared back darkly.

A secondary routine took hold, one that had been planned and simulated in her mind but never executed.

Vida popped the clasp on the holster, lifted the gun as she charged the hammer with her thumb. The barrel slipped past her lips. She tasted metal.

Her thumb danced lightly on the trigger's edge.

In the vidscreen, sad eyes pleaded with her.

Tears rolled down her cheeks, and Vida collapsed on the armrest of a nearby chair.

It's too hard, she thought. Too hard not knowing what those eyes were telling her. Were they asking her to stop? Or pleading with her to continue? To just finally do it?

Her cries echoed in the bunker.

This is no way to live.

Without hope. Without meaning.

She suddenly wished Doyle had never found her, hadn't carried her back to the bunker on his shoulder, and hadn't risked his life to ensure her survival.

Why did he care so much for her? And in the face of such overwhelming compassion, why did she care so little for him?

Routine saved her from answering. It got her up, to the kitchen, and into the pantry. She pulled out a packet of eggs and dumped them into a small bowl. She added water, salt. They tasted terrible. The coffee she made to wash it all down tasted even worse.

Sitting at the table, Vida eyed the bunker entrance, the seven-foot-tall door she had triple-locked from the inside when Doyle left. It led to a stairwell lined with sharpened sticks to discourage a quick descent. Getting out was as easy as brushing by the angled traps, but getting back in took time and patience.

Beyond that door was another which Vida had never seen. It led out into a world whose shell had broken and whose contents had spilled out into the fire. It wasn't the first invasion the United States had ever faced but was certainly the most effective. Three quarters of the population in western states had been wiped out in the first week. Civil society broke down almost immediately. Doyle referred to it as the *Shit Hits the Fan* moment. A vast majority of Americans were unprepared for the end of the world.

To hear Doyle tell it, survivalism had started as a hobby, though he had spent a small fortune on the Admiral and on filling it with food, supplies, and ammo. He admitted he had never truly believed in the doomsday scenarios the other preppers were always worrying about. When things went bad and then to worse, he still thought everything was going to be fine.

Vida pushed aside the half-eaten eggs and threw the coffee in the sink. The routine wanted her to do the dishes, maybe straighten up a bit in the kitchen, but she ignored it. She couldn't stop thinking about the gun on the living room floor, about how close she had come to escaping the confines of the bunker.

She wondered what had stopped her.

More than anything, Vida wanted to see the sun again, wanted to see it rising over the hills and setting over the sea. She wanted the pink and purple streaks, the birds flying as one beneath thin wisps of clouds. Mornings of rolling fog. Afternoons of glorious sunshine. Nights of tall buildings twinkling on the bay.

San Francisco.

Vida held her breath, tried to remain aloof to the emerging memory. It would come if it wanted to. It would wash over her and soak her with answers.

She saw a ferry cutting through calm waters, saw tourists in garish pastels leaning over the edge of railings, shielded from the sun by solar panels. She saw her own arms resting on the white rail, hands clasped, a bracelet on one wrist, a rose-gold watch on the other. Beside her stood a shadow. She turned her head, tried to take in the features, but the memory broke down.

Despite the abrupt ending, Vida smiled.

Something had been there, and *someone* had stood beside her.

It didn't matter whether that person was still alive or not. The loop had to be closed, and that was reason enough for her to keep going.

Vida walked into the living room and picked up the gun. She caught her reflection in the vidscreen and whispered, "Never again."

The gloom had almost overtaken her. Had gotten the gun in her mouth. But now, there was something beyond the gloom, something she desperately wanted to reach.

Vida engaged the safety and slotted the gun in the holster. The clasp made a satisfying *click* as she buttoned it.

And that's when the proximity alarm began to wail.

The previously dormant vidscreen came alive, showed a low-res map of the bunker and surrounding terrain. A green line swept the image from left to right, each time highlighting an approaching emerald speck.

Routine took over.

Vida hit the panic button on the wall by the door and put the bunker in silent mode. All non-essential systems shut down, leaving only the whine of the air recycler.

She played with the clasp on her holster.

There was no reason to draw her weapon yet.

The intruder would have to find the bunker first, then get through the outer and inner doors.

Then Vida would find out if there was anything worth living for.

ELEVEN

"Pinche Máquinas!"

Kagan heard Raf screaming before the elevator doors even opened, revealing a lobby in disarray, with scared businessmen and women huddled by the walls, security synths with batons extended looking for a way in, and in the center of it all, Rafael Orozco, veteran of the Máquina Wars, beating the shit out of a synthetic greeter who had nothing but its passive protection protocols to defend itself.

The synth's name was Joseph. It had worked the door at Plummer Tower for the last five years.

Kagan thought back to his morning drive, spotting Raf on the street. Then, Raf had seemed like a dying echo of the soldier and friend he had once been. The clothes, the smell, and the general disconnect with reality gave the impression of a man who had died somewhere in the MX, whose brain had checked out and left his body a walking, talking zombie. Raf used to command rooms, used to turn the heads of women—even those who had been talking to Kagan for the last half hour.

But now, on the street, post-war...

Raf reminded Kagan of a synth without its imprint. A blank sleeve.

"Please, sir," said Joseph. "I mean you no harm."

"What about Rice? And Beaux? And Martinez? Did you mean *them* no harm when you pulled their brains out through their eye sockets? When you flayed them alive just to hear them scream?"

A woman gasped.

Raf and Joseph rolled on the polished floor and slammed into the reception desk. If it hadn't been for the smell and ratty clothes, passers-by might have mistaken Raf for a professional fighter, or if he'd been in uniform, a proper American soldier. The precision of his movements. The counters and secondary counters. The way he kept Joseph's hands from getting a good grip anywhere on his body.

The man knew how to fight. Specifically, he knew the oxymoronic strategies of hand-to-hand combat with synthetics.

"Raf!" screamed Kagan, stepping through the line of synthetic security guards. He patted them on the shoulders, asked them to step back.

"He killed Martinez, K! I watched him do it!"

Kagan grabbed Raf by the collar and wrenched him backwards. Life on the streets had left the former soldier underweight. Joseph scuttled towards the waiting arms of the security guards.

Raf raised an accusatory finger. "This isn't over, you synth bastard. I will fucking erase you!"

"Hey," said Kagan, grabbing Raf by the beard. He yanked his eyes away from Joseph. "Look around you, hermano. This isn't the MX. See all these nice people? You're scaring the shit out of them with your G. I. Jose routine. You're in a civilized building in a civilized country. We don't fight synthetics here."

"I'll fight synthetics anywhere," seethed Raf. The bruises on his face threatened to swell and bleed. "Until the day I die. By God's hand or human hand. But not theirs. Never by theirs."

"Easy, now." Kagan rubbed his friend's oily hair, felt his hand come away coated in grime. "Who's my brave soldier?"

Raf narrowed his eyes. The corner of his mouth twitched.

"Joseph isn't a Máquina. Neither is anyone else this side of the Rio Grande. If they ever cross the border, you and I can fight them together. Until then, you need to chill the fuck out."

Raf's face softened; creases in his forehead relaxed.

"Now, why don't we get you home, take a shower, maybe dip you in some kind of industrial solvent. I know some good solvent people."

"Fuck you, K."

Kagan helped Raf to his feet as the crowd began to disperse. They turned to head for the door, but were stopped by Craig Turner, building manager for Plummer Tower.

"Excuse me, Mr. Kagan," said Craig. "I'm afraid I can't let this man leave."

"You want to try and stop him?" asked Kagan. "What's the problem, Turner? Nobody got hurt here."

Craig gestured to Joseph, who was standing by the reception desk and toying with a dislocated finger.

"No *human* got hurt here," said Kagan.

"I'm sorry, but I will need to call the police."

"How about we call my father instead?"

Craig bit his lip, considered the threat. His eyes drifted away, then his face, until finally the entire man was gone, off to check on his synthetic employee.

As they walked out of the towering double doors, Raf asked, "Your dad is some kind of big shit now?"

"Always has been," said Kagan. "Always will be." He spoke into his sliver. "Priya, out front, now."

A few minutes later, Kagan's yellow Maserati whipped around the corner of Plummer Tower and bit the curb right in front of him. The rear door opened automatically, and Kagan followed Raf inside.

"Let's go home."

Routing to Home, said Priya. *Estimated travel time is thirty-six minutes.*

Kagan spoke into the MESH. *Jennavie?*

Yes, sweetie?

I'm heading home, but I forgot my bag on my desk. Can you have an intern run it by the house this afternoon?

How about I bring it by later this evening? Around nine?

The MESH hissed.

Sorry, I didn't get that. We're going through a tunnel or something. Intern. This afternoon. Thanks!

What tun—?

Kagan severed his MESH link with a quick swipe of his sliver.

They rode in silence for most of the trip. Raf spent the time chewing on his fingernails.

The car turned off the major roadways and onto the winding trails of the Hollywood Hills. Wide, empty streets allowed Priya to up the speed, such that she occasionally spit out a revised ETA. They passed the imposing front gates of famous movie stars like Elise Portman, Johnny Tran, and E. Thomas Winston. They passed former clients and future clients—men and women whose pursuits of bankable beauty had led or would lead them into the offices at Vitra Synth for their best chance at eternal youth.

As if money and fame weren't enough.

Now arriving at Home.

Priya guided the car along the circular driveway and pulled up next to the front door. Kagan got out, waited for Raf to do the same, and then poked his head back inside.

"Park it in the garage."

As you wish.

Kagan turned and slapped a friendly arm around Raf's shoulders. "Ven, amigo," he said, "Mira a mi castillo."

The front doors of the three-story mansion swung open at Kagan's approach. Their footsteps echoed on the marble floors. A chorus of chimes and beeps sounded from the different rooms in the house—air conditioning, lighting, and security systems popping on and off.

"What the fuck is this?" asked Raf.

"Excuse me?"

"I'm living on the streets, and you bring me *here*? You trying to rub this in my face?"

Kagan scoffed. "You're not living on the streets anymore, brother." Then in Spanish, "This is your home. For life and forever."

Raf scowled, stepped tentatively into the polished foyer.

"It's too big," he said. "You have any smaller rooms?"

"Go up the stairs, hang a left. Any room down that hall is yours. There should be fresh towels and a shit-ton of soap in each bathroom."

"Huh," said Raf. "Place like this makes a man soft. You wouldn't last a day out on the streets."

"Hopefully, I'll never have to."

Raf nodded, started up the stairs. At the landing, he looked down and said, "Sorry."

"Por que?

"For the trouble at work."

Kagan shrugged. "Fuck 'em. The bigger question is *why* you went off on Joseph in the first place."

"It's hard to explain."

"Naw, I think you know."

Raf turned away. "Shower," he said over his shoulder, and then disappeared down the hall. A door opened and closed.

Kagan stood for another minute in the foyer, hands in his pockets, wondering how he was going to help Raf come back from the war. Properly.

"Welcome home, Honey," said Nadya. She stood in the butler's pantry that led to the kitchen, dressed in a bright, red skirt and white blouse. She held a tumbler of whiskey in one hand.

Kagan eyed his Associate with a casual glance. She was a relic of an older time when his sexual interests leaned towards the Eastern European, towards well-proportioned beauties of Ukrainian or Czech descent. Nadya had been one of the last models built before Adelai Associates switched over to the primarily Indian and Japanese varieties. Kagan had been struck by Nadya's beauty in the showroom, by her golden hair, narrow face, and perfectly rounded breasts. She'd stood there naked on a pedestal, rotating slowly, showing Kagan what a small fortune would buy him.

She had everything he could want in a partner: assumed intelligence, RealSkin technology, and an undying desire to do whatever he asked of her.

"My friend is going to be staying with us for a while," said Kagan. He turned and walked into the study, confident she would follow. "He set up in one of the rooms upstairs. Take him some new clothes and dispose of the old ones."

"Sure."

"Oh, and Nadya? Don't let him see you. He has a thing about… beautiful women."

She smiled, simulated a blush.

Kagan sat down behind the large oak desk and typed in his code on the small keypad in the corner. A vidscreen broke free of the desk and rose to a perpendicular position. His desktop loaded, showing first a supine Sepideh Ahmadi, then his icons, and finally his message and calendar programs. Before he could click on anything, Wayne's face popped up on the screen.

"Where the hell are you, Kagan?"

"Personal business."

"Well, I don't know if you're aware of this or not, but we have a *business* business running here. And now we've got cops and ambulances lined up in front of the building like some kind of circus!"

Goddamn Turner.

"No," said Kagan. "I took care of the lobby incident. Everything was fine when I left."

"What lobby incident? I'm talking about Abat, you know, the client you were supposed to be working with today."

Kagan yawned. "What about him?"

"Well," said Wayne, cocking his head to the side, "*someone* left him jacked into an orgy simulator in our corporate offices for two hours."

A chuckle bubbled its way to the surface.

"Is this funny to you, Kagan? The client is *dead*!"

The bubble popped. Kagan thought about what his father might say.

"This is the end for you," said Wayne. "I'm going to the board this afternoon. You're finished here."

"We'll see about that."

"Yeah, we will. You've killed your last client, you privileged little shit. I'm gonna see to it."

Kagan slid the call window to the side of the screen, ending it.

"Nadya!" he yelled.

She appeared at the door a minute later with her hands folded in front of her.

"Yes, darling?"

"What happened to that drink you had?"

"I thought you didn't want it. I'll make you a fresh one."

She curtsied and left the room.

Kagan stood and walked to the low couch by the window. He sat down, sunk into the cold leather.

Deep breath in. Deep breath out.

Wayne's threats were nothing to worry about. Dad needed Kagan at Vitra Synth more than he needed Wayne.

It would be fine.

Nadya returned with a tumbler of amber nectar.

"On the table," said Kagan.

"Is there anything else?"

"Yeah, shut the door. And take off your clothes."

"As you wish," she replied.

The servos in her cheeks pulled her lips into something approaching a smile.

TWELVE

It wasn't until the elevator doors closed and Sepi saw her reflection that she started thinking about her looks again. The meeting with the Sierra Brothers had been lucrative, or at least, would be. And the car ride home with Jane was exciting and optimistic; they'd traded increasingly fanciful ways of spending a hundred million dollars. Maybe buy a new car or finally, *finally*, move out of the Monarch. Not that the residential tower on the corner of Fuller and Santa Monica was a dump; it was home to many of Hollywood's mid-level writers, directors, and actors. But it was still an apartment in a building shared with many, and depending on how you looked at it, a measure of success or lack thereof.

Sepi waved goodbye to Jane, walked into the cavernous atrium of the Monarch, and entered the elevator. She hit the button for her floor and then stood face-to-face with her twenty-nine going on thirty-nine reflection. In her heart, she knew she looked as anyone her age should look—better even, than most. But her mind had a way of following the worst possible threads, digging deeper until it found a core doubt that could unravel any amount of self-confidence. There were no lines on her face, but she could imagine them. No bags under her eyes, at least not after she'd put on make-up.

Someday, her age would catch up with her, and then augmented reality really would be her only hope of keeping her career. But what kind of life was that? Would donning an augmented veneer be the same as putting on a costume? Or would she feel like a puppet master yanking on the strings, hidden off stage, in the darkness?

The elevator doors opened on the thirtieth-floor common area, a wide space that stretched across the length of the building, ending in floor-to-ceiling windows that would have given a breathtaking view of the sunset had it not been for the much taller Saleh Financial skyscraper next door. Low couches lined the walls, flanked by cherry-wood end tables with warm, yellow lamps.

A synthetic waiter who called himself Gus stood behind a circular bar in the middle of the room, hands folded on the counter, seemingly in a sleep state.

Sepi wasn't much for the common area. She knew the names of only a few people on her floor, though everyone seemed to know hers. That didn't stop her from nodding politely to those who nodded to her as she passed through. With every step, she could feel eyes on her. Even Gus woke up to gaze in her direction, a glimmer of optimism in his LED eyes. She took a breath, held it, tried to think about something else. A few more steps and she would be safe in her home.

"Good evening, Ms. Sepideh."

She turned, startled.

"Oh, Sol, I didn't see you there."

Solomon Boas lowered his oversized palette to his lap. He was an older man, in his late sixties, with a full head of hair and a thick beard, both streaked with gray. His glasses perched on the end of a long, crooked nose. Sol was a writer, primarily dramatic fiction, but he also had a half-dozen *with Solomon Boas* biography credits to his name. He was one of the few residents of the Monarch with whom Sepi had a friendship.

"I'm easy to miss down here," he said, slowly working his way to his feet. He had gained a permanent bend at the waist from an auto-driver accident more than a decade ago.

She bent to give him a hug, then held him by the shoulders.

"How are you today? How is the back holding up?"

"Little worse than yesterday," he said, smiling, "but better than tomorrow, I can assure you of that." He sat back down, groaning. "How was your meeting with uh, what's-his-name?"

"It was good. We're moving forward with a new picture. Some kind of speculative biopic about Kaili Zabora."

"And you're playing who? Krazy Kai?"

"Somehow," said Sepi.

Sol waved the doubt away, picked up his palette again. "I was reading about your BAFTA nomination. I didn't quite care for *Seven Kingdoms* as a story, but your performance in it was sensational. I'm sure you'll be bringing that award back stateside."

Sepi glanced at her watch as she nodded.

"Please, don't let me keep you," said Sol. "I know I can ramble on sometimes."

"I'm sorry," said Sepi. "That was rude of me. It's just that Nat is waiting, and I want to tell her the good news."

"Of course, of course. I'll be out here for most of the evening. Maybe if you have trouble sleeping you come visit and let me bore you to death." He gave a chuckle, coughed.

"You don't bore me, Sol. You talk to me. You don't ask me for my autograph or who I'm wearing. You don't know how refreshing that is."

"You're right. I don't." He scratched his chin. "Why do you think I keep to the common room here in the Monarch? It would be pandemonium on the streets if I went outside. Women of all ages would be throwing themselves at my feet, telling me how much they love me, how my words touched them in a very special place, how they can't wait to read my next book. When will it be out? When it's out!"

His face reddened.

Sepi smiled, touched him on the shoulder again. "Easy, Sol. The bad people can't hurt you up here."

"Thank you, darling," he said, patting her hand. "You're always there to put things in perspective. Now go on. I saw Nat come through here earlier and she seemed a little…" He lifted his hand, fingers splayed, and rotated it back and forth.

"I'll check on her," said Sepi. "See you around, Sol."

She left him sitting there with his giant palette.

Something wrong with Nat? Bad day at work? Stressed out from her commute maybe?

Sepi quickened her pace, thumbed the reader by her door, and stepped into the apartment.

It smelled of chocolate and pumpkin at first; the lavender hit as she dropped her bag and shoes in the foyer. Her stockinged feet tapped lightly on the wood floors.

"Natty? I'm home."

"I'm in here."

Sepi turned the corner into the kitchen and saw her girlfriend standing in front of the oven in her favorite red apron. She was bent at the waist, with one hand on her hip and the other on the oven door. She'd pulled her blonde hair into a low ponytail that hung halfway down her back.

"Hey, sweet pea," said Sepi. "How are you?"

"Good," said Nat, "but these muffins aren't coming out right at all. This is already my third batch." She broke away from the oven and gave Sepi a hug and a kiss. "How about you? How was the meeting?"

Sepi felt the words spill out. "I got the lead."

Nat gave her another hug, this one stronger and longer lasting.

"Awesome, baby. I knew something great would happen to you today. That's why I'm making you muffins. Assuming they come out, of course."

Nat opened the oven door and reached in with a protective mitt. She pulled out a tray of brown muffins and set them down on the white countertop.

"These look a little better," she said, "but we won't know until they've had time to cool. Did you want to change before dinner? Or do you want to go out and celebrate?"

"Maybe this weekend," said Sepi. "Tonight I'd rather just eat Chinese food in bed."

Nat checked the time over the stove. "It's a little early, but I'm sure we can find something else to do after we finish eating." Nat pulled off her apron. "I'm gonna grab a bottle of champagne from Gus. How much are they paying you? How expensive should I go?"

"Get *all* of them." She smiled as Nat raised her eyebrows. "Something Italian. I have an appointment tomorrow at eleven, so I shouldn't overdo it."

"Yeah, well," said Nat, placing her hands on her chest. "My class is doing level testing tomorrow, so I'll drink what you don't finish. And if we're going to get in the habit of buying all the champagne, then it sounds like I may never have to work again. I've always wanted to be a stay-at-home mom."

Nat clapped as she skipped out of the apartment.

When she was gone and the space was quiet, Sepi let out the breath she had been holding. She loved Natasha with every ounce of her soul, but she worried about how the influx of a ridiculous amount of money would affect the relationship. Would Nat really quit her job at Dahlstrom Academy? She loved interacting with young minds, loved working near the Berkeley campus where she and Sepi met, fell in love, and decided to be together forever.

Would the money put pressure on them to finally marry? To start a family?

Sepi went to the bedroom and slipped into the attached closet. She undressed, acutely aware of how much the prospect of marriage and children scared her. Just the idea of being responsible for someone else's life made her palms sweat. How could she watch her child go through everything she went through? How could she live seeing someone else cower at the mere presence of other people?

A child meant another person relying on Nat for a hand to hold just to get through the simplest of social interactions. Was Nat strong enough for that? Or would she buckle under the pressure, just one day say *enough is enough* and order Sepi and their son or daughter to grow up, be adults, and face the world themselves?

Sepi's social anxiety already weighed down the relationship. In the dark times, she saw herself as a burden to Nat, an anchor keeping the wide-eyed ball of excitement from all the wonderful things in the world. Natasha Kumanov deserved to have everything she wanted, and yet she'd stayed, had fallen into line at Sepi's hip and never left.

There was no doubt how much love Natasha had to give.

But Sepi wondered if she'd be better off giving it to someone else, someone who shared the same lust for life instead of being scared of it.

She placed her blouse in the hamper and hung the skirt on a wooden hanger. In the drawer beneath her slacks, she found neatly folded stacks of pajamas and pulled out a white flannel set decorated with woodland icons.

Little trees. Piles of wood. Gray snowflakes.

She cinched the drawstring on the pajamas as she stepped back into the cold bathroom. The tiles on the floor were supposed to be heated from beneath, but the elements had been broken for a month. Even at the luxurious Monarch, building management moved slowly.

At the sink, Sepi grabbed the blue pill box next to her toothbrush. The tab with the *M* printed on it was open, but the pills were still inside. She thought back to the morning and tried to remember why she hadn't taken them. Was it the excitement of the coming day? The fear of meeting new people? Or Nat in the shower pressing her butt against the glass in a way Sepi didn't really care for but that Nat found endlessly amusing?

It *had* been Nat, coming out of the shower, tiptoeing on the cold floor until she made it to the bathmat, taking up position next to the small heater Sepi was currently using while she did her make-up.

"You look beautiful," Nat had said. "Why do you waste so much time with make-up?" She put her face next to Sepi's and stared into the mirror. "You have such beautiful Persian features. Look at your eyes, baby. You shouldn't mask them."

"This is what it takes, sweet pea," Sepi replied. "It's a man's world. At least they think it is. More so in the pictures. Besides, if I don't get done up, Jane will throw a fit and I don't think I can handle that on top of everything else today."

Nat toyed with the front of Sepi's towel.

Sepi shook the memory away, grabbed the pills from the case, and downed them with some water from the tap.

"I got a Valdo," said Nat, from the doorway. Then, noticing the look on Sepi's face, asked, "What were you thinking about?"

"This morning."

"What about this morning?"

"The thing we didn't have time for."

Nat smiled, thumbed the foil on the champagne bottle.

THIRTEEN

Doyle's Journal – November 19, 2045

I never gave up on you, Vida.

Sure, there were times when I thought about letting it all go. When I woke up in darkness, in a wooden box no more than a meter and a half tall and wide, I thought *maybe this could be it*. Maybe that could have been the moment when I fashioned some kind of noose from my clothes or peeled back a sliver of wood to jam into my carotid artery. A minute of pain and then sweet release from this nightmare.

Because honestly, what did I have left to live for?

Wife and daughter gone.

The world I shared with them gone.

And what remained? Machines. Human waste.

And you.

Vida.

It sounds stupid.

I don't even know you.

And yet, I couldn't stop thinking of your face. Your pensive eyes, staring at the walls of the bunker, something on your mind that you'll never share with me. I wish I knew what was going on in your head.

I thought about how I would like to get to know you, and that alone was something worth staying alive for. You made me think of life in the abstract, of the possibility of a future.

In that box, in the never-ending shadow, I thought of your eyes, and that kept me alive, kept me wanting to push forward. I found meaning in your memory.

Even when they pulled me out. Even when they beat me, demanded to know where I came from, how many we were, and so on—questions I don't even remember anymore, those memories lost to the blinding pain.

I lost track of the days, lost most of my clothes. They were either torn off or burned off, I don't know which. It was an endless cycle of beatings, feedings, and shallow, pointless sleep.

At least when I closed my eyes, I saw a familiar face.

Sorry. That's all I can really remember right now.

Except for how I got out of there. That's pretty clear.

It started with Harlan, several days after they took me prisoner.

He was a tall man, gaunt in the face and wiry. His flesh stretched thin over rippling arms and shoulders. Scars clung to him like barnacles to a ship—he hadn't risen to his position of power through diplomacy, that was for sure.

I'd caught sight of Harlan a few times during my torture, but I never got a good look at him until that last time when he stepped out of the shadows as I hung from chains slung over the rafters. We were in a burned-out building in what looked like Park City. Some kind of explosion or crash-landing had torn a good chunk of the roof off and penetrated the second-floor ceiling. I could see the sky, see the snow as it fell.

Harlan had my Dragunov. He stroked it with a gloved hand.

"This is a fine weapon," he said, sitting on a nearby stool. "Definitely not off the shelf at Walmart. You modify this weapon yourself? Or did you take it off someone who did?"

I grunted.

"I see." He leaned the rifle against the wall. "I guess you need to be wined and dined before you put out, huh? Alright. My name is Harlan. I run Harlan's City. That chubby motherfucker over there is Nichols. He thinks we should put a bullet in your head. The man with the Vikings hat is Marks. He thinks we should flay you. Now, I've never flayed a man who didn't have it coming, but it's never something I *want* to do. So why don't you make this easy and just tell me your name?"

"Dylan."

"Dylan what?"

"Murphy. Dylan Murphy from Billings."

"Bullshit," said Nichols. "Billings is a dead zone."

"Not completely," I replied. "I holed up in a grocery store attic. Spent two weeks living in the air ducts, shitting down exhaust vents."

"How did you get out?" asked Harlan. "Máquinas have that entire city locked down tight."

"Something drew them to the south side, near the river. I saw the opportunity to slip out and I took it. Found a military convoy a few blocks north, grabbed that rifle. Been on the run ever since."

"Why didn't you mention this earlier?"

"Why waste my time with piss-ant underlings? I wanted to talk to the boss. I knew if I held out long enough, they'd bring you to me."

"Oh," said Harlan, "so this is all part of your plan?"

I tried to shrug, but with my arms pulled above me, all I could do was dip my head a little.

"If anyone's gonna let me go, it's you," I said.

"And what makes you think we're just going to let you go?"

"Why keep me? You've taken everything I have. Just give me a jacket and send me on my way. I won't make any trouble."

Harlan stepped in closer. "And how do I know you won't just run back to your people, stir them up, and march them back here?"

I shook my head. "I have no people. It's just me."

"Somehow I doubt that." He motioned to Nichols, who brought him my backpack. "According to this GPS unit, there's something at these coordinates. What is it?"

My stomach turned. I saw a flash of your face.

The GPS showed the return trip to the Admiral. If they followed the trail, it would lead them right back to you.

"Nothing, nothing. Just some provisions I stockpiled. A little food. Enough for one person. I'm leaving little caches as I move south in case I need to backtrack. There are others much closer if you need supplies."

Harlan smirked, shared a look with Marks and Nichols.

Nichols shook his head.

"I can't stand liars," said Harlan. "No respect for the social contract. And you never know what to believe when their lips start flapping. I guess the only way to find out is to send a team out there, see what they rustle up. Or maybe…" He leaned in, whispered. "Maybe I'll just go out there myself, kill every living thing I find. How does that grab you?"

"Take these chains off and I'll show you."

"Ha!" Then to Nichols. "Put him back in the box. If he tries anything while I'm gone, shoot him or flay him, I don't give a shit."

They let me down and dragged me back to my cell while I resisted the urge to yell out *don't hurt her* and *leave her alone.* I wished I had some way of contacting you so I could tell you to grab everything and run, just fucking run.

"He's not kidding," said Nichols, shutting and locking the lid. "He will kill everything he finds. If you've got a wife, family, friends… they're all dead."

I saw your face.

I believed him.

And then there was darkness for a long time.

Dreams of the Admiral came to me in my sleep. I saw you sitting on the couch, laughing at some sitcom playing on the vidscreen. Saw you dressed in Angie's clothes, eating her share of the rations.

A moment frozen in time in a dream that didn't move.

I stared at the picture for hours and hours.

Gunfire finally woke me up.

At first, it was distant, a few reports somewhere outside. Screams followed, calls for more men, more firepower. Radio chatter turned more desperate by the second. Whoever was in the room with me began clomping around. By the strain of the wood floor, I guessed it was Nichols. More people joined him, and I heard breaking glass. Gunfire filled the room, slipping in through the cracks in the box, tearing at my eardrums. I put my hands to the sides of my head, tried to blot out the sound.

I figured out it was Máquinas pretty quickly. Only their unique blend of overwhelming numbers and instant devastation could put such fear into men's voices. Nichols was screaming, pleading with people not to run.

"Stand and fight, you fucking cowards!"

Soon the words devolved into primal grunts, and I heard him unrack something heavy. Gut-rattling booms sounded in the room as he fired a large-caliber weapon, perhaps a JDJ or something even bigger. He cheered a few shots but mostly cursed and groaned. Máquinas could be fast when they wanted to be, especially when you got a group of them together. Alone, they operated on a single stream of sensory data gathered from their synthetic receptors. As a group, they had an awareness of the battlefield that humans simply couldn't match.

Any Máquina walking down the street could avoid Nichols' fire because other Máquinas were looking in that direction. They sensed the impending trigger pull, registered the muzzle flash, and calculated the trajectory. Everything else was just a matter of fast-twitch, synthetic servos.

Of which they have plenty.

You know what else Máquinas have? Ordinance.

Even with synthetics, every army needs some serious firepower if they're going to lay siege to a city. Any military force that can manufacture soldiers could certainly bring more to the fight than automatic rifles.

In the chaos, I'd forgotten all about their artillery, but I remembered as soon as the shell hit the building. Nichols' scream was swallowed up by a deafening explosion, followed by the washed-out snapping of wood. Rafters fell through the ceiling, struck my box, and pushed me through the floor. I went weightless for a moment, and with what I was sure was my last conscious thought, I considered the countless futures we could have had if only I had walked north instead of south.

Each thread I followed, however, ended in the same place: death.

So what if we had survived in the bunker for years? There would still and probably always be Máquinas to fight. Our country had fallen so easily. Where was the Corp? Where were the squids and the flyboys and the grunts?

The more I thought about it, the angrier I became. At our government. At Vinestead, for building inferior soldiers. At Perion Synthetics, for sitting back and doing nothing while the world went to shit. We could have used their tech, could have turned the tide with something innovative instead of Vinestead's blatant rip-offs.

And yet, nothing.

We were left alone, left to fend for ourselves.

I guess that's the American Way.

Every man for himself.

Except me, Vida. I would have been there for you.

Would have done anything. Everything.

I blacked out for a while and woke to crackling fire and pain in my legs.

The box had been surprisingly sturdy—had to be, to keep me from getting out. The right angles had provided just enough support to keep it from collapsing on me, though now it was off-kilter, pitched thirty or forty degrees from level. One side had come loose in the fall, and the crack was large enough for me to see I was surrounded by splintered wood and powdered drywall. I wedged an arm in the opening and pushed.

It took a few tries, but eventually I worked out enough space to crawl through. The building smelled of smoke; embers cascaded down from above. Chilly air bit at the oppressive heat as I dragged myself over and under fallen beams to the sidewalk outside. I paused, tried to ignore the cold pain gripping my chest.

Half a dozen Park City clan members were nearby, on their backs in the street, empty gazes turned to the eternal night sky.

Nothing moved. Not man or Máquina.

I tried to get up, but my arms threatened to collapse every time I put weight on them.

Get up, I told myself. *Get up and take that man's clothes and weapon.*

Myself responded with: *Why? Why should we even fight anymore?*

Because Harlan is out there. And he's headed straight for Vida.

I put bloody hands flat against the fresh snow.

Pushed.

Lifted my chest an inch from the ground.

It was a good start.

FOURTEEN

Minutes stretched into hours, and though there was silence in the bunker, the proximity alarm continued to flash on the vidscreen, strobing a sickly green that made the room feel less like a safe house and more like the bowels of some derelict spaceship drifting through a black hole. All that was missing was the tense music—a cello scraping the bottom of the bass clef—and a ten-foot alien clawing at the bunker door.

Vida struggled to keep her eyes open.

The pit that had opened in her stomach had grown to consume her, sucking in every last bit of her energy and putting out nothing but grisly images of terrible fates. Her muscles knotted, first from the crouching and later from the standing. A dry mouth sent her to the sink several times, and just that tiny act of turning her back to the door made the pit howl. Her brain maundered a series of fragmented prayers, entreating whatever deity might exist to bring her safely through this trying time. She flashed on impossible scenarios: the military breaking down the door to rescue her, her family suddenly knocking on the steel plating, or Doyle himself, tearing apart oncoming Máquinas with his bare hands.

She wanted him back.

He'd gone over the proximity alarm procedure with her several times, and yet this time she was alone, and that made all the difference. Whoever stalked the land around the bunker had been at it all day instead of just moving on, which meant they were looking for something. The routine called for shutting down the bunker when a Máquina patrol came by, limiting electromagnetic output so they wouldn't be detected, but Doyle had never said anything about a persistent visitor.

It was bad enough living in the bunker.

Life would be unbearable if she had to do it in the dark.

Vida paced between the living room and the bathroom, trying to silence the competing voices inside her head. The pit spewed its horrible visions. Her brain sought solace in a higher power. Above it all was an overwhelming desire to retreat to her room and hide under the blankets.

Shut out the world.

With each trip back and forth, she got closer to the open door leading into her room. She could see the bed under the soft glow of the emergency lights. It looked so inviting.

How bad of an idea was it?

If the stranger found the outer door, another alarm would go off. If they started messing with the inner door, she would hear it as several loud—

Knock, knock, knock.

Vida held her breath, let the whine of the air recyclers fill the bunker. Had she imagined the sound?

Again, the knocks came.

The gun was out of its holster before the conscious thought made a complete trip through her brain. She stepped out of the tiny hallway and took aim at the door. The vidscreen still showed the same proximity alarm with no outer door breach.

So if not from there...

Knock, knock, knock.

The sound was coming from Doyle's room, but not from the door itself.

Thumbing the safety off, Vida pressed down on the handle and pushed the door open with the barrel. She'd only caught glimpses of Doyle's room before, and now in the low light, it looked ominous and gloomy, like a shrine built by parents who had lost a son, who refused to change the room for fear of losing their connection to the past. The bed was made up, and everything seemed to be in place. The walls were bare except for a few pictures of Doyle and his family.

Vida had no time to study them, as another series of knocks came from behind the wall next to Doyle's bed. Close to the ground, looking more like an AC vent than anything else, was a steel panel no bigger than the flat face of a carry-on suitcase. At each corner were pins holding the plate in place. They rattled with each knock.

Violent scenes of her own rape and murder boiled over from the pit in Vida's stomach. She stumbled backwards into Doyle's closet, holding the gun out as if to prove to the intruder that she was armed—it rattled so much that she had to put her other hand under the weapon for support. The stranger had evidently found a way around the outer door and into this... what? Secret escape hatch? Doyle had never mentioned anything about it.

She wondered if the panel was bulletproof. Would it stop an entire clip from her gun? Why not just open fire now and hope for the best?

She shook her head.

What if the bullet ricocheted? There were no functioning hospitals nearby.

Exhaustion bloomed again, and Vida sank to the floor. She propped the gun on her knee, began to weep. She may not have known how everything began, but she felt deep down that this was how it was going to end. Everything that had happened in her unremembered life: the airplane, the Máquina, and Doyle—why go through any of it if she was just going to die in a bunker under the Montana dirt?

She wished herself away to the foggy streets of San Francisco where the Golden Gate Bridge had been reduced to a few orange poles disappearing into the mist. Tourists crisscrossing in front of her on streets that rose and plunged like waves. The smell of fresh seafood, fried and baked and grilled, wafting on the humid air. Street artists spray-painting with abandon—a leery synthetic cop nearby making sure they didn't hassle the passers-by.

The other world reached out for her, but at the last moment, Vida paused, certain she had heard Doyle calling out her name, urging her to come back to the bunker.

For what possible reason?

Then she heard it again.

"Vida… help…"

One last knock.

Then silence.

It was Doyle's voice. It had to be.

Tossing the gun onto the bed, Vida scrambled across the floor and pulled the pins from the four corners of the panel. It dropped off the wall, and the first thing she saw was an outstretched and bloody hand. It lay at the bottom of a vent shaft just big enough for a grown man to crawl through. Nearly unconscious and dressed in a jacket a size too small, was Doyle. He lifted his head briefly, waved his fingers at her.

Vida grabbed his hand and helped him escape the shaft, feeling like a doctor birthing a jelly-covered, fully grown adult. He landed on the floor in a heap, a mash-up of blood and grunts.

"Thank you," he said, patting Vida's knee. "Will you close up the hatch please? The sound will travel."

"What the hell, Doyle? You should have told me there was another way in."

He raised an eyebrow. "No, this isn't all my blood. Thanks for asking."

"Someone's been outside for hours," said Vida. She spoke over her shoulder as she worked to reset the four pins. "I thought you were him."

"No," said Doyle, groaning to a sitting position. Blood trickled from his matted hair. "That's Harlan. I ran into him in Park City. Chased him back here after he found my GPS. I would have put him down, but I spent all my ammo on the way here. Máquinas are crawling all over the mountainside. I've never seen so many."

Vida noticed his pants were different and ill-fitting.

"What happened to your clothes?"

"Lost them in a game of strip poker," he replied. "That was, I don't know how long ago."

"You've been gone a week."

He groaned again, tried to pull himself up to the bed, but failed. "Would you mind helping me to the shower? I need to wash this blood off so I can see what needs fixing."

Vida grabbed him by the arm and lifted. She swung her head under his arm when he was high enough and helped him out of the room. In the bathroom, he sat down on the toilet, getting blood on the pristine porcelain while she ran the water.

"Do you want me to bring some candles in here?" she asked.

"I just crawled eighty meters through a pitch-black tunnel. I can see just fine with the guide lights. Plus, I'm about to take off my clothes. Trust me, this way is better."

"How can you joke at a time like this? It looks like someone tried to kill you."

"They did," he replied, peeling the jacket from his arms. "Tied me up and tried to make me spill the Admiral's location. They beat me for days, but I never cracked. Not this soldier."

Vida turned away as Doyle unbuttoned his pants. She stepped out of the bathroom and leaned against the wall just beyond the doorjamb.

Torture.

The word repeated in her mind. She tried not to see Doyle bound and supine while a bunch of men with Máquina parts strapped to their bodies kicked him with heavy boots.

Given the blood, they'd kept at it for days.

And yet he had never given her up.

A sudden question occurred to her. "Why did they beat you?" she asked, turning just in time to see a naked Doyle stepping into the falling water. She withdrew, but not before seeing the extensive scarring, his slight paunch peppered with body hair, and his full erection.

"I told you," he said, "to find out where my people are."

"Yeah, but you said they had your GPS. Didn't they already know?"

"Huh, I hadn't thought of that." The falling water muffled his words. "Maybe they didn't find it until after they had beat me for a few days. Maybe they wanted to see me suffer and just needed a reason. I don't know, Vida. All I know is that Harlan is dangerous and if he finds this place, he's going to bring what's left of his people to burn it to the ground."

Vida glanced over her shoulder at the vidscreen.

"He's still out there," she said. "Walking around."

"Yeah, I know. I watched him for a while. He definitely knows something is here, but the outer door is well-hidden, and there's fresh snow on top of it. By the time he finds the door, I'll be showered, fed, rested, and re-armed. I'll go out the way I came in, sneak up behind him, and end this."

There is no end to this, thought Vida.

"Hey," he asked, "would you mind getting the first aid kit? There's still blood coming from somewhere. And turn the power back on. Silent mode is mostly for Máquinas. Harlan won't be able to hear us unless we scream into the escape hatch and he stands at the other end of it."

"Sure," said Vida, happy to get away from the steam and the naked man lathering himself within it.

She hit the panic button next to the vidscreen first, then headed into the kitchen for the first aid kit. The lights in the bunker graded up, and the air began to move in earnest. The fridge whined, though its fan turned off again as she opened its door. She pulled a Fruit Punch Gatorade—Doyle's preferred—and a container of fiber-rich yogurt. Vida took the items into his room and set them on the small desk. The gun on the bed beckoned to her. She snatched it up and replaced it in its holster.

The sound of rushing water abated. Wet feet exited the shower. Doyle appeared a moment later with a blue towel wrapped around his waist.

The scars and bruises made Vida turn away.

"Ah, perfect," he said, reaching for the Gatorade. "Thank you."

"I'll let you get dressed," said Vida, maneuvering past him as best she could.

The space between the desk and the bed barely accommodated one person, let alone two. She felt her skin touch his, felt what she hoped was the knot of the towel press into her lower stomach. He made no effort to move aside.

Despite the obvious attempt at a cheap thrill, Vida paused at the door and said, "It's good to have you back."

"You missed me, didn't you?" he asked, smiling.

"Not as much as you missed me," she said, throwing her gaze downward briefly.

Doyle shrugged. "What can I say? I'm just happy to be alive."

Vida pulled the door closed behind her and wandered into the living room.

It didn't seem far enough away.

FIFTEEN

A Vitra Synth hashtag started trending around five in the evening on all the major feeds, overtaking developing news of an MX incursion near Brownsville, Texas. Kagan had to kill his whisperer to keep from being reminded about the death of a man he'd considered inconsequential but whose 40-year-old trophy wife had deemed irreplaceable. She'd been on a crusade all afternoon, first blaming Vinestead's Guardian Angel chip, then Vitra Synth, and finally, after somehow getting his name, Kagan.

Son of Kagan Group founder Frank Kagan kills respected community leader.

It was total bullshit, but then the feeds were never about getting the true story out. Their goal was subscribers, individual consumers who could be fed a morsel of habit-forming news-ertainment under a heaping mound of advertisements. The fact that Abat had been old and feeble was conspicuously missing from the reports, not to mention what Abat was doing when his heart exploded.

The headline should have read: *old coot literally virtually fucks his way to the afterlife.*

Kagan sipped his third glass of whiskey in Cinema Rouge, a private theater he'd built at the back of his home. It had four rows of seats, with the back three containing four large recliners while the front row had three oversized chairs. He reclined in the center, feeling his body being absorbed by the foam cushioning. Dim lights in the ceiling and along the floors showed where each level of the room stepped down. Dark sconces on the wall dotted the space between framed posters of his favorite movies.

Titles like *Brainscan, The Remainders,* and of course, Sepideh Ahmadi's *Seven Kingdoms* and *The Dark Desert,* which was now showing on the far wall.

In lieu of a projector screen or vidscreen, Cinema Rouge used augmented reality to display the movie from wall-to-wall and floor-to-ceiling. AR glasses sat in the cup holders of each chair for guests; Kagan had made the switch to contact lenses thanks to a jovial Indian he had met in the Plummer Tower lounge.

The movie had Sepideh playing Priya Karimi opposite Claire Danes as Sarah Howard as the two traveled across the Sahara Desert discovering the hidden world and each other. The play between the older, predatory Sarah and the younger, innocent Priya was the most erotic dance Kagan had seen in a long time, and as such, the movie started playing every time he walked into Cinema Rouge. He never grew tired of seeing Sepideh's head plastered on an obvious body double for her nude scenes or the scrunched-up face of the elder Danes as she cried during the film's climax.

Kagan watched it absently, thinking about how Vitra Synth might change if Wayne tried to get him fired. Dad would step in, reorganize the company, and Wayne would be on his way out, likely as the sacrificial lamb for the Abat fiasco. That wasn't to say Dad wouldn't be pissed, but then Dad was always pissed about something.

Nadya tiptoed into the room, dressed once again in her usual uniform, holding a fresh whiskey in one hand. She set it on the small table next to Kagan's chair and smiled.

"Your friend is awake now," she said. "Should I show him to the cinema?"

"No," said Kagan, wiggling out of the chair. "I'll meet him on the veranda."

"Sure, the *veranda*." She retreated through a different door.

The Dark Desert followed Kagan out into the hallway. Nixle Chronos technicians had taken great care to ensure the house's augmented reality field extended to every corner. When he passed through the ten-foot-tall glass doors at the back of the house, the audio from the movie cut out and the sounds of a cold California evening faded in. Insects chirped, brave birds stalked the edges of the pool. Kagan sat down in a chair next to the fire pit and set his drink on the charred brick.

He took a few deep breaths, tried to think of where to begin.

High palms swayed in the slight wind. The Hollywood hills gleamed in the failing light. They looked pristine, but Kagan was all too aware of what kind of filth lay on the other side. All the depravity Los Angeles and, specifically, Hollywood, had to offer, neatly condensed into a few square miles, all ready to convince Kagan that humanity had stumbled, fallen, and never picked itself up. And beyond that cesspool of human garbage, the MX writhed with synthetics that kept finding their way over the border.

And Wayne was concerned about a fossil coming and going in a demo room.

The world had bigger problems.

"God, I needed that nap," said Raf.

Kagan looked over his shoulder and saw his friend coming out of the house while Nadya hurried away in the opposite direction. He was dressed in Kagan's sweatpants, t-shirt, and an old hoodie. With his scraggly hair and thick beard, he didn't look the least bit less homeless than before.

"Hope you don't mind," he continued, taking a chair on the other side of the fire pit.

"No," said Kagan, waving the idea away with a flick of his wrist. "You've had a stressful day. Stressful years, I'm guessing. It's time to kick back and relax. Your days on the street are over."

Raf nodded thoughtfully. "Por vida, verdad?"

"Para siempre. It's nothing you wouldn't do for me, man."

"You don't know that." Raf smiled.

Kagan made a mental note to get Raf a toothbrush and set up a dental cleaning.

"I do. I'm sure of it." He lifted his glass, waved it at Raf. "Something to drink?"

"I already asked your synthetic death machine to get me one."

Kagan chuckled, sipped, felt the burn on his lips. Speaking into his glass, he said, "I'm surprised her head's still attached. I was sure you were going to psycho out on her."

Raf groaned, shifted in his chair. "That doorman or whatever at your building was getting in my face. I just didn't feel like taking orders from a goddamn synny. Fuck all of 'em."

"Is that really it?" Kagan's chest tightened. As close as he was to Raf, he hadn't seen the man in years. Who knew what would set him off again? "Do you feel like you were in control of yourself?"

"Que?" He looked over Kagan's shoulder at the approaching Nadya. He accepted the tall glass of water when she held it out to him.

"No booze?" asked Kagan.

"Don't change the subject. What do you mean by me being in control of myself?"

Kagan set his drink down, tapped a nearby button with his toe. The fire pit gushed natural gas, and a pilot light sent a flame flickering into the sky. It settled into a low, rolling fire.

"Do you think about the MX a lot, Raf? Any nightmares? Visions?"

Again, he shifted in his chair.

Kagan continued. "You ever fly into a blind rage because some robot says you can't come into a building the way you smell?"

"Cállate el hocico," he replied. "I couldn't help it."

"Which? The smell or the blind rage?"

Raf took a sip of water, held the glass in his lap. "Both," he said.

"Fucking America." Kagan shook his head. "They drop you in a hostile environment so you can die on a lie and then when you come back bruised and broken, physically and mentally, they don't have shit for you. *You're not Uncle Sam's problem anymore*, verdad? Now you gotta make your own way, reintegrate into a world where your best friends *aren't* dying left and right. And the whole time, you've got these memories, these fucked up memories of death and destruction and general… shit-filled despair. That's a death sentence, man. Living on the street like a pinche animal? Not my people. Not my friend."

"Easy, gringo." Raf put up a hand. "I knew what I was getting into. I just didn't think I was ever coming back. The MX doesn't let people go. You know we weren't just fighting Máquinas down there, right? There's still MX infantry, soldados, they call 'em. Hijos de putas, all of them. They'd put any child, woman, or animal in front of them as a shield. I killed…" He paused, took a sip. "… who I had to kill, for the mission."

"You see their faces, don't you?"

"Para siempre," said Raf.

"What if you didn't have to?" Kagan sat up, leaned forward with his arms on his knees. "What if I could take those memories away? Leave only the good ones?"

Raf shook his head. "There's not enough tequila in the world to blot that shit out."

Kagan stood, walked to a raised brick flowerbed where various blooms struggled for survival.

"I'm not talking about getting drunk," he said, mimicking the soft, innocuous tones of a VFeed advertisement. "Do you know what we do at Vitra Synth? We transfer human minds into synthetic bodies. Shells, sleeves; call 'em what you want. Point is, it's not trivial to copy a fully functional human mind. To even get to that point, you have to know *everything* about how a brain works. That includes memories. Shit, most of what makes a person a person is memory. Responding to stimuli because of a previous experience. Did you know we didn't even know *how* a memory was stored as recently as twenty years ago?"

Raf stared into his glass, as if he weren't buying what Kagan was selling.

"James Perion figured it out in 2014, and now we can not only identify memories, but copy them. Or delete them. Wipe them the fuck out. I can make you forget about the war, Raf. Not all of it. Just the parts keeping you up at night."

Raf considered the idea, tapped his fingers on his knee. Several times his shoulders bounced, as if he were huffing to himself.

"And how much does something like that cost?" he asked.

"I wouldn't know," said Kagan. "The company's basically mine. We'll go in after hours and I'll get Glasser to take care of it."

"I'll think about it."

Kagan walked back to the fire pit, stood directly in front of Raf. "What's there to think about? I can make the nightmares go away. I can do what the government should have done for you six years ago."

He shrugged again. "It's like you said, bro. Memories make the man. Who will I be if you just take all that shit away?"

Kagan opened his mouth to speak, but the answer wouldn't come. It didn't make any sense why Raf wouldn't want to seek out a better life, a life veterans of the World Wars and Middle East conflicts never had a chance for.

His sliver vibrated minutely. A name appeared on its face.

KAGAN.

Dad was calling.

"Well, start thinking about it," said Kagan, drawing his phone from his pocket. "I gotta take this."

He walked down the steps from the veranda leading into the back lawn with its alternating rows of dark and light green grass. He took up position next to a transplanted redwood as the line clicked on.

"This is Kagan," he said.

"Mr. Kagan, this is Janet from Frank Kagan's office."

"Hey, Janet. You can put him through."

"Unfortunately, Mr. Kagan is tied up at the moment, but he wanted me to inform you that you have been terminated from Vitra Synth, effective immediately. Your personal effects will be brought to you tomorrow morning. Do not return to the building. If you have any questions, please contact your HR rep at…"

Janet's words muffled, drifted away.

Kagan looked backed towards the house, to Raf sitting pensively in his chair. He had pulled his hood up over his head.

As if that would protect him from the nightmares.

SIXTEEN

Sepi awoke with a knot in her stomach.

Before her eyes could register the room and guess at the time, her brain rattled off everything she had to accomplish that day, including a meeting with Abdul Darwish at the Nixle Chronos offices. The knot examined the potential meeting, dished out a little nausea, but seemed unfulfilled. She thought of the deal she'd made with the Sierra Brothers and the work it would entail. Her atrial tachometer sped up in response, but again, it wasn't what the knot really wanted.

It wasn't until she turned her head and saw Nat lying on her side, facing away, with the sharp rays of the sun peeking through the curtains and over her body that she remembered. It had been so brief, a passing moment as they repositioned themselves on the bed, holding each other during a mid-coital break, that Sepi had seen the flash on Nat's face. Her eyes were closed, and perhaps she had been unaware she was being observed. Maybe that's why the frown appeared for that split-second or why her chin trembled like a tiny aftershock.

Had there been tears at the corners of her welded-shut eyes?

Then it disappeared, and the intensity with which they'd started their roll in the sheets resumed once again.

Later, Chinese food. Some television. A brief recap of her encounter with the Sierra Brothers and their augmented reality room.

Sepi never mentioned the money, and Nat never asked.

All morning, Sepi wanted to say something about that frown, that momentary glimpse into the inner workings of Natasha Kumanov, but every moment seemed like the wrong one. Nat always slept until the last possible minute, and when she awoke, she barreled through her shower, make-up, and breakfast, and was out the door before Sepi had had her first cup of coffee.

"I'll see you tonight," said Sepi, standing at the door in her silk robe, watching Nat fumble with her heels.

It came out so much like a question that Nat paused, gave her a puzzled look, and said, "Of course you will. I can't wait to hear all about your meeting. See if you can steal me a pair of glasses or something."

And though Nat had smiled when she spoke, her eyes had looked everywhere except at Sepi.

The door closed, the knot wrenched, and Sepi felt the familiar panic rise up from the floor and engulf her. She tried to get away from it by turning on music, filling the apartment with the Resurgence Jazz that had been so popular the last few years. Tinkling of high-end piano keys echoed off the tall ceilings as Sepi moved from room to room. Panic followed as if attached by a chain to her ankle.

She showered, dressed in simple gray jeans and a white, low-cut t-shirt. Breakfast alone at the counter—a small container of yogurt, a glass of orange juice, and two of the hundreds of vitamins and supplements Nat swore by. She chose one for anxiety—some kind of fungus found only between the toes of Argentinian burro jockeys—and another, a root that grew six feet deep and was ninety-nine percent poisonous, for regularity, as the knot had already sent her to the bathroom three times that morning.

As the memory of the previous night faded, the knot loosened, and Sepi began to feel better. Just to be safe, she took a dose of propranolol in addition to her usual Lexapro regimen. The propranolol wasn't an anti-anxiety medication per se, but it did help with some of the physical symptoms, and that's where Sepi really needed the relief.

It was one thing to know no one in the world or on the street was out to get her, to be able to say with one hundred percent certainty that the man staring at her from across the hall wasn't going to abduct and dismember her, but it was quite another to convince her body that the threat was imagined.

"Anxiety is normal," Sophia Dahlstrom had once told her. "It's an instinctive human trait that served us well in the Stone Age when everything really *was* trying to kill us. We can civilize our brains, Sepideh, but changing our instincts could take thousands of generations."

It made sense, of course. Sepi thought about those words, and the countless words she had read in books on the subject, but nothing could ever quell the feelings inside her. It was as if she were two different people. Sepideh Prime was a normal, well-adjusted, brain-oriented human with a firm grasp on the world and how it worked. Sepideh Secundus was a scared mouse who jumped at every noise and who was so focused on survival that every person, place, and thing was seen through a veil of paranoia and distrust.

Two people living in the same body.

Plus whoever else Sepi was employed to be.

At 10:30, the intercom by the door buzzed, and a synthetic voice let Sepi know a car had just arrived for her and that it was waiting in the garage pickup zone on B1.

Sepi grabbed her purse and a light jacket and headed out. The common room was empty except for Gus. He was clearing both empty and full champagne flutes of orange juice from his bar. He paused with his fingers around a stem as Sepi approached, but she waved him off.

She rode the elevator down with the heavily modified Stella Starfall, a porn star who had only recently made the jump to more respectable pictures. She didn't say much, thankfully, but there was a slight wheezing sound coming from her pursed lips, as if her entire head were just a mask and beneath it was a shriveled old woman struggling for breath.

Stella got out at the lobby and Sepi stabbed the button for B1 until the doors shut again. In the garage, she found a lone Town Car sitting in the pickup area. By the driver's door stood a synthetic in a tailored suit complete with chauffer's cap. He opened the rear door for Sepi without introducing himself, and once she was safely secured inside, he began driving cautiously but efficiently back to street level.

Outside, Hollywood's mid-morning daze was in full effect. Neon flashes jogged down the crowded sidewalks. Homeless men and women congregated at corners to beg for money. Writers and actors masqueraded as delivery men and sign holders, struggling to keep food in their stomachs so they wouldn't starve to death before finally getting cast in a picture.

Sepi remembered the uncertainty of those days, trying to break into the business. She empathized with the struggling masses who wanted nothing more than to express their creativity. It garnered them an extra few bucks when they served her at a restaurant or delivered food to her apartment.

There was yet another crowd waiting for her at Plummer Tower when the car pulled up, but it looked like the building had added extra security for the occasion. When the gaggle of aggregators surged towards her, burly men in too-tight uniforms blocked their path. Sepi rushed inside and found the doorman holding an elevator for her. She thanked him and rode up to the Nixle Chronos offices on eleven.

The reception area was nothing more than an empty room. No desk stood ready to welcome visitors, nor were there any guards standing watch over the two doors on either side of the hexagonal space. Instead, Sepi found a young man standing by a small slit of a window to her left. Her eyes immediately sought out his name tag.

Abdul Darwish looked like he had skipped seventh-period Statistics to meet with Sepi. He was barely taller than her and had a build that suggested powerlifting and hearty meals weren't in his daily routine. Her arrival appeared to take him by surprise; he had been half-dancing to the music pumping from the whisperer in his ear. His black ponytail bobbed, swinging from shoulder to shoulder as he belted out the lyrics of the latest DJ Yz hip-hop track. The shaved sides of his head reminded Sepi of the flashback scenes she had shot for an episode of *CSI: Abbottabad* in which the extras had dressed up like cheesy, tranq'd-out skaters from the mid-90's.

"Yo, Sepideh Ahmadi, totally a pleasure," said Abdul. He held out a sweaty hand that Sepi shook weakly. "So I know you're like, crazy busy, so I'ma take you straight to the measurement room. Cool beats?"

"Cool beats," she replied, following him through the door on the right.

"Awesome," he continued, leading through a snaking hallway. "We got your records this morning, but we're still gonna measure again. When you're putting circuits next to someone's eyes, you gotta be a hundred percent USDA prime, yeah?"

Sepi didn't understand, but she nodded nonetheless. An older woman in a lab coat greeted them in the measurement room and directed Sepi to a chair.

"Hi, my name is Joy," said the tech. "Will you place your chin here, please?"

Sepi maneuvered into place, watched the lasers dance in front of her eyes.

Abdul cleared his throat. "So, even with our tech, your prescription's still gonna be the same. And you can wear these lenses indefinitely, just like your old ones."

"Oh, are you wearing your contacts right now?" asked Joy. "Can you take them out for me, please?"

Sepi turned to a nearby mirror and popped out the nearly invisible contact lenses. The world went blurry, obscuring Joy's and Abdul's faces. Now it was impossible to see what expressions they were wearing, whether they were happy or sad, judging or observing. The open door leading out of the room was now a foggy portal through which her worst nightmares could spill through.

Tendrils of panic grew up from her feet, but she took a deep breath, tried to keep them contained to her legs.

Her knee bobbed.

Sepi replaced her chin on the measuring device and watched a new light show of broad neon arcs.

The world was out of focus.

The knot stirred.

"I didn't bring my glasses," she whispered.

Abdul heard her. "We got you covered. New glasses with OcularAR built in. I'll grab 'em."

"Thank you."

When he was gone, Joy whispered to Sepi.

"You don't have to worry," she said, adjusting the knobs on the device. "It's just like wearing regular contacts. Exactly the same. After a day or two, you won't even know you're wearing them."

"Yeah, but what if someone punches me in the eye and those little bits of wire or whatever go into my eyeball?"

Joy leaned her head out from behind the apparatus. "Why would anyone punch you in the eye?"

"I don't know," said Sepi, "just if they do."

"Well, I don't know the technical term for it, but it's very safe. Mr. Vunak will be able to tell you more about it."

"He's here?" Sepi asked.

"He flew in from Austin this morning just to meet you. He's five minutes behind, but he should be here soon."

"So this isn't Abdul's company?"

Joy covered her mouth and laughed.

"Dear God, no," she said. "He's the nephew of the Regional Director who, by the way, is out with the flu. That just leaves Abdul to run the office." She sighed. "It's… trying."

"He's young."

"Yes," said Joy. "He's *crazy* young and *totally* annoying." She tapped on her palette for several minutes while the scanner buzzed. "Alright, we're done. You can sit up now."

Sepi sat back just in time to see a shadow fill the open doorway. She squinted but couldn't put order to the tall form.

The knot lurched into action.

"Sepideh, sweetheart! How are you? Welcome to Nixle Chronos!"

Sepideh Prime used context clues to infer that this person was Wade Vunak, founder and CEO of Nixle Chronos. From the booming voice and unbearable charisma, it was clear this was a man who transcended the boundaries between professional and personal. As a human, he was relatively harmless, except when it came to the health of Sepideh Prime's wallet.

Sepideh Secundus saw the blur and did nothing to stop the knot from exploding into full-blown panic. A stranger had called her out by name, had implied familiarity, and Sepi had no idea who he was or what he wanted or what she should say in return. Her muscles tensed, her calves began to ache. Panic climbed her body like a flame racing along primer cord. Conflicting electrical signals in her brain prepared her to simultaneously assume a defensive stance while casting around for possible exits. Why had she allowed them to lead her into a room with only one door? Were there any weapons around? Could Joy be used as a human shield?

"Sepideh, are you okay?" asked Wade.

Sepi struggled for breath. The blur turned to black.

She saw a flash of Nat's pensive face, the downturned lips.

Then nothing.

SEVENTEEN

Doyle's Journal – November 19, 2045 (cont.)

All too soon, I was back in the escape hatch, crawling to the surface on two fractured ribs.

A small hit of morphine while I dressed my wounds had cost me about three hours, during which I dreamed of Angie and Gretta and Vida, all of them moving around in jerky fits, their eyes glowing embers, their skin pulled taut over smooth metal. Waking to find Vida standing in my doorway caused me to see her in the afterglow of paranoia, and I started to wonder if she were a synthetic, part of a Máquina plot to infiltrate the last of the holdouts by masquerading as damsels in distress.

I'd seen movies. I knew the score.

Only, I knew that wasn't the case with Vida. I'd seen her bleed. I'd pulled charred clothes from her body and seen her full breasts beneath her sheer bra. She was as human as I was, capable of pain and love and indifference, not to mention wild mood swings in the neighborhood of a manic-depressive.

She was fragile.

Máquinas were not fragile.

And I guessed, neither was Harlan.

I came out of the escape hatch in almost total darkness; back-lit clouds raced across the sky, hinting at moonlight where they were thinnest. Snow fell casually, as if the sun would not rise in the morning and winter would last forever. As I closed the hatch and covered it with snow and branches, I chanced a quick look around with my flashlight.

The steady snowfall had hidden my footprints for the most part, though a keen observer would have been able to see the faint, dotted line stretching back towards the clearing. I followed them back to Harlan, dragging a branch behind me to wipe the new prints out. The tree line kept me hidden most of the way, but I slowed down as I got closer to where the proximity alarm had marked the intruder.

He was a persistent son of a bitch.

The fool had started a fire in the middle of the clearing and sat nearby, warming his hands. He had a small stack of firewood next to him, which he must have brought with him because nothing from the surrounding trees would have been dry enough to burn.

The fire sparked and crackled.

A horrible thought occurred to me.

Harlan wasn't setting up camp so he could continue searching the area. He was *waiting*. Maybe he knew I had escaped, or maybe he was just holding the fort until reinforcements arrived.

I hadn't been able to find my Dragunov amid the chaos in Park City, which only left me with a reclaimed MX FX-05 and a pump-action shotgun. Both would make considerable noise, but only the FX-05 could do the job at 100 meters. But could I make that shot? In the dark? In the cold?

There was no sense in taking unnecessary risks. I circled around until I was behind Harlan and then crawled out of the tree line on my stomach. Each reach of my arms set my entire ribcage on fire. Under the morphine haze, I'd probed my chest, looking for anything broken or protruding, but had found nothing. I've fractured ribs before, but that doesn't make them any less painful. My Guardian Angel chip should have kept tabs on the sensations, but the burning came and went too quickly for it to respond in time.

Snow fell. Silence filled the world.

I was only ten meters away when I heard the squawk.

"Harlan, come back."

Harlan pulled an ancient radio from his belt; it had a long, floppy antenna that whipped around his head when he put it to his ear.

"Go for Harlan."

"It's a real shit-show over here, but we checked every body. He's not here. Either the Máquinas took him, or he's headed up your way."

"Of course he is," said Harlan. "This was the only entry in his GPS."

I drew the shotgun from my back and set it down in the snow, barrel aimed towards Harlan's hunched back.

"I don't see how he could have gotten out of here with all the Máquinas around. They really tore this place apart."

Harlan lifted his wrist. "It *has* been a while. Maybe he died somewhere along the way. Tell you what. At first light tomorrow, you send two guys up this way and I'll start heading back. If we meet in the middle, then he's dead and gone. If we find him, we'll drag his ass back here and make him show us what was so goddamn important. Even if it *is* just a cache, we can use it to rebuild."

"You didn't find anything at all?"

"Just two graves," said Harlan.

My ribs stepped aside to allow my stomach to somersault.

"Nothing in them but bodies," he continued. "A woman and a kid. Neither had anything of value on them."

I looked over my shoulder at the hidden bunker entrance. The makeshift headstones I'd erected had been knocked over, and there were two piles of snow and dirt next to the holes. Even in the dark, I could see Gretta's body sitting up.

My jaw ached.

What had he expected to find under the body of a dead child? Did he think I put some kind of treasure there? Or maybe a note that read *congratulations on disturbing the grave of an innocent child you heartless cocksucker?*

I shut my eyes before I could see if Angie had been similarly disturbed. I prayed she hadn't.

"Alright," said Park City. "We'll get two on the road at first light. Out."

Harlan stowed the radio, rubbed his hands together, and held them out to the fire.

I leaned my forehead against the barrel of the shotgun, tried to hold back the tears. There was anger swirling around inside me, moving so quickly that it produced a whisper.

Kill him. Kill him now.

Suddenly I didn't want to shoot Harlan in the back of the head.

I wanted to beat him to death. I wanted him to experience a pain like mine.

You always go rushing into things, Angie used to say. It was one of her pet peeves, how impulsive I was. Act first, think second, and, if you lived, deal with the consequences third. Maybe it was the military training, the fact that when you were in the shit, you didn't have time to think. When a Syrian child is running at you in a vest full of shrapnel and a detonator in her hand, you raise your rifle and pull the trigger and dive for cover. When it's over, you can use your still-functioning brain to dissect the moment, see if there was anything you could have done better.

Usually, there wasn't.

Sometimes you just have to trust your programming.

I was standing before my eyes had opened again. Snow flitted past as I closed the gap between me and Harlan. The shotgun shifted in my hands, rotating until I was gripping the end of the barrel like a baseball bat. I wound up, stepped through the swing, and caught Harlan on the back of his wool hat. There was a wet *crack*, and for a moment I heard Dodger Stadium erupt in applause.

If only Harlan's head had come loose, soared through the air and over the 400-foot fence. Instead, he grunted like an old man straining on the toilet and keeled forward just to the left of the fire. His shoulder landed on one of the burning logs and somehow he still had enough faculty to roll away from it. He ended up on his back with blood dripping from his mouth.

"Son of a bith!"

That was rich. He had bitten off a chunk of his tongue.

I remember screaming at him. "You dug up my wife?!" The shotgun spun around; I leveled the business end at his face. "You dug up my daughter? What kind of sick fuck are you?"

"The kind that thurvives."

"Not tonight." In that moment, I'm ashamed to admit, I started laughing. I don't know why. Maybe it was the relief, the momentary relenting of the crushing need for vengeance.

Harlan shook his head, spit blood onto his chin.

"Juth get ith over with, before I puth a bulleth in your brain."

I pushed the barrel closer to his beady black eyes. "We're supposed to be working together to fight the Máquinas. *You* are the reason we won't survive this. People like you give humanity a bad fucking name."

Harlan raised a hand and flapped his fingers against his thumb.

While I was trying to decode the gesture, his other hand came up holding a small, snub-nosed revolver.

He squeezed off a shot before I could pull the shotty's trigger.

Searing metal tore through my shoulder in a painless whisper. At the same time, I watched Harlan's face explode, throwing globs of red and chunks of white onto the fire-lit snow.

The echoes of the gunshots raced through the surrounding trees, and in the distance, they were answered by the howls of wolves, or Máquinas, or both.

Blood trickled down my chest; I felt it on my back too.

That was good.

A Mr. Magoo, through and through.

I'd had a few of those lucky strikes in Syria, and another in Belarus. And those had been with real caliber weapons, not some pansy-ass .22.

I relieved Harlan of his inventory: the radio, the revolver and rifle, some matches, a knife, his boots, and various other camping gear. My intention had been to drag him a few hundred meters into the tree line, but the pain in my shoulder made me stop just outside the clearing. I covered him with branches; the falling snow filled in the cracks.

The fire bent under the weight of the Montana winter, but I kicked the logs aside just to be sure. Black smoke billowed upwards, smudging the white clouds.

I walked back to the Admiral, careful not to look at the disturbed graves. They both needed a proper reburial, but I was losing blood. Any more time spent outside and I would need a transfusion, which just wasn't possible with the first aid equipment I had on hand.

As soon as I can, I promised them, and then squeezed my way through the outer door and down the steps to the bunker. The traps and sharpened sticks slowed me down, but I managed not to snag myself too badly. I stood at the door, looking over the gleaming metal, and remembered the first time I had seen it at the Rising Sun showroom.

It had been my birthday, and I had a tradition of buying myself a nice present no one else could possibly afford. I remember it well because after the hours of paperwork, I got to go home to my above-ground house where Angie and Gretta were waiting for me with pizza and cake. Angie had bought me a watch—a black and red analog that now resided in Park City. Gretta had framed a new piece of artwork—her with mom and dad in front of a poorly drawn house. I'd hung it in my study.

I knocked on the bunker door. Three times short. Two times long.

After the pizza and the cake, after putting Gretta to bed and tearing into the champagne, Angie and I made love like it was the first time. Our desire for each other rode high on a tide of synthetic uppers that allowed us to stay in each other's embrace until the middle of the morning. When we finally collapsed, panting and sweating, I recalled thinking how lucky I was to have her, to have everything I ever wanted.

I knocked again.

Three times short.

I know now that I'll never experience such desire again.

Two times long.

And I'll certainly never hold my daughter in my arms again.

By the time you undid the locks and opened the door, I was crying. I didn't even care if you saw.

EIGHTEEN

It was midnight when Vida finally sat down on the couch in the living room. Even though Doyle had only been outside for half an hour, it had felt like a lifetime inside the bunker. It wasn't as if she could look out a window and see him fighting Harlan to the death. Instead, she had to watch the proximity alarm, watch the two dots converge with agonizingly slow speed. Then the gunshots and the silence and the lone dot walking away and back.

Earlier that day, Doyle had returned from Park City a beaten and bruised man, but he came back from his encounter with Harlan truly broken. There were tears in his eyes when Vida opened the door. Even as he showered to wash the blood and bone from his face, even as she applied the SecondSkin patch to the bullet hole on the back of his shoulder, he still cried.

When she offered him morphine for what she thought was unbearable pain, he refused, saying there was only so much of the drug left in the kit, and that what he could really use was a stiff drink. She'd poured him a tumbler full of Kentucky Gentleman and left him in peace. She found excuses to pass his door while she cleaned up; he mostly sat at his desk, bent over a notebook, with the glass in one hand and a pen in the other.

Vida reclined on the couch, put her feet up on the armrest. The knot finally began to unwind, and with her lungs free to expand to their potential, she took a deep, sobering breath. She thought about how closely she'd walked the thin line between having Doyle and facing the world alone. What if Harlan had come out the victor? What if he had set up shop on the surface so Vida could never leave?

She tried not to think about it, took a slug of whiskey from the bottle instead.

It burned, but the burning made things brighter.

Through the fire, past the flame...

Vida blinked, tried to remember the music that accompanied the lyric, but it wasn't there.

Everything was gone. And there was nothing in the bunker that would trigger her recall. For that, she'd have to make it back home, wherever that was. That meant finding out where her plane had been flying out of and finding someone there who knew her. Only, the plane was a charred hunk of metal now. And the people wherever she was from were probably all dead.

Doyle was all she had, and Harlan had tried to take him away from her.

Another drink, a pause for the burn, and then another.

The lights in the living room went out; the motion sensors had lost track of her.

Vida lay in the dark, searching for answers in the black ceiling, thinking about a future that had almost been thrust upon her. Even though she had no physical desire for him—and really she had no idea why she *should*—she realized she wanted Doyle in her life, if only to have someone to protect her from the horrible things outside the bunker.

She dozed and awoke to find the proximity alarm had cleared from the vidscreen. A digital clock in the lower right showed it was just past two in the morning. The half-empty bottle of whiskey sat on the coffee table with a smug look on its face, as if to say *that's right, I put you on your back.*

Vida screwed its cap back on to shut it up and then groaned to her feet. The lights came up; she squinted against them as she made her way to the bathroom.

Doyle's door was still open, though he was no longer at his desk. He'd crawled backwards onto his bed and was now lying in the fetal position facing the wall. The SecondSkin patch on his back had turned a dark gray—blood pooling beneath it.

Vida entered the room and pulled the blue thermal blanket from the foot of the bed, draped Doyle in it. She shut off the overhead light and went to turn off the light strip above the desk. That's where she discovered Doyle's journal, hastily abandoned in the middle of the page, the pen holding the book open. Vida was going to leave it alone, ignore her curiosity, but she glimpsed a few lines, saw her name written there in cursive so slanted it looked like the words might fall off the page.

She dropped into Doyle's chair with a loud *whoosh*, but he didn't wake, just continued to snore in that low, consistent rumbling of his.

She strained to read the handwriting.

By the time you undid the locks and opened the door, I was crying. I didn't even care if you saw.

Here, the narration ended, jumped to a new line.

I just want you to tell me it's worth it. I want to know that I killed a man for a good reason. What's the point of surviving if there's no world on the other side of this? Would you ever want a life with me? Or will you leave as soon as a better survivor comes along?

Vida crinkled her nose. He was writing directly to her. He had feelings for her, and not just the lusty kind that got him hard in the shower when he knew she was watching.

Doyle actually cared for her.

She turned back a page and started at the beginning of today's entry. Doyle had written a play-by-play of the encounter with Harlan and included far more detail than what he'd told her as they dressed his wounds. There was the radio call with the men from Park City, men who would be on their way in this direction at sunrise (he hadn't mentioned that) and a recall of a massacre by Máquinas (that either). The way he described Harlan's face exploding made Vida want to refund the Kentucky Gentleman; she tried not to imagine the bits of bone and brain matter scattering in all directions, maybe ending up on the jacket and shirt she'd had to peel off Doyle.

Then, a detail she had missed. Something about graves. She had to read it twice before she understood why Doyle had been crying. It wasn't hard to imagine that after their deaths, Doyle had felt relief that nothing could ever hurt his wife and child again. But he'd been wrong. Máquinas didn't care about graves, only that a human was in each of them. People were a different story though. In a dystopia, all bets were off, and people would turn on each other at the first opportunity, even going so far as to dig each other up.

Doyle pulled no punches pointing out that only a month ago, the people in Park City had been civilized, probably even friendly.

How easily reality shifted.

Vida felt a tear roll down her face, but she couldn't catch it before it landed on the open journal. She tried to blot it away with the sleeve of her shirt, but the ink had already started to run. In a panic, she shut off the light and hurried out of the room, closing the door behind her. She placed her hand on the wall and tried to imagine a life with Doyle.

Maybe I could learn to love him, she thought. It certainly didn't hurt that he was the only friendly face for a hundred miles. His words came back to her, and she realized he'd noticed her ambivalence towards him. He sensed her reluctance.

Vida shook her head.

She needed to show him she did care in some way.

The hallway pitched and yawed, and over the hum of the air recycler, she heard the Kentucky Gentleman calling to her in a southern drawl.

"That's a good idea," said Vida, stumbling into her room. She dressed in the dark, first in Angie's pants and then Angie's jacket. She slipped on a pair of Angie's socks and her most rugged boots.

"Appreciate you," muttered Vida, "and I'm gonna repay you. You just watch."

Doyle had dropped his bag in the living room when he came in, and from a pouch on the back, Vida pulled out a collapsible shovel. She took a pair of his gloves from his jacket and went to the bunker door. She had one hand on the first lock when she paused, reached with her other hand to her belt. Her gun was still there, clasped in tight.

A memory seeped out, showed her a dark auditorium and a stage full of smoke.

"God, send me no need of thee," said Vida, undoing the locks. "And by the operation of the second tumbler…" Her breath billowed in the outer corridor; small flakes of snow adorned the sharpened barbs around her. "… she draws it on the drawer, when *in*deed there is *no* need."

Vida paused on each step as she climbed, listening for any sounds of movement above the whine of the wind. The outer door had metal tabs for a padlock, but Doyle had removed them earlier in preparation for his meeting with Harlan. Vida pushed down on the handle and opened the door.

The stage and the faint taste of performance anxiety disappeared as a gust of cold air greeted her outside.

She almost cried.

The world smelled so fresh. The feeling of constant claustrophobia that had gripped her since the beginning of her remembered existence melted away in a sudden burst of heat. There were no birds singing in the dead of night, but she imagined their songs anyway. She took a few steps away from the door and what she saw of the world didn't even hint at an apocalypse. The open clearing gave her a clear view of a serene sky, alternating dark clouds with thinning patches where the moon and some stars shone through.

The world hadn't ended.

It couldn't have.

It was too beautiful.

Vida's tears froze, stung her cheeks.

The Kentucky Gentleman urged her to fling off her clothes and run naked through the trees.

She smiled, laughed to herself.

How wonderful it was to be back outside with the clean air and frosty snow and fragrant trees. How funny she would look running naked between their trunks, especially when she tripped, fell, bumped her head, and died from exposure.

Vida looked for a break in the surrounding trees for a good place to start running.

Her hand was on her gun before she realized it, and the gun was leveled before she fully focused on the two red dots swaying in the shadows beyond the trees. Another pair joined them, then another. Vida swung her sights around wildly, but no matter where she pointed the barrel, a set of eyes appeared.

Máquinas. Ten. Twenty. More.

Her throat tightened, and suddenly she could no longer taste the crisp air.

A clatter went up from the forest, a sound so foreign and mechanical that Vida ducked in fear. Her finger jerked, squeezing off a single round that appeared to hit nothing.

The noise stopped.

A pair of red eyes grew larger.

Vida turned and ran, taking large, awkward steps through the calf-deep snow. The eyes in the tree line moved with her, coming closer. She yanked the outer door open and found Doyle staring up at her.

"What are you doing?" he shouted. He pushed past her with a rifle and began firing. "Get inside!"

Vida nodded, started to apologize, but instead rushed down the steps and past the barbs. She heard clanging behind her, saw Doyle slamming the outer door shut. He engaged three deadbolts and raced down after her.

The heat of the bunker hit her hard, and Doyle practically shoved her onto the couch as he made for the vidscreen. The proximity alarm was losing its mind, showing a sea of green specks in every direction. Doyle put the bunker in low power mode, muttered something about an EMP, and then slammed his fist against the wall.

Vida couldn't hear what he was saying. Her mind was elsewhere, back outside in the fresh air and falling snow. She thought about the wonderful things she had seen, everything that reminded her of the beauty of the world.

But then, she started thinking about other things, things she had *not* seen.

Harlan's body, for example. Had Doyle mentioned dragging it away?

No fire either, or logs that would have supported it.

Vida's faced burned.

Doyle turned around, breathing hard, muttering an apology. When he saw the look on her face, he asked, "What's wrong?"

She couldn't answer.

In her mind's eye, she replayed her break for freedom, turning from the chorus of demon eyes to head back to the bunker. The outer doors, plainly visible on the rock formation. And to either side of them, white, pristine, and evenly distributed snow.

"Vida," said Doyle, taking a step closer. "Say something."

For the first time, Vida was able to look past the implied compassion in his eyes. Saw things for how they really were.

Ultimately, it came down to the image of the distant bunker door, and of the minute details the brain picks up on in a moment of panic.

"I'm fine," said Vida.

But inside, a different two-word answer had come to her mind.

No graves.

NINETEEN

"I wasn't prepared for the MX," said Raf, resting the rim of a Corona on his lip. He took a deep breath, filled his chest, and let the expansion tilt the beer into his mouth. "None of us were. You remember those old Vietnam films? FOBs making landfall at some glorified boy scout encampment? Nombre, the MX was nothing like that. It was shit, K. Shit from wall to wall."

Kagan nodded. The custom blend of synth he'd loaded into his Guardian Angel biochip had allowed him to mute the memories of getting fired earlier in the day. But if the conversation stalled and he started thinking back, he could remember it easily. Luckily, Raf was a good talker, and after his fifth or fiftieth beer, he'd started rambling about his time in America's Hell on Earth to the south.

Training camp sounded interesting: recruits were actually taught how to kill an MX soldado—as they were known then, when we thought they were all human—with their bare hands. It wasn't easy, and a lot of good men died trying when it came time to put their training to the test. After that was the short hop down south and a LEO jump deep in the heart of the MX shitstorm.

"I was firing before I hit the ground. That's how bad it was. Everyone, *everyone*, who had landed before us was either dead or wishing they were. The soldados wouldn't go down, no matter how many bullets we put in them. My squad landed in the mountains, and the only ones who survived were the ones who immediately went deep cover."

"You mean, you *hid*," said Kagan. He gestured to Nadya at the back door and beckoned her. She collected his empty glass and went to retrieve a new one. He put his hands behind his head and stared up into the night sky.

"Más o menos."

Kagan had expected him to lie, to lean on that Chicano machismo like a worn crutch. Instead, Raf's face darkened despite the glow of the fire pit.

"We were outgunned," he continued. "Dead. After the soldados moved on, there were only eleven of us left. Ten grunts and one officer. We collected our dead, lined them up so we knew how many crosses to make. Only thing was…" He paused, took a swig. "This kid from Philly comes up missing. His name was Hughes. I forget his first name. Something gringo like Jacob or Langdon. Come to find out, another guy, Marquis, he was from Savannah, saw him last. Said he ran out of bullets in the first two minutes, so he grabbed a grenade and gave one of the soldados a bear hug."

Kagan huffed, imagined the scene, but saw Wayne's face on the soldado. The synth he'd taken was wearing off.

"Pues, we go looking for Hughes," said Raf, gesturing around the patio. "And we find him, there." He pointed to the nearby flowerbed. "And there." In the hot tub. "And there, there, and there." Back door, outdoor kitchen, and roof.

Nadya returned with a fresh glass and set it down on the small table next to Kagan's chair. She asked if there was anything else he needed, but he waved her away. With a subtle curtsey, she withdrew.

"Blown to bits, huh?" asked Kagan.

"Simón, ese. Like shoving a firecracker up a poodle's ass. Blood and shit everywhere. But…" At this, he sat up straight, set the empty bottle down at his feet. "We also found pieces of the soldado. And that's when we knew. These things that ambushed us *before* we'd even put boot to dirt weren't soldados at all."

"Máquinas," said Kagan.

"Pinche Máquinas," said Raf. "Something completely new. And no one knew about them because no one was surviving. We had to truck a hundred and twenty klicks through mountains and pouring rain to meet another squad with a working radio. Lost three men along the way. Finally made it out in Culiacan on the Gulf of California. The Máquina parts we brought back were taken out of our hands quick, fast, and furious. I heard squawks that they ended up at Vinestead and that's how they were able to replace us so quickly."

Kagan shook his head, rifled through the code spheres in the small box in his lap. There was supposed to be a sphere for every occasion, but nothing seemed to match up with Raf's rambling tale. He wanted to stay alert so he could hear about it, but the images of Wayne and Abat kept creeping back in. Had his boss stood over the priapic geriatric and wept or laughed? He'd surely let a chuckle slip when he was informed that Kagan was no longer with the company.

"The war machine keeps churning," said Kagan, selecting a Red Mist from the deck. He gave it a gentle squeeze. A slow-burning warmth overtook him, radiating from his hands and feet to settle in his crotch. He looked over at Nadya standing quietly by the back door, hands folded in front of her skirt.

"The what?" asked Raf.

Kagan channeled his best Chicano accent. "La Máquina de Guerra. Que gira para siempre. Vinestead builds the synthetics, and the government buys those synthetics for twenty thousand on the dollar. They pit our synthetics against their synthetics from a safe distance so we'll keep going to work every day and keep paying our taxes. And you know what those taxes are for? More synthetic soldiers. It's a machine, Raf. And you and I are both cogs."

"You're a pinche cog."

Kagan laughed, held out the box of code spheres. "Quieres?"

Raf shook his head. "Won't work for me. Avenging Angels are firewalled against that synth shit."

"I thought they took that out when you got discharged."

"Nombre," said Raf, "it would have killed me." He leaned forward as he pushed the hoodie back. "Mira. Took a direct hit to my jackport from a Máquina I thought I had smashed. Shattered the port and took the AA with it. By the time we made it back stateside, the scarring had fused it with my brain stem."

"Come on, there's gotta be a procedure or something."

"Sure," said Raf, drawing out the word. "There's a procedure alright. They've got lots of procedures for Jacobs and Langdons. But for Rafael? Y Julio? Chale. We're on our own like San Antone. That ain't never gonna change."

"You're not on your own, hermano. Delts por vida."

Raf lifted his empty bottle. "Para siempre."

Kagan sat up and slapped Raf on the knee. "That's about it for me, my friend. I'm gonna hit the sack. Long day ahead of me tomorrow. All that groveling and shit."

"I'm gonna stay up for a bit." He tapped the side of his head. "Bad dreams."

"Bueno." Kagan stretched, checked his sliver. It was almost three in the morning. "Well, Nadya's coming with me, so if you need anything, you know where the kitchen is."

Raf glanced over his shoulder, gestured with his thumb. "You really take that thing to bed?"

"Every night," said Kagan. "Well, most nights."

"Huh. I can't believe you're sticking it to a robot. What would La Madonna think of that?"

"Shit, Madonna's damn near 80 years old. If it ain't a synthetic giving her the business fortnightly, then I feel sorry for the poor chump who is."

"One day," said Raf, "that thing is gonna malfunction and her pussy's gonna snap shut." He slapped his hands together. "And bam, you're walking the earth a dickless wonder."

Kagan nodded, walked past Raf's chair and put a hand on his shoulder. "It's like my daddy always says: don't knock it until you're balls deep. But not with my girl. You get your own."

"I'll stick to manual mode," said Raf, pulling up his hood. He used the strings to draw it tight around his face.

"You'd rather have Manuel? Shit, he'll be here on Tuesday. I'll let him know you're expecting him."

Kagan was almost to the door when the code sphere came flying from the fire pit. With Red Mist coating his biochip, his reflexes were too slow to handle the incoming projectile.

Instead, it was Nadya who reached out with a deft hand and snatched the sphere out of the air. She raised an eyebrow at Kagan and followed him into the house.

"You didn't tell him," she said, as they climbed the stairs.

"Tell him what?" His fingers worked at the buttons on his shirt.

"That Madonna is a synthetic."

Kagan grunted as they cleared the landing on the third floor. He kicked off his shoes, which Nadya picked up and carried with her free hand. "It would have killed him," he replied. "Big *Papa Don't Preach* fan. Loves all that Day-Glo 80's shit."

The lights in the bedroom came up to a soft glow, but Nadya dimmed the overheads back to nothing and let the baseboard LEDs illuminate the room.

Kagan walked through the adjoining bathroom and into the closet where he stripped down to his boxer shorts. Back in the bathroom, he brushed his teeth, kept spitting until the taste of whiskey and toothpaste was gone.

"Should I start the shower?" asked Nadya.

"In the morning," he replied. "You can get changed."

She nodded, exited the bathroom through a third door that led into another closet. Her blouse and skirt went into a hamper, and her bra took its place amongst the other lace and velvet pieces. She returned to the bathroom in her underwear, rubbing at the slight red marks the bra had left on her RealSkin. A minute later, the marks were gone.

Such were the benefits of synthetic skin, something Kagan always pointed out to any dope with a bottomless wallet who would listen. At least, that's what he used to do. If Dad had been serious about firing him, and all signs pointed to that being the case, then Kagan's days of selling immortality to the rich were over.

Nadya's swaying backside drew him into the bedroom. She crawled onto the bed and he followed right behind her. The sheets were soft, laundered that morning.

As the baseboards faded to black, Nadya said, "You're sweet."

"What's that?" asked Kagan, his eyes already closed, his mind already reaching for the distant shores of the dream world.

"You care so much for your friend. It's sweet of you to want to help him."

"That's what brothers do for each other."

"It's very kind."

"Thanks."

"You're welcome."

A playlist of ambient music spun up, filling the room with dulcet tones that drowned out the occasional helicopter or drone fly-by.

Nadya stirred beneath the sheets. She slipped a hand into his boxers.

"In the morning," he replied. "Go to sleep."

"Okay, but I'll be thinking of a plan."

Kagan turned on his side, sought out her face in the dark. "A plan for what?"

"To help your friend. You said you would take him to work, but your father fired you."

"And?"

"So you don't have access to the equipment anymore."

He reached out and pushed a strand of hair away from her eyes. She was so much like a real woman. The idea of not obeying the rules simply didn't occur to her.

"Do you really think I'm going to break my promise just because they quote-unquote fired me? I've spent the last eight years at Vitra Synth. I know that place inside and out. People there are loyal to me, not the company."

"I hope you're right," said Nadya.

He scoffed, rolled over. "You don't have hopes. You're a machine."

"Una máquina humana."

"That's one way to put it," said Kagan, closing his eyes. The Red Mist had dissipated, and now he just wanted the day to be over. The problem of Rafael Orozco could wait until tomorrow.

"There's another way to put it," whispered Nadya.

"What's that?" asked Kagan, already drifting away.

He barely heard her response under the tinkling music.

"Esclava," she said.

Slave.

TWENTY

"I'm so embarrassed," said Sepi, placing a rattling teacup back on its saucer.

"Don't even worry about it," said Wade Vunak. He sat across from her in a deep leather chair with one leg crossed over the other. Now that Sepi had put her contacts back in, she could see he was an older man, likely in his mid-50s, with faded blond hair, large ears, and lazy blue eyes. He looked a little goofy, and with his Texas accent, he sounded a little goofy too.

"I'm actually flattered," he continued. "It's not every day a woman swoons from my mere presence. More like every third day, but you take my point." He watched her struggle to put the tea down on the coffee table. "Are you sure you don't want me to call someone? The building has synthetic EMTs on staff."

"No, I'm fine." Sepi waved a shaky hand at him. "This isn't… the first time." She felt cold even though all of the shades were up in the office.

"Pardon my impropriety, but what exactly was that? Are you given to fainting spells?"

"Panic attack," said Sepi, "but I'd appreciate it if you'd keep that between you and me."

"Only thing worse than a cow that won't give milk is a cow that won't keep secrets," he said, reaching for a hat he wasn't wearing and then deciding to smooth out his hair instead. "You know, I bet your biochip did a soft reset. As much as I hate 'em, Vinestead does put a lot of work into handling brain chemistry and dealing with things like panic attacks, but the way I hear it, medical science doesn't completely understand them either. And if *science* can't treat those attacks with drugs, surgery, or psychotherapy, then well, I'm not sure how a tech company like Vinestead expects to handle them with a little code on a tiny little chip."

Sepi half-smiled. "Isn't that what you guys do here? Sell code on a little chip?"

"No ma'am. Augmented reality is not intended to prevent, diagnose, or treat any medical condition. It's more like a coating over everything you see. It's the wave of the future."

"That's what the Sierra Brothers told me. I'm going to be in their next picture, but they're going to cover me up with your…"

"Augmented reality, or AR," said Wade, sensing her struggle. "It's a hoot, right? No more long hours in the make-up chair to look like someone else. No costume changes. No green screen. You'll look in the mirror and *see* the character. We've already got half a dozen smaller production companies using the tech, but getting Sierra Brothers onboard would go a long way towards breaking into the big five. And once that happens, well…" He rubbed his stomach, as if he were anticipating a tasty meal.

"I see." Sepi kneaded her palm with her thumb. "So this is going to be one big product placement for your company?"

"And also a movie, if there's time," he replied, winking.

A knock sounded from the open door and they both looked over at a subdued Abdul Darwish. He had a small box in his hand and a mirror in the other.

"We're done crafting your lenses," he said. "Would you like to try them on, madam?"

"So formal," said Sepi.

Abdul smirked and set the mirror down on the table. He handed the box to Sepi.

Inside, she found a glass contact lens case with a laser-etched *L* and *R* on each compartment. She opened one of them, pulled the lens onto her finger.

"Ain't that something?" asked Wade. "First generation lenses had visible circuitry. People knew when you were wearing them. But not these. Without a microscope, you'd be hard-pressed to tell the difference between them and your regular ones. It's like I said, Ms. Ahmadi, wave of the future."

Sepi removed and replaced the new contacts one at a time, careful always to keep a good one in her eye so she could see the room. Once she finished, she gave her surroundings a second look.

"It's still the same," she said.

"Yep," said Wade. "That's because you're in single-user mode. That's great if you're the creative type or you live alone, but the real value is in multi-player." He picked up a palette from the table, tapped a few hundred times. Finally, he turned it around and handed it to her. "Can you put in your VNet password please? That's how we can sync everything up. We're working on integrating it with the MESH to make it truly ubiquitous, but that's a few years away."

"I'm not on the MESH," said Sepi.

"It's overrated," he assured her.

She keyed in her password and handed the palette back.

Wade took it, furrowed his brow, and said, "Alright, welcome to the next version of reality, Ms. Ahmadi." He tapped a button, and liquid neon spilled into the world.

Sepi gasped.

Previously off-white walls graded down to an impossibly deep black. They intersected the ceiling and floors in thick, bright green lines. The furniture shifted, turned blood red with black outlines. Wade's slacks became blue jeans; his white button-up swirled and settled into a pattern of barely visible longhorns. Hazy blues turned to piercing. His hair sparkled like gold.

Abdul remained pretty much the same, though he seemed proportionally larger.

"That's the face," said Wade, gesturing to Sepi. "That's why we do what we do." He stood, pointed to the wall. "Come, let me show you something."

Sepi joined him as he drew a rectangle on the wall with his finger. Within it, the black strobed a few times and became what looked like a computer desktop. He poked around, brought up a folder, and then enlarged an image.

"Savannah Kessler AKA Bonnie Diaz AKA Kaili Zabora," said Wade, "from her Perion Synthetics ID card. Last known photo of the Butcher of Burbank, if you don't count that video that came out during that APOX nonsense in '16, which I don't."

Sepi nodded as if the reference meant something.

"Abdul, the mirror."

He brought the mirror to Wade, who held it up for Sepi to see. She was surprised to discover the augmented reality was visible in the mirror as well. For some reason, she hadn't expected it to be.

"Now, if you don't mind, I'm just going to touch you on the cheek right quick. This isn't gonna hurt one bit, I guarantee."

"Sure," said Sepi. "I've done this before."

Wade flashed disappointment but proceeded.

Sepi watched her reflection snap into that of Savannah Kessler. With no clunky glasses to get in the way, the effect was indistinguishable from reality.

She sighed. "My God." She touched her face, earlobes. The holes were plainly visible, but she felt nothing but unbroken skin.

"I'm no God, Ms. Ahmadi. I'm just a man with a dream who has waited a very long time to see it succeed."

"This is amazing," said Sepi. "I don't know why we aren't using this all the time."

"Your contacts cost $256,000," said Abdul. "Each."

She couldn't help but laugh. "That better not be coming out of my talent fee."

Wade shook his head. "Quid pro quo with the Sierra Brothers," he explained. "We give them our tech for free and once the movie is done, they tell all of their friends, and the feeds, how Nixle Chronos' OcularAR revolutionized their industry. And then, steaks for everyone."

"I'm a vegetarian," said Sepi.

Wade put his hand over his heart and sighed.

A digital clock appeared on the wall next to the picture of Savannah Kessler; it flashed as it changed from 11:59 to 12:00.

"Pardon me," said Wade, "but I've got another meeting downtown. I'm sorry we have to cut this short, I really am. Let's do lunch in a couple of weeks so we can see how the contacts are working for you. Abdul will set that up. And if you have any other questions, he's at your disposal."

"I think I'm good," she replied, shaking his hand.

He gave her an extra squeeze, said, "I won't forget about the cows."

"Thank you," she said.

As soon as he was gone, Abdul came back to life.

"Sweet," he said, "now we can totally max this baby out."

"Actually, I'm not feeling too good. Would you mind calling me a Viking?"

He shook his head. "We'll take you home, Ms. Ahmadi. No worries."

Sepi nodded to Joy on her way out. The woman returned a weak smile. Abdul insisted on escorting her to the lobby and outside, all the while talking about Nixle Chronos and how it would change the world forever. Silence didn't come until she was alone in the back of the car and crawling back to the Monarch.

And even then, it didn't last long.

The phone rang, and though Sepi didn't feel like talking to anyone, she couldn't refuse a call from Jane.

"Hey, Jane."

"Sepi, sweetness, how are you?"

"I'm okay," she lied. Her heart had never really settled since the panic attack, and the embarrassment of fainting in front of Wade still lingered in her mind.

"Are you sitting down?"

"I'm in the car headed home, so yes."

"Good, that's good. Here's the thing. I spoke to Richard Sierra this morning about some of the finer points of your contract. And I noticed they stuck in a full-frontal nudity clause way down on page 112."

Sepi groaned. She hadn't done nudity since *Lost in Your Eyes*, and had no intention of ever showing off her private bits on the big screen again.

"I know," continued Jane. "That's why I called him up and gave him hell. He tried to spin some story about the augmented reality preventing people from ever *really* seeing you naked, but I kept pressing him. He wasn't playing straight with us, Sepi, and I made it clear we were unhappy about that."

"So what happened? He didn't change his mind about hiring me, did he?"

"No!" Jane practically yelped her answer. "Gracious, girl, no. They're still committed. They still *need* you. I just had them take the clause out, and also, as a sign of good faith, instead of the five percent upfront, they're giving us fifty."

Sepi's throat dried up. She croaked, "How much is that?"

"Minus my fee? About forty-seven million, before taxes. It'll be in the bank in two or three business days."

The car shrunk and expanded. Sepi's face ached; she was smiling.

"Speechless?" asked Jane.

"Yes," replied Sepi. "I have to tell Nat."

"Yes, you tell her. Go out and celebrate."

"We already did."

"Well, do it again. I've got some other calls to make. I'll check in on you tomorrow."

"Thanks. Bye Jane."

A fog wrapped itself around Sepi, but instead of being cold and stiff, it felt more like a warm blanket, a feeling of easiness that allowed her to float out of the car, into the lobby of the Monarch, and up the elevator to her apartment. She hardly noticed Stella Starfall riding up with her again or Gus giving her a nod from the bar.

Sepi thumbed the pad outside her door and went in, her stomach still full of butterflies. The money had seemed abstract before, but in a couple of days, it would be as real as the lavender in the air, the heels by the front door, or Nat sitting on the couch.

She paused, squinted to make sure she was seeing the world correctly.

Nat looked over from the couch, her face full of sadness and surprise.

"You're home early," said Sepi, dropping her purse on the counter. She approached the couch and noticed the tears in Nat's eyes. "Hey, what's wrong?"

"I thought your meeting was going to last longer," said Nat. "I'm sorry. You weren't supposed to see me like this. I thought…"

Sepi sat down, put her hand on Nat's knee. "What is it? Did something happen at Dahlstrom?"

Nat shook her head.

"Sweetie, tell me. Don't make me cheer you up."

"You already cheer me up," she replied, placing her hand on top of Sepi's.

"Yeah, but now I've got forty-seven million more reasons you should be happy today."

Nat dabbed her nose with a tissue, raised an eyebrow.

"We'll have the money in a few days. I was thinking we could take a vacation before shooting starts. Maybe something tropical? Or to Vail?"

"Yeah," said Nat, her voice distant. "I'd like that."

Something was off.

It was only when Nat was in real trouble that Sepi didn't experience any symptoms of anxiety, as if her instinct to protect overrode her instinct to survive. Her stomach felt fine, there was no headache, no high-pitched whine in the distance. All she felt was concern for the woman she loved.

She reached out and touched Nat's quivering chin.

Nat burst into tears.

Sepi pulled her close, let her cry it out.

"Whatever it is," she whispered, "we'll face it together. You and me, babe."

"You can't help me," said Nat. "My doctor can't help me. I'm alone."

"Hey! You are not alone, you hear me?"

Nat squeezed Sepi's back, said, "I'm sorry I was keeping it from you. I thought it was nothing. But they got the tests back today. I have a… um… a type of brain cancer."

Sepi sighed. "They can fix that, sweetie. Easily."

"Not my kind," she whispered. "It's too deep, too big. Like Patrick's, just… worse."

Sepi made a soothing sound, hugged her tighter.

"The doctor said…" Nat paused; years passed. "He said I only have a few months left, maybe less."

"We," said Sepi, her voice breaking. She felt her eyes water. "*We* have a few months. But not *left to live*, do you hear me, Natasha? Wc havc a few months to figure this out, to find a way. Forty-seven million buys a lot of doctor visits."

Nat didn't respond, just cried harder.

Sepi felt her stomach lurch, but she tightened her abs, held it together.

She had to be strong for Nat.

Had to figure out a way. Because a world without Nat was not a world Sepi could live in.

Wade's voice echoed in her mind.

Welcome to the next version of reality.

The corporate cowboy had no idea how right he was.

TWENTY-ONE

Doyle's Journal – November 22, 2045

I'm writing tonight from Jake Magnuson's shit shack on his ranch, about five kilometers northwest of the Admiral. From the outside, the shack looks like any old rickety outhouse, complete with a jagged quarter moon carved into its front door. Inside, the subterfuge continues with a roll of toilet paper hanging on a rusty nail next to a board perched across two tall blocks of evercrete.

The putrid smell of human waste is real, but the plumbing is not. Neither is Jake Magnuson, for that matter.

There are certain precautions you have to take when building a bunker underground. Power loss is a concern in the post-apocalypse, so life support systems better have a manual backup. Even though every electronic device in a two-kilometer radius had been rendered moot by an electro-magnetic pulse, the Admiral still had solid walls, locking doors, fresh water, and breathable air. In fact, Vida is probably hard at work keeping those systems going, giving the air recycler a good crank every hour or so.

We should all be so lucky.

After life support, there's mind support. What does the human brain need to retain its sanity? In a word: stimulation.

As the EMP shot outward, it left a trail of destruction in its wake. Short-term, it absolutely ravaged the dozens of Máquinas trying to break down the bunker door. But it also took with it the vidscreen, the audio system, palettes, media server, and even the goddamn microwave. The ultimate kicker was the complete loss of the Admiral's CPU. Without its brain to keep the bunker functioning, Vida and I were left to rely on candles and each other's company.

Some might have seen that as romantic.

And it might have been, had Vida wanted to talk to me at all. I still feel like I should have been the one to be angry, that I should have given her shit for even going outside at all. Instead, she disappeared into her room and didn't come out. A day passed. Then another. I had to stand at her door and tell her I was leaving to get supplies, that she would have to crank the air recycler or she would die.

I know, that sounds bleak, but there is so much more to live for now. And I think I'll finally be able to convince her of that.

But I'm getting ahead of myself. Back to the beginning.

After the EMP and a couple restless nights, my first priority was getting the Admiral back online. Before I could do that, I spent half a day covering Máquina bodies in snow—that's gonna be a problem come spring, but that's for Future Doyle to worry about. The other half of the day I spent hiking through the hills to the ranch of one imaginary Jake Magnuson.

I'd invented Jake as a way to store supplies near the bunker without raising any suspicion. No one lived on the ranch, and if they had, they probably would have been killed during the first week of the invasion. It would have cost too much to build another Admiral on the land, and the location would have been terrible anyway. Instead, I'd buried some key electronic components in an underground vault beneath the shit shack, about twenty meters behind the main house. The entrance was hidden under the floorboards, themselves covered in carefully arranged toilet paper that I'd decorated with red, yellow, and brown paint.

The hike through the hills was uneventful but slow. Considerable snow had fallen overnight, and my right boot sprung a leak after I caught it on an exposed tree root. Each time I had to stop and wring out my sock, it cost me ten minutes between unlacing my boots and peeling off the sock and putting the whole mess back together. Turned out it was a blessing in disguise because it stopped me at the edge of the tree line. Beyond that was open ranch ground, just an endless flat sea of dirt where a tall, burly man such as myself would stick out like a dickless synthetic at a porno shoot.

While I sat there vigorously rubbing my foot, I saw movement on the horizon.

A dark speck floated above the white fields, dipping left and right, but growing bigger by the second. I used binoculars to track it, and when it got close enough, I identified it as a Blue Eagle, one of the first iterations of the Air Force's autonomous drones. It was big, bulky, and maneuvered like a wet sponge. The two drones flanking it were Perros Grandes, the aptly named Big Dogs of the MX arsenal. They were primarily drone hunters; their 50mm rounds could shred almost anything in the sky.

They were good at their job.

Already, the Blue Eagle was shedding debris, as if its hull were coming off in tiny slivers that caught in the wind and fell to the earth like maple seeds. It dove for the ground, hugged the terrain, close enough that had any of the cows in the pastures been standing up, it would have been a mission-ending collision. The Perros banked, rolled, crisscrossed each other's flight path to keep their guns trained on the Eagle.

I rooted for our country's tech, but I knew it was outmatched. If the Perros didn't bring it down soon, more drones would show up. That was how the MX had managed to decimate us, through sheer numbers. It used to be that a country's military was limited by the size of its population, but not anymore. Something had happened in the MX that not only allowed them to build advanced synthetics, but to mass-produce them on a scale never before seen.

It must have cost a fortune.

I didn't see the end of the dogfight. The metal birds flew near but then turned suddenly northward to follow the mountain line. The wake of debris hung over my head, suspended in air longer than I thought possible for shards of metal. It wasn't until fragments started coming down among the trees that I realized they were papers, leaflets really, made of strong stock and laminated for protection against the elements.

One landed near my backpack. I picked it up, glanced at the American flag on one side, and then read the text on the other.

Read. Held my breath. Read again.

This is what it said:

To all human Americans, let me be the first to reassure you that your country has not abandoned you. We are working tirelessly to drive the MX menace from our lands. Unfortunately, the intrusion zone now stretches from the West Coast to the Mississippi River. For those of you caught within this zone, you have two options. The first is to head east to our fortifications along the river. Do not go north; the MX invasion has stopped one mile from the border and is preventing anyone from leaving. For those of you who cannot make it to the free zone, your second option is this: stay put. Run, hide, survive.

We are coming for you.

Sincerely, President Meyer.

I couldn't move. I stood there, reading the message over and over. The snow stung my bare foot, but I didn't care.

We are coming for you.

The words evoked something deep in the pit of my stomach, something warm and hopeful. For the first time, I felt like it wasn't me versus the entire MX army. Half of the country had survived; the government was still intact. And most importantly, they were still fighting.

All we had to do was survive long enough to be rescued.

I resisted the urge to scream.

"Bless you, Blue Eagle," I whispered. And yes, I really did say that out loud.

I'm sure the drone had been long destroyed by then, but its mission had been a success. It had given me hope, and I wanted to share that hope with you, Vida. If you only knew there was a future waiting for you, maybe you'd stop hiding in your room. Maybe you would come out and keep me company. Maybe you'd even relax and stop being so paranoid all the time.

I snatched up five more leaflets as I made my way across the open land to Jake Magnuson's farm. They were reassuring to look at, and if I did more traveling in the coming weeks, I could deliver the leaflets somewhere else, give any passers-by a ray of sunshine in this synthetic cloud-covered world.

Okay, I admit it. I was giddy, and I hadn't felt that way in a long time. Not even my simultaneously wet and frozen foot could bring me down.

The perimeter fence was still intact as I crossed Coles Road. I had to cut the barbed wire myself to make an entrance. After that, I trudged through the snow directly to the shit shack. There was nothing in the house I needed, and if any MX patrols came by, that's where they were most likely to look anyway.

I had to hold my breath to step inside, which made the physical tasks of moving the toilet paper and lifting the hatch more difficult than they should have been. A ladder carried me down three meters until the space opened up into a musty, reinforced shipping container. Deep shelves lined each side, stocked with multiple copies of electronic parts for the Admiral. More hung from the ceiling in black nets; they swayed as I brushed past them.

The air hardly moved, and the stench from the shit shack had settled into a pungent, almost tactile presence. Luckily, I'd filled the shelves myself, and having made a list prior to setting out, I knew exactly what we needed. I grabbed parts for the Admiral's CPU, PCB for the vidscreen, and two palettes. The media servers were at the back of the shipping container, and as I was opening boxes, I saw a collection of vacuum-sealed bags full of undershirts, boxers, and yes, socks. These were hung on long, metal pegs stuck into corkboard. Next to my rack was Angie's, then Gretta's.

I'm not ashamed to admit I considered opening a bag containing one of Angie's bras. She used to leave hers scattered about the house, always slipping it off somewhere between walking through the door and making dinner. Seeing pink lace hanging off the back of a chair always made me smile, because somewhere in the house, her breasts were swinging wild and free under a blouse or t-shirt, and that was something to get excited about.

My outstretched hand hung in the air, my fingers closed into a fist, and I pulled it back.

Angie was in the past, and the bra in the bag was new. She had never even seen it, let alone worn it. There would have been no reason to open it, no sentiment attached. I would have been a grown man standing in a shipping container under a shit shack fondling an unremarkable white cotton bra in the twilight of an LED headlamp.

How fucking pathetic.

So here I am, sitting on the cold, steel floor, writing in my journal and trying not to breathe. I keep staring at my fully loaded backpack, thinking about the leaflets, but mostly thinking about the palettes and the media server. When I'd created the disk image, I'd thrown every piece of media I owned onto it. Photos dating as far back as my childhood. Some of Angie's. Pictures from our time together in college, to our wedding, to Gretta's birth. Terabytes of videos and photos of my little girl.

Movies, new and old. Ancient classics like *Jaws* and *Christmas Vacation*. Barely year-old pictures like *Star Wars: Dark Republic* and *Cars: Electric Avenue*. Enough books to last a lifetime. Every song I'd ever heard or ripped from music streaming sites. Eight different educational programs covering K through 12. Games that would have kept Gretta busy for years.

I can see the menu, all of my media rigorously organized and cataloged. But if you click to the right a few times to a blank tile, then up twice, left once, and up three more times, you'd land on a tile with no image and no text. Clicking on it would bring up my personal Library of Congress of pornography.

I don't know why I included it. Maybe I thought *Stella Starfall Makes a Wish* needed to survive the apocalypse. Maybe I thought future generations would suffer without my tens of thousands of pictures of Ukrainian beauty Luba Hegre.

That's not true, of course. I know why I included them. I'm sure you do too, Vida.

I love and loved Angie; there's no doubt in my heart about that. And though I couldn't imagine ever needing more than her, I also knew her pretty well, knew that during times of stress and depression, her sex drive ground to a screeching halt. That would invariably be followed by my pleas for attention. Once she grew tired of those, I would pretend they were all jokes, that I was just horny and that she drove me crazy and that I didn't care we weren't having sex as often anymore.

This probably wasn't what you, Vida, or you, random stranger, were expecting to read when you pulled this journal off my mutilated corpse. But it's the truth. It's part of what makes me human. I hope a Máquina reads this and realizes how limited their world is.

They'll never get to experience love and lust and reciprocity.

So yeah, lots of pornography in case things got rough in the bunker. It called to me, but I couldn't answer it here in the shipping container, not without a network and certainly not with a ghost's shit-covered fingers jammed up my nose.

I'll wait until I get back to the Admiral.

It's better that I take my sexual frustration out on myself rather than Angie. Or I guess now... you.

TWENTY-TWO

As evening approached, Vida grew tired of her new, simplified routine. It consisted of two actions: crank the air recycler and wait an hour. The waiting was the worst part. Because of the time frame, she couldn't sleep for long, and the dreams that came were vivid and fragmented. In those flashes of fantasy, green grass stretched to the horizon to meet with the pink and purple hues of a sunset. Short but billowy trees waved their leaves at her, unlike the high pines around the bunker that swayed in the heavens. The ground was free of snow, and the clear sidewalks beckoned her to take a walk around a small pond.

Normally, such images would have spawned a round of questions about how she had imagined such a scene, whether it was from memory or spontaneously created in her mind. Vida didn't need to ask in this case. All she had to do was go back to her bedroom, sit down on the bed, and look up.

Doyle had intended the room for his daughter Gretchen. And though it lacked the vibrant colors and rounded edges typically found in a child's room, it did have one piece of decoration the other rooms lacked. On the ceiling, to the right of the LED strip that bisected the room, and directly over the bed, was a watercolor mural of a verdant meadow just after sunset.

Where Vida's dream had been hazy and liquid, the strokes of the paintbrush above her were sharp and detailed. She could pick out the individual reeds of the plants surrounding the pond, the green and white posts supporting young trees, and the lolling tongues of two dogs, one black with a white stripe, the other white with black markings.

The first time she saw the mural, Vida thought it was an odd choice for a child's room. Why not some kind of cartoon? Or horses and puppies? Why such a simple image?

"I wanted to remind Gretta of where she came from," Doyle had explained to her. "Every night before she went to sleep, I wanted her to know the world was good once and that it could be good again."

It hadn't had the same effect for Vida.

Most nights, she could barely stand to look at it, couldn't fathom how far away she was from that world. And yet the image continued to seep into her dreams. There, free of the bunker's trappings, she rejoiced in the open air, running along the banks of the pond like a deranged Julie Andrews, rolling in the soft grass as the dogs pounced on her and tried to lick her face.

Sometimes she floated several feet off the ground, higher and higher, until she could see miles of green in every direction. Birds flew in formation, stopped to alight on distant power lines. Clouds rolled over the horizon, over the entirety of flat earth.

It was heaven, the place Vida hoped to go when she died, which would hopefully be any day now.

Or today.

Today was a good day to end the clanking and bright lights and stuffy air and cold chills and distant explosions that seemed to rattle around inside her head constantly.

Whatever this nightmare was, there was too much of it.

She stared at the air recycler's crank.

It would be so much easier to stomach and make less of a mess than a bullet in the mouth.

All she had to do was go back to her room, shut the door, and go to sleep. Sometime in the ensuing hours, the carbon dioxide buildup would overwhelm her, and she would pass peacefully inside the dream world.

Vida turned the handle, wound up the recycler, and headed towards the bathroom.

She had bought herself another hour to ponder her limited knowledge of carbon dioxide poisoning. She knew carbon monoxide could kill silently, but hadn't she seen movies of people coughing and hacking? Suffocating? Was the true same for carbon *di*oxide?

It was too much of a risk; she didn't know enough to assure herself a painless death.

Instead, she took a shower by candlelight. The plumbing was purely mechanical, but the water heater was fully electric. The hot water lasted for only a few minutes; in that time, she was able to scrub her face and rinse away three days of sweat and oil from her skin. As the water turned frigid, she felt her breath leave her body.

Her skin cried out in agony, but she remained in the shower, letting the icy stream of water fall on her neck and chest. She put her hands over her breasts, felt the goosebumps leap from her flesh.

Though the cold penetrated to her very core, Vida endured the torture. It was something to feel, something to focus her mind on instead of the thunderous machinery of her waking nightmare. She shut her eyes, tried to imagine the mural and the dream, but instead, saw a choppy sea from the deck of a swaying boat. A strong breeze over the bay sent ice crystals flying across her face. In the distance, a small island peeked through the fog, its rocky shores giving way to decrepit buildings that looked a lot like—

"Alcatraz," stammered Vida.

The prison in San Francisco. Before it reopened in 2028, it had been a tourist attraction. Vida had gone there when she was younger, but how young? Was that in college?

In the vision, Vida caught a glimpse of someone in her periphery. She tried to turn her head, but the movement slowed the harder she pushed.

Her stomach shuddered.

The memory shifted perspective. She could almost see the person standing next to her.

Vida gasped, unable to stand the freezing water any longer. She shut off the shower and stepped out. She grabbed her two towels from the hooks on the opposite wall, wrapping one around her shoulders and the other around her legs. Cold and shivering, she sat down on the closed toilet and hugged herself.

Warm tears drifted down her cheeks.

She hadn't been able to see exactly who the person in her vision was, but she knew in her heart it was someone special. But where was that person now? They could have been dead, either before the war or worse, in the plane crash. Vida buried her face in her lap as she thought of this familiar stranger being out there somewhere, missing Vida as much as she missed them.

But that was impossible.

How could she miss someone she couldn't even remember?

The question consumed Vida. She returned to her room, absently drying off while she thought about the holes in her memory, how the images had disappeared, but the feelings were still there. She dropped the towel on the bed and sat on its edge, her eyes unfocused and drifting.

Fatigue drew her onto her back; she stared at the mural on the ceiling, struggling to stay awake.

In the dim light, she imagined creases in the artwork, as if it were painted on a crumpled piece of magazine that someone had tried to smooth out. The lockers to her left, though made of wood, glinted like steel. Everything was so spartan, so much like a jail cell. Vida wondered why she hadn't made that connection before.

The mural wavered, expanded, and became a world through which she could float. She was naked in the dream as well, but the air was warm and the only eyes on her were those of the two dogs. They sat watching her from a bench where their owners had placed them. Vida approached the edge of the water, and with a little mental manipulation, brought up a miniature of Alcatraz Island halfway across the pond. Again, she felt the presence beside her. Again, she tried to turn her head.

Distant noises roused her from her sleep.

A panel fell to the floor. Footsteps approached the door.

Vida held her breath.

"Vida, are you awake?" asked Doyle. His boots cast shadows beneath the threshold of the door. "Sorry I was gone so long. But I got everything we needed from the stash. Plus something I think you'll want to see."

A change in his voice, as if his forced optimism had become real.

Vida sat up and pulled the covers to her chest.

"Okay," he said at last. "I'm going to start replacing components so we can get power back up. Shouldn't take too long. In the meantime, if you want something to read in there, give this a try."

The shadows moved, and a slip of plastic shot out from under the door. It slid along the floor and landed near Vida's bare feet. She picked it up, held it close to the candle so she could read it.

To all human Americans…

The letters danced in place, spinning around each other. She squinted, tried again, and as the words turned to sentences turned to meaning, her pulse quickened. Shallow breaths came fast and stilted.

We are coming for you.

The sign-off disappeared under the haze of tears filling her eyes.

She choked on a sob and laughed. Giddy, joy-filled laughter. The idea that someone was coming for her, coming to free her from this post-apocalyptic prison, filled her with so much happiness that she wanted to scream. Even though there might not be a San Francisco to go back to, at least she would be out in the world again, back in civilization where she belonged.

Vida stood, pulled the blanket around her shoulders, and shuffled out of her room. She found Doyle standing next to the table with his hands behind his back, expecting her.

"Well, hey there," he said, the smile on his face stretching from one side of the bunker to the other.

Vida held the leaflet out to him, her happiness tempered by the memory of unbroken snow outside the bunker doors.

"Is this real?" she asked, her voice breaking. "Please, I have to know."

"It's real." He produced five more leaflets from behind his back. He splayed them out, some still wet, others marked with dirt and burns. "One of our drones dropped them near the stash. Two MX birds chased it away, but not before it released these." He licked his lips. "You know what this means, right?"

Vida felt her legs go numb. She faltered, but Doyle was there to catch her as she fell.

"I'll take that as a yes," he said, lifting her to a standing position.

She stared up into his face. His beard was still damp, and there was red in his skin. His cheek bones looked on the verge of blistering.

Angular and rough; those were the words that came to Vida's mind. She had never found such features attractive before. But now… now a halo bloomed around Doyle's head and golden light pierced his short, wavy hair.

"Don't get too excited though," he said, releasing her shoulders. "Who knows how long it will take them to get to us. We could be looking at months, maybe a year."

"But they're coming?" she asked.

"All we have to do is survive, Vida. And once I get the Admiral back online, our worst problem will be trying to fill the time. I won't go out unless I need to. We'll hole up together for a while, watch movies, read books, play games. Anything you want."

I want to walk outside, she thought.

"But, I'm going to need your help," he continued. "I can't stand this distance between us. This isn't how I expected life to turn out either, but if you can just set aside your worries for a little while, it'll make our time go by faster. Once we're rescued, you can get the medical attention you need to get your memories back. For now, I need your optimism and if you can manage it, your enthusiasm."

Vida closed her eyes, leaned into him.

He hugged her.

Attraction or not, there was comfort to be had in his arms.

"I know," she said. "I'm sorry. It's just…"

"You don't have to explain to me. I'm sorry I can't do more for you."

"You've done plenty." She looked up at him. "You saved my life, you've kept me sheltered and fed. And now…" She lifted the leaflet again. "You've brought me hope."

"And champagne," he said, gesturing to the table.

Vida eyed the black bottle.

"Krug 2035," said Doyle. "Trust me, it's fitting." He patted her back. "Will you drink with me?"

"To what?" she asked, acutely aware of how close her lips were getting to his.

"To us."

Vida put her head against his chest and nodded.

"To us," she whispered.

TWENTY-THREE

The email arrived at 7:54 p.m. on Tuesday, January 23rd.

Kagan was standing in front of the dresser in his bedroom fixing the cuffs on his button-up when his palette chimed.

You have a new message from Janet Kline.

Finally.

After two weeks of emails and phone messages, Janet, and by extension his father, had finally responded. Kagan clicked on the notification and brought up the email. His eyes skimmed the text.

"Fuck," he said.

His fingers flexed around the palette, nearly cracking the glass display.

"Is everything alright?" asked Nadya.

Kagan gave her a cold glance. "Dad got me a new job."

"That's good news, isn't it?"

"No, *Nadya*, that's not good news." He threw the palette down on the dresser. It slid off and landed on the hardwood floor face-down. "He wants me to go work at one of our subsidiaries in fucking Belgium."

So that was the old man's game. Ship his negligent son off to Europe to minimize the fallout from one tiny oversight.

"I hear Belgium is beautiful," said Nadya.

"Shut up," he replied, sitting down on the bed. He put his hands to his face. "Just shut up a minute so I can think."

There was no way Kagan could leave Los Angeles, especially not for some NATO-controlled disputed zone that didn't even have consistent access to VNet.

"I think it would be nice for us to get away for a while," said Nadya, wistfully. "It's always good to try new things."

Kagan dropped his hands and looked over at the synthetic.

She was on her hands and knees on the floor in front of the bed, naked as the day she rolled off the assembly line, and facing away towards the vidscreen on the far wall. Both ankles were wrapped in thick leather cuffs, dotted with silver holes for the buckle. Chains connected the cuffs to the metal loops on the floor, which were usually hidden under a square ottoman. Her wrists were similarly bound and tethered. To keep her from slouching in this pose, a single metal bar ran horizontally just under her stomach. After two weeks, she had begun to lean on it more and more.

"*We* are not going anywhere," he said. "I may send you in my place if you love eurotrash so much, but this is my home, here at the center of the universe. Everything worth happening happens here."

Kagan stood, began unbuttoning his shirt. He pulled it out of his pants and tossed it on the bed. Kicking off his slacks, he stalked angrily to the closet and came out wearing shorts and a gray undershirt.

As he approached the door, Nadya asked, "I could fix you a drink if you let me up."

Kagan paused, glanced back.

Her hair was messy and hung clumsily over her face.

"Eres una esclava?" he asked, admiring the curves of her synthetic body. "Then be a slave."

He slammed the door behind him and walked out into the hall.

Goddamn synnies.

Nadya had broken the unspoken agreement between humans and their products to never discuss the reality that one owned the other, especially when it came to synthetic companions. If someone wanted a fuck doll, they bought a fuck doll. But if they wanted something deeper, they got themselves a top-of-the-line Associate, treated it with a healthy level of respect, and formed a pseudo-relationship. Adelai Associates prided themselves on the lack of self-awareness in their products; it was usually the human who told the synthetic *he* owned *her*.

At no point was the synny supposed to say it felt like a goddamn slave.

Kagan took the main stairs to the second floor. He glanced down the hallway but didn't see Raf. He continued to the ground floor.

If Nadya wanted to be a slave, then he would treat her like one, and had, for the past two weeks. Stripping away the artifice of a supposed relationship had been liberating. There were no rules to follow anymore, nothing he couldn't do to her. He'd subjected her to alternating periods of lust and frustration, during which she hadn't protested or tried to tell him that what he was doing was in any way wrong.

At least Adelai Associates had gotten that part right.

On the other hand, maybe it was time to replace her with a newer model.

Kagan found Raf in the lounge, standing at the bar, adding a clear liquor to a glass of soda water.

He turned around and saw how Kagan was dressed.

"What's up, man?" he asked. "I thought we were going out."

"Change of plans." Kagan gestured for Raf to follow.

They walked single file down a hallway leading to the back of the house, then turned right down a flight of stairs. The basement covered the entire footprint of the house, and contained, among other things, half of a basketball court, two bowling lanes, pool tables, and a well-cushioned boxing ring. At the far end of the room, two identical immersion chairs hung from the high ceiling. Each of the egg-shaped chairs pointed slightly outward towards a table with immersion rigs and feedback gloves.

Kagan led Raf over to the chairs and gestured to the one on the right.

"I need to show you something in VNet."

"Nombre. I don't really fuck with VR anymore."

Kagan spoke through gritted teeth. "Just sit in the damn chair. I'm trying to help you here." He eased into his own chair and slipped the rig over his face. The goggles held tight to his eyes, blocking out all incoming light. He pressed the button on the right side of the rig just above his ear and felt the chair slide out from under him.

A moment later, he was standing in his virtual homeroom decorated floor to ceiling with moving images of Sepideh Ahmadi. A full-scale model of the actress stood in one corner of the room, wearing only a hand on her hip and a smirk on her face.

Raf blinked in next to her.

"Fuck me," he muttered, taking in the room. "Someone's obsessed, aren't they?"

"And?" asked Kagan, walking to the door.

"Can't be healthy, bro. All I'm sayin'."

Outside, the homeroom's porch extended five feet into the empty ether of Vinestead's virtual reality. Floating just beyond it was Fartsicle, Kagan's VNet-assigned Personal Assistant. He'd named his PA when he was thirteen, and it had become funnier with each passing year.

"Good evening, Mr. Kagan. How are you today?" asked Fartsicle. He wore a green alligator trilby hat with a black band and an ill-fitting suit of pearlescent crimson.

"Fan-fucking-tastic," said Kagan. He pointed to Raf. "I need a guest pass for my friend here."

Fartsicle lifted a monocle to his left eye and surveyed Raf. "There is no need. VNet is free to all active and retired military personnel. Thank you for your service, Mr. Orozco, and may God continue to bless America."

Raf rolled his eyes.

"Where can I connect you to today, gentlemen?"

"I need a private copy of the Plummer Tower in Hollywood, California. Can you set that up for us?"

Fartsicle nodded. "There is an active version in A-Prime. Copying will take approximately three minutes. Where would you like me to load it?"

"Out there is fine. Give us some ground to walk on too."

Kagan watched as evercrete floated up from the black abyss below to form a street, then a sidewalk. A gray haze reached for the horizon, forming the foundation of the building. The Plummer Tower grew up out of it, reaching high enough that Kagan had to step out of the homeroom and onto the porch to continue tracking the progress.

Fartsicle had closed his eyes to execute the copy, but now they opened and settled on Kagan.

"Is there anything else I can provide, sir?"

"No, leave us."

Fartsicle blinked out; the sound of squeaky flatulence punctuated his departure.

Raf chuckled. "I remember that."

Kagan wished he could join his friend in reminiscing, but Janet's email kept scrolling in his mind. He still wasn't sure how his father could be so callous.

"This is where you work, right?"

"Yeah," said Kagan, "only there aren't any synnies in the lobby for you to beat up."

"Lucky for the synnies."

"Alright, Macho Burrito, come on."

Raf followed, but not without asking, "Why *are* we here, K?"

"Dad fired me the day you started that shit in the lobby," said Kagan. He didn't speak again until they had walked through the foyer and were riding the elevator up. "Which yes, means I can't just walk you into Vitra Synth and unscrew your lightbulb like I said I would. And now, he wants to send me to Belgium to sell artificially intelligent backscratchers to political derelicts."

"Well," said Raf, inspecting his avatar's smooth hands. "Send me a postcard, I guess."

The doors opened onto the empty offices of Vitra Synth. The desk where Jennavie usually sat had been wiped clean.

After a moment, Kagan said, "This is the only way into the offices. There are emergency stairwells on the east and west sides of the building, but synnies are always guarding the bottom floors and the doors only open from outside the stairwell. All other traffic has to come from here."

Raf walked to the reception desk and put a hand on it, testing its presence. "And you're telling me this why?"

"Because, amigo, it's clear to me now that my father has no intention of giving me my job back, even though I consistently brought in the most clients. That means if we want to get you fixed up, we're going to have to break in and do it ourselves. I know a guy who works in the Blender room. His name is Earl Glasser. Little punk owes me a favor."

A smile crept across Raf's face. "Why don't we just come in guns blazing? Take out the synths in the lobby, hold everyone here hostage until I can get the procedure."

Kagan shook his head. "Yeah, you let me know how that movie ends."

Past the double doors, Kagan led Raf to the left of the cubicle farm and into a small hallway that branched into several offices. A door marked *Supplies* stood at the end of the hallway.

Kagan opened the closet and turned on the light. He pointed to the ceiling.

"You see those panels up there?" he asked. "In the actual office, those come loose and you can get up into the ceiling. About ten feet that way is a hollow support column used to run fiber and other telecom cables. It leads upstairs to the forty-first floor, which is conveniently unoccupied right now. We can slip in during the morning rush hour, hang out on forty-one, and once everyone leaves that evening, we'll come down here and do the deed. After that, we can just walk out the front door."

Raf huffed. "But there will be synnies in the lobby."

"I know. And if we can get out of here without you trying to kill any of them, we'll know the procedure worked."

"Sounds risky."

"Life's a risk."

"Says the pinche silver spoon guero." Raf examined the ceiling. "How do you even know about this?"

"I bang the receptionist in here sometimes. Sometimes we shake a ceiling tile loose."

"Shut up, man."

"She's a thrasher, what can I say." Kagan looked over his shoulder. "I'll mark off the path we'll need to take once we come out of the closet. We should probably trace it out a few times before we do the real thing. I'll reach out to Glasser tomorrow, make sure he'll run the procedure for us."

"If you can't, I'm out."

"What do you mean, *you're out?*"

Raf put his finger in Kagan's chest and seethed. "The last thing I want is your grubby fingers in my head. God knows what you'd do in there."

"Whatever," said Kagan, walking back down the hallway. "You want my fingers inside you. Just admit it."

Something heavy hit Kagan in his back just above his waist. He pitched forward, rolled painlessly into a nearby trashcan. A thick arm slipped around his neck and began to squeeze.

Raf laughed into Kagan's ear.

"Admit it," he chuckled. "You never banged the receptionist."

"*You* admit it. You never banged a woman."

Raf let out a comical yell, released his grip just enough to let Kagan slip it.

The simulated violence lasted half an hour, and Kagan was all too happy to indulge his anger and frustration.

More importantly, he wasn't thinking about his father, Belgium, or whether the procedure would even work.

TWENTY-FOUR

Seven doctors in five cities all said the same thing: Natasha Kumanov was going to die.

Each time the prognosis came back, Sepi grew a little bit angrier. Nat had been born in 2008, a full four years after the Guardian Angel bill passed, which meant her GA biochip had been installed at birth, watching her every move, collecting vitals, for twenty-seven years. And in all that time, it never saw the mass growing in her brain? Never picked up on anything amiss in the one place where it mattered most? If the cancer were in her lungs or spleen, the biochip would have registered it immediately, allowing her enough time to get a replacement from a donor or a bio-med farm.

But to miss it in her brain? Less than four inches from the biochip itself?

The tumor was practically tapping its foot on the Guardian Angel's doorstep.

Some of the doctors offered their own reasoning as to why the biochip didn't detect it. Dr. Saldana, who had been Nat's GP for several years, said computers were unreliable and that they didn't adapt well to situations they weren't expecting. Dr. Larson, who flew in from Denver, blamed the grow-wire that encased Nat's brain, showing Sepi on the MRI where the wires missed the affected area completely. Dr. Huang in San Francisco blamed Vinestead International outright for giving people a false sense of security. The other doctors, likely fearing lawsuits from Vinestead, chose not to comment on the failure of the biochip.

"It doesn't matter how we missed it," Dr. Conner had said. He was an aging specialist living in Carmel, with a thick beard and eyes that never seemed to focus on anything. "What matters is it's there, and we need to do something about it. Now."

He'd been the only one to openly suggest transcendence. The others had merely waved their hands around vaguely while mentioning *other options*.

Sepi had done her best to ignore the suggestion. If there was one thing she was certain of, it was that she loved Natasha for what she was now, in human form, flaws and all.

They didn't talk about it on the drive back from Carmel, and when they arrived at the Monarch, Nat went right to bed, citing a weariness from all the procedures and tests she had been put through that morning. Sepi left her in the dark bedroom and set up shop at the bar in the kitchen with a glass of wine and her palette.

She was online only a few minutes before Jane messaged her.

"I'm in the area," she wrote. "I'm stopping by."

"It's not a good time," Sepi wrote back.

"Sweetness, this is the kind of conversation we need to have in person. Also, I have some things for Natasha that I wanted to drop off."

"Okay. I'll meet you in the common area."

Sepi slipped out of the apartment with her wine glass and walked barefoot down the hallway. It was nearing midnight on a Thursday, but there was a good crowd sitting at the circular bar conversing with Gus. Solomon Boas raised his glass from across the room as Sepi found a seat near the window.

She stared at the twinkling streets below, trying to see past her own reflection. Helicopters darted across the sky, some with spotlights pointed down at the writhing masses, others chasing the small drones that were trying to spy on celebrities in their apartments. Aggregators had no shame when it came to getting an exclusive picture; technology only emboldened them.

Sepi sipped her wine, tried to keep her mind from wandering, only to be struck by the image of a synthetic Nat leaning in for a kiss.

Would her lips still feel the same? Would they feel real at all?

"Rum and Coke, Gus. And double it up for me."

Sepi turned at the sound of Jane's voice, saw her lumbering across the common area with a Gucci purse swinging from one hand and a Whole Foods bag in the other. Her pantsuit buckled and stretched as she navigated the chairs and low tables. Finally, she plopped down into the seat opposite Sepi and set the Whole Foods bag down on the circular table.

"What's going on outside?" asked Jane, retrieving a handkerchief from her purse. "My car had to drop me off three blocks away. I had to walk here with all manner of street rats accosting me. You know, now that you've got some money, I think it's time you consider moving to the Hills. I hear Colin Hanks will be putting his house up for sale soon. Something to think about."

Sepi leaned back in the chair, rested the wine glass against her chin. "I have plenty to think about," she said, feeling her eyes moisten.

"Tell me," said Jane, nodding to Gus as he deposited her drink on the table.

"You first."

"Alright." Jane took a sip, scrunched her face, then took another. "I had a meeting with the Sierra Brothers this afternoon. Very last-minute."

"They called you?"

"Their lawyer called me," said Jane, stirring her drink. "A real smarmy guy by the name of Bolet. They had the audacity to sic their legal team on us, as if we haven't responded to any of their inquiries already."

Sepi nodded. She knew the Sierra Brothers were pissed. They'd given her money to star in a new picture and Sepi had spent a small portion of it flying Nat to see doctors. Their two-week medical world tour had set the start of filming back a similar period, and with other actors, locations, and equipment already paid for, the Sierra Brothers were losing money.

It was a serious situation, but for some reason, Sepi found it hard to care.

"So," continued Jane, "I told Bolet to french a goat and hung up. Then I found out where the Sierra Brothers were having lunch and had myself a little pop-in."

"Did you put them in their place?" asked Sepi.

Jane pursed her lips, narrowed her eyes. She gestured to Sepi with her glass. "No. I apologized on your behalf. Richard said he understood, but he seemed real eager to lay it all out for me again. I know it's not fair with what's going on with Natasha, but we *are* holding up production, Sepi. They've got location holds that are costing them tens of thousands of dollars a day. And that's been since day one. At the most, we can stall another few days, but if you're not at call next Monday, they're going to shut the picture down. And then I'll probably hear from Bolet again asking for their money back."

Sepi let out a deep breath. There was no way she could work, not with Nat counting down the days. She had already lost so much of her carefree attitude; the smile she wore now bent at the edges, as if a frown were always hiding just beneath the surface.

"Did you tell them my girlfriend is dying?"

Jane reached out and put a hand on Sepi's knee. "I told them about your situation week before last. They're both sympathetic."

"I just hate all these doctors," said Sepi. "What do they know about saving lives? If someone could tell me, yeah, there's a chance she might survive, that there's an operation we could do, then maybe, maybe I could go back. But not if they have no answers for me. They take your money, look at some blurry pictures, and then just shrug their shoulders."

She sat up, put the wine glass down on the table.

"Do you know what this last doctor told us?" Sepi continued. "He said we should look into transcendence." She put her hands up. "Abandon ship, everyone. This body is a lost cause."

"Richard said the same—" began Jane.

"No," said Sepi, holding out a finger. "I'm not sleeping with a machine. I'm not kissing a machine good night. I'm—"

"This isn't about you, Sepideh!"

Sepi felt her throat tighten, felt all eyes in the room turn to her. Their silent judgments made her heart tremble.

Jane sighed, sat back in her chair. "I'm sorry, sweetness. I didn't mean to yell. I know you're having a hard time, but you have to remember that Natasha is the one we're trying to save here. She needs our support and our selflessness. We have to do what's best for her, even if that's not the greatest thing for us."

Tears fell, and Sepi put her hands to her face to stem the tide. When she opened them again, Jane was holding out a cocktail napkin. Sepi took it, blotted her eyes.

Jane gave her a minute before continuing. "Richard and I spoke for a long time today about Natasha. He suggested we at least schedule a consultation at Vitra Synth in Plummer Tower, you know where you went to get your contacts?"

Sepi nodded.

"Same place. They've been doing synthetic transfers for almost a decade, and Richard says many of the actors he's worked with have made the transition. He's going to make the switch himself at thirty-five. I guess he doesn't want to enjoy the pleasures of old age."

"Huh," said Sepi. "I thought Nat and I would experience those pleasures together. Get married, have children, grow old. That's what I wanted." She looked up and saw Jane cocking her head to the side. "But you're right. It's not about what I want. If this picture hadn't come along, I wouldn't even be in a position to consider a synthetic body." She paused, took a deep breath. "So, I guess I do owe these guys."

"Just show up," said Jane. "Just star in their little picture and make that jump to the next level of fame."

"I don't know if Nat would even go for transcendence. She didn't say anything when the doctor suggested it."

"Well, then that's your mission, isn't it?" asked Jane. "Modern medicine has failed her, her Guardian Angel chip has failed her, but now Vitra Synth, or whoever you decide to go with, has an answer. It's not the best answer, but I think you're being dramatic when you say you won't have sex with a machine. Ed died ten years ago, Sepi. I've been having sex with machines ever since. Beats dating, I'll tell you that."

Sepi shut her eyes, shook her mental Etch-a-Sketch.

"But I get it," continued Jane. "I really do. It wouldn't be the same as it is now. And really, it would be up to Natasha. You can put the glass down on the table in front of her, but she's gonna be the one who has to drink. I know three synthetics personally, Sepi, and I couldn't tell you how they're different from the way they were before. But then, I'm not intimate with them, so that might be an adjustment." Again, she reached for Sepi's knee. "But you can handle that, can't you? For her?"

"I don't know."

And she didn't. While she understood that she shouldn't be selfish, there was no ignoring the worries and doubts welling up inside of her. They weren't rational thoughts produced by her brain, but rather emotional objections raised by her heart, the very thing that had led her to Nat. How could she ignore it now?

Minutes passed in silence. Jane sipped her drink. Sepi stared into hers.

Residents came and went, though none of them approached the two women sitting quietly in the corner. Solomon did come by, asking forgiveness for interrupting them, just to wish Sepi a good night. Sepi finished her wine, and Gus collected the glass shortly after.

"I brought some things for Natasha," said Jane, motioning to the bag. "Just some herbal remedies, some sweets, and this new French-Italian fusion salad they have at the deli. I've had two this week. They're really good."

"Thank you," said Sepi.

"Well, sweetness, I should be going." She stood and slung her purse over her shoulder. "You call me if you need anything, alright?"

"There is something."

"Name it," said Jane.

Sepi stood, hesitated for a moment, then put her arms around Jane.

"It's going to be okay," said Jane, squeezing tightly.

"It won't be the same," said Sepi.

"Nothing ever is."

Sepi shut her eyes tight, but that only produced a blank canvas on which to paint a horrifying image of Nat with her mouth opened wide in a silent scream, the gizmos and servos around her teeth and tongue plainly visible, the skin on her throat glowing bright orange from some internal heat source.

A mechanical Natasha Kumanov.

Sepi could live with it, laugh with it, and maybe even sleep with it.

But love it?

No technology could be that advanced.

TWENTY-FIVE

Doyle's Journal – November 23, 2045

I'm thinking a lot about Angie tonight.

Before I met her, I thought all relationships were temporary, that you loved someone for as long as it lasted and then moved on to someone else. Angela Ballard was different. She was headstrong and infinitely loving, and I couldn't help but pour everything I had into her. We had our fights, our disagreements, but we got past them all.

I became a better man for Angie.

And when we had Gretchen, I became better for her too.

I swore to myself I would never abandon them, that I would never love any woman as much as I loved them.

It wasn't just a feeling that drew me to them.

I *chose* to love Angie and Gretta.

And now, I choose to love Vida.

Normal relationships have no place in this fucked up world anymore. If she and I were still in pre-apocalypse days, we probably never would have spoken to each other. But, this is the situation we find ourselves in, with a world hell-bent on killing us and only each other to lean on for support.

There's something about Vida that makes me want to protect her, to throw my arms around her waist and shield her from all the wrong. I could stabilize her ups and downs, provide her a foundation of happiness and optimism that she could rely on.

I know how vulnerable she is, how much she needs me.

It was never like that with Angie; she didn't need me in the slightest. I knew that if I died before her, she'd be just fine.

Vida, not so much.

At the same time, I need her too. Honestly, there isn't much reason for me to carry on, except for my moral opposition to suicide. But I remember those nights in Park City, when I most needed strength, that I thought about Vida and found a way to keep going. She inspired me to survive then and now, and that's exactly what I need in my life.

If we can just hold out until rescue comes, or failing that, if we can find a way to the Ole Miss, then we have a chance at a normal life. We can only do that together, even if we go our separate ways after this is over.

I'll be honest.

A selfish part of me doesn't want to let her go.

But it's not up to me, is it? All I can do is love her in my own way and hope she feels—or chooses to feel—the same. It may not be the greatest love she has ever known, but it would be what we have, and that's worth something in a world where we have very little.

I'm not trying to justify myself to Angie. Her face is and always will be etched in my mind. I see her when I close my eyes. Every time.

I will never forget her, even when it may seem like I have.

It wasn't my intention to sleep with Vida.

We just got caught up in the moment. She hadn't had a happy thought in weeks. She couldn't remember who she was or where she belonged. There was nothing on the horizon for her except more time in the Admiral. And then I brought home those leaflets and it was like a mask had fallen from her face. She forgot about the horror show outside and threw her arms around me.

I hadn't felt a woman's arms in so long.

We were kissing before I knew what was happening, and then her wet hair was slipping through my fingers. The sheet she was wearing fell to the floor, and I saw she had nothing on underneath. In the candlelight, Vida looked ethereal, almost too perfectly assembled, as if she were some average of what beauty could and should be.

A long neck that ended in visible collar bones. Petite, rounded breasts with nipples only slightly darker than the surrounding skin. A flat stomach. An empty piercing above the belly button.

The rest of her was lost in shadow.

Oh god, Angie. I'm so sorry.

Vida helped me out of my jacket, then my shirt. I closed my eyes and saw your face, and when I opened them, Vida's lips had become yours. The soft back I ran my hands over was your back, Angie. I withdrew, but she pulled me close.

We ended up in the bedroom. At first, I worried she might lead us into mine, where pictures of you and Gretta still hang on the wall. Instead, we went into Gretta's room and onto the bed where our daughter should have been sleeping.

It was hard not to think of you two.

But Vida was so inviting. She had my pants off, had reached into my boxers as we kissed. There was no going back. We sat down on the bed, hands exploring each other, lips locked.

When Vida pulled me down to the bed, I ended up on top of her, my elbows falling on either side of her head. I felt her tug me closer, pulling my hips down. I touched something wet, and then I was inside her.

She gasped, told me to be gentle.

Any other woman, any other place, and I would have been happy and excited and ready to put on a show.

But with Vida, I could only stare at the pillow behind her head, unable to close my eyes anymore. I didn't want to see you, Angie, not while this was happening. It was physical pleasure and mental anguish in equal measure, and I just couldn't lean either way.

I came in just a few minutes, but I kept moving my hips like some kind of synthetic companion stuck in a program loop. Vida moaned as I kissed her neck, shoulders, and breasts.

My erection returned, my tempo increased, and Vida began to pant.

She whispered something under each breath, and it sounded a lot like she was calling me *daddy*. Before I could ask her about it, her orgasm built to a head, and her long fingernails dug into my back. I climaxed again, and our bodies relaxed simultaneously.

I slid onto the sheets between her and the wall, held her in my arms.

In the low light, I could see the sweat beading on her neck. I ran a finger down her arm to her hip.

A deep silence took over the bunker. I felt like I should have said something to her, but what?

Thank you?

Was it good for you?

Ultimately, I kept my voice soft and tried to tell her that it was going to get better, that from this day forward, things would start to improve. We had found a meaning to our lives, something to look forward to other than merely surviving. I promised her I would get her to safety, that I'd stay until she figured out who she was and whether her people were still alive.

She nodded a few times but said nothing.

Sometime later, she excused herself to the bathroom, pausing at the door to look over her shoulder at me.

I wish I could write that she had been smiling, but the look on her face was more curious than anything else. Her eyes scrutinized me, making me aware of how dirty I was from the trip to the shit shack. I probably smelled even worse.

When she came back, she sat at the foot of the bed, not looking at me. The silence dragged on. Finally, I told her I needed to shower, but that I could make her some food once I was out. After that, I'd get the bunker back online.

She nodded, didn't look up when I passed her.

I showered in freezing water, scrubbed off the stink of the shit shack, and wrapped a towel around my waist. When I came out of the bathroom, I found Vida's door closed.

Such a brief awakening.

I dressed, made some food that Vida refused, and then started in on the electronics. It took an hour to get the lights back on, and two more before everything else was fixed. The microwave still didn't work, so I had to make tea the old-fashioned way on the electric stove.

The couch sighed as I collapsed into it. The vidscreen resisted at first, but after some insistent mashing of the power button, it turned on and loaded my media center's dashboard screen. All the movies, pictures, and music were still there, so I clicked through to my collection of television shows. I picked a sitcom at random, let it play while I reclined on the couch and stared at the ceiling.

Angie, if you're looking down on me, I hope you forgive me.

Vida, if you ever read this, I hope you forgive me for writing it all down in detail. Being with you makes life worth living again. I never want to forget this night we shared together.

The way your hair clung to your face.

The way your back arched.

The way your moans echoed in my ear.

Daddy… daddy… addy… addy…

TWENTY-SIX

None of it felt right.

Vida had been so sure of herself before, standing in the living room, the words from the leaflet still fresh in her mind. Had stood there looking at the man named Doyle who had brought her the good news. Had looked into his eyes with such appreciation and admiration that she mistook it for something else.

She let him hug her. Let him kiss her.

And then they were in bed, naked, and she was staring up into his face, watching him grimace and smile. His eyes had looked bolted open, but at the same time far away, as if he were thinking of something else.

Doyle smelled like an open sewer, his body hair borderline repulsed her, but there was something undeniable about the pleasure she felt as he hovered over her and rocked his hips slowly. Except, the feeling seemed completely separate from him as a being. It was more abstract, like a remembrance of a sensation lost in the dark corners of her mind.

Vida reached for the memory but couldn't wrap her fingers around it. She felt herself withdraw from the situation, felt the pleasure wane. The rote mechanics of intercourse stood out in stark contrast to what she remembered— no, felt—sex to be. It had been, at one time, an intimate experience shared with a loving partner.

Sweet. Tender.

Nothing like the man grunting on top of her.

Vida wanted to be out of the bed, the room, and the bunker, but looking up into Doyle's face, she couldn't think of a way to extricate herself. He'd already climaxed once—the thought of his goo sloshing around inside her made her stomach lurch—but he seemed to be picking up steam again.

He pressed hard against her, ground into her pelvis. She let out louder and louder moans to urge him on in the hopes he would finish quickly and leave. Strangely, a familiar feeling started to well up inside her, and the pleasure returned.

She put her hands to his face, smoothed back his hair.

Then she saw it.

A flash of lightning in the dark room.

His hair turned golden blond.

His skin paled, eyes softened, and lips thinned to a taper.

He was someone else completely, almost elf-like in appearance.

Doyle pulled back and shook his head. In a blink, his normal face returned.

Vida called out the syllables of a name she couldn't remember, and the more she repeated them, the more hopeless it all seemed.

Finally, she cried out in mock ecstasy, did her best to shudder, and went quiet. Doyle followed, then fell into place behind her, draping his muscular arm over her body, his hand cupping her breast. He likely meant it as a protective gesture, but it made Vida feel trapped. Their relationship had crossed a line, and the grass was dead on this side.

She excused herself to the bathroom, wanting to sit down on the toilet as soon as possible. When she returned, Doyle left to take a shower, and Vida took the opportunity to close and lock the door. She blew out the candle on the desk and laid back on the bed. The comforter was still on the floor in the living room, but the room was warm, muggy, and smelled of stale sex.

In the darkness, she spoke to the ceiling.

"Who are you? Where have I seen your face before?"

The mural stared back, unspeaking.

"I've seen your eyes blink, your lips smile. I've seen you push your hair over your ear."

Then it hit her: the ferry in San Francisco. The person standing next to her. Was it a man or a woman?

She felt a rush of excitement as the pieces fell into place. Recalling the memory, she tried again to turn her head, and this time she saw the features she had seen on Doyle's face on a waif of a boy beside her. He was small, like a Peter Pan from a recent movie. He had no voice, no other identifying features.

All Vida knew was that he was holding her hand, and it felt right.

Felt like home.

She ignored Doyle's knocking when he returned with food some time later, and instead fell asleep thinking about the Golden Gate Bridge, Alcatraz, and her Peter Pan boyfriend.

In the morning, the lights buzzed on at six thirty, as they had almost every day since she arrived. Vida fell into her routine without thinking, and was showered, dressed, and eating breakfast at the table when Doyle came out of his room.

He wasn't wearing a shirt, and his wounds from Park City were still fresh on his skin. His flannel pajama bottoms sat low on his waist, giving Vida a view of the ridges along his hips. The loose material did little to hide his partial erection.

She looked away as he approached.

"Good morning," he said, opening the fridge.

Vida nodded.

He took out a glass and placed it on the table, poured himself a drink. "So, last night, huh?"

Vida looked away.

"Hey," he said, "look, I get it. Neither of us were thinking clearly. Hell, if you had been some *guy* I saved from a plane crash, I probably still would have kissed you. Maybe not ended up in bed, but who knows? People do crazy things when they're happy to be alive."

The words rolled off his tongue as if he had been practicing the speech all night.

"I know this doesn't change anything between us, Vida. And I'm not expecting anything from you at all. As far as I'm concerned, this was a one-time indiscretion. I, um… I appreciate what you did for me. I know I'm not much to look at, especially after what I've been through."

Vida looked up, saw Doyle taking inventory of the scars on his chest and stomach.

"It's not that," she said. "Last night was… something I wanted, at the time."

"And now?"

She shrugged. "I don't know. It's hard to think. So much is happening at once. I can't keep everything straight. The government is coming to save us, we end up in bed together, and I start remembering things…"

Doyle put his glass down. "What things?"

"Bits and pieces mostly. San Francisco. The bay. Alcatraz. I was there before, with someone special to me. We rode the ferry out to the island."

"To Alcatraz?" asked Doyle. "That had to be like, twenty years ago, right? They turned it back into a prison in—"

"I know," said Vida. "It was, and yet, it feels like just yesterday."

"Memories can be weird like that."

"I can smell the water," she said.

Doyle sat down on a stool and furrowed his brow. He asked, "So how do you think you made it all the way up to Montana from there? You think you were in San Fran on vacation?"

"Maybe."

"Well, it's good progress. Here's to your speedy recovery." He raised his glass of orange juice in a toast.

Vida clinked her cup of water against it.

"So, I got the Admiral back online."

"I see that," said Vida, lifting her eyes to the LED lights in the ceiling. "I was beginning to think we'd be living in darkness for the rest of our lives."

"Yeah," said Doyle, his shoulders slumping. "Our real problem though is those Máquina bodies we toasted on the surface. I buried at least twenty in the snow, but that'll only hold for so long. The sooner I can get them away from the Admiral, the better."

"I could help you," offered Vida.

"Very kind of you, but I've got it covered. If anyone or anything shows up asking questions, I want to be the only one who has to answer. Besides, it's all downhill. Maybe I can just roll the bodies. There are a couple of boarded-up exploratory mines down there, from back when they thought there was gold in these hills."

"Was there?"

"If there were, we'd be standing in the Fleet Admiral 990-XLS instead of the Admiral 640. About three times as big, multi-level. Even has separate bathrooms."

"How luxurious…"

"Yeah, well," said Doyle, draining his glass. "Maybe if I had worked harder." He put the glass in the sink. "I'm gonna get geared up and head outside. You gonna be good here without me?"

Vida patted the gun on her hip.

"Easy, Shooter. You don't want that thing going off in here. Bullet will ricochet off these walls like a pinball. Then, bam!" He jammed his finger into his forehead. Smirking, he headed to his room, but didn't bother to close the door as he changed clothes.

Vida pulled the gun from its holster and dropped the clip into her other hand. She inspected the bullets, found them to be in good order, and reinserted the magazine. With a slight tug of the chamber, she was able to look inside and confirm the gun was charged and ready to fire.

It was part of the routine to check. She hardly even noticed herself doing it anymore.

Doyle returned in a white snow jacket, made a flat joke about the weather outside, and left through the bunker door. Vida watched the clock on the vidscreen count out fifteen minutes and then went to his room.

She hesitated in the threshold.

Photos from Doyle's past dotted the wall, but the one Vida cared about hung over his pillow. It showed Doyle in tan cargo shorts and a blue button-up sitting on a picnic table. Beside him, a wispy woman with long, blonde hair sat with her arm over his shoulder. Standing behind both of them, with her face pressed to their shoulders, was a little girl with big eyes and pigtails.

She found his journal laying open on his desk. It looked like he had just finished a new entry and she wanted nothing more than to see what, if anything, Doyle had written about their night together.

He didn't disappoint.

Though his description was more graphic than she would have liked, and he got a few of the details wrong, it also included insight into what he was thinking as he loomed over her.

The poor guy. Haunted by his dead wife.

The last thing Vida wanted to do was get in the way of Angela's memory, and if Doyle felt guilty for sleeping with her, then it must have been for a good reason.

And love? Did he really write that he loved her?

Vida shook her head, backed away into the hallway.

It was much too soon for that, wasn't it?

The walls of the bunker took one step towards her.

The way your back arched.

The way your moans echoed.

Vida shuddered and hurried back to the kitchen. She reached for the bottle of Kentucky Gentleman in the cupboard and was relieved to find it still had a few shots left in it. She pulled directly from the bottle until it was empty. The warmth spread over her chest while she stood perfectly still.

The bunker leaned.

"He really had his way with you, didn't he?" asked Peter, breaking the silence.

With her eyes closed, Vida could see the boy standing next to her on the ferry, his dark eyebrows dipping at the center.

"And now that he's had a taste, he's going to want it again and again and again."

"No," whispered Vida. "He said—"

"He *said*. Men will say anything to get in your pants, you know that. And you're the only pants around for miles. You make sure that gun stays on your hip, because sooner or later, when it's dark and you're groggy from sleep, he will come for you. And if you don't give him what he wants, he *will* take it from you."

"No. You're wrong about him. You don't know him."

"And you do?" asked Peter.

"I know enough."

Vida sat down on a stool, dizzy from arguing with herself.

"If you really want to know him," said Peter, "you should ask his wife and daughter."

Her eyes drifted to the bunker door; it bulged and receded.

"If they even exist," said Peter.

TWENTY-SEVEN

Lucasz Abat was personal friends with three of the eight board members at Vitra Synth, including Kagan's father. When news and circumstances of his death hit the media feeds, an emergency meeting was called at the Kagan Group offices in Sacramento. According to the internally released minutes, only three of the board members attended physically; the others appeared in their seats as augmented reality projected onto three-dimensional stand-ins. After a brief discussion, during which Frank Kagan said very little of note, the next senior member, Elan Roark, called for the immediate termination of the offending employee.

If it had been anyone else, the employee might have ended up in a ditch on the seedy side of Umbra. But as a general rule, no one told Frank Kagan how to run any of the companies in his portfolio, especially those in which he had a personal interest.

As a compromise, Frank offered to suspend his son from work until such time as he could find him a position elsewhere. The board agreed, and Frank told his assistant to call Kagan with the bad news, only she was to tell him he had been fired outright.

On paper, Kagan still worked at Vitra Synth, and his coworkers likely assumed he was just on another impromptu vacation. And since building security hadn't been told otherwise, they had no reason to prevent him from entering Plummer Tower. Both he and Raf strode right in through the front doors, albeit in hats, aviator sunglasses, and popped collars. Raf claimed it made them look suspicious, but Kagan had insisted on playing cloak and dagger.

They cut across the main lobby and headed directly for the elevators. Kagan mumbled *forty-one* as they entered. They rode up in silence for the benefit of the camera in the ceiling. When the doors opened, Kagan bent his arm ninety degrees and held up a closed fist. He gestured with two fingers into the darkness.

Raf groaned.

The forty-first floor had previously been home to the social networking company Pattrn, which had gone out of business in 2033 after a five-year legal battle with privacy groups who accused then-CEO Edward Chen of handing over personal data to government agencies for profiling. Their assets had been in legal limbo for more than a year, leaving the space above Vitra Synth empty.

Amber guide lights ran the length of the hallways, angling off to the left and right to show the borders of an open floorplan. There was just enough glow that Kagan didn't have to use his flashlight.

"The column should be on the east side of the building," he said, closing his eyes to see the map in his head. "Reception would be here, main doors down there. Break room, copier, and there, supply closet."

Unlike the floor below it, forty-one had no room adjoining the support column. Instead, it occupied a quarter of the real estate inside the office's worst cube. Kagan dropped his bag onto the desk and pulled out a screwdriver.

He knelt to work the four corners. Over his shoulder, he noticed Raf slumping to the floor, his back against the fabric wall.

"What's wrong?" he asked.

Raf shrugged. "No se. This just seems like a lot of risk for me. No offense, but you were never the kind of guy to stick his neck out for someone else."

The screwdriver paused. "That is true. I'm actually not doing it for you; I just want to prove a point." He resumed his work. "You've suffered from PTSD for how many years? And all because you didn't reach out to me like you should have, whether or not you thought I would help you. Because I would have then. I could have saved you some pain. So when I do get you in that chair and make the bad memories go away, I want you to admit you should have done this sooner. You suffered unnecessarily."

"I don't have PTSD," said Raf. "That's just something they made up for people who can't handle their shit. Yeah, I've got some bad dreams, but that's the price you pay for being a warrior. Nobody forced me to enlist. When they put a rifle in my hand and told me to go kill my own people, I could have run out. But I didn't. I knew what I was getting into."

"Well, that's the other thing," said Kagan, removing the last screw. He tapped the metal plate; it fell free of the wall. "Nobody forced you to go, I agree. That was just one of those classic Raf dumbfuck decisions. But what happened after you did what they told you to do? After you sacrificed your life for 'merica? What did they give you? A street to sleep on? Dumpsters to get your meals from? Contempt from people who probably never fought for anything in their lives? Chale, Raf. They abandoned you."

"Ah," said Raf, tapping his head against the wall, "so this is civil disobedience for you? You want to make yourself feel good by helping a vet like me?"

Kagan peered down into the open column and saw crisscrossing lines of light below. He pulled his head out of the column and rested on his heels.

"Alright soldier, we've got an ingress point," he said, gesturing with the screwdriver. He put his hands on his thighs and considered Raf's last statement. "Okay, let's just say this is a protest. If that's true, then I don't really need *you* do I? I could have grabbed any prior-service grunt off the streets and brought them in. God knows there're plenty of them lining Santa Monica. Naw, I'm not protesting shit. I'm helping my friend, mi amigo pendejo, get himself out of the mess he got himself into. Why can't you just accept that I want to help you?"

Raf reached into his jacket and pulled out a flask. The cap clinked against the metal side as he took a swig.

"It's not you, K. You don't help people. No rich gringo does."

"You're not just people. Eres mi hermano. And I can be nice once in a while. Just ask…"

Kagan blanked on an example.

"Whatever," he continued. "I'm only risking my freedom over here. If you don't want to go through with this, so be it. You know where the elevator is. Otherwise, let's have some dinner."

Raf reached into his bag and brought out two foil-wrapped stacks of pizza. After tossing one to Kagan, he tore into his own.

"How long are we gonna be here?" he asked.

Kagan looked at his sliver. "It's seven now, we'll head down there around ten to make sure everyone's out. In the chair by eleven. The rest is up to Glasser."

"Can we trust him?"

"Considering how many bad-batch synthetic bodies he's taken home over the years? Yeah, I think he's going to do what I tell him. He's got too much to lose."

At twenty-three years old, Earl Glasser was the youngest person at the company. He'd graduated from Umbra Technical with degrees in Computer Science and Mathematics. Although the technology for synapse manipulation had been tuned long before Isaac Glasser ironically changed his name to Earl, he was the first to perform a complete wipe in under sixteen minutes. For whatever reason, the kid knew his way around a brain. If the subject had any bad memories, for example, five hellish years in the MX, Glasser could root them out with surgical precision.

He was the right guy for the job, but far from a sure thing.

Kagan tried not to think about the two percent margin of error Vitra Synth had been unable to eliminate over the last few years. He asked Raf to tell some stories from the MX, an activity Glasser had recommended in the hours preceding the procedure. Something about the subject recalling the offending memories helped them show up better on the scan. Even though Kagan had heard many of the tales, he still listened intently, kept probing whenever Raf struggled with a detail.

He was in the middle of a story about an incursion deep into the MX when he suddenly fell silent. His eyes jumped rapidly from side to side.

"That's the one, isn't it?" asked Kagan.

Raf looked up, his eyes reddening. "Huh?"

"The memory that keeps you up at night. Tell me about it."

"No."

"Hey, man, it's me. Say that shit out loud. Get those neurons firing, and Glasser will rip it right the fuck out of you."

Raf tilted his head back, took a long pull of water. Kagan saw the scars running the length of his throat, the uneven holes around his left carotid artery. The damage was more prominent now that he'd begun shaving again and cropping his hair close to his head. Those damn Máquinas had really done a number on him, but at least he'd survived. Many of the men he fought beside hadn't.

"Remember I told you they sent me home when the Vinestead synthetics started arriving? That wasn't the whole story. Truth is we were encamped near Lago Colina, way beyond the front lines, cut off from everyone else. The Máquinas were jamming comms, so we had no way to call for support. It was all quiet that first night, but come the following evening, we found ourselves surrounded. All sides. Every point of the compass. Hundreds of synthetics, K. All these little red eyes looking out from the trees."

Raf crushed the empty water bottle in his hand.

"Our squad leader was a Dominican named Arnel. Something Arnel. Can't remember. He told us to form up, huddle together. The Máquinas laid down fire and marched forward. Our cover started to go. Arnel screamed something like 'suck our metal dicks.' Then he hit the EMP and those fucking Máquinas dropped like someone had upped the gravity. It was too effective though; all of our weapon systems went down. If we'd had fully mechanical rifles, like an AK or something, we would have been okay, pero no. Too caught up in technological progress, I guess."

Kagan checked his sliver. It was getting close to ten.

"We were too tired to march. Arnel gave us two hours of sack. I remember going out like a light but waking up with a Máquina grabbing my shoulder. I fought back, thrashing, punching, kicking. No gun, no knife, just my bare hands. By the time they pulled me off Arnel, he was already dead. I'd choked him to death. And that was it for me, K. I was broken then."

"But you didn't mean to kill him, right?" asked Kagan.

"What the fuck do you think?" His eyes flashed red.

"Then what are you beating yourself up about? The military trained you to be a killing machine. That's what you did. Sometimes machines don't work the way we intend them to, but that doesn't mean we discard them out on the street. We *repair* them. Fix 'em up so they can fight another day. And that's what I'm gonna do for you, man. No one breaks my best friend except me!"

Kagan held out his clenched fist. Raf bumped it.

"Let's go. Glasser is probably pissing himself waiting for us."

Raf nodded, slipped his bag onto his back.

Kagan's headlamp put out a narrow beam of light, but it was enough to navigate the cramped crawlspace in the column. He gripped thick bundles of cables as he descended, careful not to snap anything crucial or touch anything electrical. At the bottom, through a series of muscle-exhausting moves, Kagan reoriented his body horizontally and traveled the ten feet to the ceiling over the supply room.

He pulled the ceiling tile up and peeked inside. Nothing but darkness. Sliding the tile out of the way, Kagan dropped his feet into the room as if he were testing the water in his pool. His boots thudded on the carpeted floor when he landed, but the sound didn't echo beyond the closed door.

Raf dropped in behind Kagan.

With a finger over his lips, Kagan made a series of military hand signals that made no sense to either of them. He opened the door slowly.

The corridor was dark, but a bright flash appeared at the end of it. A low, booming voice rolled down the hallway.

"That's far enough, assholes."

TWENTY-EIGHT

The synthetic loomed over Sepi.

As far as she was concerned, she had two options. Either let the synthetic tear her limb from limb, or roll to the side, pop up next to the copier machine, and use it to vault herself over the synny, all while wrapping a length of wire around its neck.

She let the decision-making process play out on her face, waving her eyebrows and flaring her nostrils.

As the synthetic reached for her, she made up her mind.

Sepi lunged and rolled, grunting as her broken shoulder hit the floor twice. She used her good arm to push herself up, took a running leap at the copier, and launched herself into the air, executing a perfect backflip. Blood-soaked hands came apart, pulling the network cable taut between them. She wrapped it around the synthetic's neck. Sepi lowered her center of gravity, got just enough leverage, and pulled the synthetic over her shoulder.

It crashed into a glass window, shattering it.

She made one last desperate grab for the gun on the floor by the table, and once she had it in hand, she lay sideways on the ground, aiming with one eye closed, and emptied the entire clip into the synthetic's head. Her scream filled the room and echoed long after Richard Sierra yelled, "Cut!"

A shrill bell rang out from the rafters above. Synthetic crewmen rushed in to reset the scene.

"Powerful take, Sepideh," said Richard, coming down off his chair. He stepped around the camera and smiled. "Loved the intensity on that yell. How were the wires? Did they get in your way?"

Sepi accepted the outstretched hand of a synthetic and climbed to her feet. The harness on her waist had begun to chafe, and the complexity of the last stunt had left her inner thighs bruised.

"No," she replied, "they were fine. How was the shot?"

A stylist dropped a tall chair next to Sepi and waited for her to sit down. She removed the excess blood from Sepi's hands while the continuity specialist took photos.

Richard gave her a thumbs up. "Great work. I think we only need a couple more takes for coverage and we should be done. I appreciate your effort on this one. I know it's a demanding shot. But hey, better now than when you hit your thirties and it all starts to fall apart."

Sepi raised an eyebrow.

"That's what they tell me, anyway. Nothing for you and I to worry about just yet." He glanced at a palette an assistant put in front of him. He groaned. "Goddamn union breaks." Touching his headset, he said, "Alright, people. That's an hour and a half for lunch." His voice boomed over the set.

The stylist switched gears and placed her dainty fingers on Sepi's cheek, reverting the Savannah Kessler veneer back to Sepideh Ahmadi. Satisfied with her work, the stylist put her bag down on a nearby table and walked away.

Sepi followed Richard to the warehouse entrance. Outside, the California sun hung hot and heavy overhead. The Sierra Brothers lot slowed to a crawl; for everyone except the synthetics, that is. They continued to rush between buildings, setting up for new shots and tearing down the old ones.

A golf cart sat dormant next to the entrance. Sepi climbed in behind Richard.

"Talent trailers," he said.

The cart responded with a flash of green light, reversed, and rolled leisurely down the main avenue of the lot. It turned left, then right, and finally came to an open area bordered by large, well-appointed trailers. The cart stopped near the loading zone, which happened to be next to the day's food truck, a Brazilian take on stuffed hamburgers.

Sepi inhaled the aroma; her stomach grumbled at the fresh onions.

Lawrence Sierra stood by the food truck, staring off into space and absently eating a hamburger. When he saw Sepi, he nodded and gestured to her trailer with his thumb.

"You have a visitor," he said.

"Your ball-busting agent?" asked Richard. "I mean, sweet Ms. Zimmerman?"

Lawrence shook his head. A smirk crept onto his face.

Sepi recognized the look, had seen it on the faces of a thousand men anytime she and Nat walked into a room. For as invasive as aggregators were, they had never caught wind of Sepi's sexual orientation, had always referred to Nat as a *friend of film star Sepideh Ahmadi*. But when people finally saw them together, in person, it was hard to miss the connection.

"Grow up," said Sepi.

Lawrence took another bite, shrugged, and walked away towards a table full of supporting actors. They eagerly made room for the man who held their destinies in his greasy hands.

"Do you remember the last time I apologized for him?" asked Richard.

"I do."

"Then I don't have to repeat it." Richard sighed. "I guess that was his way of telling you Natasha is here."

"Why does he have to be a child about it?"

"I don't know. I think he thinks we're more important than everyone else. That's the funny thing about success and money, Sepideh. You take two men, with similar DNA and upbringing, and give them the kind of career we've had. Their responses to that can be so dissimilar that you wonder if they're even brothers at all."

"You guys are important," said Sepi, "but that's no excuse for being a homophobic twat."

Richard laughed. "Excuse me?"

"Sorry," said Sepi. "That was Kaili Zabora talking."

"Method actors," he replied. "Alright, I'll talk to him. Go see your girl."

She nodded farewell and walked across the blacktop, acutely aware of the eyes of her co-stars glued to her back. Instead of thinking about Nat waiting for her in the trailer, she thought about her walk, whether each foot was hitting the ground properly, one in front of the other. Was her ass swaying too little or too much? What about her costume? Had any of it fallen away, revealing something she didn't want revealed?

This is just how your body is.

The mantra came out of the gloom like the engine of a classic car finally turning over. Its gravelly growl drowned out the noise of her own mind assessing the situation and allowed her to hear the words of her therapist, Sophia Dahlstrom.

Sophia was one of the four founding sisters of the Dahlstrom Academy where Nat worked. She saw Sepi for a reduced rate and for twice the amount of time of her usual patients. At first, Sepi had gone to see her during a period of miscommunication with Nat, wanting to know how the woman she felt so connected to could be so far out of reach. As the relationship improved, the conversation turned to Sepi's anxiety, turned to synth and chemical treatments for what Sophia claimed was a natural physical trait.

"Your body was designed to respond to stimuli," she had said. "That's its core function. But evolution hasn't caught up to modern times. Our bodies don't realize we don't face the same threats we did thousands of years ago. Crowds aren't necessarily dangerous. People aren't out to get you. *You* know that, but your body doesn't. It wants to protect you. If you really want to move past this, you're going to have to start accepting your body's defense mechanisms for what they are."

"And what is that?"

"Lies. Don't fight them. Just thank your body for informing you, then move on. Don't let it overrule your mind. Say *this is just how my body is* and *this is who I am*. You are Sepideh Ahmadi, a highly sensitive woman with hyper-vigilant tendencies. We may never know *why* you are this way, but we can change the way you cope with it."

Sepi took a deep breath, told herself *this is who I am*, and continued to the trailer with relaxed shoulders and an effortless gait. The mantra worked for small situations; in the bigger ones, the mantra was just the electronic starter for the larger engine of self-fulfilling anxiety.

Sepi opened the trailer door and started up the steps.

"Nat? Natty?"

The air conditioner had the AirStream at a cool 73 degrees. A cleaning crew had come through and tidied up the kitchen and living areas while Sepi worked. Down the narrow hall, she spotted her bedroom door ajar and could see two pale legs hanging off the side of the bed.

"Sweetie?" she called again, approaching slowly.

Nat looked up from the bed, her face wizened and eyes red. Her hair hung like drapes on her cheeks, so silky and lifelike that few would have known it was a wig.

Sepi sat down on the bed next to Nat, put a hand on her thigh.

"How are you?" she asked.

Nat's lips smacked when she spoke. "These treatments are going to kill me before the cancer does. I don't even know why I'm doing it. I should be living my last days to their fullest instead of spending them in hospitals." She put her hand on Sepi's.

"We can do that, if you want," Sepi offered. "I can ask Richard to let me slip away for a week while they focus on the scenes without me. We could go somewhere tropical or overseas. Whatever you want."

"No," said Nat. Her artificial hair waved as she shook her head. "Not if I just have to come back to this. Three weeks of treatments, Sepi. I can't stomach it anymore."

Sepi bit her lip, said nothing.

Nat cleared her throat. "I thought more about what you said."

"And?"

"I don't like it." Her voice broke. "I don't want to be a machine. But I also don't want to lose you. So what am I supposed to do?"

Sepi recalled how violently opposed Nat had been to the idea of Vitra Synth. That was weeks ago, and they hadn't spoken of it since.

"I think," continued Nat, "that I don't really have a choice." She looked up, stared into Sepi's eyes. "I'm selfish. I haven't had enough time with you. But what kind of life would it be for you? Living with a synthetic? Growing old while I stay the same age?"

"It would be fine," Sepi replied. "I would love to see you—"

"No." Nat raised a finger to Sepi's lips. "Don't try to make me feel good about it. I've made my choice."

A warmth spread through Sepi's body. Could Nat really be agreeing to go through with the transfer?

"But I have two conditions." Nat held Sepi's hand in hers. "First, I want to get married. Before. As humans. It's something I've wanted since the day I met you. And it needs to be public. No more me just being a friend on the feeds. I want the world to know you are mine and I am yours."

"Okay," said Sepi, nodding. "Yes, of course, I will marry you. I don't know why it's taken us so long." She smiled, gave Nat a soft hug. "I'm so excited."

"Good." Nat went into a coughing fit, reached for a nearby box of tissues on the nightstand. "That makes me happy, Sepi. You have no idea." She wrapped her arms around her own stomach and shivered.

Sepi waited for the fit to pass. She patted her future wife gently on the back. "And the second condition?"

Nat wiped her mouth with the back of her hand.

"I want to be with you for the rest of my life," she began, her eyes glued to the floor. "That's an easy thing to want when we only live a hundred years. But if I become a machine, I'll be more or less immortal. And just like right now, I can't simply choose to die, not when there's another option. I don't think I'd be able to make that choice in the future. So that will be my life. Watching you grow old and die. Then living on, forever and ever, without you."

The comforting warmth dissipated, replaced with a sensation that turned Sepi's blood to ice.

There were tears in Nat's eyes when she looked up.

"I can't do this without you," she said, squeezing Sepi's hand. "I'll give up my God-given body for the sake of our life together, but only if you come with me."

"You want me to transcend too?" Sepi tried to keep the panic out of her voice.

"It's the only way. Together forever."

"Oh, honey, I don't know if I have enough money for—"

Nat fell towards her, buried her face in Sepi's chest. Her thin arms poked into Sepi's ribcage.

"Find a way," she sobbed. "Find a way or watch me die."

Sepi ran her fingers through Nat's hair, wondering if her synthetic body would have the same kind of artificial texture.

"Please," Nat whispered.

"Okay. Okay, I'll do it. For you."

"For us," said Nat, looking up. Her face was streaked with fake blood.

Sepi focused on the image, tried to hold it in her mind—anything to avoid thinking about the implications of what she'd agreed to. The negatives rattled off like bullets from a tommy gun, each jacket plinking on the trailer floor, echoes building upon echoes.

But then, a dud jammed the gun. She pulled out the bullet and examined its markings.

This is just the way your body is.

Sepi almost smiled.

This body had been nothing but trouble.

Maybe it was time for a new one.

TWENTY-NINE

Doyle's Journal – November 24, 2045

So much for the afterglow.

No matter how good you feel about sleeping with a beautiful woman, a Montana winter can knock you back down to pissy in no time flat. Snow that had been languid and ethereal the day before was now sharp and biting. Even with full gear on, I felt the bloated flakes tapping me on my shoulders, on my cheeks. The cold clung to me like a wet shirt, burning deeper into my bones as I tried to uncover every Máquina I had buried.

All told, there were twenty-nine machine bodies in the snow. Each of them weighed about 100 kilos, more if their clothes were saturated, which most were. I scavenged each corpse for anything we could use, found mostly guns and ammo. The supplies made a sizable pile at the bunker entrance by the time I was done. None of the Máquinas had the equipment you'd usually find on invading soldiers. All of the comm systems were baked right into their heads, along with their nav and data management. Occasionally, a Máquina might have a collapsible shovel on his back or a specialized weapon like an auto-shotty or revolver.

I tried fitting all of it in the bunker, but there just wasn't enough space in the storage bins. Most of it went into the escape tunnel; I'll have to move it to the Magnuson ranch when I get some time.

Once the Máquinas were properly looted, I began the laborious process of dragging them through the snow about 400 meters down-slope, letting gravity do most of the work. If I'd been smarter, I could have fashioned some kind of sled to help me. Though, dragging Máquinas with a rope tired around their necks did give me a small amount of satisfaction. Each step was a *fuck you* to their electronically fried faces.

After the last visible Máquina had been moved, I stalked around the perimeter of the bunker, testing the deep snow with the butt of my rifle. Twenty-nine seemed like an odd number of Máquinas (yeah, I know, *technically* it is), a little too random to be a full squad. Number thirty could have been the Máquina that ate it in Park City, and after this squad leveled that town, they had come up here to finish off Harlan or me.

I don't know. I guess it was possible.

Máquinas are a strange bunch. They don't talk out loud, so you can't learn anything about how they operate. They work equally well in groups of two and two hundred, all controlled by a seemingly centralized source, but based where? In the MX? How do they communicate and organize over such great distances?

I remember the ramp-up to the war, when reports were coming out of the MX almost daily. Cutting-edge synthetics laying villages and small cities to waste. Tourist towns overrun by synthetics virtually indistinguishable from humans except for their mechanics, the way they moved. But they kept getting better. Cabo San Lucas, Cancun, Puerto Vallarta; all ground zeros for the worst American massacres since Calle Cinco de Mayo.

That was when we started sending troops in. They came back broken men and women, with stories and nightmares to last a lifetime, images of hollowed-out skulls glinting in the moonlight. An entire generation of soldiers crippled by PTSD.

But what could we do about it? The U.S. already had a crisis on its hands. Máquinas were coming over the border on the weekly. At first, it was only one or two slipping in with illegals. They'd get ferried north some ways, into New Mexico or Texas, infiltrate a populous area, and then just go to fucking town.

So many civvies died.

Even in the Lone Star state, where a majority of the citizenry openly carried firearms, the death tolls were staggering. It turned out many of the guns were just for show, meant to intimidate other humans. When it came time to actually fight, a lot of those guns stayed in their holsters while their owners bled out in the streets.

It was six weeks, maybe a month before the end, when the rumors started coming out of the MX, stories of a leader of the machine army. Grainy images made the rounds, showing a beat-to-shit synthetic standing tall over a sea of newly minted Máquinas. Popular opinion held that this synthetic was the head of the beast, and that if it could be killed, the rest would lay down their arms.

We never got a chance to test that out.

Instead, the Máquinas overwhelmed the border like a swarm of locusts, spreading out over the southern states before the feeds even knew what was happening. They pushed all the way to the northern border but stopped shy of actually entering Canada. Now, the U.S. is infested with Máquinas, and it's each American's duty to kill as many as they can. I'd racked up three before Vida showed up. Now my tally is up to thirty-two.

That makes me the biggest patriot this side of the Mississippi.

It's a good feeling, knowing I'm doing my part.

Even if that included tearing rotted boards off the entrance to a defunct gold mine so I could stash inert Máquina bodies inside. Every nail that passed my hand was rusted to the core, and a quick mental inventory of the bunker's medical supplies came back with a big ol' *fuck if I know* when it came to tetanus toxoid. By the time I finished with the boards and dragged *twenty-nine* synthetic bodies deep into the mine, I was sweating like a cold beer in the Montana sun.

At least I was out of the harsh wind, and deeper in the mine I found some old crates whose wood hadn't rotted too badly. A little coaxing with my fire-starting kit got a healthy blaze going. The high winds outside helped suck the smoke out.

When the fire was big enough, I removed my jacket, gloves, hat, and face mask. Both my body and clothes were soaked, and I needed them not to be, even for the short trip back to the bunker. The cardinal rule of survival is to minimize opportunities to die. If anyone showed up on the way back, if a Máquina squad was waiting for me, I'd have to make a run for it, to God knows where, and with only a few supplies to tide me over. The chance to get in front of a fire again might not come for a long time. In the meantime, I'd die of hypothermia as my sweat froze to my skin.

Hell of a way to go.

Vida would probably venture out of the bunker eventually, maybe find my popsi-corpse leaned against some tree, an outstretched middle finger pointed south towards the MX.

While I dried out in the cave, I ate the second of the two MREs (that's Meals Ready to Eat for you civvies) I'd brought with me. Although stashing the bodies had taken the better part of the day, I'd made sure to stop for meals and to keep my liquid intake high. The last thing I wanted was to succumb to exhaustion.

If you've never had an MRE, the food is as terrible as you can imagine. Actually, take whatever you're imagining and double it. That plus six Skittles gets you an MRE.

It was around the third course (two salt-free crackers) that I started feeling like I was being watched. At first, I thought it was the pile of Máquinas just around the corner. I kept looking back at them expecting to see one creeping along the ground, a serrated knife held between its porcelain teeth.

Then I started hearing noises further down the cave. I grabbed my rifle and followed them. The beam of my flashlight cut through the darkness but bounced off arrays of spiderwebs and dangling roots. Crouching, I turned a few corners and froze solid.

Someone was living there.

A ratty, green sleeping bag occupied the center of a small alcove. Set around it were various knick-knacks, a mini stove, some books, and what looked like a solar charger. Long, knotted sticks leaned against the earthen walls, their tips sharpened to points. Off to the left, piles of clothes sat atop two suitcases, both of them beige and dirty, as if they had been on a long safari.

"Are you armed?" asked an echoing voice.

I gritted my teeth, moved my index finger from the safety position to the trigger.

"I am," I told the voice. "Well-armed. Are you?"

"No." He sounded disappointed. "Take what you want and go. Serves me right for not sleeping with a spear."

"Is that all you have?" I asked. It was hard not to pity him. A spear was really only good against something you could poke holes in, something that could bleed.

"Used up the last of my ammo coming up from SLC. Maybe you could just leave me a day's rations?"

"Why don't you come out slowly with your hands in the air? I promise I won't shoot you."

"I don't believe you." His voice seemed to come from all directions at once.

"The way I see it, I can take all your supplies, and you'll die of starvation, or you can come out and I'll shoot you in the head, in which case you'd die painlessly. Or, third choice, you come out and share my bounty of Skittles."

The pile of clothes swelled as the man pushed himself out. He was older, with gray hair and a thin build. His clothes were stained green and brown, but there were no holes—an impressive feat for someone who had trekked across the wilderness alone.

Empty hands reached into the air.

I motioned for him to sit on the sleeping bag, and he obliged.

"What's your name, friend?" I asked, tossing him the packet of Skittles.

"Loren, Loren Pilsky."

"Lauren? Odd name for a dude."

He shook his head, tore at the plastic wrapping. "Loren, like in Lorenzo. Been in my family for generations."

"You came up from Salt Lake City? You Mormon?"

He looked up, narrowed his eyes. "Is that a problem?"

I shook my head, watched my candy disappear between his chapped lips.

"Well, then, yeah. Family's been a part of the church for a hundred years, and will be for a hundred more. Doesn't matter what laws they pass. And you, stranger? What's your name?"

"Thomas Cook."

"I usually ask people how they managed to stay alive so long, but it looks like you're well-prepared for this kind of world, Mr. Cook."

It was a nice thing to hear. Not that Vida hadn't been appreciative, but she certainly wasn't in awe of what I had done.

"Got a rifle, some food, and a place to crash," I said. "That's what makes a man a king these days."

"Wouldn't have any spare ammo, would you?"

"No such thing anymore, I'm afraid."

He nodded, resigned. He put another Skittle in his mouth, savored it.

"How'd you get in here anyway?" I asked. "Took me half an hour to get the boards off the entrance, and it didn't look like they'd been put on recently."

"You came in the back way." Loren gestured further on down the mine. "There's a switchback about a hundred paces that way, leads back up to the surface on the other side of this ridge. I covered it with some branches and stones. The robots haven't noticed it yet. I actually thought you were the first."

"No," I said, crouching to rest a knee on the ground. "I'm no Máquina."

"Just a human like me, right?"

I shrugged. "Don't know what kind of human you are, Loren."

"I like to think I'm a good person, and just like everyone else, I don't deserve to be living like this. I put doing right over surviving. How about you?"

"You don't save humanity by destroying your own," I said, though I used different words at the time. The poetry of the moment didn't come to me until I was writing this entry.

"You strike me as a good man, Mr. Cook. That's refreshing. Some of the people I met coming up here, especially the survivalists at Yellowstone, weren't so good. Oh, here." He reached for a rusted box next to the wall, flipped the lid, and pulled out a flask. "The one thing I still have from home. Glenfiddich 2042. Burn your teeth right out of your mouth, but it's good."

I pulled my rifle close to my chest, reached out for the flask with my free hand.

And that's when Loren lunged at me.

THIRTY

Vida leaned against the wall between the bathroom and her room, watching the proximity sensor on the far side of the bunker. It hadn't shown any activity in three hours, and she had used that time to dress in multiple layers, stealing snow pants from Doyle's room that she'd had to cinch with a long belt. Her bulky jacket would keep her warm outside, but inside the temperature-controlled bunker, it was slowly baking her to death. The only part of her that could breathe was her face and hands, and those were covered in nervous sweat.

Her stomach sloshed, rolled over on itself.

A memory came into focus.

Vida was thirteen before her father got her an account on VNet. For the first few years, she was only allowed to access it for an hour a day, and that included research time. None of her friends had the same restrictions, so Vida found herself sneaking in as often as she could, mostly when her parents were away or when she stayed home sick from school.

She always feared getting caught, was never sure when her father might walk through the door and catch her jacking in.

It felt like that now, except Doyle was no father figure. Vida's imaginary friend Peter had claimed Doyle was holding her hostage, which she had refuted without being able to present evidence. The absurd argument had gone on for some time, with Peter's final words on the subject being: *what about the graves?*

That was when Vida decided she had to know for sure. Doyle was her best chance for survival, and he'd been nothing but kind and accommodating, but if he had an ulterior motive, she wanted to know about it. His journal hadn't provided any real clues, just pages upon pages of how he'd sacrificed for her on a daily basis.

Part of her hoped it was just her imagination running wild, that she'd go outside and find two graves and know Doyle was telling the truth.

Another part of her shuddered at the thought of what it would mean if there was nothing but unbroken ground *just to the left of the bunker door*, as Doyle had described.

The clock ticked past 1530. Vida kicked off from the wall, took a step forward, and then ran back into the bathroom. She barely got the lid on the toilet seat up before she started vomiting. Deep spasms in her abdomen squeezed her internal organs, creating a pain so intense she had to grab both sides of the bowl to keep from falling over.

Lunch and breakfast came spilling out of her. She tried to breathe between spurts.

She thought of Peter, his blond hair, his elvish ears, his androgynous cheekbones.

When the spasms subsided, she flushed and got up to wash her mouth at the sink. In the mirror, she watched the redness in her cheeks fade away.

"What's your problem?" she asked herself. "You have every right to walk out of this bunker whenever you feel like it, whether that's to leave him completely or to verify his story. If the Máquinas catch you, at least you'll die trying to figure out the truth instead of living with the doubt."

Vida stared herself down, waiting for an answer.

It took only a minute for her to realize she didn't need one. It didn't matter if Doyle was out there or not. If he challenged her, she'd tell him exactly where he could shove his EMP.

Vida barely glanced at the proximity sensor as she headed for the door. The click of the opening locks echoed in the bunker; the door groaned as she pulled it back. She stepped into the stairwell and left the door slightly ajar, fearing there might not be enough time to enter the codes if an army of Máquinas showed up.

The wind howled beyond the outer door, pitching into a wail with every step she climbed. The cold steel of the door handle rattled in her hand, reminded her to slip on her gloves. She turned the handle; the wind caught the door and pulled her outside.

Snow cut across her bare face. For a moment, she considered going back inside, saving the expedition for a day with better weather. The wind seemed to be conspiring against her, pushing her down into the snow.

I have to know.

With a glove over her mouth, she pushed forward.

There was no world outside the bunker, just the roar of the wind and the oppressive snow. A white haze obscured everything: trees, the sky, and even her own footprints in the snow. It reminded her of half-instantiated constructs in VNet where the white was bright enough to blind even virtual eyes.

Remembering her childhood gave Vida a sense of calm. She could almost see her bedroom, see the rest of the house she had grown up in. Her life was coming back to her.

Vida turned right, putting the wind directly at her back. As she took a step forward, a gust pressed hard on her shoulders, sending her tumbling forward again.

She spit snow and tried to stand, but only got a few steps before another gust put her back on the ground. Finally, she decided it was easier to just crawl, despite the thick powder. Ten feet from the door, she started pushing away the snow to reveal cold dirt.

The plan was simple: find a starting point and dig out crisscrossing channels covering two of her body lengths. Vida pulled the drawstrings on her hood tighter and got to work.

She distracted herself by rooting around in the gloom for more memories. It wasn't surprising that VNet would be one of the first to return. After all, she'd been exposed to it during the intense, hormonal stage of puberty, a time when everything was the best version of itself. Foods tasted better, popular music peaked as an art form, and the things she loved meant more to her than life itself. VNet— being with her friends—was one of those things. Another was photography, split equally between shooting wildlife and taking pictures of her girlfriends. Portraits spoke to her, mostly through the eyes.

Vida recalled sunsets at a lake, her subject standing at the end of a rickety dock while the strange light of dusk danced on her face.

The beauty of that moment made her pause, sit back on her heels. She looked around at the grid she'd created, surprised by progress.

Her breathing quickened.

She'd been thinking so hard about taking pictures that she hadn't noticed what she'd discovered: absolutely nothing.

No graves.

No disturbed ground.

No indication whatsoever that two bodies had been buried there.

Vida bit her lip. She must have heard Doyle wrong. The graves were probably on the other side of the bunker door.

Turning into the wind, she kept her chin to her chest to avoid the stinging snow. Several paces away from the door, she fell to her hands and knees again, repeating the grid process. This time, she couldn't shift her focus to happy memories. Each drag of the glove through loose snow made her heart sink further, until its bottom edge started pushing through into her stomach. Line after line revealed unbroken ground. No hastily made tombstones. No marker indicating *here lies Angela, devoted wife and mother.*

Vida stood, her strength renewed by anger or frustration or both, and began kicking at the snow, sending plumes into the air for the wind to ferry away.

Still nothing.

She tried to scream, but her mouth and throat felt tight, almost frozen. Stumbling through the snow, Vida made her way back to the bunker door, scanned the empty, white horizon for a moment, and then headed inside. By the time she got down the steps and back into the bunker proper, her hands and face had begun to ache.

It doesn't mean he's lying.

Peter replied in a soprano lilt, "Actually, it does mean that. If he lied about the graves, what else has he lied about?"

Vida put her hands to her ears, hurried into her room, and shut the door. She shed the cold, wet clothes and put on fresh everything. Diving under the covers, she pulled herself into a fetal position and tried to shiver herself towards warmth.

* * *

Vida snapped awake, chased from her dreams by a swarm of questions that stung at her from every direction. There were so many, each following on the heels of the other. She sought escape in her pillow, burying her face until she couldn't hear them anymore.

Tears filled her eyes, to which she whispered, "No."

She balled her hands into fists and pressed them hard against her eyes, but the tears would not stop. The more she cried, the more she pressed, until a sharp pain stung her left eye—a stray eyelash perhaps.

Another memory from childhood. Long eyelashes, even as a young girl. The envy of her girlfriends who had to artificially extend their own stubby lashes.

Vida held the afflicted eye shut as she climbed out from beneath the blankets. She hurried to the bathroom where the lights were brighter and put her face close to the mirror.

With her index finger, she pulled her lower lid down, revealing an eyeball streaked with red. Her vision was blurry, but she didn't see any black lines on her eye or eyelid. Instead, she saw a small fold, as if someone had pinched her iris. Vida switched fingers, dabbed at the fold, and moved it to the side.

She caught it with her nails, pulled.

The small sliver of plastic fell into the sink.

Vida started to follow it down, but her reflection in the mirror held her attention.

Everything looked wrong, as if she were seeing two worlds at the same time.

In one of them, her image was sharp, detailed, and her brown hair looked positively bronze against the backdrop of bright white walls. In the other, her hair was deep black, blurry, and framed by tan walls. In the haze behind her, she saw a stainless-steel toilet instead of a porcelain one.

Vida turned, stepped closer to the shower.

Reddish-orange soap scum stained the plastic walls; black mildew grew out from the drain floor.

She alternated eyes, closing one and then the other in rapid succession.

The shower shifted. Tile to plastic. Clean to dirty.

Holding her hand over her good eye, Vida took her bad vision back to her room to look around.

The white underwear that filled the shelves was now gray. The sheets with their floral pattern were beige and looked cheaply made. On the floor, the carpet lost its grid of blue and white lines.

Everything appeared muted, even the light.

So many changes, so much hidden from her before.

Vida sat down on the edge of the bed, on the verge of hyperventilating. This couldn't be. What was that thing in her eye? A contact lens? But if it was, why did taking it out change the world so much?

A little blurred vision was to be expected, but this?

I'm losing it, she thought, and shut her eyes tight.

Panic surged within her, and all rational thought was swept away with it. She moaned into her hands, pleading for answers to the questions running roughshod through her brain.

Nobody answered.

She tilted her head back, screamed loud enough to be heard in heaven.

Stopped. Stared.

The mural on the ceiling that Doyle had painted for Gretta had turned translucent. Only her good eye could see the lake.

In her other, there was nothing there but glass; it threw back a faded image of the room below.

Beyond that visual echo was something else, a shape.

A man.

Not Doyle. Someone else.

Someone who was simultaneously there and not there.

Vida saw the whites of his eyes, then reached for the gun on her hip.

THIRTY-ONE

Time slowed as Kagan stared into the harsh light and wondered how in the hell he was going to keep Raf from killing whoever was on the other side of it. Breaking and entering wasn't a crime that was taken lightly in the City of Angels, not with the amount of tech and potential for privacy invasions in every building. Frank Kagan would be able to buy his son out of prison, but Rafael Orozco had no such benefactor. He might end up in San Quentin, or worse, in Folsom as a ReTread.

Familiar laughter built from behind the light.

"You son of a cock stain," said Kagan, sighing.

"Yeah," said Glasser, "but you should have seen your faces."

"You have no idea how close you were to being killed by my friend here." Kagan dropped his arm as Raf relaxed.

"I would have died laughing and pissing," said Glasser, lowering the flashlight, "as the prophecy foretold."

Earl Glasser was a younger guy, and his sense of humor came with a lack of general regard for everyone around him. Not that he wasn't in awe of the power and money of the older generation, but he didn't subscribe to the idea that their status made them any better than him. He'd crack a joke about Jennavie as easily as one about Kagan. They weren't always funny jokes, but then the kid only cared about his own amusement.

Like most technophiles his age, Glasser was heavily augmented; his short-throw mag eyes had built-in augmented reality support as opposed to the contact lenses Kagan wore. His sliver glowed an eerie green in the dim light, and when Kagan looked just to the side of him, he could see emerald neon tracks on Glasser's skin, as if the excited gas ran through his veins. His hair was cut short on the sides and stood up straight at least five inches on the top of his head, as most of Generation 1-0 wore it.

Kagan stepped forward, gestured when the men were closer together. "Raf, this is Glasser. Glasser, Raf."

"Quién es este nino, hombre?"

"Soy el jefe, papi chulo," said Glasser.

"Do I look Puerto Rican to you?" Raf stepped forward abruptly, but Glasser didn't flinch.

"What does it matter?" he asked. "They're all played by Cubans in the movies anyway."

"Hey!" snapped Kagan, as Raf took another step forward. "We didn't hire him for his people skills, Raf, so cut the gringito some slack."

Raf took a deep breath, threw a hand up.

"Let's get this over with before the uniforms show up," said Kagan.

Glasser nodded, mustered a fake salute, and turned on his heels. He led them down dark corridors to the prep room on the far side of the floor. They passed Wayne's office, and Kagan was disappointed to find it locked because that meant he couldn't squat over his former boss' desk and let him know how he truly felt about his management skills.

The prep room lit automatically as they entered. Vidscreens filled an entire wall of the room, while the others housed suspended racks of servers behind floor-to-ceiling plexiglass. Once the procedure started, the servers would heat up, causing a mixture of liquid nitrogen and dark magic to drift down from the ceiling. It was far more efficient than using standard air conditioning or water-cooling, and as a bonus, it gave the impression of staring into a foggy aquarium where LED fish blinked on and off.

"Welcome to the Brain Blender," said Glasser, gesturing to a leather chair in the center of the room. "My new Mexican friend can sit here. Kagan, if you don't want to be wiping his drool for the rest of his life, you can find a quiet place and put your hands in your pockets."

Kagan scratched his cheek with his middle finger.

"Good," he continued. "Now, KK tells me you have an Avenging Angel in your neck, right? And it's fried?"

Raf adjusted himself in the chair, nodded.

"Alright, well, that's a problem."

"How big a problem?" asked Kagan.

"Easy, Trust Fund," said Glasser. "I wouldn't have agreed to this if I couldn't make it happen." He turned back to Raf. "Usually, we just piggy-back on the Guardian Angel, or Avenging Angel, whatever, to get this done, but since yours is burnt toast, we're going to have to patch in manually."

"What does that mean?" asked Raf.

"Like um, needle and thread, you know, grow-wire, and your cerebral cortex. You won't feel a thing with the local I'm gonna give you."

"Save it. I'm not scared of a needle."

"Yeah, no," said Glasser, "it's a big fucking needle."

Kagan laughed, saw that even though Raf kept a straight face, his body relaxed a little. There was a chair by the back of the room for nervous spouses; Kagan sank into it with a satisfied grunt. He crossed one leg over the other, leaned his head back against the wall.

It took half an hour of prep before Glasser put Raf under. He'd been asking him questions about the MX, and Raf's answers had been getting more curt by the second. Finally, the vet passed out, and Glasser let out a soft whistle.

"Wow, for a minute there, I thought your friend was a synthetic. This drug can put a horse to sleep in under a minute. He lasted twelve."

"You know Puerto Ricans," said Kagan. "They put coke on their Rice Krispies instead of sugar."

"Is that racist?

"No, I can say that. I have Puerto Rican friends."

"You don't have friends," said Glasser. He tapped on the palette, bringing the vidscreens behind him to life. Raf's vitals appeared in the upper left-hand corner of each one.

"How long is this going to take?" asked Kagan.

"Longer than usual, since we're going in over grow-wire. There's a reason biochips need to be right on the brain stem. But, I don't know, we should be out of here by three or four. Take a nap if you want. Your office is still like you left it, couch and all."

"Fine, but you take care of him. Anything goes wrong and there won't be an augment in your body strong enough to stop me from tossing you out a window."

"Aww," said Glasser, without looking up from his palette. "I really have missed your convoluted threats of violence."

Kagan took one last look at Raf and then left the Blender room. He followed the amber guide lights past the cubicle farm and conference rooms until he arrived at his old office. The doors were locked, but the prox-sensor still recognized his Guardian Angel. Two deadbolts retracted from the ceiling and the double doors fell away as Kagan pushed forward.

His office really had been untouched, except by the cleaning crew. Kagan walked around the desk and sat down, barely glancing at the twinkling Hollywood hills outside. His terminal came alive, the vidscreen filling with a nude Sepideh Ahmadi lying face-down on a bed, most of her body hidden in shadow, while a disinterested Claire Danes stood nearby, a length of satin cloth in her hands.

Emails appeared in the upper right portion of the screen, while nearly transparent media feeds began scrolling on the left. Out of curiosity, Kagan logged into the Pre-Sales opportunity tracker to see what final notes had been logged for Lucasz Abat.

Opportunity lost. Client expired.

Kagan was surprised he hadn't been called out by name. After staring at the record for a minute, he highlighted the text and hit the backspace key.

Dirty old codger dies doing what he loved: young girls.

He left Wayne's name tagged as the note's author and saved the file. The screen cleared, revealing the queue's dashboard underneath. It listed the currently scheduled demos, as well as potential leads from the pipeline. Normally, Kagan would have spent the time at his desk perusing the pipeline, using a script Glasser had helped him put together to automatically search VNet records for the names listed. It would then sort them by how old they were and how much they were worth.

Kagan scanned the potentials absently, hoping he wouldn't see someone famous or powerful amongst the candidates.

Charles Morgan, Richard Davis, Tong Chen…

"Fuck me sideways," said Kagan.

He blinked a few times, but the letters remained the same. Her name *was* written there amongst the nobodies.

Allison Lipton, Natasha Kumanov, Sepideh Ahmadi…

Kagan pushed back from the desk, stood, and began pacing. It couldn't be. There was no way Sepideh Ahmadi would show up at Vitra Synth less than a month after he'd been fired. If Lucasz Abat hadn't been such a vigorous fornicator, Kagan might have had the opportunity to meet the woman he'd fantasized about for years. He could have shaken her hand, smelled her perfume, gazed into her eyes…

He struck the desk with his fist.

Lucasz fucking Abat.

Or should the blame have been on Raf? After all, he was the one who started the fight in the lobby that pulled Kagan away from the demo.

Maybe it was just fate.

The world was unfair, so it made sense that Kagan should want something for so long, have that thing come almost within reach, only to have it pulled away at the last moment. Plans filled his head, ideas on how to show up at Vitra Synth on the right day to at least catch a glimpse of Sepideh in person. He could wait for her in the lobby, pretend to still work for the company, and accompany her upstairs.

Kagan went to the window, banged his forehead against it. The world shimmered and settled.

He knew she lived somewhere in Los Angeles, though he'd never run into her at any of the fancy restaurants the other stars went to. Media feeds tried to keep tabs on her, but whenever they announced a sighting, Kagan would always be late to the party.

He was destined to admire her from afar.

Some things were just so.

It didn't snow in L.A.

The good guys never won.

And Kagan would never hold Sepideh in his arms.

Unless…

He sat down at the desk again, pulled an actual sheet of paper from the drawers, and began scribbling. The pen scratched across the desk in a flurry of deep, crisscrossing lines. Over the next two hours, Kagan wrote out the details of his plan, following eventualities to their conclusion and then working backwards to solve the original problem. By the time he was done, he had twelve sheets of paper, all of them smudged and wrinkled.

On the last page, with his hand aching, he wrote: *this could work.*

Exhausted, Kagan collected the notes and walked over to the couch to lie down. He held the papers to his chest, closed his eyes, and imagined Sepideh in a long, flowing gown, its white sequins catching the light and throwing it in every direction. The ballroom in which she stood swelled with dancing men and women. Classical music—a waltz—filled the air. Kagan saw his non-body reaching out a hand to her, saw her reaching back.

The dream was all too brief. Before long, someone was shaking him awake.

"Somebody shot the President!" screamed Glasser.

Kagan sat up, looked around.

The laughter coming from Glasser modulated and settled. He put a hand to his forehead. "Oh, hey, it's time to get up. Your friend is going to be awake soon. We need to haul ass as soon as he can walk, unless you're game to carry him out together?"

Kagan blinked, waited for Glasser to come into focus.

"What do you know about Sepideh Ahmadi?"

"Your girlfriend? Nothing really, just that she has an obsessed fan who keeps nudie pics of her on his work computer."

"She's on the pre-sales schedule for a consult next week. Why didn't you tell me about it?"

"Oh, I know this one. It's not my job? I'm not stalking her? I didn't want to see her chopped up into a dozen pieces in your freezer?"

Kagan sat up, collected the papers from the floor.

"I'm going to need your help again," he said.

"I don't think so. This was a one-time deal, K-ster. We're friends and all, but I could get into some deep shit."

"I'll pay you twice what I'm paying you tonight."

"Two hundred grand? For what?"

"That's just for starters," said Kagan, "just for information. I want to know everything that goes on with Sepideh Ahmadi's case as it happens."

"Why—"

"I'll pay you another fifty to not ask me any questions."

Glasser frowned, scratched his forehead.

"Two hundred large would buy you a shiny new augment," said Kagan.

"Two hundred and fifty," said Glasser.

"Yeah. I assumed you'd spend that extra fifty on a proper haircut. So are you in or not?"

"Are we going to break any laws?" asked Glasser.

"We're gonna lose count."

He shrugged, extended his closed fist. "Bump it like you mean it, bitch."

Kagan obliged, rolled the papers in his hand, and thought about the words on the final page.

This could work.

THIRTY-TWO

The visit to Vitra Synth was not unlike any of the other dozens of visits Sepi and Nat had made to hospitals and private medical companies over the last few weeks. Someone greeted them in the lobby or at the front desk, hurried them away from the general public to some private office or conference room. There, they would be treated to coffee and donuts (or finger foods, if it were later in the day). Curious office workers or medical staff would find excuses to walk by the open door or windows to steal a glance at a movie star and her ailing lover.

The routine was always the same.

Only the name of the company changed.

Vitra Synth's ringmaster was a six-foot-six towering tree of a man with dark eyes and stark-white hair named Wayne Demeyer. Despite his lumbering frame and skeletal features, he was actually quite friendly, and most of his attention focused on Nat. How she was doing. If there was anything he could get her. Sepi was an afterthought to him, and rather than being offended, Sepi was relieved.

Nat often lamented how invisible she felt when she and Sepi were out in public. It never bothered her much before, but after the illness and Death's warm breath on her neck, she had started wanting to be noticed more, to feel like she was part of the world she was about to leave. The desire had likely always been there, but Nat had written it off as the price of dating a famous actress.

The last thing Sepi wanted was for Nat to feel disregarded.

Wayne somehow picked up on the imbalance, and after greeting them both, had sat on the couch across from Nat and spoken directly to her. He talked about the process of moving a human consciousness from an organic body into a machine chassis. He described the advances in sensory receptors, how the new body would be more in tune with scents and tastes.

Sensations, like fingernails tracing down the small of her back, would feel a hundred times more intense. If anything, moving to a synthetic body would allow both of them to experience the world far more intimately than an organic body would.

It was the same spiel the ads on the media feeds whispered directly into her ear day and night.

Not so much the content as the general idea that *our product will solve all of your problems*. It was the same promise Nixle Chronos had made about their augmented reality lenses, which while useful for filming movies, didn't have much application off the set. In Los Angeles, there were only a dozen destinations where augmented reality was used. To really feel the impact of the technology, Sepi would have to travel to a more tech-oriented city like Umbra or Margate.

Vitra Synth was just like everyone else; they would say anything to get her money. Only this time, they actually had a product Sepi wanted for Nat, who was weakening and withering by the day. Sepi wanted to flash Wayne some kind of sign to hurry things up, but he kept digressing into meaningless tangents. An hour went by before he took a breath.

"Do you ladies have any questions for me?" he asked.

Nat looked to Sepi.

"How soon can we do this?" asked Sepi.

Wayne picked up his palette from the cushion next to him and scrolled through a calendar.

"Shouldn't be too long," he said. "Most of the lead time goes into building the sleeves; those have to come direct from Perion City. At the fastest, about seven to ten business days. Let's see, today's the twentieth, so that would put us into early March. Maybe the week of the fifth?"

"That's the absolute fastest you can do it?" asked Sepi.

"Well, this isn't the kind of thing you want to rush." He leaned forward, gestured to Nat. "If we can speak frankly, I understand we're up against an ambiguous clock here. But that doesn't mean we should ignore protocol. When you wake up in your new bodies and hold each other for the first time, I want those bodies to be perfect. I want it to feel just as it feels now, if not better. All I ask is that you give me the time I need to make it perfect."

Nat sighed.

Sepi squeezed her hand. "We'll do our best," she said to Wayne.

"That's what we like to hear. Two weeks, ladies. That's all I need. Then we'll have you in new sleeves ready to take on the world. In the meantime, why don't I show you around the office?"

He stood and gestured to the door.

Sepi helped Nat to her feet and led her by the arm into the hallway.

Wayne adjusted his pace accordingly.

They passed cubes, offices, and a small break room before veering off through two large doors.

"Inner sanctum," said Wayne. "This is where we store the new sleeves until we're ready to transfer. Each comes factory-sealed from Perion Synthetics. We unpack it, inspect it, and load it up with a base personality to test its motor functions. Perion will have already done their own testing, but we like to be thorough. If it passes all tests, we wipe it clean and prep it for the big show."

Black steel cases lined one side of the room like obsidian obelisks. They had no identifying marks except a sticker with a bar code on it and an arrow indicating which way was up.

"These are the four sleeves we'll be activating this week. And if you'll come around here, I can show you the loading bay."

He led them around a small partition to a brightly lit area lined with vidscreens. In the center stood an operating table; loose, leather straps hung from the sides.

"We call this the Gray Maker. There are only twelve such chairs in the United States, all of which are leased from Perion Synthetics. This is where the actual magic happens. We feed in the data, and a synthetic human comes out the other side."

"You don't know how it actually works?" asked Sepi.

Wayne smiled, shook his head. "No one really does, Ms. Ahmadi. I mean, we understand the concepts, why it *should* work, but the actual mechanics are a closely guarded secret. So much so that a majority of the Gray Maker's actual brain is back in Perion City, connected to us via high-grade fiber. If anyone were to steal this chair, they'd find it completely useless when they got it back home. I guess that's just part of the world we live in."

Nat looked around at the bare, white walls.

"This is where we're going to wake up?" she asked.

"No, of course not," he replied. "As soon as the last synapse is transferred, we induce REM sleep. You'll actually start to dream as a synthetic. Let me show you the recovery room."

They returned the way they came; Sepi's forearms prickled as they walked through a field of cubicles. At the end of a wide hallway, Wayne thumbed a scanner and stood aside as the door swung inward.

Tall plants stood in the corners of the room. In the center, water burbled from the wide mouth of an azure, ceramic jug. Spread about the room were black chaise lounges with smooth white padding. All were empty.

"Notice the fresh flowers, the candles," said Wayne. "You'll awake here as if coming out of a refreshing nap. We like to hit you with some sensory data before you remember what happened. Our clients report thinking of the procedure as some kind of wild dream because what they experience in here is *too real*. No one fully appreciates what synthetic bodies are capable of until they're inside one." He cleared his throat. "Once you're awake, we'll bring you water, champagne, chocolates—anything you'd like. The sooner you put your senses to the test, the better you'll feel about your choice."

"Will Sepi be there when I wake up?"

"If you wish," said Wayne. "The timing is such that one of you will wake up before the other, but there's no reason we can't do Ms. Ahmadi first."

"That's fine," said Sepi. She felt Nat lean into her.

"Alright, on with the tour."

Sepi noticed the faces peeking over the cubicle walls as they walked through the office again. Groups of workers just happened to be congregating at the right corners to watch them go by. Most had smiles on their faces, but others had blank faces Sepi could only interpret as judgment.

This is who I am.

Despite the mantra, she couldn't stop thinking about what they were saying in their hushed whispers. Were they talking about Nat? About how terrible she looked? Or about Sepi herself? And how she was walking around the office hand-in-hand with a woman?

Sophia had recommended Sepi up her anti-anxiety medication, and the new dosage made short work of the physical reactions welling up inside her. In previous situations, her stomach would have turned on itself. This time, it merely gurgled, as if the meds had it in a tight headlock and it only had enough oxygen to gasp. The thoughts were harder to push away, but Sophia had warned that Sepi needed to learn how to deal with them herself. One day, she would go off the medication, and if she wasn't prepared to outsmart her anxiety, the cycle would start all over again, maybe even worse than before.

"Through here is the Prep Room, though our techs refer to it as the Brain Blender. I don't care for the term; it really doesn't capture what we're doing here."

He pushed through the double doors and led them into the room. Standing next to a reclining chair in the center of the space was a young man with spiky hair. He covered a yawn with the back of his hand.

"Ladies, I'd like you to meet Earl Glasser, one of our most talented technicians. He will be performing both of your procedures. Earl, this is Sepideh Ahmadi and Natasha Kumanov."

Earl held out his hand to Sepi.

"I know who you are. I'm a big fan of your work."

Sepi shook it, waited for him to do the same with Nat, but he didn't. His eyes remained glued to Sepi.

"Earl, would you like to tell our new friends here about the transfer process?"

"Sure," he replied. "How versed are you in metaphysical synaptic transference? Quantum simulacrum?"

Wayne crossed his arms.

"Just kidding," said Earl. "Here, check this out." He walked over to a wall full of vidscreens and tapped on the center display. He brought up windows, and with a flick of his hand, shot the images onto the other vidscreens. "This is a brain scan of an average adult female. This represents the culmination of a hundred years of medical science, and it tells us no more about what makes us human than ripping a brain out of a skull and unfolding it on a table. However, with the advent of the biochip and brain-stem interfaces, we're now able to use the body's neural network as our own.

"That means we can traverse the network as well as map it. Follow the billions upon zillions of neural pathways, recreating each twist and turn, and you can create a perfect, complete copy of a human mind. Think of it like this: the brain is a coiled fuse. We light a match at one end and watch as the flame travels."

"You burn our brains?" asked Nat. She looked to Wayne.

"He's speaking metaphorically. However, the process *is* destructive. We're currently operating at three nines, that is, a 99.999% success rate. When we do have an issue, it's usually something small.

"What happens to our brains after the transfer?"

Wayne turned, touched his face briefly.

"Well, there is no going back if that's what you're asking. Once the procedure is complete, the original brain is no longer viable. Do you have a specific concern?"

"Yeah," said Sepi. "I don't want to go to sleep in that chair and wake up still in this body."

Nat's face blanked, as if she hadn't considered the idea before.

"No," said Wayne. "It doesn't work that way. This is a move, not a copy. We put your bodies to rest, respectfully, and you continue on in your synthetic body as if nothing happened. If you'd like, I can put you in touch with previous clients. I assure you, a little anxiety is normal."

"Who said she wasn't normal?" asked Nat.

Earl chuckled, suddenly became interested in his own shoes.

"Um," continued Wayne, "how about we move on to the demo room? We've got some virtual reality material that I think you'll both enjoy. Really gives you a sense of how your new bodies will feel."

Nat shot a glance at Sepi, her eyes drooping.

"No," said Sepi, "I think we've got everything we need for today. Can you give me a call when you have a definite date?"

"Absolutely. I'll make it my highest priority."

"Sepideh, do you mind if I get a picture with you?" asked Earl. He already had his phone out and the camera app loaded. "For a friend," he explained.

"I do mind." Sepi tugged lightly on Nat's hand and led her out of the room, through the offices, and to the reception area.

The receptionist, Jennavie, wished them a pleasant afternoon as Wayne looked on.

As they waited for the elevator, Sepi leaned over, kissed Nat's earlobe, and whispered.

"You are *not* invisible."

THIRTY-THREE

Doyle's Journal – November 24, 2045 (cont.)

Thou shalt not kill.

I don't know if a man ever went up to the top of a mountain, spoke to God, and returned with ten holy commandments. I heard it was originally fifteen, but I also heard it was complete bullshit. It doesn't seem like something a god would do. Humans don't take well to laws, even those handed down by a deity, and especially laws that make no sense. Telling people not to kill shows a lack of understanding about human nature, which God himself was supposed to have created.

This is why I have a problem with religion in general. The rules don't really take our nature into account. Why can't we covet a man's wife if we're biologically predisposed to mate with as many partners as possible? Why should we have to honor our mothers and fathers if they are coked-out streetwalkers and coked-out Wall Street wolves?

And why shouldn't we be able to kill when someone is trying to kill us? Or when someone stands between us and survival?

The only reason we stopped senseless killing is because we banded together into tribes, communities, cities, and societies. And that worked fine, for a while.

Instead of a commandment, we should just ask people to do their best, something like: *welcome to Los Angeles, try not to kill each other.*

Because what happens when society breaks down? How does a system of rule stay in place when the enforcers of those rules are all dead or on the other side of the Mississippi? The western United States is now a warzone, and the rule of society no longer holds sway here. The only rule now is survival, and to follow that rule, we must lie, steal, and kill.

It was no surprise that Loren jumped me, and honestly, I don't blame him for it. He knew I had the upper hand, and he firmly believed he would not be surviving the encounter. What other choice did he have? In that split-second, it didn't matter that I was bigger, stronger, or better equipped. He just wanted to survive. And when a man just wants to survive, he can accomplish great things.

I've had time to think a lot about that fight, and my preference is to rewrite history for the sake of my pride. Vida, I know you read my journal and I don't mind. It lets me say things to you in print that I could never say out loud. So I have you in mind as I write this. I want you to think I was brave, strong, and fearless, but in all honesty, I thought it was the end of the line for me.

Ultimately, the blame is on me. I let my guard down. Loren reminded me of someone I knew in the before time. Most people weren't ready to abandon their million-dollar mansions and fancy cars to live a life in the cold wilderness. They just weren't built for it. Loren struck me as that kind of guy, and I admit I felt sorry for him. After everything that had happened in Park City, everything with the Máquinas, I just wanted to connect with someone.

Maybe that was too much to ask.

At the very least, I just wanted to not have to fight someone.

It's so tiring, Vida. Constantly being on guard. Sometimes you just want to trust people.

But that's how you get killed, I guess.

Loren was no stranger to killing, but he was even better at ensnaring prey. After the first blow to my nose and the subsequent wiry fingers around my neck, with their sharp fingernails drawing blood, I began to realize the entire thing had been a farce. Loren was a trap-door spider, and the mine was his den. He had everything arranged just so: a lone sleeping bag to convince people it was just him, the sharpened spears to suggest no other weapons were available, and the pile of clothes… well, I don't know what that was supposed to mean. Maybe that was really how he lived.

I've had my nose broken before, but you never really get used to it. When Loren's fist connected, I fell backwards, trying to avoid the headlight of a train that had come hurtling out of the darkness. My boots slipped on the loose dirt, and I hit my head on a wooden support beam. I saw stars through the rain, and then those fingers found their hold on me.

Loren couldn't have weighed more than sixty kilos, but in my blinded state, I had trouble getting a good hold on him. In desperation, I rolled like a crocodile, tucked my head into his sinewy arms. The mine graded downward, helping us along. Finally, I was able to pull my knee up between us and kick. Loren went over my head and smacked into the earthen wall. His fingernails pulled some of my flesh away.

I put my hand to my neck, felt blood, but it was barely a trickle.

Once he rolled over and reoriented himself, he came at me again. By that time, I could almost see, so I was able to parry his grabs. His momentum took him into the other side of the shaft. He struck it with his shoulder and fell to the ground.

"You don't have to do this," I told him. "We're on the—"

He lunged again, and this time I snaked my arm inside his and used my other hand to force his head down. The move sent him somersaulting into the dirt.

"Don't make me kill you!" I screamed.

He shot forward in a boxer's lunge, wrapped his arms around me ineffectually.

"You kill me or I kill you," he grunted. "That's how this works."

I told him it didn't have to be that way, that we could work together to fight the Máquinas, survive long enough to be rescued. Either he didn't care or didn't believe me.

"I don't want to join you," he said. "I want your bunker. I want the woman you keep in there."

It took me two tries to snap his neck.

On the first, he gave a quiet, almost forlorn yelp, followed by a string of curses no Mormon had any business knowing. I dropped him to the ground, and he just lay there unmoving but still cursing. Not wanting him to suffer more than necessary, I dropped into place on his back and got a better grip. The second try produced a loud pop, and the cursing stopped.

I climbed off, sat with my back against the mine wall, and tried to catch my breath.

Thou shalt not kill.

Maybe if it had just been me in the bunker, I could have lived with the uncertainty of whether Loren might come back and try to break in. But knowing he had staked out the Admiral, knowing he knew about you… well, I just couldn't allow it.

I think of everything in the bunker and realize you are the most precious. I'm not going to lose you the way I lost Angie.

My headlamp had come off in the scuffle; it lay some five meters away, casting light back the way I had come. The wind still howled in the distance. I listened to its soothing, rhythmic roar as I closed my eyes.

The adrenaline left me achy and uncomfortable.

Then I realized…

Piece by piece, I'm dying out here. Everything that makes me human is being stripped away by the daily horrors of this new world. There is no one to trust, no one to rely on. No military protects the borders. No police force protects the streets. I am a lone tree on an open plain in a ceaseless wind. With every passing second, it is tearing the flesh from my body, and my branches are reaching out for the ground.

Soon enough, I will fall, and when I do, I won't be the same man I was when I first stood up. I will be a half-remembered echo of a man, pared down to his very bones, wasted away to nothing.

At some point, I will lose who I am.

Everyone does.

After the fight, I treaded the border between wake and sleep, and in those shallow dreams, I watched the wind tear me apart to reveal a shiny skeleton beneath. I stared into my own glowing red eyes and screamed.

Humanity is finished.

Loren, with his head turned the wrong way around, is the future of our species.

After the aches had dwindled and the trickles of blood on my neck had ceased, I got to my feet and smacked my head on the low ceiling. I tried to breathe through my nose and got a painful hissing in return. It took a few attempts to put the bones back in their proper place, but once I had done that (as well as blown out all the blood), I was able to breathe better.

I left everything except my rifle in the mine. The pile of Máquinas. The broken human. Turned my back to them and made my way back to the real world. At the opening of the mine, I paused, peered into the white haze.

Visibility was zero. Montana winters are no joke.

My hope was that the high winds had masked any sounds of struggle from inside. I worried that a Máquina might walk in at any moment and kill both me and Loren. I wonder how pissed it would have been to see so many of its brothers laid low.

Probably not pissed at all.

Máquinas didn't have feelings, after all, and no sense of loyalty to each other.

Maybe I'm overthinking this humanity thing. I don't know why its absence bothers me so much. I cling to this idea of a social contract as if it's the only thing keeping me sane. After Angie and Gretta, what else do I have besides my convictions? How would I honor them if I just started massacring people left and right?

Thou shalt not murder.

Yeah.

It's not me that has to survive all of this, it's my humanity.

Without that, I'm just a tree without leaves, a metal skeleton glinting in the sunlight.

Well fuck that.

I did my best to stack the boards against the mine entrance, but without tools, I couldn't nail it shut like before. The wind and snow had taken my footprints from the bunker; I had to find my way back using the angle of the slope and the lean of nearby trees. By the time I got back to the clearing, I was frozen to my core again. My neck ached something fierce, and I couldn't feel my nose at all.

I didn't want to tap it to see if it was still there.

Some of the snow around the entrance to the bunker was disturbed. I assume that was you, Vida.

I don't know what you were doing outside, but I hope it was worth it. My words of warning aren't enough to keep you from venturing out, so I'll just wait until the worst happens. One of these times, we won't have an EMP to save us.

I won't be able to save you.

I'll try though, and maybe I'll die in the process, but it will be worth it, because that's what humans are supposed to do for each other.

Please read this entry carefully and try to understand how dangerous it is outside the bunker. I don't want to kill anymore, but I will keep doing it if that's what it takes to protect you.

Every time you step outside these walls, you may be signing someone's death warrant, be they Máquina or human.

Think about that.

In the meantime, I'm back safe and sound in the bunker, sitting at the table writing this entry while you sleep in your room.

I wonder what you dream about.

I wonder if you dream of me the way I dream of you.

THIRTY-FOUR

Vida squeezed the trigger.

Nothing happened.

She tried again, and yet the trigger still refused to move. Pulling the gun back to inspect it, she found the safety was still engaged. With a swipe of her thumb, she shifted it to the off position and raised the sights to the ceiling.

The man was gone.

All that stared back at her was her own reflection, hazy, cut with the darkness beyond the glass.

She experimented with using just one eye to see. The mural reappeared when she used her right and disappeared when she opened her left. Over and over, Vida winked like a maniac.

She thought of the bunker. Doyle had left that morning, and though he'd been expecting a lengthy excursion, he had asked that the bunker door stay only half-locked.

"You sleep so much these days," he had said. "I don't want to wake you if I come back and you've already gone to bed."

Vida rushed out of the room, her heart trying to break through her ribcage like a firefighter shouldering his way through a locked door. Each *thump* echoed off the evercrete walls of the bunker, loud enough to have come from an external source. In her heightened state, she misjudged the corner of the sofa and banged her knee into the wood framing. The gun went flying as Vida fell over the coffee table, landing on her back on the other side.

Despite the pain in her leg, she was able to crawl to the bunker door and use its many locks as handholds to drag herself up. She used her right eye to inspect the locks, all of which had been engaged from the inside.

Had Doyle returned while she slept?

Vida turned her attention to the proximity sensor and found it dormant. Though the green power indicator on the vidscreen glowed brightly, there was nothing on its display. It was as if an EMP had wiped it out again. She looked around the room, for other fried electronics. Her eyes fell on the table, lit from above by two crisscrossing strands of LED lights.

There, with the pages opened to the current entry, was Doyle's journal.

Vida approached, turned the journal around with a shaky, outstretched finger, and began to read.

So much for the afterglow.

The words jumped off the page at her, reminding her of the night before, of the other face she had seen when she looked up at Doyle. The memory made her shiver. She skipped ahead, started reading about the thirty some-odd Máquinas Doyle had to drag down the hills to a mine. There had been so many out there, ready to kill her, and he'd used his most precious weapon to wipe them all out.

And then, in the aftermath, he'd cleaned up the bodies all on his own. He really was a survivalist, ready to do whatever it took to ensure he saw the next day, even when someone as disruptive as Vida came into his life.

She read about the man in the mine, Loren Pilsky, and how he'd tried to take Doyle out. Words scribbled in the margin asked tough questions.

Had Loren been staking out the bunker?

How did he know about Vida?

That there were no answers to these questions bothered Vida enough to make her hold her breath; she didn't release it until she got to the part about Doyle killing Loren in a brutal wrestling match. The scariest part of the entry was not how close Doyle had come to death, but how easily Doyle justified killing.

So much of his entry was dedicated to explaining away *why* he was allowed to kill Loren.

Too much of his entry was like that.

Even after Vida read of his injuries—broken nose, bruised ribs, cuts up and down his neck—she couldn't accept his nonchalance at having taken another man's life. She didn't expect him to mourn or even cry, but to throw God under the bus as unfair? To claim the society to which he pledged his good behavior was now gone?

It's not me that has to survive all of this. It's my humanity.

Vida shook her head. Didn't he realize it was already too late?

A rustling from behind drew her attention, and she turned to see the bathroom door opening. A wet and weary Doyle stared back at her. He was draped in a white towel below a slightly protruding stomach. There was a light dusting of chest hair, topped by large, curvy shoulder muscles. His thick neck, glistening from the water, bulged under the weight of his Adam's apple.

Vida blinked.

Broken nose.

There was no indication Doyle's nose had suffered any injury. It didn't look off-center or even swollen. No bruises grew beneath his eyes.

Scratches on his neck.

Again, unbroken skin, with a damp five o'clock shadow.

It wasn't until Vida switched eyes that the blood and the scars appeared.

Other injuries rattled off in Vida's brain, culminating in the bullet hole in his left shoulder that healed and reappeared depending on which eye she had open.

"What's wrong with your eyes?" he asked.

Vida swooned, reached out for the barstool for support.

"Are you alright?" He had a thumb inserted into the lip of the towel, which pulled it low enough to just see the start of his pubic hair.

Was he really trying to entice her?

Vida looked away, tried to make sense of the words she had read and the simultaneously there and not-there wounds on Doyle's body. It was as if the scars and bruises had been nothing but make-up, washed away by a few minutes in the shower.

"I'm f-fine," she stammered, despite every fiber of her being screaming the opposite. "I thought I heard a noise, so I…" She pointed vaguely to the door.

"Huh," said Doyle, leaving damp footprints as he approached. When he was right next to her, he pointed to the vidscreen and said, "Proximity sensor isn't showing anything."

Vida looked over her shoulder, half-expecting to see the vidscreen working again. Instead, it was blank. Doyle was staring at nothing.

"Don't worry," he continued. "If anything comes within a half-mile of the Admiral, we'll know about it. I took care of those Máquina bodies, so I think we're gonna be all right. Maybe in a few days I'll make another trip out to look for other survivors, but I think I've earned a few days of sack time. Hope you don't mind having me around here."

Vida's skin writhed with heat.

"No," she whispered. "That will be nice."

He touched her chin unbidden, lifted her face.

"You'd like that?" he asked, smiling.

Vida clenched her jaw. "I would."

"How about I get dressed and make you some dinner? Or, if you'd prefer, I could *not* get dressed."

I hope you dream about me the way I dream about you.

It had sounded like a profession of love, but now, staring into his empty eyes, Vida saw nothing but raw, untempered desire. Her heart renewed its attack on her ribs. By the smirk on his face, Doyle probably thought she was trembling for him.

"Clothes," she said. "You wouldn't want to burn yourself."

He clucked his tongue. "You're the boss lady."

Vida watched him go, but it wasn't until he'd entered his room—removing his towel a split-second before—that she finally relaxed. Tension broke into a million little needles, stinging every inch of her body as muscles tried to untie their knots. She turned and put her elbows on the table, buried her face in her hands.

This was all wrong: Doyle, the man in the ceiling, the decorations missing from the world. Somewhere along the line, the world had splintered off into this hell where nobody told the truth, where strange men spied on her from above while she slept.

Had she died in the plane crash? Was everything that came after that moment just her own little slice of purgatory?

Jahannam.

The word clicked into place.

A fire whose fuel is people and stones.

She threw her hands up. *Nothing* made sense. Anything was possible. Maybe her entire life was a lie, maybe Doyle's journal—

She grabbed the pen he had left on the table and turned to a blank page. Her cursive stood in stark contrast to Doyle's leaning print.

Doyle is a fucking liar.

Vida slammed the journal shut and slid it across the table. It fell over the edge, hit the floor. The pen rolled a few feet away.

"I need to get out of here," she said, the words echoing the thoughts in her head, as if saying them aloud would make them more real.

She stood and walked slowly to the intersection of the two bedrooms and bathroom. Doyle's door opened inward, so there was no way to block his exit with something. She could tie his handle to her bedroom door, but the only rope they had was in the storage crate in his room.

Vida stared, begged her brain to think of a solution.

In his room, Doyle shuffled around noisily.

The nerve of that psycho.

Walking out of the shower like some kind of Adonis. Throwing the door of the bathroom wide so the world could bask in his glory.

The solution leapt out at her.

Vida pulled the bathroom door open. It had to swing into the hallway because there wasn't enough room in the actual bathroom for it to go the other way. Fully open, it covered about three quarters of Doyle's bedroom door.

Once the doors were touching, she ran back into the living room. At first, Vida considered moving the entire couch, thinking more weight would be harder to force out of the way. But, the corridor was so small that even the single armchair could wedge itself nicely. So long as the frame held, Doyle would literally have to crush several lengths of laminated wood to get out of his room.

As Vida reached for the chair, she noticed the gun laying on the cushion. She picked it up, holstered it.

Were it not for the adrenaline fueling her muscles, Vida never would have been able to carry the chair to the corridor and set it down. Her back screamed in protest, and her arms went numb as she stepped away. The difference in widths between the chair and the corridor was only an inch, two at most. Doyle would have a hard time squeezing out of it.

She climbed over the chair and into her room. There wasn't much time to pack, so she grabbed the go-bag Doyle had prepared for her shortly after she arrived. It was only supposed to be used in emergencies, like if the bunker got overrun. There was ammunition, food, a first aid kit, and a few changes of socks. The rest of her clothes she'd have to carry on her back.

It was like a bad dream the way she dressed. Nothing went in the right hole. Everything caught and pulled in the wrong places. All the while, the sweat poured out of her, drenching the inner layers.

Finally, Vida grabbed a black headband and pulled it over her head to cover her left eye. Whether or not her right eye showed her a skewed version of reality, at least it was in focus.

Vida stepped back over the chair and nearly stumbled as Doyle opened his door.

He chuckled. "What's this?"

His face appeared in the opening. The smile faded when he saw the way she was dressed.

"What are you doing, Vida?"

"That's not my name!"

"I know," he said, reaching through the door for her. "I'm gonna help you remember—"

"Liar! You fucking liar!" Tears streamed down her face, clouded her vision. Short steps took her backwards; she was unwilling to turn her back on him.

"I don't know where this is coming from. Are you leaving? Is that it? After everything I've done for you?"

She nodded, unable to form words anymore.

"Are you sure you want to do that? It's dangerous out there."

Her leg hit the couch again, softer this time. With only a few feet between her and the door, she turned and ran. The locks clicked open one by one.

A gust of cold air entered the bunker as she opened the door.

"Vida, please! Please don't leave me. I love you."

Doyle's words followed her up the steps. At the threshold of the outer door, she looked back one last time, bid farewell to the Admiral.

"I won't miss you," she said.

She pulled the latch for the outer door and recoiled when the wind yanked it open. Outside in the blinding snow, she struggled to close the door. Doyle hardly deserved the courtesy, but she wasn't going to make life easier for the Máquinas.

Vida fought the wind, used all of her strength, and finally managed to get the door shut. She engaged the outer latch and turned around.

Saw *him*.

He was dressed in jeans and a t-shirt, and his face was covered with a red bandana and reflective sunglasses. Snow dotted his close-cropped hair.

"Who—?"

The man grabbed Vida by the jacket and flung her face-first into the snow.

THIRTY-FIVE

The road will end in two thousand feet.

Kagan looked up from his palette. The Ponderosa Pines were growing closer to the road; they rushed by his window at a brisk sixty-five miles per hour. Light snow covered the road while large banks on either side pushed ever closer to swallowing it. Soon, the last half-mile of the state-managed blacktop would end, coming to a head right at the edge of the Kagan property.

After that, Priya would take a back seat to the all-wheel drive of Kagan's Land Rover.

"We almost there?" asked Raf, from the passenger seat.

"I thought you were asleep," Kagan replied.

Raf pressed a button on the door and brought his seatback up to its normal position.

"I was," he said, "but your lady woke me up. Jesus, it looks cold out there. My people don't belong up here."

Kagan tossed the palette aside and took hold of the steering wheel. He relieved Priya of her duties and met the accelerator pedal as it came back up.

"Any dreams yet?"

Raf shrugged. "Some. Bits and pieces. But they always cut out. Still just… foggy… in there." He gestured to his head.

"Glasser said it would take some time for your brain to heal. Now that you don't have those memories of the war, your PTSD should start to die down."

"That's good to hear, Dr. Kagan."

"Don't hate just because you went into the service and I learned how to read books." He slipped into a southern accent. "I know all they is to know about PTSD."

"I don't get it."

"Well," said Kagan, slowing as the road came to an end. Bulky wheels dug into the mixture of snow, gravel, and dirt. "Certain experiences, which are stored as memories, affect our future responses to certain stimuli. You encounter a situation that was previously dangerous, like being in a crowded room, and your brain tells you to kill every fucking thing you see. That might have saved your life in the MX, but back here, they'll lock you up for it."

"I know what PTSD is, asshole. I don't get the reference. Is that from a movie?"

Kagan continued unfazed. "The memory feeds the conditioning feeds the response feeds new memories. At some point, you have to get inside that cycle and break it up. But how do you do that if those memories come back to you every night in your dreams?"

"Brain blending?" asked Raf.

"Yes. The finest mind-fuck money can buy."

Kagan guided the SUV through the ever-decreasing space between the pines. Overgrown limbs reached out and scraped against the Land Rover's mirrors and many antennas. When they could drive no further, Kagan stopped the car and asked Priya to put it in low power mode.

Quiet fell over the cabin. Kagan stared at the falling snow, the dusted pines, and the gray-blue sky beyond.

"What do you think of my father?" asked Kagan.

Raf shook his head. "Don't know the man. But if he shares your DNA, then I'm sure he's a privileged guero like you."

Kagan rested his hands on the leather steering wheel. "I don't blame you for thinking that. Most of the world thinks of him that way, but if you read his Wikipedia entry, you'll find out he's the All-American Dream. Started from nothing. My grandfather, William Kagan, was an immigrant, came to this country with a sack full of potatoes and a penchant for whores and gambling."

"He came to the right place."

"No doubt, but the point is, *I'm* the privileged guero. I didn't work for any of this. And like your PTSD, my experiences and memories tell me I can have anything I want, and when I don't get what I want, it upsets me, which in turn lowers my quality of life."

Raf took a deep breath, tapped on his door handle. "Are you trying to say you're in love with me, K? Is that why you took me to Vitra Synth?"

"It'd be funnier if you weren't serious," replied Kagan, shaking his head.

"Answer the question."

"No, Raf, I'm not trying to fuck you. *We* broke into Vitra Synth to help *you* live a better life. You've been my friend for more years of my life than not. I wouldn't put my life on the line for just anybody. You understand that men can be friends, right? Not everyone in this world is trying to fuck or fight you."

"You are," he replied.

"Argh," said Kagan. He smacked the horn twice.

Raf laughed. Continued to laugh.

"Ungrateful, homophobic… cocksucker!" Kagan opened his door and stepped out into the wilderness.

Fresh air filled his lungs, and the deep cold in his body reminded him of teenage years spent on the land. Frank Kagan had purchased the four hundred acres twenty years prior, mere days after the reports from Perion City began hitting the feeds. Here was a man who controlled his own destiny, who knew business and money like the back of his wrinkled balls, who feared no man on the planet, and yet who cowered at the idea of synthetic humans running amok.

"The writing is on the wall," he'd told Kagan. "And it's written in blood."

Frank Kagan feared the coming synthetic apocalypse and decided to build his own safe haven far from the overcrowded cities. He'd hired a team of biologists and survivalists and any other *-ist* that would listen and had them design the perfect safe house.

Twenty years later, its entrance had become buried under fallen trees and loose dirt.

"This is it?" asked Raf.

Kagan nodded, started pulling branches away.

"I thought you said everything was ready to go. We can't do this in a week, man." Raf looked around. "All of these trees would have to come down. That takes a crew, a *synthetic* crew. And then you want to build the box over it? Naw, you need a different plan."

The metal doors rattled as Kagan pulled them open.

"There's no time. Let me worry about the prep. I don't need you for that."

"Of course not," said Raf. "You can just hire someone for the legit work, but when it comes to breaking the law, why not fuck over the vet? He's lived through hell already. Prison will be nothing for him."

"A hell you can't remember," said Kagan. He stepped down into the darkness, followed the stairs to the inner door. It took a minute for the key code to come back to him. "But I get it. I'm asking you for help, but if you want to say no, then whatever. I can always hire a gun."

The lights came up as Kagan stepped into the miniature living room. To the left was a couch and an armchair. To the right, a small coffee table hid under a fine layer of dust. Beyond the living room, shadows swallowed the kitchen and island table.

Kagan felt a hand on his shoulder, paused to look back.

"Oye, hermano," said Raf. "I'm with you 'til the end. Por vida, para siempre." His eyes softened. "But are you sure you want to do this? I mean, Nadya is one thing. She's a synny. But…"

"What drove you to fight those synnies at Plummer Tower when you came to see me that first day? Was it anything conscious?"

Raf shook his head.

"No, it wasn't, was it? You were acting out of a pre-programmed response, a biological imperative you couldn't ignore. Well, I've got one of those too. Unlike you, though, I don't fantasize about ripping robots apart. I fantasize about Sepideh Ahmadi."

"That doesn't sound healthy."

"It's not." Kagan walked to the table, triggered the kitchen lights. "It's called a parasocial relationship. Do you know what that means?"

"Pendejo, *my* daddy's name wasn't on our library."

Kagan returned a glare. "Look, at least I make an effort to understand myself. How long would you have lived on the streets never trying to improve your position? I've been to therapists who said I should just forget about her, who said I should find a nice girl and settle down. But that's just it, Raf. Nice girls don't want to settle down with me. Even Nadya thinks she's a goddamn slave. Even a synthetic who has been programmed to serve my every whim can't stand to be with me. Do you have any idea how fucking frustrating that is?"

"I haven't crushed a skirt since boot," said Raf. "You learn to live without it."

Kagan opened a cabinet, peered at the dried goods inside. "It's not about sex. I can buy sex. I could buy sex every night for the rest of my life. It's about the connection."

"And you feel a connection with an actress?"

"I do, and I know she'd feel it too if she knew I existed." He pointed to the ceiling. "Cameras, here, here, and there. We'll need full three-sixty view, in the beginning at least."

Raf took a seat on a dusty barstool and unzipped his jacket.

"This isn't gonna go down the way you want it," he said. "You're putting a lot of faith in that punk kid."

"Glasser knows his shit," said Kagan, turning to lean against the counter. "I wouldn't have let him work on you if he didn't have the chops. All he has to do is a copy instead of a move, then blank out the important bits."

"What if her memory starts coming back?"

Kagan waved the question away. "You worry too much about the future, Raf. It's a solid plan. Just help me get her out of Plummer Tower. I'll worry about reintroducing her to the world." He smiled to himself. "It's gonna be so fucking perfect. I will be her personal Jesus."

"Isn't she Muslim?"

"Muslims are cool with Jesus. But that's besides the fucking point. We need to focus on *how* we get her here. We've already got one guy on the inside, but interrupting the transfer process at just the right time is going to be tricky, even with his help."

"What usually happens to the bodies?"

Kagan folded his arms. "Well, our official story is the transfer kills the brain, so they die pretty much right after. The bodies are cremated and disposed of, anything to keep the new synthetic from having to face the fact they're no longer human. Their contract states they don't get to see their bodies after the procedure. We claim the trauma would be too much, but who really knows?"

"What's back there?" asked Raf, pointing over Kagan's shoulder.

"Beds and bath. The one of the left is slightly bigger. That's where me and the wife would have slept. Come on, I'll show you."

He led Raf to the small corridor and opened the bedrooms. "I was thinking Pamela or Angela, something folksy for the wife. She'd be here on the left with me. Over here, my daughter. I'm thinking Gretchen; that was Abat's nurse's name."

"The law would never allow you to have a daughter." Raf stuck his head inside the smaller room. "You actually think the great Sepideh Ahmadi is gonna live in here?"

"She's going to love it. Million-dollar penthouses don't have shit on a twin bed with real cotton-poly sheets. And look at this, a little desk to write on. What more could she want?"

Raf groaned, walked the short distance back to the kitchen. "She's gonna want Egyptian sheets, caviar, champagne—"

"Ah, there's your problem. You're seeing the bunker as it *is*, not how it will look once I layer on some augmented reality. We know she's got the contacts, so I can pretty this place up and make it livable. As for the booze, I've got fucking booze."

Kagan walked to a cabinet and opened the low door. He pulled out a bottle of Kentucky Gentleman. His pocketknife made short work of the plastic seal. From another cabinet, he grabbed two plastic tumblers.

"Make mine a double," said Raf. "It's not every day I agree to the absolute worst fucking idea since…" He paused, grimaced. "Since some memory I can't even remember. I swear a saw a movie with this same setup."

Kagan filled both tumblers halfway, slid one across the table.

"There were actually a lot of movies with this setup," said Kagan, taking a sip. "But in most of those cases, the captors were actually insane. As you can see, I am not."

Raf mumbled into his glass. "That's what they all said."

"And, *and*, they didn't have the Brain Blender. This will be true amnesia—irrevocable." He burped. "The lack of memories will give her doubt, and the augmented reality will sell the illusion. It'll be the first movie where the captor and captive live happily ever after."

"I give it ninety minutes at the most."

"If you're talking about the sex scenes, then I'll agree."

"*Stolen Love: the true story of Sepideh Ahmadi and Doyle Kagan.*"

Kagan smirked, lifted his glass in a toast. "I'll drink to that."

THIRTY-SIX

"I didn't know," said Sepi. "How could I have known? You follow a guy around for a while and you think you've got a good bead on him, but you don't. How can you?"

"Cut!" yelled Richard. "Reset the train."

Next to her on the bench, Jaime Borrego sat up and wiped the drool from his lips. He smiled at Sepi, said, "I thought that was good."

She nodded her thanks, turned to Richard as he approached.

"We're not quite getting it," he said, taking a knee in front of her. "This is a man you love, and it's that rare, immediate, unexplainable love, the kind you'll carry with you for the rest of your life. He has shown you there is more to life than getting revenge, and a huge part of you wants to go with him into this other world, live there, and forget all of this."

"I know," said Sepi, folding her hands in her lap.

"And you, *you* Sepideh, have sentenced him to death. You've killed him already. Someone you love deeply is going to die."

She looked up, met his gaze. Dared him to continue.

"I know," he said. "But we could really use that emotion here. You hate me, don't you?"

"You're just doing your job."

He nodded, stood, and gave the hand signal for first positions.

Make-up techs added slight drool back to Jaime's face. Sepi used the delay to turn her attention inward.

It had been almost two weeks since the meeting at Vitra Synth, and each day since then had left Sepi with shorter fingernails. Nat more or less stopped fighting once they got home, as if she had just crossed the finish line of a marathon and had nothing left to give. The question had become whether she could hold out until their new bodies were ready. Some days, it didn't seem like she was going to make it.

Sepi tried not to think about Nat dying before she could transfer, but the nights of relentless coughing, moaning, and crying had pushed the scenario closer to reality. Richard was right; it did mirror the scene in some ways. Here, Kaili

Zabora was in love for what might have been the first and last time. And she had to watch the object of her desire die.

"Are we ready?" asked Richard.

Jaime slumped into the seat as if he were drugged.

Sepi took a deep breath.

"Action!"

She counted to three in her head, then looked up at Jaime's face. Bit by bit, she changed his brown hair into blond, softened his features, colored his lips, until she could see Nat sitting across from her.

The words spilled out of her.

"I didn't know," she said, her voice breaking. "How could I have known? You follow a guy around for a while and you think you have a good bead on him, but you don't. You can't."

Jaime's throat contracted, but the sound he made didn't resemble speech.

"And it's not like this is my first time or anything," she continued. "I've done a few before. I've earned my stripes. Why did I have to draw you?"

For this scene, Jaime did nothing but move his eyes, widening them to ask questions, narrowing them to express dismay.

Sepi looked away, delivered the lines into her chest. She removed his wedding ring, slipped the tungsten loop onto her thumb. It was so bulky, so unlike the thin ribbon of rose gold both she and Nat usually wore. Wardrobe had made her take it off for the scene; it hung from a silver chain around her neck, safely hidden beneath her costume.

"Sepi?" asked Richard.

She looked up, saw him motioning in her periphery. "I don't know how," he mouthed.

"I don't know how to stop Vinestead," said Sepi, lacing her voice with bass now that she was talking about Kaili Zabora's favorite subject. "I don't know if we can really bring that scumbag corporation to its knees. They're so many. We're so few. But that doesn't mean we shouldn't fight. This is who we are." She choked up, squeezed her eyes tight. "This is just who we are. Goddammit, Rick. We warned them. We told them we'd kill every Vinestead employee from the boardroom to the mailroom. And they… they just abandoned you, treated you like you didn't even matter."

Sepi closed her hands into fists.

"They should have told you. I didn't know you didn't have a choice. I thought you were just being stubborn. But you were clueless. God, you all were."

She thought of how she had left Nat that morning, with a synny nurse standing guard, holding a cool washcloth to her forehead. Nat had barely opened her eyes when Sepi said goodbye.

Heavy globs of salty tears rushed down her cheeks, fell on her blouse.

Her voice broke again, became shrill and panicked. "I wish I could take it back! Please, God. Let me take it back!"

She put a hand to Jaime's face, imagined she was caressing Nat's. Her cheeks rose to meet her eyes, pulling her mouth into a warped smile.

"But I can't. I can't do a goddamn thing about it. As much as you mean to me, as much as I love you, I have a job to do. This is who I am, Rick. And this is bigger than both of us."

The gimbaled set pitched forward, giving the impression of the train coming to a stop.

"Cut!" yelled Richard.

A smattering of applause broke out amongst the crew. Jaime sat up and looked at Sepi. "Are you alright?" he asked, putting a hand on her shoulder.

"Yes," she replied, covering his hand with hers. "Just acting."

He raised an eyebrow, said nothing.

"Sepi, baby! That was incredible." Richard offered his hand.

She took it, stood, and thanked him for the compliment.

"I don't think we're gonna do any better than that today," he said, checking his sliver. "And all before noon. We'll see you in the DR next week, right?"

Sepi nodded.

Richard held her by the shoulders. "Enjoy your last twenty-four hours as a human. I hope your new body can act as well as this one."

She crossed her fingers but couldn't find words to accompany the gesture. Too much emotion had been poured into inconsequential words, and Sepi didn't think she could handle saying anything else. All she wanted to do was go home, check on Nat, and spend the rest of the day holding her.

Continuity held her for several minutes while they took pictures of her costume, and then wardrobe came with a makeshift tent to strip her down. It was fifteen past noon before she got into the car on the north side of the lot and told Franklin to take her to the Monarch.

On the way, she called the nurse and asked for a status update. Nat, for the most part, was fine, had slept most of the day away, but recently she had been asking for Sepi. Vitals were all good, all within limits.

Sepi relaxed, even as the car swerved in and out of traffic. Franklin had been literal in his interpretation of *get me home as fast as possible*. His auto-drive protocols barely kept him from jumping the curb in front of the building.

The Monarch doorman waited an extra beat to make sure the car was stopped before approaching Sepi's door to open it.

"Welcome home, Ms. Ahmadi. You might want to get your car looked at."

Sepi nodded and hurried inside. The lobby bustled with midday activity, residents heading out to lunch or coming home from an audition. Stella Starfall nodded from the lounge area as if they were longtime friends. In the elevator, tinny music accompanied her up to her floor.

So many little actions. So much to accomplish before getting to Nat.

The doors parted. Sepi slowed her walk, tried to calm the anxiety building inside of her.

"So tomorrow's the big day, is it?" asked a deep voice.

Sepi paused at the entrance to her hallway, turned and saw Solomon sitting in his usual chair. His smile sucked her in.

Without moving, she replied, "It is."

"Are you nervous?"

"Is this an interview?" she asked.

He chuckled lightly, scratched his beard. "No, but a biography about one of Hollywood's hottest young stars would probably be a bestseller. People love stories of devotion and sacrifice."

Sepi held her purse in both hands, looked down.

"So you think I'm being foolish?" she asked. "Sacrificing too much?"

Sol shook his head. "For love? You should sacrifice everything. From what I hear, there's not much difference between a human and synthetic existence. A few minor changes, a few things feel different, but what really matters is your wife. Her living on. You taking a stand against biology and genetics. It's a battle worth fighting."

Sepi stepped closer to him, spoke in a low voice. "I haven't told Nat, but I'm really scared."

"As you should be. All great accomplishments require a certain amount of bravery. Otherwise, everyone would do them, and they'd become commonplace. Imagine if everyone could act as well as you do."

She smiled, but instead of thinking about the whole world as actors, she imagined them all as highly sensitive, socially anxious, and borderline depressed. What kind of world would that be if even half of them were like her?

"I wouldn't worry too much," continued Sol. "You have to focus on what's important here. Life is an adventure, and you and Natasha are about to embark on one of the newest and least charted adventures ever conceived. Immortality, Sepideh. It's what humans have yearned for since caveman days."

"I will never grow old," she added. "My looks will never go. I won't get sick. Never get a cold again."

"That's the spirit."

Sepi swallowed hard. "And none of it will be real. I'll walk, talk, and look like a human, but I won't be. We'll never pass our DNA onto our children, never experience the highs and lows of growing old together, learning to rely on each other more as the years drag on. You make it sound like some kind of grand experience, and maybe it is, but at what cost?"

"You seem to know already," he replied.

"Yeah, the human experience. That's what we're giving up."

"You're a brave woman for doing this, and I promise I will always be there to share stories of my bad knee and failing kidneys should you ever need reminding of where you came from."

"Thank you, Sol."

"If you have time tomorrow, send me a message, let me know everything went according to plan. I'll be praying for you and Natasha."

Sepi nodded, withdrew slowly despite the urgency she felt, and continued down the hall to her apartment.

The nurse greeted her just inside the foyer.

"No change since we last spoke," she said. "She's awake now."

Sepi thanked her, dropped her purse and jacket on the bar. She kicked her shoes off and padded her way to the bedroom.

The blinds were up, and the sun was casting abbreviated beams of light on the carpeted floor. Nat lay in the middle of the bed, covered up to her stomach by the thick, white duvet. She wore a pink tank top bordered in black.

"Are you hot?" asked Sepi. She tapped the panel by the door and turned on the ceiling fan.

"A little," said Nat. Her voice had weakened over the past few days. Everything about her seemed to be tapering off.

Sepi crossed the room, climbed onto the bed at its foot, and crawled across the duvet to lay by Nat's side. She brushed her hair with her fingers.

"I've been waiting for you," said Nat.

"Oh yeah? I've been waiting to see you too."

Nat smiled, nuzzled Sepi's cheek.

"I've been waiting to say goodbye."

Sepi pulled back, looked into Nat's sleepy eyes. "What?"

"I feel it coming. Something pulling me away. I really did try to hold out, but I'm so tired now."

"No," said Sepi. "We're doing this tomorrow. You can make it until then, I know you can."

"I'm sorry, sweetie. I know how much this meant to you, but I've made my peace with it. I already called my parents."

Sepi sat up, her heart pounding. "You can't leave me here, Nat. I won't be able to go on without you. *I have no life* without you. Don't you get that?"

Nat smiled, closed her eyes. Her lips were dry, cracked.

"I can't fight it anymore," she said. "I will always love you, Sepideh. To my dying breath."

The world blurred. Sepi's throat contracted.

This couldn't be happening. To have come so far, come so close.

How could Nat just give up like this?

Sepi covered her mouth.

"No," she said. "If you give up, I'll give up."

Nat opened her eyes, sought out Sepi.

"I'll stop acting. I'll move out of the city, get a shitty cabin in the woods, and I'll just sit there until I'm dead. I won't go out. I won't find love again. I'll refuse to live."

"Don't be stupid," said Nat.

"*You don't be stupid!* You've got a chance at a new life, and you're just giving up the day before?"

Nat frowned. "I've made my choice. You'll change your mind when I'm gone. Love will find you again. You're just that kind of—"

"I swear to you it won't."

Nat turned away. "If you're just going to argue with me, then go. Let me die in peace."

"No!" screamed Sepi. She crawled off the bed, felt her limbs tingle as she walked to the door. It had barely closed behind her before she burst into tears and collapsed on the floor.

She sobbed, loud enough to attract the nurse. The synny tried to comfort her. Sepi wondered if this is what it would feel like. A synthetic hand on her shoulder. Would it have the same effect?

"Can you get me my phone?" asked Sepi.

The nurse complied, returned a moment later.

Sepi held it to her ear.

"Call Wayne Demeyer," she said.

The phone rang, rang some more.

A recorded message played.

Sepi hit the *END* button and redialed. This time, Wayne answered on the second ring.

"Ms. Ahmadi, how are you?"

"Today," she sputtered.

"Excuse me?"

"It has to be today."

"I'm sorry. I don't think we can accommodate—"

"She's going to die, Wayne," she said, borrowing a deep voice from Kaili Zabora. "She won't make it to tomorrow."

"I'd have to bump—"

"Do it."

"It'll cost us—"

"Just do it!" she screamed. "Please!"

"Okay, okay," said Wayne. He was silent for a moment, then said, "Your sleeves arrived this morning. We'll do as many system checks as we can before you get here. Do you have your own transportation? Or should we send a car?"

Sepi looked over her shoulder at the bedroom door.

"Send an ambulance," she said, and hung up.

THIRTY-SEVEN

Doyle's Journal – November 24, 2045 (cont.)

Doyle is a fucking liar.

THIRTY-EIGHT

Vida inhaled snow.

She came up to her hands and knees in the midst of a coughing fit, and despite the pain gripping her chest, was able to start crawling away from her attacker. Gloved hands sank six inches into the snow, each time bringing her exposed face closer to the ground again. Finally, after pumping her legs for what felt like forever, she chanced a look over her shoulder.

The man had retreated to the outer bunker door and made short work of unlatching the locks. He pulled the metal panel open—against the wind—as if it were nothing. He turned, squinted through the whiteout, and spotted Vida.

Numb fingers fumbled for the gun on her hip. She pulled it out and pointed in the man's general direction.

Either he didn't see the weapon, or he didn't believe she was capable of pulling the trigger.

"Stay back!" she yelled, her voice trembling. "I'll shoot!"

The man sighed, his shoulders slumping as if he were about to start a chore he didn't want to do. The wind tore at his thin t-shirt, but he didn't seem to notice.

San Francisco rose and fell in Vida's memory. Images of the bay, of cold mist rippling across the observation deck of a ferry, scrolled through her head. She saw Peter standing next to her, saw his features melt away. His cheeks hollowed out; dark circles appeared beneath his blue eyes.

"Do it," said the man.

I can't, thought Vida. *This isn't who I am.*

Peter's hair grew long and wispy.

"This is who you have to be," he assured her. "Come back to me."

Vida squeezed the trigger until it gave way. A gunshot rang out in the clearing, but didn't echo back.

The man smirked, continued his approach.

The gun rattled off nine more shots, but the bullets had no effect on him. No matter where Vida thought she was aiming, nothing seemed to land. Either she was a terrible shot, or the man wasn't a man at all.

When he reached down to grab her, Vida thrust the gun into his face and pulled the trigger again. This time, he winced and knocked the gun out of her hands. It landed somewhere in the snow and disappeared.

"Dick," he growled, hoisting her up by the jacket. In one swift move, he bent and lifted her onto his shoulder.

The world turned upside down. Vida looked around frantically for the gun, saw nothing but blinding snow. She clawed at the man's blue jeans, tugged at his belt. Her gloved fingers slipped while trying to tear his t-shirt. He shook her a few times in response.

Vida felt the Admiral pulling her back, felt the confrontation with Doyle rushing out of the darkness like the first tendrils of a nightmare. At any moment, it would encompass her completely, compressing her existence into a single point of blinding anguish.

They passed the threshold of the outer door.

She pleaded with him, tried to explain that Doyle wasn't who he said he was.

"None of us are," said the man, slowing to avoid the barbs in the stairwell.

"He can't keep me here. I don't deserve this!"

"How do you know?"

Vida beat on his back with her fists, leaving only the slightest of red marks on his skin.

"You're a wild one, aren't you?" he asked. "I can see why he likes you."

Vida flashed on the idea of returning to bunker life. She screamed, reached for one of the barbs on the side of the stairwell, and managed to dislodge it from its mounting.

She held the pike in both hands, pulled it back as far as her arms would stretch, and then jammed it into the small of the man's back.

He screamed, faltered, dropping her to the evercrete steps. Her shoulder hit first; a sickening cracking sound followed the impact. As the man tumbled down the stairs, she tried to get up, felt her hands slip on something wet.

"Pinche concha!" The man was on his stomach, reaching ineffectually for the wooden pole sticking out of his back. The wound gushed blood, coating the barb in a slick red.

Vida looked at her hands; her gloves were now crimson.

She gagged, scrambled up the steps again, unable to use her left arm to find purchase. A blast of wind greeted her outside, and she used her body as a sail to push herself along.

The go-bag lay where it had fallen; Vida scooped it up and ran through the snow, ever outward, further away from the screams emanating from the bunker.

A chill seeped into her clothes, made her skin itch.

She ran and ran, unsure of where she was going but trusting the wind to take her far away.

Then she saw them in the snow.

Footprints. Hers.

Somehow, the wind had been changing directions, leading her in a circle. Off to the right were footprints heading back to the clearing, including the odd, red handprint where she'd stumbled.

Vida stood for a moment, staring at her own tracks.

It wasn't possible, not unless the storm was actually a tornado and spinning directly above the bunker.

She turned ninety degrees, put the bunker at her back, and began walking. The more the wind tried to push her off course, the more she leaned against it. Above her, the tree-tops swayed precariously, as if they might fall over at any minute.

Maybe they would. It wouldn't surprise her.

She thought of Peter, thought of the face she could barely remember.

"I'm going home," she said, her teeth chattering.

Vida picked up her pace, repeated the mantra every few breaths.

Soon, she was running flat out, leaning into the biting wind, watching the haze carefully to avoid any trees that might suddenly jump out at her.

The faster she ran, the more she remembered of San Francisco, the more she became convinced she had lived there at some point and had shared an ice cream sundae at Ghirardelli Square with an effeminate man named Peter.

She saw him just beyond her vision, in the haze. His arms open and inviting.

Running, running, running.

"I'm going home," she screamed. "I'm going—"

Vida slammed into something cold and stretchy. It absorbed her for a moment, then flung her backwards into the snow. Her shoulder cried out as she tried to control her landing.

"What the fuck?" she asked, climbing to her feet.

In front of her, the forest wavered, as if vibrating. It extended into the infinite distance, shrouded in a white haze. She approached slowly, her good arm outstretched.

An invisible barrier stopped her hand from going any further. She pressed on it, skewing the forest, warping the trees around her finger. Nothing in her memory explained how any of this was possible. The barrier didn't feel very strong, and yet she couldn't grasp it or find any kind of seam.

Vida slung the go-bag off her back and dropped it on the ground. In one of the outside pockets, she found a small folding knife in a fire-starting kit. Running back to the barrier, she stabbed at it. The first try slipped, but the second tore a three-inch gash. She inserted the knife again and used her weight to pull it towards the ground.

A blast of heat hit her, as did the glare of daylight. Vida tore at the gash, watched as the forest fell away. She stared at the portal to another world, saw the bright blue sky, so big and empty. A shimmering sun hung low. Tall pines stood stoic in their dark-green dress.

Vida looked behind her, at the swirling snow, the oppressive storm.

She heard his voice.

"Vida!" said a faraway Doyle. "Vida, where are you?"

She dove for the go-bag, hitched it over her good shoulder, and stepped through the gash into the alternate reality. A few steps away, she turned and looked back. Her mouth fell open.

A wall of silver material grew three stories out of the ground. In both directions, it went on for hundreds of yards. She could hear the wind inside, see the blusters of snow dribbling their way out of the tear in what looked like plastic sheeting. Even without seeing the other sides of the structure, Vida knew what she was looking at.

Her eyes slowly filled with tears.

"I don't…"

"Vida!"

His voice was close enough to force her legs into motion. She ran, awkwardly dumping her outer and inner coats. As she did, she changed direction, ran through the trees, meandering around them at random—anything to make the trail harder to follow. The heavy go-bag beat against her back, but she didn't tire. Freedom was just beyond the tree line. If she could make it that far, she would be away from Doyle forever.

It didn't matter if there were Máquinas still roaming the countryside; she would just run away from them, hide out until she could continue moving east. There were people waiting for her there, people who would protect her from Doyle and his domesticated Máquina.

"Come back!" His voice was small and distant.

Vida smiled, changed directions again. The trees thinned, and noises filtered in over the sound of her ragged breathing. A roar built off to her left, far away but vaguely overhead. She stopped to listen to it, put a hand against a tree.

As the sound reached its peak, Vida looked up through the pines at the blue sky. A small, glinting object cut across the dome, leaving a trail of white smoke behind it.

Was it one of those drones Doyle had told her about?

"That's an airplane," said Vida.

But how?

She hurried on, dodging smaller trees, listening to the shrieks of small birds as she ran past. Finally, she came to a division in the land where a large swath of forest had been clear cut. She stood at the top of a long slope, looking down on a valley in the distance.

She gasped. Fell to her knees.

Vida lifted the headband from her left eye to make sure she was seeing the real world and not some illusion.

Buildings, like jagged teeth, on the horizon, still standing.

Roads cutting between them, undamaged by Máquina carpet bombing.

Tiny blips of white, red, and gray flitted past each other; cars going about their business as if the world hadn't ended.

Above, birds soared, flying over the land in wide, sweeping arcs. Higher still, white contrails crisscrossed the sky.

How long were we in that bunker?

Had the war come and gone? Was it not as bad as Doyle had made it seem?

Vida shook her head.

She thought about the last entry in his journal, the one she had put there herself.

Doyle is a fucking liar.

A black hole of anxiety opened in her stomach. She tried not to think about the pain, but the sweat came anyway, then the ragged breathing, and finally the thundering heartbeat.

I'm going to die right here.

She was seconds from an anxiety-induced heart attack.

After everything she had been through, it was going to be a panic attack that sent her over the edge. Vida collapsed, stared at the blue sky, and tried to imagine herself as one of the truly free birds flying above her.

She panted.

The gray crept in.

She tried to speak, couldn't get the words out.

She screamed for Peter across the infinite void of her memory.

What the fuck is happening?

THIRTY-NINE

Kagan paced the loading dock behind Plummer Tower with his hands shoved deep in his pockets. Darkness had long fallen over Los Angeles, and in the gloom, nocturnal creatures were now stirring. They passed like zombies in the alley behind the building, casting hungry glances at the nervous man scrolling through a palette.

With each turn, Kagan passed the open doors of an Econoline van where Raf sat with his feet dangling. A cigarette lit his face as he took a drag. Raf had given up smoking when he joined the service but had returned to the habit a few days after the procedure. He claimed it calmed nerves that had been set on edge by constant uncertainty. His time in the MX was now lost to the ether, but its echoes tormented him, brought a low, nagging rumble to his everyday life.

It was a small price to pay to sleep through the night.

Raf checked his sliver.

"2300 hours," he announced. "Anything yet?"

Kagan swiped his mail app out of the way to bring up his messenger on the palette. "No," he replied. "But he said it would run longer than usual."

"This doesn't feel right. We never should have moved up the plan."

"It's the only way," said Kagan. He scanned the body of an email, read a few lines about a man going toe-to-toe with a synthetic soldier. "Besides, tomorrow would have been too late. At least this way, we don't have to go into the building ourselves. Glasser is gonna roll her out to us and then we're gone."

Raf shook his head, took another drag. "Pues, when has it ever been that simple?"

"Hey, man. Ask no questions, tell no consequences. You dig?"

"No," said Raf, pushing himself off the van's metal bed. "I don't dig. I don't dig at all. We're exposed out here, K. How do you even know what he said about Sepideh was true?"

Kagan waved the question away with an impatient hand. He tried to concentrate on the emails from the writing service, on the fabricated stories he would have to hand-copy into a journal, but his mind kept going back to the frantic phone call he'd received from Glasser earlier that day. Something about Sepideh pushing up her appointment. It had taken several minutes to calm Glasser down, but once he could breathe again, he began to formulate a new plan all by himself.

"We're getting started later in the day," Glasser had said. "Which means by the time we get them transferred and out the door, it'll be way late, like nine or ten. Bio-waste comes at six, so the bodies will have to sit overnight. Wayne's not gonna like leaving them unattended, but if I sedate her, he won't suspect anything. Once everyone is out, I'll put her on a gurney and bring her down."

Both Kagan and Raf had been in Montana at the time, putting the finishing touches on a three-story tall superstructure they'd dubbed *The Black Box* even though it was gray. The plastic sheeting that formed the outer shell of the Box billowed and bulged under the self-contained weather system inside, but three days of testing had revealed no leaks. Outside, the temperature was just slightly above freezing, typical for an early March. Inside the box, snow whipped around enclosed trees, laying a fresh coat of powder on a small clearing. The thermometer read minus twelve.

Figuring the Box was as ready as it would ever be, Kagan and Raf took the jet back to California, landing at Bob Hope Airport just outside of Burbank. After that, it was only a matter of telling the synthetic crew to refuel while they picked up the van they had rented.

Despite the change in plans, Kagan couldn't help but feel giddy. Raf did have a point about making last-minute changes and about exposing themselves in the alley, but none of it really mattered. They were too close now. At some point, Glasser would appear through the rear doors with a sedated Sepideh Ahmadi, and for the first time in his life, Kagan would get to physically touch her.

The very idea of his fingers on her body filled him with nervous energy. The words in the emails danced to the point where he could no longer read them.

Kagan took the palette to the van and tossed it inside.

"2330," said Raf. "That punk bailed on us, hermano."

Kagan's sliver vibrated.

Heading down now, the message read.

"Fucking A," said Kagan. Then to Raf, "Start her up. He's coming down."

An electronic whine filled the air as the Econoline's systems switched on. From underneath, a low rumble ran along the frame—an add-on for commercial vehicles to help blind pedestrians hear them coming.

Two minutes later, the service door opened and a wrecked Earl Glasser poked his head out. He nodded to Kagan and turned around to pull something through the door.

A stretcher. On it, lay a black body bag.

Kagan's smile faltered.

"What's this?" he asked.

"It's a bag full of stupid questions," said Glasser. He pushed the gurney to the end of the loading dock and hit a hidden lever under the bed, collapsing it. He gestured to Raf. "Can you take it from here?"

Raf nodded, guided the gurney across the small gap from the loading dock to the back of the van.

Glasser sat down on the edge of the dock and sighed. "What a fucking day," he said.

"Everything go alright?" asked Kagan. He stepped into the van and searched the body bag for a zipper.

"With her? Yeah, everything's Steve Aoki-dokie. Did a smooth one-to-one copy, and then cut out the pieces you wanted gone, which was a lot, man. *That* was a lot harder. Like, double my price harder."

Kagan opened the zipper, revealed the dark hair and smooth forehead of Sepideh Ahmadi. "If you did like I asked, then there might be a bonus in it for you."

"It's done," said Glasser. "She won't remember anything about her previous life, maybe just a few things from childhood. He knows what it's like, don't you?"

Raf nodded. "Fucking sucks."

"Gotta pay to play. Grass is always greener. All that shit."

Kagan traced a finger down Sepideh's cheek. Touched her dry lips.

"Now," said Glasser, "the woman *after* her was a total nightmare. She had one foot in the grave when she came in, almost completely unresponsive. I had no idea how I was going to get a good brain scan. But I fucking did it." He nodded to himself, his eyes pegged open. "Because I'm a genius. A Certified Fucking Genius. A CFG from the LBC, ain't none of you bitches can fuck with me."

His shoulders bobbed.

"Vámanos," said Raf. Then, mumbling, "No tenemos tiempo para esto." He walked around the van and got into the driver's seat.

"What did he say?" asked Glasser.

Kagan looked up. "He said West Coast rap is dead. Get over it." He gestured to the doors. "Give me a hand."

Glasser groaned, kicked the door while Kagan closed the other one.

"If she's like you said, I'll send another thirty K. If she's not like you said, or if you mention this to *anyone*, I'll send him." He gestured over his shoulder.

From the front seat, Raf mimed a gunshot into the rearview mirror.

Glasser nodded, rolled onto his side, and stood up.

"Enjoy the raping," he said, a crooked smile on his face. He turned and hurried back inside.

Kagan left the body bag open so Sepideh could breathe. He made sure the wheel locks were engaged and then slipped into the passenger seat.

Raf kept to the side streets until they were out of Hollywood, then turned onto the 101 heading north. Dark hills scrolled by, lit occasionally by million-dollar homes with no regard for energy conservation. Midnight traffic was light, and soon they were turning off Vanowen to hit the private hangars on the backside of Bob Hope.

The jet idled in the hangar; Kagan could see the pilots going over systems checks in the cockpit as the van pulled up. Waiting by the small staircase leading up into the cabin was Nadya, looking prim in a faux stewardess uniform she'd crafted from previous years' Halloween costumes.

Raf drove the van right up to the plane, positioned the rear doors next to the stairs.

Kagan stepped into the back and pulled the zipper on the body bag the rest of the way down, revealing Sepideh Ahmadi in all of her paper gown glory. The rear doors opened and Nadya peered inside.

"This is she?"

"Yes," said Kagan. "Get her on the plane and put her in one of the beds. Once you've done that, I want you to dress her in those clothes I set out."

"Are you sure?" asked Nadya. "They're so ratty and torn. It looks like they've been in a fire."

"Just do it."

Nadya nodded, pulled the gurney out of the van. The legs unfolded automatically. Without even so much as a grunt, Nadya picked up Sepideh and carried her up the steps.

Raf stood by the back of the van, reached for another cigarette. A tech from across the hangar called out, "You can't smoke in here," but Raf ignored him.

"Well?" asked Kagan. "That went better than I expected. You still convinced something's gonna go wrong?"

Smoke billowed from Raf's nose as he smiled. "We're not out of California yet."

"I guess I don't blame you," said Kagan, putting his hands in his pockets. "You've got this inclination to see the worst possible outcomes and you don't even know why. Meanwhile, back here in the real world, away from wars and books and movies, we don't have wrenches flying at us from every direction. Most of the time, shit just works out, man."

"Maybe for you."

"Para nosotros! Tú y yo, cabrón!"

Raf pointed with his cigarette. "There's something wrong with you, hermano. Seriously, down deep."

"Ah, fuck that," said Kagan, picking up his palette. Another five emails had come in, each with a different version of a post-apocalyptic world. "We're all a little messed up. You should know that better than most. The difference between us and them is that we have everything we want. We have the means. After this is over, we're gonna find you a new job, something to fill the time. You'll meet a woman, or we can build you a male sexbot, and you'll be happy."

"Yeah," said Raf. "You picked a homeless guy up off the street, brought him home, clothed and fed him, and I'm the gay one."

Kagan continued in a monotone. "I love you like a brother. Mi hermano. You know that."

"Por vida," said Raf.

"Para siempre," said Kagan. "Come on, Sepideh Ahmadi's got a date with a plane crash, and I don't want her to be late."

"Why do you have to say shit like that when we're about to get on a plane?"

They walked up the steps single-file, and Kagan nodded to the pilots as they entered the cabin. Towards the back of the jet, he could see Nadya standing over one of the two beds on either side of the aisle. Over the idle engine noise, he heard her saying something.

Kagan walked towards her, but when Nadya reached out and slapped Sepideh in the face, he broke into a full run.

"What are you doing?" he yelled

Nadya glanced back, slapped Sepideh again. "Wake up!"

Kagan pushed her away; she hit the bathroom door but didn't fall. He checked Sepideh, found her still unconscious.

"It's not right," said Nadya. "You can't do this to her."

Kagan squinted, tried to see past the façade to the pseudo-artificial intelligence behind Nadya's eyes.

"What's the problem?" asked Raf.

"She's not a *thing* to be kept!" screamed Nadya, looking as panicked as any synthetic could. There were calculations going on in her head that Kagan couldn't account for.

"Raf?"

"Yeah?"

"You know that nagging feeling you have to kill synthetics?"

Raf paused for a moment. "Didn't know you knew about that."

"I think now would be a good time to exorcise those demons."

"With um, her?" he asked.

Kagan continued to stare at Nadya. "Problem with that, soldier?"

"Nope."

"Good," said Kagan. "Then please escort my companion off the plane. She seems to have suffered a critical failure and needs recycling."

Raf stepped forward.

Nadya remained still, but she knew as well as Kagan did that she couldn't resist. She may have wanted to, but desire and being a synthetic were mutually exclusive.

Kagan barely listened to the struggle as he stroked Sepideh's forehead.

FORTY

Sepi opened her eyes and cringed.

For what felt like hours, she had been hearing the dulcet sounds of a muted piano echoing from far above the catatonic hole in which she'd awoken. There, without the least bit of sensory input or motivation, she'd come into being with a single repeating thought in her mind.

This is who I am.

From there, Sepi assumed that despite what her body was telling her, she did, in fact, exist. Not only that, but she knew her own name: Sepideh. That piece of information led her to another, and another. Fractal branches spread out in front of her like bolts of lightning tearing through the clouds. Her memory took the form of a sprawling mansion, and Sepi spent what could have been minutes or eons running through the rooms, slapping the rocker switches, illuminating another part of her life.

Then the piano had come in, drawing her attention upwards. The tiniest glint of light shone from overhead, and Sepi felt herself rising to the surface of consciousness.

She became aware of her eyes. Opened them.

The room hit her all at once. The grayish walls; white curtains; four white chaise loungers; tables adorned with tulips; a serving counter with glasses and a sweating pitcher of water; dark slats across expansive windows; motes of dust floating in the low rays of a dying sun; her body reclining under a floral afghan; a white box by her bare feet; speakers in the ceiling; LED strips set to low.

Jasmine. Conditioned air.

Tinkling of piano keys. Distant conversations.

The sensory data crashed into her like a tsunami, knocking her feet from the earth and the breath from her lungs.

Only, there was no breath to contain and no lungs to contain it. In her new synthetic body, bio-electrical approximations of life-support systems did have their place, but their roles had changed to that of security blankets. Breathing was no longer required, but the act of bringing in air and expelling it was so ingrained in human consciousness that being without it would create a debilitating amount of panic.

Sepi recognized Wayne's words echoing in her brain, the way he'd described what it would be like to wake up in a synthetic body.

"We'll bring your new body online for the first time in our recovery room," he'd said. "There, we've done our best to balance the sensory input. No flashy colors, no complex smells. Over time, we pipe in a little more auditory input, to let your new brain adjust. Clients have reported a crispness to those first few hours. What we don't realize as humans is how, over time, our bodies are simply diminishing. We accept it because it happens over such a long scale, but now we'll be resetting you back to prime. You're going to be amazed by how much you were missing."

Sepi sat up, marveled at how quickly her body moved. No straining, no blood rushing to fill pinched veins. She put her feet on the floor, felt the thick rug between her toes. She stood and her connection to the floor seemed magnetic, as if nothing could put her off balance.

Between the slatted windows hung a long mirror bordered in distressed, white wood. Sepi approached it, stared at her reflection, at the paper gown that reached down to the tops of her thighs.

This is who I am.

She could see only a few minor differences between her human self and the new synthetic version. The skin was clearer, the eyes a little brighter, and the long, black hair had a brilliant luster to it.

Thin fingers reached for the collar of the gown and pulled it off. Sepi brought both hands to her shoulders, explored the nooks, traced over the synthetic bones. She touched her chest, tested the shape of her breasts, and smoothed out the skin on her stomach. Her fingers paused at the border of her slight pubic hair as a knock sounded from behind her.

The door opened a crack, and Wayne stuck his head in.

"How are we doing, Ms. Ahmadi?" he asked, sotto voce.

"Admiring your work," she replied, flinching at the unnaturally high timbre of her own voice.

Her nudity didn't appear to concern him. Wayne stepped inside and shut the door.

"Now you understand where the money goes. Twenty years ago, when something like this was only starting to become possible, the costs were well out of reach for everyone except half a dozen billionaires. It's still pricey today because there's only so much cost-cutting you can do. That right there is a top-of-the-line synthetic body that'll carry you through the next few centuries without a hiccup. And if anything were to go wrong, you have a lifetime warranty with Vitra Synth that reverts back to Perion Synthetics should our company ever go under."

Sepi nodded, turned back to the mirror.

"How are you feeling otherwise?"

"Muted," she replied. She saw his face scrunch and relax behind her.

"Huh," he said, "that's an interesting way to describe it. You don't feel the crispness? The intensity?"

Sepi tapped on the mirror, felt the sensation ride the nail into her finger, hand, and arm.

"Not like before. I felt everything before. Noises. Movement. Things like that. Now it's like I'm missing something."

Wayne took a step forward; his eyes went to her feet and came back up.

"Perhaps you're just missing your better half."

"Maybe," said Sepi, smiling. She thought of Nat, how she would look with her health restored. She put her hands to her breasts as her nipples stiffened.

Wayne chuckled. "It's like learning your body all over again. You can expect some knee-jerk reactions like that for the first few weeks or so. After that, your brain will adjust to how little work it has to do to elicit a response."

"How is Natasha?"

"The transfer went well. Earl is finishing up with her now. We'll bring her in shortly." He motioned to the box on the chaise. "We put your clothes in here, but I'd advise against bright colors until your wife has had some time to adjust. There are cotton robes in the cubbies over there if you'd like to put something on."

Sepi followed his gaze to the corner of the room where plush fabric hung over the lips of small, square cubes.

"I need to step away for a few minutes," said Wayne, "but if you need me, your new sleeve is equipped with MESH technology. Just send me a message."

"I've never used the MESH."

"It's pretty easy. I'll send you home with some literature." He gave her a reassuring nod and left the room.

Sepi looked herself over again, marveled at the realistic skin and the subtle muscles below it. They'd even transferred over the slight birthmark on the front of her left knee.

The robe she pulled on was warm and enveloping; she felt the soft cotton on every part of her body. The tingling sensation it produced forced her to sit on a nearby chaise. When the feeling finally subsided, the afterglow stayed with her for several minutes. Sepi found that just by thinking about the feeling, she could recall it with perfect clarity and send her body into a tizzy over and over again.

She was still thinking about it when another knock came from the door. This time, it was Earl who opened it. He rolled in a chrome gurney on which Nat reclined, stoically, as if etherized. Following him was another tech Sepi didn't recognize, but realized soon enough that he was there to lift Nat from the gurney to the chaise lounge.

"She just needs a few minutes," mumbled Earl. He sighed, stretched his back, and left the room.

Sepi thanked the tech for his help, but he wouldn't meet her eyes. She joined Nat on the chaise, placed a hand on her leg, and began to caress it.

"And I'll be dancing in the rain with you, my love," she sang, struggling to find her whisper voice.

Nat stirred; her eyes fluttered.

"Hey, sweetie," said Sepi. "Can you hear me?"

"Sepideh," said Nat, though for one horrible second, her voice modulated into something unrecognizable. She opened her eyes and immediately began to cry.

"What's wrong?" asked Sepi, scooting closer. She tried to touch Nat's face, but was rebuked.

"I can't believe you did this," said Nat. "You should have let me die."

Sepi gasped a hollow, empty sound. "How can you say that? *Why* would you say that?"

"I'd made my peace," said Nat, shaking her head and looking away. "I was ready to go. I *asked* you to let me go. And you brought me here. It's like what I want doesn't even matter to you. I'm still invisible to you."

A knife sliced Sepi's synthetic heart in half. On one side, it ached for the pain Nat must have been feeling. Throughout their relationship, Sepi had worked to cultivate empathy for the woman she loved, and despite their occasional arguments, had always come to see Nat's point of view, even if she didn't agree with it. To not be seen, to feel disregarded, must have made Nat feel like the absolute worst. It was a fate Sepi didn't wish on anyone.

The other side of Sepi's heart, however, balked at the ungratefulness of a woman who was supposed to love her. Sure, she'd heard Nat say she was ready to die, but what did that really mean coming from a dying woman who was not of "sound mind and body?" How was Sepi supposed to simply give up that which she treasured over everything? She'd spent millions, traded away her own humanity, and granted Nat another chance at life.

In what reality did that mean Sepi didn't recognize Nat or not hold her in the highest regard?

Sepi put her hands in her lap, turned to face the windows. The motes were now invisible, having lost their backlight.

"I'm not sorry I saved you," she said. "Even if you hate me now and forever, at least you're alive to do so. You're the only part of my life that matters. I would do anything for you."

"Except give me what I wanted."

"If what you wanted was to die, then yes, I would give you anything except let you die. Not when I can prevent it."

"You're selfish."

Sepi wiped her eyes. "I'm in love."

The music in the ceiling shifted to something more orchestral. The shrill whine of a violin filled the room.

Sepi forced herself to think of the possibility of a life without Nat. What if she had just let her die? Could she have really lived without her? Even with augmented reality, Sepi's looks would have eventually faded. She was a good actress, but talent had been losing out to young and sexy for the last thirty years. She would have eventually made the switch to synthetic just to maintain a marketable appearance. And then, with Nat gone, she'd be forced to live out the rest of eternity alone, with no hope of recovering the one part of her life that made her feel human.

A hundred years from now, she'd look back on the moment and decide she should have saved Nat's life when she had the chance.

Sepi was sure of that.

"Do you hate me?" she asked.

The pause lasted forever.

"No," said Nat. "I would have done the same for you. I would have been stubborn too."

"You should see yourself, Natasha Kumanov. You're so beautiful."

Nat covered her face, cried softly.

Minutes passed. Ten. Twenty.

Finally, a knock. Wayne and Earl stepped inside.

"Everything alright?" asked Wayne.

"We're fine," said Sepi.

"We've got a car waiting for you downstairs," said Earl, glancing at his sliver. "If you'd like to get dressed, I can walk you out."

"May we have some more time?" asked Sepi.

"Take all the time you need," said Wayne, ushering Earl out of the room despite his protests.

"Let's go home," said Sepi.

Nat peeked between her fingers.

It was an opening, a small one, but Sepi took it. She leaned in and kissed Nat's new lips. Though they gave like they used to, even tasted the same, there was something missing.

Some layer of reality.

"It's like the first time I kissed you," said Nat.

"Yeah," said Sepideh, though for her it was more like a replay of a memory with the sound turned down.

No, that wasn't right.

It wasn't the memory that was lacking.

It was reality that was muted.

FORTY-ONE

"Hijo de puta!"

Raf pawed at the keypad on the inner bunker door, trying to steady his hand long enough to punch in the code. He knew Vida had stabbed him in the back, but he couldn't figure out why the pain kept crashing into him. It would subside for a moment, as if the nerve endings were gathering their collective breath, and then it would return as a massive squall of noise and crippling torment. With the barb still in his back, he knew he wasn't losing too much blood, but if he didn't find a place to sit down and get it out of him, he would soon pass out.

Finally, his shaky fingers hit the right sequence, and the electronic locks inside the door snapped open. He fell inward through a gust of warm air, stumbling into the coffee table. He heard Kagan screaming from the bedroom, and even though the lights were beginning the dim, he managed to make his way over to a wedged chair and pull it out of the small alcove formed by the two bedrooms and bathroom.

Kagan burst out of the room.

"Where is she?" he asked, barely pausing for an answer.

Raf raised a bloody finger, but Kagan was already through the bunker door and climbing the steps to the surface. His voice echoed down.

"Vida!"

With a groan, Raf tried to lower himself into the chair, but the barb was too long and caught on the seatback. He cursed, stood up, and decided to kneel on the cushion instead. As the strength left his legs, he angled himself towards one of the armrests and fell over it.

"Meat blanket maneuver complete," he muttered. "Awaiting further orders."

Raf slowed his breathing, focused on the pattern on the floor, on the intersecting lines of gray and black, on the specks of dirt and dust—anything but the pain.

Heat built in the back of his neck, and for the first time in six years, he felt his Avenging Angel come online. It fought back against the sensory overload, cutting off pathways until everything dulled into a minor ache. Raf felt his muscles relax, felt saliva drip from his mouth.

Then, nothing.

Then, Kagan shaking him awake.

"What the fuck happened to you?" he asked.

Raf spit, tried to speak. "Your girlfriend stabbed me."

"I see that. Does it hurt?"

"Of course it fucking hurts."

Kagan ran to the kitchen, threw open the cabinets, and pulled out all the medical supplies he could find. Raf watched him through half-open eyes. Kagan dumped the collection behind Raf.

"Take it out or leave it in?" he asked.

"Pinche maricón," said Raf.

Kagan laughed, but it was tight and brief. "I can get the barb out and dress the wound. That should hold you until I find Vida."

"Chale, K. I need a hospital. Now."

"You don't even know how bad—"

His words cut out as he took hold of the barb and pulled.

Raf screamed, cursed every god he could name. Through gritted teeth, he asked, "How bad?"

"Definitely a heavy flow day," said Kagan. "Looks like a single wound, inch in diameter. Barb went in about three inches. Dunno if it hit anything vital."

Raf squeezed the armrest. "You know who will know? A fucking doctor!"

"Do you think you can drive yourself?" He pressed something soft against Raf's back.

"You better be joking." Raf heard tape coming off a spool, felt it pull the skin on his back.

"The bird is out of the cage. The turtle's eaten through the box. If we don't find her before she makes it back to civilization, that's it for us."

Raf let Kagan pull him until he was kneeling again. Tape circled around him several times.

"If you don't get me to a hospital, that's it for me. Por vida, no para Vida, recuerdas?"

Kagan paused, his attention jumping to the bunker door for a moment. He studied Raf's eyes, as if looking at a friend whose face he didn't recognize.

"Well," he said, sighing, "if I'm going to jail, better to go with a friend. You can totally be my bitch."

Raf watched Kagan's face begin to melt. He was suddenly aware of how little he was aware of. The ocean of pain had calmed, and now there was nothing but sand between his toes, warm and comforting. He reached out for Kagan, who caught his arms.

"What did you do?"

A thin smile spread across his friend's face.

"What I had to do."

Raf raised an arm, tried to throw a punch, but it fell harmlessly between them.

"Jesus, Raf. It's just morphine, man, for the pain. We've got a hike to get back to the Land Rover. I sure as shit can't drag you if you pass out."

"Motherf—"

Kagan snaked his arm under Raf's and pulled him close. They walked to the bunker door and up the steps.

The weather outside had calmed to almost nothing; Kagan must have shut down the environmental systems when he got back from chasing Vida. Emergency lights shone down from the top of the Black Box, highlighting the gray, plastic sheeting that formed a canvas on which augmented reality showed an artificial sky. The last flakes of snow, caught up in the residual breeze, floated lazily through the trees.

When they finally reached the north entrance, hidden far behind the back of the bunker, Raf realized there would have been no way he could have made it without the morphine. For a terrible moment, he'd thought Kagan had poisoned him or was trying to kill him. Instead, he'd just been trying to save him some pain.

Raf looked over at Kagan, who smiled as he pushed the door open.

The sun was half gone, casting long shadows in the makeshift parking lot. There, Kagan's Land Rover sat next to the Jeep he had bought Raf so he could make trips into town. Beyond the cars sat a trailer that gave all appearances of being related to construction. If anyone were to look closely, however, they'd find a trapdoor that led down into a tunnel, which in turn led back to the observation room just above the bunker.

From that room, an occupant would have full view of every room in the Admiral, as well as control over electricity, water, temperature, ambient noise, and of course, the layer of augmented reality that covered most of the bunker's surfaces.

Raf had called the observation room home for most of the last month. It had been his job to keep an eye on Vida when Kagan couldn't or didn't feel like it.

Life in the room hadn't been too bad. There was a comfy cot in the corner, a bathroom that shared plumbing with the Admiral, and all the free entertainment he could handle.

He smiled, thinking of Vida in the shower and the way she would stand there absently, staring at the wall, hands perched on her breasts.

Kagan pulled the passenger door open and shoved Raf inside.

"Priya, find the nearest hospital," said Raf.

I've located a hospital in Billings, Montana. It is thirty-two minutes away with traffic. Would you like me to alert 911?

Kagan climbed into the SUV and growled, "No." Then to Raf, "I can do it in twenty."

Hungry wheels bit the dirt as Kagan put the Land Rover into reverse and gunned the engine. They accelerated backwards, came to an abrupt stop, and then shot forward down the road. It was dirt for at least two miles, and every bump and dip made Raf's back spasm. He arched to keep the wound off the seat.

"You good, soldier?" asked Kagan.

"Five by five, if you don't count the hole in my back."

Kagan laughed to himself. "She literally tore you a new asshole, didn't she?"

"You didn't tell me she was a fighter."

"I didn't know!" Kagan shook his head. "How do you know someone you've only seen in movies and interviews? I bet *she* didn't know she was a fighter. I guess if you push someone hard enough, they remember."

Tendrils of sickly pain spread throughout Raf's abdomen. His muscles contracted and released in rapid succession.

"So what's the plan?" he asked.

"Billings ER," said Kagan. "I'll drop you off and head back up here. Vida is alone and scared. She won't get very far."

"And when you find her?"

"I'll take care of it," said Kagan.

Raf leaned his head against the window. "What does that mean?"

"It means we stay out of prison."

"So you're just gonna kill her?"

Kagan nodded. "She's just a leftover, man. Even if I kill her, Sepideh Ahmadi is still alive."

Raf considered the nonsense for a moment but then understood the poorly packaged meaning. As far as the world was concerned, Vida had been cremated and her ashes sent to a disposal company. Her synthetic counterpart, Sepideh Ahmadi, was still out there in the world, living and quasi-breathing.

Vida simply didn't exist.

You couldn't kill something that didn't exist.

"Cold," said Raf.

"You want the heater?"

"Nombre, *you're* cold. I thought you loved her."

Kagan shook his head. "I told you we have a parasocial relationship. It's different."

The Land Rover transitioned to paved blacktop and accelerated through the pines. When it came out into verdant hillside, Kagan flipped down his sun visor.

The Kagan Ranch roads had wound back and forth through the terrain, but now that they were back on public lands, the road turned southerly, putting them just a half mile from the Admiral point to point.

Raf watched the grass scroll by, saw something moving in the low brush. He debated keeping his mouth shut, but the more he thought about it, the more he realized Vida couldn't be left alive. She didn't necessarily have to be killed—they could just take her back to the bunker—but she couldn't be allowed to return to civilization.

"Allá," he said.

Kagan let out a string of curses, and suddenly they were off-road.

Pain raced through Raf's nervous system, bombarding his Avenging Angel with more data than it could handle. Bits and pieces of the damage warnings made it through the digital gate, and Raf screamed.

"What the fuck?"

"I can get her," said Kagan, leaning over the steering wheel.

Through the windshield, Raf saw Vida running over rough terrain. She'd noticed the Land Rover and was heading straight down the mountain towards Billings.

"Dammit, K! Stop!" Raf put a hand on his back, felt fresh blood.

"I can get her," he repeated, over and over, even as the Land Rover pitched and yawed, striking bushes and rocks and small animals.

Raf could barely see anymore; the gray had pushed in from all sides.

A fallen tree launched the right side of the Land Rover into the air. The SUV jerked upwards, caught an outcropping of rock at the wrong angle, and began to roll.

Neither Raf nor Kagan had taken the time to buckle themselves in; their bodies bounced in the cabin like bricks thrown into a washing machine.

Kagan screamed, but it was lost under the sound of breaking glass.

The wrenching moment encompassed Raf completely. Just when it seemed the Land Rover would never stop rolling, a hand reached up from the gloom and stopped it on its hood.

The world went on for a time without him.

When he awoke, an intense burn had settled on the back of his neck. The Avenging Angel was hard at work, but there was far too much to keep up with. One of his legs felt numb, and an arm was either fractured or dislocated. Blood flowed down his face, which was pressed to the leather-lined roof.

"K?" he asked.

No answer.

Gritting his teeth, Raf lifted his head and looked around.

Kagan was nowhere to be found.

FORTY-TWO

Sepi put off going back to work as long as she could, but after a week of lounging around the house with Nat, Richard had begun filling up her phone with voicemails. He and the rest of the production team were already on location in the Dominican Republic, and they were ready to start shooting Kaili Zabora's Astoria scenes. Richard offered to let Sepi bring Nat to the nearby resort, but Nat had politely refused in a despondent way that made Sepi not want to leave her side.

Except that she'd already spent all the money the Sierra Brothers had paid her. Every last dime. The money had bought them new lives, but what kind of lives?

Nat did her best to force a smile now and then, but when she thought Sepi wasn't looking, her eyes dimmed, and her mouth turned down. Whether she wanted to admit it or not, Sepi was sure Nat was still upset about not being allowed to die. Sepi assumed it would just take time for her to come around and recognize the gift she'd been given.

Sepi didn't have the luxury of waiting alongside her.

Ten days after the procedure, Sepi was alone in the Dominican Republic, sitting on the beach and staring into the endless sea, wondering when things would go back to normal. Her co-stars did their best to keep her company, but Sepi found she had little in common with them, even though they were playing the two most important people in Kaili Zabora's life.

The only thing that saved her was the job. Playing Krazy Kai let her escape from her normal life, let her pour her anger and disappointment into a woman who was rage incarnate. Weeks rolled by, turned into a month. In that time, she saw Nat every few days, mostly in VNet where their avatars still resembled their much younger, human bodies. Nat seemed more comfortable there, as if the almost cartoonish virtual reality were preferable to her actual one.

By the end of March, their meetings had begun to dwindle. In April, they fell off completely, but not because of any rift between them.

It was a Tuesday evening, and the balmy air of the Caribbean flowed in through the open windows of the Riu Palace's dining hall. White curtains billowed. A mishmash of smells filled their air: spaghetti, steak, rice, and fresh fruit. Sepi sat with an empty plate in front of her and watched her human counterparts enjoy their buffet dinner.

Richard joined them twenty minutes after eight; it was the first time he'd ever been late to one of his own meetings, including informal meet-and-eats. Despite the long hours, Richard had taken too much sun in the past month, and even though the stars were already out, he still wore a large-brimmed hat, dark sunglasses, and blotches of white sunscreen on his nose and cheeks.

"Listen up," he said, raising a hand in the air. He waited for the noise to dim before continuing. "Just got off the phone, an actual land line, with the embassy in Santo Domingo. Things have gotten worse over there, and they may start clearing out any day now. So far, the unrest has been limited to the capital, but we're starting to feel the effects out here as well. You may have noticed your VNet connections stopped working this morning. It turns out all of the DR's network traffic runs through a central hub in Santo Domingo. Protesters torched it last night."

"What about sat-phones?" asked Sergey. He played one of the goons who kidnapped Kaili and haunted her dreams.

Richard nodded. "Sat-phones are still working, so we're not completely out of touch. They are overworked at the moment though. That's why I had to call the embassy on the land line. And obviously the MESH is working, but you won't be able to talk to anyone off-island."

Sepi put her hand in the air.

He acknowledged her with his eyebrows.

"Does this mean we're heading home?"

Richard smirked, said, "I know we all miss our families, but we're a three-hour drive from Santo Domingo, and the police force here in Punta Cana has assured me they are on high alert, especially after the large donation they just received from Sierra Brothers Productions. There is no immediate danger to us. Everybody got that? The HID don't have a problem with foreigners being in the country. They have a problem with the government. Shooting will resume tomorrow as scheduled, but we'll keep monitoring the situation and let you know if anything changes. Any other questions?"

Jaime Borrego asked, "Are we getting hazard pay?"

"No," said Richard, shaking his head. "In fact, most of your pay has been spent paying off hotel security, so... there's that."

Pockets of nervous laughter broke out, died.

"Alright, back to business as usual. Enjoy the rest of the evening. Tomorrow we're gonna hit it hard."

The actors resumed their meals, talking amongst themselves sarcastically about their impending deaths.

Sepi pushed her chair back and stood up.

"Are you coming out with us tonight?" asked Ever Jovovich. She was playing Anela Zabora, Kaili's older sister and impetus for Kai's vengeful journey. She looked so much like her mother, an actress Sepi had idolized since childhood.

Beside Ever, Malina Birch wiped her mouth and nodded vigorously. Her long, blonde hair bobbed around her shoulders. "You *have* to," she said. "Everyone is going. It wouldn't be the same without our star."

Sepi raised an eyebrow. "You're leaving the resort? Is that safe?"

She asked the question out of habit as she imagined all the horrible things that could happen just outside the resort's high walls. But, just as she had been noticing ever since the transfer, the accompanying physical reactions were missing. Normally, it was a black hole in her stomach that prompted such questions, but now her synthetic body did no such thing. The missing *layer* she had been struggling to understand had started to take shape, almost enough for her to put her finger on it.

"It's safe," said Ever, her hazel eyes sparkling. "The security crew is going to come with us anyway. And… of course… Jaime will be there."

"He's got it bad for you," said Malina. "I wish he had it bad for me."

Sepi fingered her wedding band in demonstration, to which Malina simply shrugged.

"If you don't go," said Ever, "then I'm going to have to watch Malina bat her eyes at him all night. And I don't want to do that. I want to go up to my room, change into something that barely constitutes clothes, and go dance with some sweaty Dominicans."

"Fine, I'll go. But I'm not rubbing up against sweaty anythings."

Malina clapped her hands and smiled.

"The bus will be here at ten," said Ever. "Meet you out front?"

"Yeah," said Sepi. "I'm gonna call home." She nodded to the girls and excused herself.

As she walked out of the dining room, she felt a collective gaze on her back. Sepi braced for the chills, the shortness of breath, but neither came. Instead, her synthetic heart just kept beating as normal. Her new brain, instead of feeding her images of women with the backs of their hands held to the sides of their mouths and men with their arms over each other's shoulders snickering and cracking jokes, delivered to her a patina of Caribbean life, complete with twinkling stars and salty water, all wrapped in the vague scent of spiced rum.

Sepi smiled to herself and turned right to take the stairs up to the third floor. There was an elevator, but the extra exercise didn't faze her much anymore. Her synthetic body's energy was endless. If she didn't consciously choose to sleep each night, her body could just keep going, keep dancing with the Dominican hardbodies until her power supply was exhausted, which according to Wayne at Vitra Synth, would be long after his grandchildren were dead and gone.

In her room, she plopped down on the king bed and reached for the phone. She asked the operator to patch the call through the communal bank of sat-phones. The phone rang twice, then nothing. She called back, tried again, but the call never went through.

Chalking it up to Richard's speech about the lines being jammed, Sepi went to the bathroom to freshen up. She'd been out on the beach all day, despite her skin hardly tanning anymore. It did sweat, however, so Sepi took a quick rinse in the cavernous shower. She toweled off, tried the phone. Brushed her hair, tried the phone. Dressed in a tight-fitting, pink dress that ended only a few inches below her crotch, tried the phone.

At five of nine, she slammed the phone down on the receiver and sighed. Sitting on the beach was one thing, but going out to a club without Nat just felt wrong.

"No," said Sepi, looking at herself in the mirror. "You just miss her."

And it was true. Their calls had become infrequent, suggesting for the first time that they might be able to live without each other. Sepi knew that wasn't true for herself; how could it be? She thought of Nat daily, thought of how much she wanted to be back home in bed with her. Ever, Malina, and even Jaime were fine friends who knew how to have a good time, but they were no replacement for the *lack* Sepi felt.

The bus is leaving soon, said Ever, through the MESH.

Coming down, said Sepi. She cast one last look at the phone, thought of trying another call. Perhaps later, when she returned, most people would be asleep, and the satellites wouldn't be as congested.

She left the room and skipped down the steps to the ground floor. The lobby bustled, filled with the excited chatter of American tourists psyching themselves up for a night on the Dominican town. Sepi didn't recognize anyone in the crowd, so she gave them a wide berth and moved towards the door. Outside, Ever stood by the bus holding the door open. Inside, the driver was yelling at her in Spanish.

"Hurry up, before this crazy guy kills us all," she said.

Sepi climbed onto the bus, saw it was packed, and headed down the aisle. Near the back, Malina waved a hand. When Sepi got to her row, she saw an empty seat next to Malina and one next to Jaime across the aisle.

She chose Malina.

The bus lurched forward as Ever stepped out of the aisle; Jaime and Sepi reached out for her just in time to keep her from falling. She cursed at the driver in Ukrainian and sat down. A smile replaced the flash of anger.

"So where are we going?" asked Sepi.

"Some dive," said Ever, adjusting her shirt. True to her word, she'd picked out a sheer, white top and wore nothing underneath. The points of a silver, glittery star barely obscured her nipples.

"It's not just some dive," said Jaime. "Coco Bongo has been the biggest attraction in Punta Cana for decades. They even moved their downtown to be closer to it."

"Sounds like a weird zoo," said Malina.

"It kinda is," said Jaime.

Ever gestured for quiet and leaned in towards Sepi. "It's just a little dance club. They put on a show. No big deal. We'll grab a quiet table in the back if that's more your style."

"Thanks," said Sepi, wondering if that was still her style.

The bus drove through the LED-lit highways of Punta Cana, surrounded by an endless sea of darkness. Tourism had brought so many changes to the area, mostly in transportation, and then mostly only between the resorts and Punta Cana International. Everywhere else, poverty still reigned, and electricity was a luxury most couldn't afford. Sepi felt the required amount of guilt about being ferried around in a comfortable private bus in a country whose residents mostly walked.

They turned off the highway, and Sepi got her first glimpse of the Coco Bongo monstrosity.

It stood three stories high and had enough red neon to put Vegas to shame. Spotlights whirled in drunken circles on the roof, illuminating stray clouds in the night sky. The bus pulled alongside a sprawling courtyard where eager revelers stood waiting to get inside. A line snaked from the doors of the club to a hundred yards back where the bus had stopped.

"So many people," said Sepi.

Ever reached across the aisle, grabbed Sepi's hand. "Just hold onto me, okay? I'll keep you safe."

Those hazel eyes.

So beautiful.

So endless.

FORTY-THREE

Kagan sat up in the rough grass and put a hand to his head. The world was blurry, the colors all wrong. For a moment, he thought there must be something wrong with his OcularAR contacts, that they were somehow skewing his reality. A green sky spread out in front of him while pink smoke billowed from the engine block of the Land Rover. The SUV was on its roof; clumps of grass and dirt filled its grill, clung to its bumper.

"Raf?" said Kagan, his voice hoarse.

When no response came from the SUV, he pitched forward onto his hands and knees. The ground felt gelatinous, as if at any moment he might sink through it to another world. He tasted blood, realized it was running down his face from a wound on his head.

The windows on the Land Rover had busted during the roll; shattered glass littered the approach path. Kagan tried to get to his feet, but the ache in his head prevented him. Each pause in his movement came as a surprise, as if his brain couldn't process what was happening.

"Raf!" he called again.

Sinking to his stomach, Kagan lay on the grass and stared into the open driver's side door. He could see Raf upside down, held in place by a leg pinned under the glove box. There was blood dripping from his short hair like a pipe with a slow leak.

Drip, drip, drip.

Orange blood oozed from his leg. Kagan kept blinking until the blood turned red again. He took a deep breath, let it out, and watched it billow in a puff of blue smoke.

Rafael Pancho Orozco was dead.

The wind carried the smell of gasoline.

Kagan pushed himself back onto his knees and looked around for Vida. The Land Rover had missed her completely. For all he knew, she was still running down the hill, bound for what she thought was safety from the mad men chasing her.

Raf gone.

Vida gone.

There was nothing left.

Kagan stood, stumbled, and began walking back up the slope towards the road. He cut across the asphalt, kept his path headed towards the Black Box, even though he couldn't see it through the tall pines. By the time he reached the tree line, the bleeding from his head had stopped. The throbbing subsided as well, and he became more aware of his body.

Colors returned to normal.

There were aches and pains he couldn't pinpoint, but he suspected a mirror would show bruises up and down his body. Not wearing a seat belt had been reckless, but trying to run down Vida had been sheer lunacy. He tried to retrace his exact thought process, tried to understand why his foot had floored the accelerator instead of hitting the brake, jumping out, and pursuing on foot.

It wasn't until he saw the Box peeking through the trees that he remembered.

Vida couldn't be allowed to live.

If she escaped, which seemed inevitable now, she would eventually lead the police right back to the bunker. He and Raf would go to prison for the rest of their lives despite the best efforts of the Kagan family lawyers.

Kagan followed the gray sheeting to the right, turned a corner, and headed for the small parking lot and trailer.

His only option was to bury the project. The day before bringing Vida to the bunker, he and Raf had spent hours rigging remote charges every twelve feet on the outer enclosure. Once triggered, they would separate the framing and fabric into small pieces that would simply disappear beneath the pines.

The trailer door beeped as Kagan entered the code. He yanked it open and stepped inside. The hatch took a while to figure out, even though he'd been going in and out of it regularly for the last month. Eventually he was able to climb down the steel ladder and stumble into the adjoining corridor. It went on for what felt like miles, always twisting slightly to the left. At its end, Kagan stepped through a curtain into the bunker's overwatch room.

Guidelights illuminated the floor, while vidscreens cast soft blue tones onto a single desk. Kagan sat down in the high-backed chair and woke the computer.

A grid of video feeds filled the screens, each showing a view of the bunker from inside. An empty living room, empty kitchen. A shower. Vida's bed.

Kagan pulled up a terminal; the cursor blinked on a new line. He struggled to remember the right commands. The harder he concentrated, the drowsier he became, until finally his head pitched forward, and he crumpled onto the desk, mashing the keyboard with his face. Plastic dug into his skin, but he merely closed his eyes, thought about Vida, and remembered their time together.

For years, Kagan had fantasized about a relationship with Sepideh Ahmadi. Though he felt a small amount of shame about his obsession, he also knew that no one else in the world really understood how he felt about her.

It had started with a few pictures on his desktop, then full-motion videos playing when the computer was idle. Whenever Kagan worked, whenever windows filled his screen, he'd catch glimpses of Sepideh behind them. The computer cycled through her photos every ten minutes, producing a random ear or mouth or eye in the gaps between his programs. Kagan would minimize every window just to stare.

They had a connection, whether or not anyone else acknowledged it. Kagan first thought the connection was between Sepideh and the photographer, but over time, that seemed less and less likely. Instead, Kagan believed she was looking back at him, gazing lovingly into his eyes the way he gazed into hers.

Then, the *I love yous* started. The first one happened by accident. He'd just sat down for work, and before his windows could load, the desktop background shifted to a medium shot of Sepi laying her head on the armrest of a red velvet sofa. She wasn't smiling, but her shoulders were bare and the look on her face was one of contentment and longing.

"I love you," Kagan had said to the screen.

Sepideh didn't reply, but did continue to stare. Over the next year or two, the interaction repeated. Kagan was often overcome by her beauty, whether in her expression or in the curves of her body. More *I love yous* came, mostly muttered under his breath.

Sometimes he imagined her moaning back at him, the way she might had she woken up in his bed after a night of vigorous sex.

Imagining a life with Sepideh was easy. He'd hired writers to get him started with his journal, but over the weeks, he'd found writing about a post-apocalyptic world to both scare and comfort Vida to be as easy as closing his eyes and imagining an ideal life. He'd invented a hundred different lives, possible outcomes of chance meetings and passing glances. He wanted to see himself in the role of Sepideh's savior, the man to whom she turned when the world flipped upside down.

And it had worked, for a while at least. It hadn't been easy; finding excuses to leave the bunker so he could rejoin the real world had become more difficult. The original idea of leaving every few days to scavenge for supplies had been made moot by the overstocking of the bunker. The staged Máquina attack and subsequent EMP ruse had given him plenty of reasons to venture outside, but by then, things had started to unravel.

He didn't even know why.

They'd taken every precaution.

The journal and its wild stories, the simulated weather, and more augmented reality than the demo room at Nixle Chronos. They'd reconciled everything, from the mural above Vida's bed to the bullet holes on Kagan's body. It should have reinforced the illusion, but somehow it hadn't been enough.

I just wanted to love you, thought Kagan.

"You wanted to *own* me," said a feminine voice.

Kagan bolted upright, looked around the room. It was empty; the only sound came from the small space heater running in the corner. He sighed, the echo of Vida's exotic Persian lilt still running circles around his heart.

The terminal showed a random sequence of characters; Kagan backspaced through them all. The cursor blinked.

 # the end -m 20

His finger hovered over the *ENTER* key.

It was useless.

Vida didn't know his full name, but it wouldn't be too hard to figure out that a man named Doyle had kept her captive in a bunker on land owned by Frank Kagan. Even if he destroyed everything, they would still find him eventually, or worse, they would come for his dad, who in turn, would probably hire a squad of Russian assassins to take Kagan out.

He pushed back from the desk, stood up.

On the wall by the door, a rack held a small arsenal of firearms: a few rifles, two shotguns, and a matched pair of silver 9mm Glocks. He pulled the handguns, put one in his waistband, and carried the other with him to the observation window. He looked down at Vida's room in the bunker, at the messy bed where they'd had their one perfect night.

He missed her.

The bunker missed her.

Kagan charged the Glock and made the long trip back to the surface.

Outside, night had fallen. He'd passed out for longer than he'd realized.

Raf's Jeep rumbled to life, its engine burbling with excitement. It took Kagan a minute to relearn the manual transmission, but soon he was flying down the bumpy roads again. He took advantage of the Jeep's high beams as well as the four ultra-LED spotlights mounted to the roll cage to keep his path lit.

Back on the main road, he pushed the Jeep to its limit, trying to speed through the memory of the crash. He passed the overturned Land Rover, but didn't stop to consider or imagine Raf. There would be time to deal with that grief later. For now, his one objective was somewhere further down the hill, stumbling alone through the wilderness, not sure of where she was or who she was.

After two switchbacks, Kagan slowed the Jeep to cruising speed and scanned the surrounding landscape. Vida might still be running, or be hiding, but the most direct path to sea level took her through the area. The Jeep slowed.

He thought of calling out to her, decided against it.

The road straightened out, pointed towards Park City, so Kagan made a u-turn and headed back towards the main highway. He was coming up on the right turn for Billings when he saw her.

She stood by the side of the road, one arm raised feebly to the night sky.

A steely hand closed its fingers around Kagan's chest. He struggled for breath as he turned on his hazard lights and eased the Jeep over to the shoulder.

Vida repositioned her hand to shield her eyes from the light. She ran to the passenger door.

"Please, please help me," she said.

Kagan had the Glock raised and trained before her eyes could adjust.

"Get in," he said.

Vida's mouth fell open.

He made a show of pulling back the Glock's hammer. "The Máquinas are coming, Vida. If they catch you, they'll torture you until you give up the Admiral. I can't let that happen. Get in or die here, now."

She shook her head minutely.

A flash in the rearview mirror got Kagan's attention. Vida saw it too.

"Now!"

Vida took a step backwards.

He looked between the mirror and Vida. "I swear to fucking God—"

She bolted, shifting to the rear of the Jeep and then off the road. Kagan climbed out and chased her a few feet into the brush but lost her in the darkness. He fired randomly, screaming.

The headlights bloomed into flashing reds and blues.

"They're coming for you, Vida! The Máquinas are coming! I can protect you!"

From the shadows, she screamed, "Fuck you!"

He fired in the direction of her voice until the clip was empty.

A siren ramped up.

Kagan jumped back into the Jeep, cut the lights, and sped off into the shadows.

As the wind whipped through the open cabin, he stifled his tears.

"Vida," he whispered, "I love you, you fucking bitch."

FORTY-FOUR

Vida hugged the earth as if it were tilting and she might fall off at any second. The smell of cold dirt filled her nostrils while loose branches from nearby brush poked her arms and legs. Her shoulder throbbed, but it was the only pain she felt. Despite describing himself as a crack shot in his journal, Doyle hadn't managed to score a single hit. Most of the bullets had pinged into the dirt ten or twenty yards away.

A wailing siren approached, and Doyle's Jeep roared in response, peeling out into the darkness. She waited until its engine had faded completely before lifting her head to take a clean breath.

The siren cut out, but in her periphery, Vida could see the flashing blues and reds tinting the tips of the surrounding brush. A door opened, closed.

Doyle's words ran through her mind.

The Máquinas are coming for you.

What if she had imagined the planes in the sky? Or the cars on the road? What if the Máquinas had stolen police cars and were using them to canvas the countryside for humans?

Vida looked towards the road, saw a silhouette moving through the grass. He had a man's build, with thick shoulders and large arms. She noticed his eyes right away: white pinpoints surrounded by a lattice of red LEDs.

She gasped.

It *was* a Máquina.

There were escape routes all around her, but Vida wasn't sure she could outrun a machine, even in the best of times. It would catch up to her, kill her, and then wear her flesh as a trophy.

She beat the dirt with her good arm, moaned quietly even though she wanted to scream. Nothing made sense. Since when did planes still fly overhead? Since when did Doyle have a Land Rover or a Jeep? What the hell was happening to the world?

"Is anyone out there?" asked a modulated voice. "Are you hurt?"

Vida froze, held her breath. The Máquina was closer now; she could hear its heavy footsteps in the dirt. She hadn't run in a straight line from the road, and yet the machine had come right to her, stood only ten feet away.

"My name is Deputy Roberts. I am with the Yellowstone County Sheriff's Office. I'm here to help."

Here to wear my skin, thought Vida.

The Máquina came closer, as if he could sense her thoughts. Vida watched his eyes scan the area around his feet, sweep out in all directions. Finally, the white pinpoints settled on her.

The breath she had been holding came rushing out, carrying with it an alarmed yelp. She flexed her legs and good arm, tried to push away.

"Please," said Roberts. "You don't have to be afraid."

"You're one of *them,*" said Vida, her voice trembling. "A Máquina."

"That's generally not a term we use for ourselves, Miss. I'm a Perion Synthetics Gantz-class Automated Guard, and I was built right here in the United States. More importantly, I'm here to help you."

Vida shook her head. "You're going to wear my skin!"

Roberts chuckled. "Miss, I assure you your skin would not fit on my chassis. Are you feeling alright? I've already requested medical assistance, but if you have any injuries, I'm well-versed in first aid."

"Stay away from me!" She pushed back again as Roberts approached.

He stopped short, spread his hands to the side.

"Alright," he said. "I won't come any closer, but I will stand here to ensure your safety until backup arrives." He looked towards the road. "Do you know who was shooting at you?"

Vida considered staying quiet. Telling the Máquina about the bunker would probably get Doyle killed.

"His name is Doyle. We've been waiting out the war in a bunker up on the mountain. I ran away this morning and he... he didn't want me to go. He says you Máquinas aren't safe to be around. There was another man too, who chased me, but I don't know his name."

Roberts crouched, put a knee in the dirt.

"Which war are you referring to? The current conflict in Iran?"

Vida sat up, pulled her legs under her. There was always a chance her strength might return, and she could make a run for it.

"The invasion," she said. "The Máquinas have taken over the U.S. from here to the Mississippi."

Roberts frowned. "Miss, there hasn't been an invasion. The MX threat is contained south of the Rio Grande. America is safe."

"I don't believe you."

"Miss, do you know who the current President is?"

"What does..." She paused, thought about the leaflet Doyle had shown her. "President Meyer, right? Or Fitz-Hume?"

"Not quite," he replied. "Do you know the current date?"

"I don't know exactly, but it's November 2045."

The deputy stood and cocked his head as if listening to someone whisper over his shoulder.

"The EMTs are almost here. Are you able to walk?"

"Do I have a choice?"

He smiled, held out his hand.

Vida put her fingers in his glove and felt her body lift off the ground. He led her gently by the inner arm, escorting her over the uneven terrain to the road. As they approached his truck and came under the glare of its spotlights, she glanced at his profile, saw he was light-skinned and clean shaven. Dark eyebrows sat over deep blue eyes that looked black in the harsh light. If he hadn't identified himself as a synthetic…

… virtually indistinguishable from humans. Only your lover will know for sure…

"Did you say something?" she asked.

Roberts glanced at her, shook his head. He opened the back door and pulled a blanket from a pouch on the back of the seat.

Despite being overdressed for the temperature, Vida accepted the blanket and pulled it tightly around her shoulders. She let Roberts lead her to the front passenger seat of his truck.

"Rest a moment," he said. "If you get cold, I can turn on the heater."

She thanked him, and Roberts smiled again—so lifelike, so human. He closed the door and walked out into the road. Vida tracked him through the driver's side mirror as he stepped to the rear of the truck. In the distance, a pinprick of yellow and red blinked on and off.

Vida settled into the seat, stared into the darkness through the windshield. The deputy's truck was cramped, packed full of small vidscreens and physical keyboards. She noticed a shotgun next to her elbow, wondered if it was loaded and whether it could take down a Máquina. More than looking authentic, the cabin felt like it was still in use, like everything still worked.

Why would the Máquinas need this antiquated equipment to communicate if they could speak telepathically?

She tapped a hanging keyboard and woke the vidscreen above it. The emblem of the Yellowstone County Sheriff's Department appeared, showing an eagle soaring over the edge of a cliff above a pristine stream. Beneath the logo, the screen read:

Terminal locked by Deputy 9338 Roberts.

Enter password:

Vida's eyes widened.

Last login: April 3, 2035.

She blinked, read it again. Before her brain could process the date, a flash of light drew her attention to the windshield. A pair of headlights had appeared in the oncoming lane; they grew larger by the second. She saw Roberts turn around in the mirror and come back to the front of the truck. He put a hand up to shield his eyes while the other went to the gun on his hip.

At first, Vida thought it might have been another traveler on the road, but the growl of the Jeep's engine had been burned into her memory. It sounded like a prehistoric animal leaping from its ambush spot deep in the jungle. She screamed out for Roberts, just loud and panicked enough for him to look away from the road for half a second.

The Jeep veered out of the oncoming lane and side-swiped the truck, first tearing through the side mirror and then through Roberts. Vida saw the deputy get thrown backwards. Glass exploded inside the cabin; Vida shielded her face with her arm, wrenching her shoulder.

She screamed. Metal howled.

The truck lurched sideways onto the shoulder, bit like it was going to roll over, but held its ground. It swayed back and forth on its suspension for several seconds before settling.

Tires screeched on the asphalt. Brake lights bathed the rearview mirror in a red hue.

Vida reached for the shotgun, tried to pull it free of its harness, but it wouldn't budge. She fumbled in the dark for some kind of release or clasp.

"Come on," she pleaded, yanking the barrel.

The shotgun came free just as the passenger door opened behind her. Rough hands clamped down on her shoulders, sending a bolt of pain down one arm. Her fingers lost their grip on the shotgun, and she fell backwards out of the truck. The impact knocked the breath from her lungs.

"Vida de me vida," said Doyle. He took a deep breath, belted into the night, "Me enamoré, la primera vez, que te vi…"

"No!"

He grabbed her right leg and dragged her through the dirt and chipped asphalt. Vida felt chunks of rock dig into her back.

"Let me go!"

Doyle replied with the same maniacal singing.

He yanked her onto the road, then bent down and grabbed her by the jacket. As he lifted her up, Vida struck him in the face, tearing her knuckles on his teeth.

Doyle grimaced, wiped his mouth, and slapped Vida back to the ground.

The sting took a lifetime to subside; it radiated from her cheek into her neck and shoulders. The cold road held her tight, and Vida suddenly wished she could just stay there, face-down in a heap. It wouldn't be the worst fate to die like this. At least she wouldn't have to go back to the bunker. At least she would never have to see Doyle again.

"We have a connection," said Doyle, his voice soft and close. "I loved you from the moment I first saw you, and that love grew with every minute we spent together. I saw the same love in your eyes when I told you about the leaflets. But I guess you were just pretending, weren't you? Just acting? You never loved me, Vida, even when you were fucking me, moaning my name like I meant something to you. *Daddy, daddy…*"

A memory clicked. A name rolled off her tongue.

"Natty," said Vida. "I was calling for Natty." She tried to connect the name to a face, but nothing came. Every time an image started to coalesce in her mind, she saw Peter's face. Was that his name? Natty? Nathanial?

"Of course you were," he said. "You're such an ungrateful bitch. I don't know what I ever saw in you. I should have let the Máquinas have you."

"Then just leave me here," said Vida, still reaching for the memory, now starting to cry. "Just let me die." She gasped as a powerful hand pushed her face into the asphalt.

"After all the money I've poured into you? After everything I've risked? You are *mine*, Vida. You don't have a place in this world anymore except by my side, in my bunker."

"You're a lunatic."

Doyle flipped her onto her back. His face was drenched in sweat and marked with dirt.

"Love makes us do crazy things," he said. "You're going to learn that tonight."

Doyle pulled back his fist and swung a wild hook directly at her chin. The sudden impact sent the world spinning into darkness.

FORTY-FIVE

When the four o'clock bell rang, Natasha looked up from her desk and noticed her entire classroom was staring at her. Prior to setting herself adrift in a rough sea of introspection, Nat had assigned them what she thought was a lengthy reading selection in their textbooks. Students of Dahlstrom Academy, however, were renowned for being quick readers, and at some point over the last fifty minutes, they had each, one by one, finished the reading, put their books away, and sat quietly with their hands folded on their desks.

Though the eight and nine-year-olds gave every indication of being synthetics—down to the dead-eye stare of an ornery paper towel dispenser—they were, in fact, as human as Nat used to be. Their behavior was not a limitation of their bodies, but rather a conditioning instilled in them from the age of four. They were attentive, shockingly intelligent, and completely antithetical to what children should have been.

Nat stood and smoothed out her dress.

"Thank you for your time today, class," said Nat.

"Thank you, Miss Natasha," said the students in unison.

They stood and filed out of the classroom like passengers deboarding a plane, each one taking care to let the person in front of them go first, each reserving their conversation until they had cleared the threshold of the hallway.

So orderly. So polite.

Like a well-oiled machine.

Nat sat down, pulled the chair closer to the desk, and put her face in her hands. She inhaled the faint lavender scent of her moisturizer, which she had been happy to discover still made a difference in the feel of her skin. She listened to her artificial breathing and tried to pick out shapes in the complete lack of visual input.

Little by little, the hallway conversations dimmed, and Nat was able to focus on the almost subsonic droning of her whisperer. She had never used one before, and after suffering its buzzing for a few days, had intended to go back to Vitra Synth to have them turn it off or rip it out of her ear. But then VFeed had learned about her and started feeding her stories she found interesting.

Trashy celebrity gossip became recently published papers on advancements in rapid-development pedagogy. Entertainment news, at first a wide net encompassing every actor and musician on the planet, narrowed its focus to one Sepideh Ahmadi and the new Kaili Zabora biopic she was rumored to be filming. That led to a discussion about *where* she was filming, which led VFeed to start peppering in stories about civil unrest in the Dominican Republic.

Nat listened to the reports of protesters taking out power stations in the capital city of Santo Domingo, and how that had subsequently knocked out the island nation's entire telecommunications infrastructure. The government— allegedly—was working hard to get everything back up and running.

None of this was news to Nat. Within a few hours of losing contact with the DR, the production company Sepi was working with had reached out to the American embassy. Word got back to the main offices in the U.S., and a cheery-voiced receptionist had made calls to the agents of every cast and crew member affected by the situation. That had led to a call from Jane who repeated several times that Sepi was in no danger, that at worst, Nat would just have to go a few days without speaking to her wife.

An ad for a synthetic Zoloft took over the feed; Nat lifted her head and focused on something else.

"Natasha?"

Sophia Dahlstrom stood in the doorway to the classroom, hands folded in front of her black skirt, dark twists of red hair hanging over the deep neckline of her white blouse. The diamond stars on her necklace (the same worn by all four Dahlstrom sisters) sparkled under the LED lights.

"Good afternoon," said Nat. She pushed back from the desk and stood.

Sophia ran the ontological wing of the Dahlstrom Academy, with a heavy focus on what made people tick. To keep her personal practice up, she saw clients one-on-one on occasion, catering exclusively to former students as well as the rich and powerful. Sepideh Ahmadi was hardly rich, but Sophia had turned out to be a fan of Sepi's work in *The Dark Desert*. The opportunity to look inside the mind of a woman whose profession required her to be other people was just too good to pass up.

"Sorry to interrupt," said Sophia. "You appeared to be in deep thought."

Nat nodded. "Just missing my better half." She sighed, looked away. "It's like we were only married a couple of weeks before she had to jet off to the Caribbean."

"I know the feeling," said Sophia. She smiled appreciatively. "Jonas and I were married on a Friday before a WHO conference in Lillyhammer. I was eight months pregnant, so they wouldn't let me fly. Then it was delays, delays—that big El Niño of '22, remember?"

"Vaguely, but then a lot of my memories are vague."

This admission made Sophia's eyes widen; she slunk into the room as if a secret meeting had been called.

"Really? My sisters and I have been wondering about that. Victoria, in particular, is fascinated with how your situation differs from her ReTreads. Will you tell me about it?"

"Sure," said Nat. "How about over coffee?"

Sophia cocked her head, puzzled. When she finally gestured to the door, Nat followed her out into the hall. They walked past the Summer lockers, reserved for their second-stage students, generally children between seven and ten, and turned a corner into the Winter wing, where pubescent boys and girls walked together holding hands at a respectable distance from each other.

There was no graffiti on the lockers, no decorations of any kind. Students spoke in hushed tones, subdued almost to the point of being lifeless, as they had been trained. Even those facing away from Nat made room for her in the hall as she approached, using a well-honed sixth sense that gave them complete awareness of the hall and everyone in it.

Outsiders might have been troubled by what those gigantic brains were thinking about in those tiny bodies, but not Nat. She knew they had bigger things to worry about than a synthetic teacher walking down the hall with one of the Academy's founders.

Double-doors parted automatically as they approached the east end of the building. A low porte-cochere opened into a sprawling plaza of manicured grass dotted with hundred-year-old transplanted redwoods and a variety of benches, chairs, and loungers. As the school day had just ended, many of these seats were taken by students who, now free of the Academy code by virtue of being outside, had reverted to normal children, laughing and talking as if they couldn't give Vinestead's Lassiter Intelligence Collective a run for its money in a game of Go.

Sophia waved to students who waved to her and then shared some anecdote with Nat about who the student was, how they were doing in classes, and how they viewed themselves as a sentient being.

They passed out of the plaza and into a private garden reserved for staff. A young boy noticed them and hurriedly made his way out.

"Fabrizio Pellicciotti," said Sophia. "His father is Presidente del Consiglio. Very wealthy family, not to mention nearly flawless genes."

"Cute kid," said Nat.

Sophia nodded, led Nat to a circular arrangement of benches in the center of the garden. They sat opposite each other as the water feature between them kept a marble statuette glistening.

"Yes, cute, but also troubled. He's at that stage where he's learned enough about the world and his place in it to start feeling the first pangs of existentialism. He has barely learned the word for it."

"Poor thing," said Nat. "I didn't learn that life was meaningless until much later. Kinda spoils his childhood, don't you think?"

Sophia shook her head. "A childhood exists regardless of its conditions. Every Dahlstrom student experiences a childhood outside of what normals would call typical. But let's not gloss over the fact that you thought life was meaningless. How old were you?"

"Sixteen, before I really knew what I was… *how* I was."

"That must have been difficult. Did your parents object?"

"No. They never said it was a bad thing, but they never said it was a good thing either, so I just didn't know. I was relieved afterwards, but every moment leading up to telling them was just confusion and anxiety. Like, maybe I wasn't even really part of this world."

A synthetic waiter approached with light footsteps. He greeted the women and offered to get them something to drink. Sophia ordered two lattes. She returned her gaze to Nat and waited.

"Like I didn't even exist."

Sophia smirked, wiped it away. "Sorry, I didn't mean to make a face. I just find it interesting the juxtaposition of you and Fabrizio. He doesn't see a reason to exist, and you don't think you do exist. When did logic prevail for you? When did you grow out of this feeling?"

Nat shook her head.

"You still feel this way?"

"Now more than ever." Nat looked around the garden; there were no other teachers or staff in sight.

"You can consider this a private session, if you'd like. I assure you nothing from this conversation will be repeated, to my sisters or Sepideh."

Nat shrugged. "I just can't shake the feeling that Natasha Kumanov died already, and that whatever I am is just… wrong." She dabbed the corner of her eye. "You see? It should feel weird to refer to myself in the third person, but it doesn't. I feel so separated from her, and from Sepi. From the world."

"Is it the memories? Do you not feel connected to who you were before?"

"In some ways. Same body, same voice. But the memories feel different, not exactly foggy, but…" She searched for the right words. "You know dreams…"

"I'm familiar with them."

"When I was human, I remember dreaming and feeling like I was participating in them. *Actively* participating. I felt the beaches, I smelled the burning rubber. I heard thunder booming—all of it. But ever since the switch, I feel like my dreams are just little movies being played to pacify me. I'm a spectator, not a participant. And just that small difference has changed my enjoyment of dreams completely."

"You don't like who you are now, do you?"

Nat nodded. "Sepi keeps telling me I'll get used to it, and I *should* believe her, but I don't."

"Why do you think that is?"

Nat had been studying the rocks at the foot of the fountain but now looked up to meet Sophia's gaze. She replied, "Because Sepi also died that day. Killed herself, actually. We both did. She used to be this wonderful mix of empathy and anxiety, so wonderfully, beautifully flawed."

"And now?"

"I don't know. It's like she doesn't need me anymore."

The waiter reappeared with the two steaming lattes. He handed one to each woman, produced a subtle bow, and retreated.

Nat sipped her drink. Sophia held hers in her lap.

"Do you still love her?"

"Which *her*?" asked Nat.

"Sepideh. The current one."

"Oh. Of course I do, in some way. Voluntary love is easy to maintain, but that chemical attraction that drew us together in the first place is gone."

"It's hard for you to see her humanity when you don't recognize your own."

Nat considered the idea.

Sophia cleared her throat. "This may sound like a strange question, and I apologize if I offend you, but hear me out."

"Okay…"

"Sepideh is standing in the middle of the road, wearing headphones so she can't hear anything. Behind her, an auto-driver has gone haywire and a truck is barreling down the street. You have no way to call out to her, but you can run and push her out of the way. However, if you do so, the impact will leave you in the path of the truck, and you will be killed. What do you do?"

Nat felt her eyes roll. "Are you asking me if I would die for her?"

"The urge to protect, to care for and nurture, is instinctual, and indicates a low-level form of love necessary for all successful relationships. Whether or not you would give your life for Sepi would give us insight as to whether that love still exists."

The latte was hot, but Nat was in no danger of burning herself. She took a long pull, felt a myriad of sensations flow over her tongue, none of them real.

"I would push her out of the way," she said at last.

Sophia smiled. "Then you do love her."

"No," said Nat, taking another pointless sip. "I would do it because I've already died, and you can't die twice." She looked away at the sun sizzling the tops of nearby trees. "No matter how much you may want to," she whispered.

FORTY-SIX

Sepi recalled a time when she struggled to keep up with the activity happening around her. Then, it had all been too overwhelming: tracking the blurry faces, watching for sudden movement, picking out scents amongst the jumble of cologne and perfume, and generally just feeling the vibe of a place, its warmth or coolness. Being unable to process all of this data simultaneously and efficiently had made Sepi anxious, which her brain then took as a sign of danger, which in turn, only made her struggle harder to make sense of the input.

In particularly bad cases, these moments turned into full-blown anxiety attacks, where even the simple, autonomic act of breathing became something to worry about.

As a synthetic, Sepi no longer had such limitations. Even as Ever led her by the elbow through a milling crowd to the back of the Coco Bongo line, Sepi was able to recognize, categorize, and prioritize every sight, smell, sound, and sensation. Her synthetic brain processed this information automatically, storing it for recall later. At first, Sepi dove into this data as if it were a pile of pillows, finding comfort in the way total situational awareness kept her safe.

Over time, she realized she had not asked for the data. There was no instinctual, physical reaction in her body that said *there is potential for danger here* and thus asked the brain to assess the situation.

Sepi had accepted the data out of habit, but now, she actively ignored it, even as they shuffled slowly through the plaza, passing drunk tourists and synth-hawking locals, listening to conversations that had nothing to do with them, hearing the low *thump-thump-thump* of a bass line coming from inside the club.

A waitress approached wearing a serving tray and little else. Lined up on the tray were neon glasses containing who-knew-what for only five dollars American.

Ever waved the waitress over and handed her a twenty. She passed out shots to Sepi, Jaime, and Malina.

"To Kaili Zabora!" she announced.

They raised their glasses to the clear night sky and drank.

Malina whooped, started bouncing up and down, her petite breasts threatening to rise over the low-cut, sparkling blue dress she was wearing.

Sepi felt a wave of warmth spread out from her stomach. Though the alcohol had no real effect on her synthetic physiology, the sensors in her stomach knew when it was present and adjusted accordingly.

As the line inched forward, they passed various art installations—reproductions, of course—from the DR's most prestigious artists. Sepi stared for a long time at what was ostensibly a tree, though it was made of bundled metal slats, bound tightly in the center and growing laxer towards the ends.

"How are you doing?" asked Ever.

Sepi nodded, said nothing.

They approached the final turn in the line and came upon a small stage with a garish Coco Bongo sign hanging above it. To the right, a frog stood upright, casually tipping his hat. To the left, a Dali-esque palm tree leaned and melted over the top of the sign. Flashing red, blue, and gold neons assaulted their eyes.

Ever pulled Sepi onto the stage, along with everyone else. They got a guy visiting from New York to take the picture. When he asked them to smile, Sepi inadvertently looked out over the line, saw it was even longer than when they'd arrived, and almost started to worry about whether everyone would fit inside.

Started to, out of habit.

Stopped, by force of will.

Ever nuzzled her cheek into Sepi's neck, and the man snapped the picture.

The line started to move faster, and they had to hurry off the stage to reclaim their spot. They followed a group of Venezuelans up a long, wooden ramp to a set of double-doors that had been wedged open. The music itself was still muted, but the bass poured from those doors like water from a bursting balloon.

Inside, the air grew more humid, and the luxurious personal space of the outside world transformed into a suffocating throng of sweaty bodies. Sepi felt men and women brush her from all sides. They didn't exactly push, not in any way she could characterize as aggressive, but the pressure was constant, as if the club owners were trying to utilize every inch of real estate.

Once they had their clutches inspected at a security checkpoint, they turned a corner and were hit with the full force of blaring oldies. The Black Eyed Peas' *Let's Get it Started* roared over the excited crowd who jumped and pumped their fists in the air as a nude dancer spun around a pole suspended from the ceiling.

Ever led the way into the crowd; they formed a train by holding hands. Sepi had Ever in front and Malina behind. Jaime had graciously volunteered to bring up the rear.

The crowd was surprisingly welcoming of their arrival. They parted as much as the space would allow, leaving a sliver of a pathway into the heart of the dance floor where a square bar supported a cadre of drunken women, each doing their best to steal the crowd's attention from the main show.

Halfway to the bar, Sepi bumped into a tall man with thick eyebrows hanging over beady eyes. He sported a traditional Sunnah beard and short, cropped hair.

Sepi smiled at him, tried to make an apology, but his face remained impassive. She couldn't keep his gaze, not with the way his eyes bored into her. He was still staring when Jaime bumped him to the side, redirecting his attention.

When they reached the bar, a security guard standing near a small set of steps pointed aggressively at Ever and then gestured to the dancing girls behind him. She refused, Sepi shook her head, but Malina didn't hesitate. Her black heels clicked along the wet bar as the song cross-faded into Flo Rida's *Low*.

"She's insane," screamed Ever.

Sepi watched Malina jump and gyrate, her long, blonde hair fanning out around her. When her face was obscured, Sepi was reminded of Nat and wished her wife still had a tenth of the lust for life that Malina had, that kind of fearless *come-what-may* attitude that led into one adventure after another.

Nat had changed so much, from vibrant human to dour synthetic.

Ever turned around and joined in the dancing, pulling Jaime over so the three of them could form a triumvirate of uncoordinated bodies. The people around them radiated heat, excitement, and desire, all of which made Sepi feel enclosed, trapped. Just as the feeling was becoming too much to bear, nozzles in the ceiling activated and freezing jets of air shot down into the crowd.

The world disappeared behind the fog, and Sepi reached out to Ever and Jaime. She found their stomachs, felt her way up their torsos, and took hold of their shoulders. They screamed, she screamed, and the three of them began jumping up and down.

Sepi bumped the people around her, spilled their drinks, but didn't give a damn.

All at once, the lights, music, and jets cut out. Panic built exponentially in the crowd over a matter of milliseconds until a spotlight cut through the darkness to illuminate a rhinestone-clad Elvis. He'd risen from the center of the bar on a small, circular pedestal and towered over both the girls on the bar and the rest of the crowd. A small pike behind him kept him from falling off as he shook his knees from side to side.

Amber floodlights exploded in the ceiling, strobing as *Hound Dog* reached a crescendo. A line of burlesque dancers shuffled along a walkway that had been lowered from the ceiling on the other side of the bar.

Sepi felt Ever grab her by the waist, her fingers digging into the flesh just above her hip bone. Ever pulled her gently in time with the music, and then another hand appeared on the opposite hip. Sepi closed her eyes, imagined Ever dancing behind her, close enough to smell, close enough to feel the fabric of her skirt rub against her legs.

The hands circled her stomach, rose slowly to flirt with the undersides of her breasts. Sepi took a breath, held it.

"Isn't this fun?" yelled Ever, her voice coming from the wrong direction.

Sepi realized the auburn up-do to her right was, in fact, Ever, and not some random girl who shared similar features.

But that meant…

Something stiff pressed into her backside. Sepi bucked away as if it were a hot poker.

"Hey, what the fuck is your problem?" asked Jaime, thrusting a hand into the chest of the Persian man.

He reacted by knocking Jaime's hand away and swinging a gold-laden haymaker. A ring worth more than Sepi's car clipped Jaime on the nose, flew off course, and connected with her soft cheek. Pain sensors went off the charts, informing her synthetic brain that something terrible had just happened.

Sepi, Jaime, and the Persian stood paralyzed, unblinking.

For most of her life, Sepideh Ahmadi had lived with the fear that people were out to get her, that they were judging her or wanted to do her harm. Walking down the street, shopping in malls, or getting money out of the ATM always provided opportunities to imagine what it would be like if she were attacked. She'd learned a thing or two doing stunt training later in life, but those early years had been bleak and stressful.

What if a man tried to grab her purse? Would she fight him? *Could* she fight him?

All of the collected anger and impotence of her adult life compressed into a single ball of fury in the pit of her stomach.

Her fist shot out, caught the Persian on the chin. Her hand opened, rotated, slipped around the left side of his neck, and closed. She pulled him forward and down while slipping her other arm under his armpit. Her knee came up, struck him in the nose, then again, and again.

Sepi's knee was comprised of RealSkin over fibrous tissue over artificial padding over a microlatticed magnesium alloy. Standard human bone and tissue stood no chance against it.

She pushed the Persian away; he fell backwards onto the floor, his hands held to his face, muffled howls blowing bubbles of blood between his fingers.

A heavy hand fell on Sepi's shoulder. She reacted by ducking and slipping to the left. At the same time, she shoved her elbow backwards, striking her assailant in the throat.

The security guard dry heaved, gulped—anything to get air to his lungs. More guards sprung out of the crowd and circled Sepi. They held up their hands palms-out as if she were a dangerous animal.

"Are you okay?" asked the guard directly in front of her.

"Yes," said Sepi, turning to face the guard she'd hit. "I'm sorry."

"Are you sure?

Sepi whipped around, asked, "What's wrong?"

Ever touched her lightly on the arm, squared her up. Her eyes didn't quite meet Sepi's. They drifted down and to the left. She touched Sepi on the cheek; her finger came back coated in a black-red mixture of blood and synthetic juices.

Sepi put a hand to her face, felt the flap of skin hanging loose. There was no real pain to speak of; she had to rely on the wide-eyed looks of bystanders, most of them with hands pressed to open mouths.

Their eyes burned holes into Sepi's chest. She felt the sparks ignite the gunpowder, felt the explosion ripple through her throat.

"What the fuck are you looking at?" she screamed.

No one in the crowd had a response.

"We should go," said Ever.

Cold tears sprung from Sepi's eyes, rolled over her cheek and around the open wound. Her head dipped.

Ever grabbed her hand, dragged her through the widening gap in the crowd. Jaime followed behind them, his hand on Malina's back.

Outside, the silence held for only a few minutes before the *thump-thump-thump* of the bass returned.

Sepi let Ever embrace her, let Jaime and Malina wrap their arms around the two of them.

"Sorry I ruined the night."

"Fuck that guy," said Jaime.

"I shouldn't have done that. It's not who I am."

"We love who you are, Sepi," said Ever.

Who's Sepi, she wanted to ask, but didn't, because the only person who really knew the answer was thousands of miles away, facing a synthetic life of her own.

Sepi shut her eyes, pulled an image of Nat leaning over the rail of the ferry that had taken them out to Alcatraz Island. Of all the trips they had made to various doctors, the stop in San Francisco had stood out above the rest. The other destinations were just that, places to go. But in San Francisco, they'd taken a break from the race to save Nat's life, and instead focused on enjoying what was left.

How beautiful Nat had looked that day, with the sun blazing behind her, creating a halo around her head, setting her hair on fire. The flaming strands cut across her ears, giving her elven features, made her look almost boyish.

"Do you need anything?" asked Malina.

"Natty," said Sepi. "I need Natty."

FORTY-SEVEN

Kagan wiped the sweat from his face as he tapped a steady beat on the Jeep's clutch.

The way the floodlights hit the forest made the trees look ominous, made shadows stand out like faces, each one turning to watch a man abduct a woman for the second time. Thin branches stretched out like spindly limbs, reaching for the Jeep as it tore through the loose dirt heading up the mountain.

As if they were saying *stop, think about what you're doing.*

So Kagan thought about it, glanced at an unconscious Vida slumped in the passenger seat, and shrugged his shoulders.

"She doesn't exist," he told the judgmental trees.

The way he saw it, Vida was a discard, a body thrown away by the very woman who used to inhabit it, the one who should have cared for it the most. She was a woman out of place in this world, an artifact that would have been burned to ash had he not saved her. In a way, he had given her the chance at another life, one where she wanted for nothing. She'd have food, shelter, entertainment, and a man who loved her dearly, who would fight a legion of synthetic soldiers just to keep her safe.

So maybe it was wrong to abduct a woman and keep her hostage, but Vida wasn't a woman, not in the legal sense. She was just a lingering echo. So why couldn't he take her and keep her?

Kagan switched hands on the steering wheel and let the Jeep cruise in fifth gear. With his other hand, he scratched the hair on his chin.

Part of him wanted to tell Vida what had really happened, mostly to see the look on her face but also so she would understand just how alone she really was. According to the United States government, Sepideh Ahmadi was alive and well, living as a registered synthetic in Los Angeles. As far as Kagan knew, there hadn't been any cases where the original human survived transcendence. Which side would even win that legal battle?

His phone rang as he steered through the last hairpin turn. Kagan switched the audio to his whisperer so he could hear over the Jeep's flapping exterior.

"What's up, K-diddly? You call me?"

"I did," said Kagan, doing his best to sound cheery. "I need you to redo a memory wipe."

Glasser sighed heavily. "What does he remember?"

"Not him," said Kagan, flashing on the image of the overturned Land Rover. "This is for Vi—Sepideh."

"Huh," said Glasser. He was eating something crunchy. "Well, you know, it's not an exact science. You have to expect *some* memories to return after a while. The brain is always finding new pathways around damage, so that's something you're just going to have to—"

"The erasure was fine." Kagan slowed the Jeep as the trees opened up. He pulled in next to the trailer and killed the engine. "She doesn't remember anything about her previous life."

"So then what's the problem, man?"

Kagan closed his eyes, clenched his teeth. "The *problem* is that I want her to forget the last month or so. I want to go back to that first moment where she woke up after we took her away. And, obviously, I won't be able to fly her back to Los Angeles to have this done. I'm going to need you to come up here."

There was silence on the other end. Glasser took a drink of something.

"That's not how it works, K-Mart. I'm a neuromechanical engineer who works in a lab. I don't make house calls. Do you really think there's some kind of device I can pack in a bag and take with me to… to wherever you are?"

"I have a hundred thousand friends who think it's possible."

"This isn't about money. The equipment is specialized, on loan from Perion Synthetics. It's about as mobile as the Plummer Tower."

Kagan slapped the steering wheel. "Are you shitting me, Glasser? Is there *no* way you can make this happen?"

"If that kind of technology existed—unlicensed and mobile—then you'd have people getting mind-wiped all over the planet. It would be anarchy. End-times type stuff."

"Fuck!" He hit the steering wheel again and again. "Fuck, fuck, fuck!"

On the other end of the line, Glasser let out a quiet chuckle.

"Is this funny to you?" asked Kagan. "Get this straight. If I can't roll Sepideh back to the way she was before, completely wiped of her memories, then I am uppercase-F fucked. If you don't find a way to do this remotely, we both go down hard."

Glasser continued to laugh. "Man, you are seriously messed up. I thought you were just a little off because your daddy is a one-percenter who never said no to you, which is still true, but now I see you're also certifiably deranged." He sighed. "Oh well, that's not your fault. You can't help what you are."

"I would choose my words very carefully right now," said Kagan.

"Yeah, yeah, yeah. I got your threat. Loud and clear, Captain Insane-o. I don't blame you; this is actually my fault. I chose to get involved with an entitled mental defective because it paid a shit-ton of money when I should have just kept working on my side projects so I could sell the next big thing to Vinestead. But no, you're right, this is more important. I'll start working on a remote wipe, but don't hold your breath. If anything, you might want to start learning how to relax your butthole. I have a feeling we're both going to end up in prison, and I don't care who your daddy is, I'm nobody's bottom bitch."

The line cut out, and the whisperer resumed breaking news about an MX incursion into Nogales, Arizona. Scores dead, twice as many injured. Máquinas responsible: three.

Kagan unbuckled his seat belt and got out of the Jeep. As he walked around the front, he noticed the open door of the trailer; blood was smeared on the doorjamb. His hand went to the holster on his hip. Weapon drawn, he approached the trailer, as if Jack might jump out of the box at any second.

No doubt whoever was inside had heard him pull up. With a quick glance around, Kagan confirmed there were no other cars; the intruder had arrived on foot.

The trailer was quiet and still, but the whirring of distant fans floated up from the trapdoor. Blood surrounded the opening, as if someone had crawled backwards along the floor to get on the ladder. Kagan climbed down, twice feeling something wet and sticky on the metal rungs. At the bottom, he flipped the safety off and aimed the gun down the tunnel.

Nothing.

Silence.

Kagan walked the length of the tunnel as fast as his tiptoes would allow. He used the barrel of the Glock to push through the curtains leading into the observation room.

"You fucking left me."

Kagan relaxed, lowered the gun. "Raf, thank god you're alive."

He was sitting in the chair at the desk, leaning to his left as if the room were tilting.

"Now you care? What about when I was unconscious and bleeding out? Look at my fucking arm, K." He made an effort to hold up his mangled arm, but it just flopped around below the elbow. "Do you know how much blood I lost? Or how fucking hard it is to make a tourniquet with only one arm?"

Kagan waved the question away. "You're an American soldier. Aren't you trained for this?"

"Is that a fucking joke, puto?" He groaned as he straightened up.

For the first time, Kagan noticed the gun in his lap.

"What's the big deal, compadre? You're alive. I'll take you down to Billings right now and see if the docs can patch you up. If not, we'll go to Umbra and get you a new arm, even better than that one."

"The big deal? You chose her over me!" Raf's face turned bright red as he screamed. "You think I don't know *why* you left me there to die? It was so you could chase after your fucking sex slave. It was supposed to be *you* and *me*, ese."

Kagan holstered the Glock and put up his hands. "Is this some kind of gay thing?" he asked, smiling.

"Fuck you!" Raf lifted the gun; it rattled in his outstretched arm. "Tu y yo, Delts por vida, para siempre. Or was that all bullshit?" He stood and stumbled forward. "Why did you pick me up that day? Why did you make me a part of your fucked up world?"

"Because you're my friend," said Kagan, implying with his curt delivery that Raf should have already known the answer.

"I'm your accomplice. I helped you kidnap a woman who did nothing wrong except be the object of your obsession. And you know what? The only reason I'm not putting a bullet in your brain right now is because she got away, and it's only a matter of time before the cops show up here. And when they do, you and I are going to be sitting right here, waiting for them."

Kagan huffed, put his hands in his pockets, and drifted to the wall of vidscreens. He jerked his head towards the feed from just outside the trailer.

"Well," he said, "if that's the only thing keeping you from killing me, I shouldn't tell you that Vida didn't get away. She's sitting in the passenger seat of your Jeep."

Raf narrowed his eyes.

"You see, Raf. I *had* to leave you there. I had to go after Vida. I knew you had enough training to keep yourself alive. I wanted to get you fixed in a regular hospital by a trained synthetic, not a prison doctor who's been keistering OxyContin for inmates. I got her, Raf. All I need to do is get her into the bunker, lock the door, and then we can go get you fixed up. She means nothing to me compared to you. Bitches come and go; amigos son para siempre."

"Para siempre o para Vida?" he asked, gesturing to the vidscreen with the gun. "It can't be both."

"What do you want me to do, man?" Kagan spread his hands plaintively. "Lock her in here and throw away the key? Jet us back to Los Angeles and turn my house into the ultimate bachelor pad? This is something I *want*, Raf. I need your help to make it happen. Somewhere down the line, there's going to be something you want, and I'm going to pour my father's fortune into making it happen. Claro?"

Raf lowered his arm, shifted his gaze to the floor.

For a minute, he said nothing, until finally a weathered groan escaped his lips. He shuffled back to the chair and sat down.

"It ends here, man," he said, placing the gun on the desk. "I don't know what kind of soldier I was." Raf turned and locked eyes with Kagan. "But I know we were better friends than this. If you're gonna choose your obsession over me, then yeah, maybe we shouldn't be friends anymore. I won't rat you out. I'll just go."

Kagan eyed the shotguns on the wall, knew they were all loaded and ready to fire. It would have been trivial to grab one and turn Raf's head into a pile of bloody mush. But that wouldn't be necessary. Kagan had given him too much, had plucked him out of destitution and set him on a new path. Raf was the perfect partner in crime: well-trained, physically imposing, and crafty. The idea of abducting Sepideh Ahmadi and convincing her the world had ended hadn't even crossed his mind when he found Raf living on the streets.

And yet he had stopped the car.

Now Raf wanted to know why.

Kagan wondered if it would break his hardened Mexican heart to hear the truth.

Raf wasn't in Kagan's circle of friends.

Raf was in Kagan's debt.

FORTY-EIGHT

Vida was unaware of the complex processes taking place in her brain as she lay slumped in the passenger seat of Doyle's Jeep. The entire mechanism of conscious thought had derailed down the side of a steep mountain, and the primal parts of her brain were in a panic trying to restore communication with distant synapses. Signals were routed, rerouted, and tried again, faster and in greater quantity than any synthetic mind could have hoped for.

The mission was simple: find a way to restore her natural state of consciousness.

As impulses spread over her gray matter, they touched ablated parts of her brain they had avoided in the past. The sudden influx of new inquiry was enough to needle through the damage and unlock memories Vida thought she had lost forever.

She saw her family clearly: Dad bald but sporting a massive mustache, and Mom, looking regal in a beautiful blue and gold sari. There was a white woman there too, with short blonde hair and middle-aged girth. She moved towards Vida in a nowhere space and smiled. Lights pricked from all directions, erasing the ethereal faces and replacing them with a dark hallway in a hotel or apartment building.

A door appeared, and as it swung open, Vida felt a familiarity that made her heart race. A blinding glow spilled out of the room, sending a slender, feminine figure into silhouette.

It hissed.

Vida snapped awake, her legs kicking out involuntarily, slamming her right knee into the glovebox. One hand pulled hard against metal, skimming a layer of flesh from her wrist. Her eyes focused; a handcuff and a steering wheel came into view. An emblem in the center of the wheel identified the vehicle as a Jeep.

She opened her mouth to speak, almost passed out from the pain. Her jaw buzzed as if she had swallowed a nest of bees. Flexing the muscles in her mouth made them all sting at once.

Darkness lay beyond the windshield, but the moon provided enough light for her to see a temporary building with an open door. Maybe ten or twenty yards beyond that, the world shimmered and rolled.

Her throat closed up.

It was the gray tarp structure, the one she had cut her way out of to escape. Doyle had brought her back to the bunker.

Vida's heart seized; pain radiated throughout her chest.

"Jeep," she said, trying to keep her jaw closed, "turn on."

The car remained dormant, as if it hadn't heard her.

She began to wonder, given its faded leather and cracked windshield, if the Jeep was a vintage gas-fueled machine that pre-dated auto-drive. It had no vidscreen for displaying speed and fuel and even lacked an ignition button. Instead, it had a chrome circle on the side of the steering column. There was no way to start the Jeep without a key.

Vida whimpered, looked up at the stars through the plastic sunroof. Against the backdrop of an infinite universe, she felt small and distant, as if the rest of the world was light years away. So much of her memory was still shrouded. She hardly knew who she was or even when she was, and it seemed Doyle wanted to keep it that way.

Why else would he bring her back? There obviously wasn't any war going on, so there was no reason for the two of them to stay in the bunker. He hadn't opened his arms to her for her protection; he'd done it so he could keep her. If she let him put her back in the bunker, the arrangement would be the same, except this time she would know she was a prisoner.

Vida clenched her teeth, winced.

"No," she said.

The stars twinkled, shook loose of their black backing, and fell, streaking across her field of view. Some dashed in straight lines while others circled lazily, growing bright as they turned their faces to her. All the while, these loose stars grew bigger.

It wasn't until the blue and red lights came into focus that Vida realized they weren't stars at all. She checked the flashing colors against her memory, passing first through shame, then authority, and finally settling on the police. She thought back to Deputy Roberts.

She imagined him bending unnaturally against the hood of Doyle's Jeep.

Maybe he wasn't a Máquina.

Of course Doyle had lied about everything.

That's why drones and helicopters filled the sky. They were looking for whomever had run down one of their own, and they wouldn't stop until that person was found. But how would they find them in the wilderness, with all the tall trees?

The small light inside the temporary building was hardly bright enough to cut through the canopy. And the gray structure had no lights at all, inside or out.

Light.

Vida reached for the Jeep's vidscreen, forgetting it had none. Instead, two plastic poles stuck out from either side of the steering column. She pulled them at random with her free hand, spraying the windshield with cleaner. Finally, she pulled the left stick towards her and flashed the high beams.

She sighed, tried to steady her breathing, and began tapping out a constant tempo.

The gray structure in front of her appeared and disappeared in fuzzy green afterimages.

Over the gentle rush of wind through the Jeep's cloth shell, she heard the distant whine of engines. A meandering white light broke off from its heading and started towards her. It got close enough to blind her with its spotlight.

Vida pushed the stick forward to leave the high beams burning. She struggled to contort her body without ripping more skin from her wrist, but soon she was in a position to put enough force on the Jeep emblem.

The horn blared, echoed through the trees. She didn't know if the helicopter would be able to hear it over the chattering of its own blades, but she had to try. Something in her heart told her this was it, that rescue had finally come, and the nightmare would soon be over.

She looked up into the spotlight, saw the silhouette again, and reached out to take its hand. Familiar fingers wrapped around hers. Vida imagined them, and more features followed, until she was staring into the eyes of a woman she had mistaken for a boy.

"Natasha," said Vida.

"Nope," said Doyle, ripping the Jeep's driver side door open. He punched her on the side of her head; the horn cut out.

Vida screamed as he pulled her from the Jeep. When her wrist caught on the handcuff, Doyle cursed and fished a brass key from his pocket. Once free, he threw her down on the dirt. She rolled a few times, came to rest next to the boots of another man.

He looked down at her, scowled. A pistol gleamed in his right hand.

"You just left her up here alone?" he asked.

"Shut up, Raf," said Doyle. He cut the lights on the Jeep and looked up at the circling helicopter.

"And now the law is here."

Doyle considered the aircraft, lifted his gun, and fired a dozen rounds. The helicopter broke off, took cover behind the trees.

"Problem solved," he said.

Vida scrambled to her feet and started to run but only got a few steps before she tripped over Raf's outstretched foot. She fell hard, putting her face into the dirt again. Looking over, she saw Raf pointing his gun at her. She realized he was the man who had tried to drag her back into the bunker, the same one she had stabbed in the back.

A drone made a low pass over the parking lot, close enough for Doyle to duck involuntarily.

Raf kept his eyes on Vida.

"Let's end this, K," said Raf. "Blow the Box and let's get the fuck out of here. We'll head south and spend the rest of our lives fucking Caribbean bitches on the beach."

Doyle smirked. "I *do* love Caribbean bitches."

Another drone skirted by. This time, Vida ducked, pushing her jaw into the ground. She stifled the scream.

"Please let me go," she said. "Just leave me here and go. No one has to die."

"Someone always dies," said Doyle.

A helicopter rose above the lip of the gray structure and zipped overhead. Vida saw men standing on the landing gear, leaning out over empty space like trapeze artists waiting for their turn to swing.

Doyle fired at it, got off only a few shots before his clip went empty.

"Fuck," he yelled, focusing on Vida. "All you had to do was stay in the fucking bunker!"

"They're coming," said Raf, motioning to the hovering helicopter some hundred yards away.

Doyle turned to face the darkened road, put his hands out to the side, and screamed, "Let them come!"

"You're insane," said Vida, the words slipping out before she could stop them.

"You keep saying that like it's going to change anything!" He stowed his gun and charged at her with arms outstretched. In one quick movement, he picked her up off the ground and slung her over his shoulder.

Vida beat him on the back with her fists.

"That's right, baby," he said. "You keep pounding away. I know how you love your foreplay." Doyle started towards the temporary building, but Raf held out an arm.

"We don't have time for this," he said.

"Well, I'm sure as hell not going to shoot her, and if you do it, I'm liable to shoot you in a moment of fire-hot passion. I'll be right back. Let me just put her away."

"Let me go," pleaded Vida. "Why are you doing this to me?"

"It's like I've told your pictures for the last five years, Vida. You're too beautiful to be left alive. Women like you can't exist in a world like this." He maneuvered down a short ladder into an underground room. "Everything in this world gets corrupted, even you. I thought I could preserve your honor, but I was wrong. You're too *you* for this to work out."

Vida watched the evercrete floor float by, tried to keep her bearings despite being upside down. Doyle carried her into a larger room; vidscreens and terminals dotted the walls. He used his foot to lift a metal grate and pushed it back against the wall.

"Going down," he said, dropping her into the hole he'd uncovered.

The drop was shorter than expected, and when Vida's feet hit the corrugated metal, she found her shoulders still level with the floor. Her arms splayed out, preventing Doyle from pushing her in.

He drew his gun again and pointed it lazily in her direction.

"Tell you what I'm going to do for you, Vida de mi vida. You can either climb down into that escape hatch and follow the green arrows back to the bunker, or I can put a bullet between your eyes and end the story right here."

Vida shook her head. "You said you couldn't shoot me."

"Yeah, but Raf is kinda forcing my hand here. It's you or him, and you're pretty much a lost cause. I failed you. I'm sorry about that. But at least now I get to start over, do it right."

His eyes narrowed, pushed into tiny slits by a monstrous smile. He laughed a little, surprising himself.

Vida sank down to her neck, but thinking about some other poor woman in her situation made her stop, look back up at a man she thought she had known, who had seemed so honest and protective.

"Please don't do this," she said.

"Come on, it's not so bad in the Admiral. She's a good ship."

"No, I mean, don't do this to another woman. Keep me hostage if you want, but don't bring someone else into it."

Doyle smirked. "I have no interest in anyone but you. And the *other* you."

"What?"

He opened his mouth to reply but got distracted by an explosion on the surface. The vidscreens on the wall went white.

"Law's here," he muttered. "Time to go."

He stepped forward and put his heel on her face.

Pain rippled through her jaw as she drew away, sinking down into the tunnel. When her head was clear, Doyle slammed the cover down. Metal scraped against metal as he locked it.

In the resulting darkness, Vida considered crying.

FORTY-NINE

Thunk.

Raf turned his head to what sounded like a distant boulder dropping into water. It wasn't until the whistling started ramping up that he realized what had just happened.

A metal cylinder dropped into the dirt next to him and rolled a few feet, giving Raf a clear view of its Swiss cheese exterior. His legs tensed, prepared to dive out of the way, but he was too slow. The flashbang exploded before he could even close his eyes, and the resulting light and sound sent him sprawling backwards. He lifted a foot as he fell and rotated his body to land on his good arm.

Something about the afterimage—the dull green on deep black—was familiar, but those memories had been torn out of him by Earl Glasser. Left in their place were damaged synapses, microscopic sections of gray matter that had been burned to a crisp. In normal life, there was no reason for electrical signals to travel down those pathways, let alone even try. But something about the flashbang evoked an instinctual response, and his brain immediately reached out to his memories of training.

Raf rolled as he hit the ground and came up on his feet. He took cover behind the Jeep's hood and yelled for Kagan. No response came from inside the trailer. Behind him, he heard the crunch of boots on the gravel road.

"This is Deputy Roberts of the Yellowstone County Sheriff's Department," said an amplified voice. "Throw down your weapons and put your hands in the air."

Raf sniffed the smoke around him, heard Captain Arnel's voice in his head. *That's war, son. Take a good whiff.*

The trailer was only a short distance away; he could cover that in just two seconds if he really hauled ass. From there, the underground tunnel would take him all the way to the bunker observation room and other exits. He could be out and running for the far end of the Box before the law even realized he was gone.

"Fuck that," said Raf. He was an Orozco, and Orozcos didn't run from a fight, especially against a synthetic force of unknown size and lethality.

Unlike the Máquinas in the MX, the Yellowstone County law men probably weren't aiming to kill him. There was advantage in that.

Raf dropped to the ground and put his stomach in the dirt. Under the Jeep, he saw five figures silhouetted by the glare of a spotlight. They walked methodically in a slow crouch, rifle scopes held to their faces. Red lasers shot out from their muzzles, crisscrossing the road as they swept the area.

Six bullets for five Máquinas.

That meant at least four headshots, which was nearly impossible for a revolver at this distance.

Raf smacked the dirt, looked over at the trailer, and called for Kagan again. Still nothing.

He was probably too busy raping and murdering Vida to care about what was happening on the surface. How that piece of shit had convinced him that taking a movie star hostage was a good idea, Raf had no clue. Did Raf really owe him that much? His life on the streets wasn't that bad. As far as the streets went, Hollywood was as good a place as any to be homeless. Mild summers, mild winters, and people with deep pockets walking by every day. The only thing Kagan had done was rid Raf of the memories of the war.

Memories that would have come in handy right fucking now.

Raf extended his arm under the Jeep, took aim at the middle synthetic, and squeezed off three shots. The first one missed, as did the third, but the second hit the synny in the leg, forcing it to a knee. The others took up defensive positions around him.

So much for headshots.

Raf emptied the remaining bullets into the sky, hoped idly they would fall back to earth and put him out of his misery.

"What the hell are you shooting at?"

A shadow appeared in the trailer doorway. It was Kagan. He held an AR-15 against his shoulder with one hand and carried another loosely in the other. Once he had Raf's attention, he tossed the rifle towards the Jeep.

"Where the fuck have you been?" asked Raf.

Kagan squeezed off a short burst, then retreated when the synnies answered with a volley of their own. Holes appeared in the trailer's pre-fab walls.

"Any day you wanna help me out," he yelled.

Raf pulled the AR-15 into position and aimed down the sights. Two of the synthetics had dropped to prone positions, but the others were still kneeling. Raf focused on the damaged synny and sent two rounds towards his head. The bullets pinged off its helmet. It threw its head back and fell.

"Nice shot," said Kagan, "but they've got gear."

"And what the fuck do we got?"

Kagan fired again, took cover. "I've got an idea," he said. "Does that help?"

Raf rolled onto his back, lifted his head towards Kagan to get a look at his face. The son of a bitch was grinning.

"Come on," said Kagan, waving. "Get over here. I'll cover you."

Raf rose to his knees, and the ground between the Jeep and the trailer began to dance. Divots appeared as dirt leaped into the air. A loud *thack-thack-thack* tore through the trailer wall; Kagan disappeared inside, diving backwards. As soon as the mini-hailstorm died down, Raf broke for the trailer. He felt tiny animals nip at his heels as he ran.

Kagan filled the doorway at the last second, couldn't get out of the way as Raf entered. They collided, spilled over each other, and landed near the hatch. Raf cursed as Kagan took hold of his broken arm.

Smoke filled the trailer.

Flames licked the rim of a plastic wastebasket nearby.

"You started a fire?" asked Raf.

"Tactical destruction," he replied.

"That's not a thing."

"It is today." Kagan nudged him towards the hatch.

Raf climbed onto the ladder and got halfway down before he jumped. Above, Kagan closed the metal hatch and locked the deadbolt. He joined Raf at the bottom of the ladder and smiled.

"That buys us a little time," he said.

Raf reached out, wrapped his fingers around Kagan's neck, and squeezed. His rifle clattered to the floor.

"Are you enjoying this, huh? Is this fun for you?"

Kagan gasped, replied, "They're just synnies, Raf. What's the big fucking deal? No human will ever go to the chair for damaging property."

Thunder rained down from above. Raf let go of Kagan and looked up. An imprint of a fist had appeared in the metal hatch.

"No fucking way," said Kagan.

Another fist. Then another.

"Move!" said Raf, pulling Kagan by the shoulder. They cleared the falling hatch by a fraction of an inch and ran through the subsequent dust cloud towards the long corridor. Behind them, Raf heard the plink of another flashbang landing at the foot of the ladder. He counted to three and then shut his eyes tight against the blast.

The concussion waves sent the liquid in his inner ear sloshing; they tumbled together to the left side of the corridor. Raf took the impact in his broken arm. He held his breath, watched Kagan continue to wobble forward.

When the dizziness cleared, Raf ran after him down the endless tunnel, watching the LED strips in the ceiling sway with each footfall. He passed Kagan, giving him a wide berth.

Raf cursed himself for dropping his rifle, but as he turned into the observation room, he remembered the rack of weapons on the wall. He pulled another AR-15, checked its magazine as best he could, and then pulled it into position. He was back at the corner with the rifle trained just as Kagan was stumbling in. Once he was clear, Raf opened fire.

The sound clawed at his eardrums, but Raf didn't care. There were Máquinas somewhere in that distant cloud of dust, and he wanted them all dead.

Shapes emerged, giving Raf a target to aim for. He chose his shots more carefully, loosing short bursts at the hulking figures.

The rifle clicked empty. Raf dropped the gun between his knees, ejected the mag, and tossed it aside.

"I'm out," he announced. When Kagan didn't respond, Raf turned and found him sitting at the desk, still holding his head. There was an emptiness in his eyes that Raf knew all too well. He'd seen it on the streets of Hollywood, in the eyes of the other vets who shared his operational theater.

"Hey," said Raf. "Get in the fight, soldier!"

"I'm not a soldier," replied Kagan. "You're a soldier. *You* get in the fight."

Raf ran to the rack, grabbed another magazine, and tried to slot it on the way back to the corridor.

The Avenging Angel sent out the alarm before Raf could even process what he was seeing.

A synthetic had just covered the entire length of the corridor in the time it took Raf to reload. It had lost its weapon or slung it over its back, leaving its arms free to swing like an Olympic sprinter's. Armored legs pumped soundlessly against the evercrete, the tips of its boots barely touching the ground.

The synthetic slammed into Raf, who didn't even get a single round off. They rolled to Kagan's feet, but he just stood and backed away.

Raf wrestled with the synthetic, but even with two good arms, it would have been a challenge.

"I am Deputy Roberts of the Yellowstone County Sheriff's Department, and I'm placing you under arrest."

"Pinche tu madre," said Raf, striking Roberts in the face with an open palm. It had no effect.

Roberts grabbed hold of both of Raf's arms and squeezed. The previously broken but subdermal bone tore through Raf's tricep and splintered. He tried to wrench away, but Roberts' grip was too tight.

"Stop resisting," said Roberts.

Raf lifted his legs one at a time, placing his feet against Roberts' chest. He flexed, pushed with everything the Avenging Angel could give him. He felt fingers slip on his right arm; the left had long since gone numb.

Pulses shot through damaged synapses, found alternate paths around burned memories. Repressed images of the MX came flooding back to him.

Are you gonna take that from a Máquina, private?

With a guttural cry, Raf kicked out.

Roberts lost his grip on Raf's left arm, allowing him to spin away towards Kagan and the desk. He caught sight of his friend's face, saw the eyes go wide, saw the blood splatter across his cheeks.

Raf turned back to Roberts, saw the synthetic was now holding half of a human arm.

Even Roberts looked surprised.

"K?" asked Raf, feeling an icy cold rush into his body. "Ayudame…"

FIFTY

Sepi leaned her head against the window, watched the dark streets of Punta Cana scroll by as the bus ferried them back to the resort. She barely heard the conversations taking place around her, which in a moment of introspection, struck her as odd. Long ago, her brain couldn't not keep track of everything being said within earshot. And now it was as if her brain didn't care at all.

Odd.

So many things were odd.

Ever laughed in response to something Jaime said. Even though Sepi wasn't actively listening, she found she could rewind the conversation and listen to it in real-time.

"I'm tired as hell," said Jaime.

"When I get back to the resort, I'm going straight to bed," said Ever, projecting to be heard over the excited hollering of drunk tourists.

Malina asked Jaime, "What did she say?"

"She said we should go skinny dipping when we get back to the resort."

"Cool," said Malina.

Sepi turned away from the window to see if Ever would correct Jaime's interpretation, but she simply laughed. She noticed Sepi staring.

"How are you feeling?" she asked. "Your cheek is looking better."

The bus driver had offered his first aid kit when they boarded, and with Ever and Malina's help, Sepi was able to get a bandage fashioned that ran from her chin to the top of her head. The right side of her face radiated heat; her self-healing RealSkin was hard at work trying to repair the damage.

Sepi replied with a few nods of her head and turned to the window again. She flashed on memories of the fight. How quickly she had moved. How hard she had been able to hit. The fight suggested a future in which she didn't have to be scared of anyone. She could walk down Ventura Boulevard with impunity, confident any bum or gangbanger who tried to hold her up would think twice after the first hit from her synthetic fist.

She squeezed her hand, felt the tendons slide over her knuckles.

Ever covered the fist with her hand, patted Sepi gently.

The bus turned off the main highway and started snaking through the outer resort roads. Sepi watched stray cars veer dangerously close to the bus, all without using their horns or brights. The hydraulics hissed as the coach pulled up to the resort and lowered itself.

They walked together through the candlelit lobby; night owls sat in small groups in the many chairs and couches while human waiters hurried back and forth with their drink orders. Ever nodded to the bar as they passed into the next room and asked if anyone wanted a drink.

Jaime made a face that meant *no mas*. Malina hid behind a thin smile and blushing cheeks.

"I'll take one," said Sepi. She felt Ever's gaze wash over her and became self-conscious of the bandage.

"Two Mama Juanas coming right up."

Sepi drifted to the stairs leading down to the courtyard. She caught sight of herself in a gold-framed mirror, saw the red-black stains on her bandage. Touching her cheek lightly, she sensed the heat had died down, and without really thinking, she tugged at the tape and gauze.

Jaime let out a low whistle.

The flap of skin had melded back onto her face, and the jagged lines in her flesh had softened into a light-gray mesh of cross-hatching. The flap itself was still red, still burning like a fireplace ember, but for the most part, the damage had been undone.

In less than thirty minutes.

Without a trip to the hospital.

Ever returned with the drinks and nodded approvingly at Sepi's unbandaged face. "Like it never happened," she said, taking Sepi by the arm.

Two circular staircases led down into an atrium, which opened to the resort's main plaza. It was empty now; chairs sat upside-down on small tables. The four of them walked quietly through the dim lights and tall palms, feeling more like patrons in a museum than guests at a party-all-night resort.

Sepi squeezed Ever's hand between her arm and body.

Gardens gave way to deserted swimming pools. Without their lights, the water seemed to go down forever into the murky shadows. They paused at the end of the decking, removing their shoes so they could feel the soft sand between their toes. The maintenance crew had neatly arranged the many lounge chairs on the beach, giving them a straight path to the slumbering ocean. Waves that had crashed and delighted earlier in the day now lapped gently at the shore.

The ocean stretched out in front of them, the many peaks of its waves shimmering under the full moonlight. Sepi focused on the horizon, on the meeting of heaven and earth, and wondered how this moment would have felt had she still been human. There was a breeze in the air, the water was cold, and down the seemingly infinite beach, there was nothing but darkness. So many things to feel and yet she could only think of Nat.

"So, how are we doing this?" asked Malina.

Beside her, Jaime shrugged and undid the buttons on his shirt. He tossed it aside, pushed his shorts and underwear down to his ankles, and then took off running and screaming into the water. He let out a howl as a wave crashed on his chest.

Malina turned her back to Ever. "Can you get my zipper?"

Ever had to use both hands to pull the zipper down from Malina's shoulder blades to the small of her back. Once done, Malina pushed the dress down and ran it to a nearby lounger.

"I knew she wasn't wearing any underwear," said Ever, leaning into Sepi conspiratorially.

Malina approached the water with her arms crossed over her breasts and tested the temperature with her toes.

Jaime whistled his approval.

"Like he's never seen her naked before," said Ever.

Sepi felt her take the inside of her arm again, lean into her. The contact warmed her. It was nice to have that electric sensation sparking her nervous system.

Ever downed the last of her drink and asked, "Shall we join them?"

Sepi wondered if Nat would disapprove.

"You're thinking too hard," said Ever, digging her empty glass into the sand. She pulled her t-shirt off in one smooth motion and tossed it into the air. She wiggled out of her tight jeans. Her red underwear was lined with sequins that caught the moonlight. She slipped them off and kicked them away with a dainty foot.

Sepi watched her walk slowly to the water.

What Nat didn't know wouldn't hurt her.

Sepi set her drink beside Ever's and took off her pink dress. Standing naked on the shore, the wind suddenly felt colder—the water, even more so. It took a few minutes of encouragement from Malina and Jaime to give Sepi the strength to wade into the water.

"Have you been swimming since you crossed over?" asked Ever.

"No," said Sepi, bending her knees to get her chest below the water. "I was never much of a swimmer before anyway."

"That's so wild," said Jaime. He swung his arms forward and started floating on his back.

Malina splashed water at him. "Put that thing away, you animal."

"Bring it closer?" He chased her through the water. The current drew them away.

At first, Sepi thought Malina was struggling against Jaime's advances, but soon she realized it was just a game. They embraced, kissed.

"Do you still love Natasha?" asked Ever.

Sepi nodded absently. "Of course. Why would you ask that?"

"No reason. I just always wondered if we could still love once we transitioned to a synthetic body. Everyone I've talked to say it's possible, but I have a hard time believing it." She leaned her head back, stared at the night sky. Small waves rolled over her breasts.

"I can still love," said Sepi. "I'm no different than anyone else."

"I didn't say you were." Ever brought her legs up, began to float. She reached out and grabbed Sepi's arm to steady herself. "I just worry about the stuff that doesn't transfer over. Did I tell you my dad is synthetic? He didn't really have a choice. Loves us just the same though."

"Neither did Nat." Sepi tested her buoyancy, decided to keep upright instead. "And I think she still loves me the same, but she's…" A moment went by where there was nothing but the sound of waves and the occasional giggle from Malina. "Neither of us are who we were before."

Finally saying the words out loud lifted an immense weight from Sepi's chest. She'd been struggling for so long to describe their new synthetic lives, and now she'd summed them up perfectly.

"I like this new you," said Ever. "Before, you were a little, I don't know, jumpy I guess. Mmm, like you were worried all the time. This new you is more relaxed and confident."

"Those are the last things I am." She looked away from Ever's profile. "I was flawed, but Nat loved me for those flaws. Now I'm *better* and she's depressed because she feels invisible and useless."

Ever swam up behind Sepi and put her hand on her shoulders.

"There you go," she said. "She doesn't feel needed because, well, maybe you don't need her anymore."

Sepi glared over her shoulder.

"I may be full of shit," said Ever, "but that's just what I'm seeing from this side. As humans, you two were perfect for each other. As synthetics…"

"So what?" asked Sepi, turning around. She fought to keep her tone even. "I should just accept my new synthetic life and be with someone else? Someone like you?"

Ever shrugged in response, sought out Sepi's hands beneath the water. "Is that so crazy?" she asked. "Two A-list actresses taking Hollywood by storm?"

Sepi felt a tug on her hands, and soon her palms were pressed against Ever's hips.

"I'm married."

Ever smirked. "You're swimming naked in the ocean off the coast of a foreign country, one big wave away from being in a bona fide foursome." She gestured with her head to Malina and Jaime, who had left the water for the stability of a lounger.

"No."

"Just…" Ever lifted Sepi's hands, placed them on her breasts. She pushed in closer, planted a soft kiss on Sepi's lips. Ever retreated slightly.

"This isn't me," said Sepi.

"It is now."

They kissed.

Warm hands roamed Sepi's body as waves rose and fell around them.

Ever laughed. "I never thought I'd make out with a machine."

Sepi turned away, looked towards the beach at a shadowy Malina sitting tall atop Jaime, her shoulder blades catching the moonlight. "Where are the aggregators when you need them? They'd make a fortune off her."

"And the Sierra Brothers know it too," said Ever. "I heard Lawrence brought her in just to have an excuse to show more skin. She's doing her own nudity, did you know that?"

Sepi shook her head.

"She's a sweet girl," said Ever, "and I love her, but she really needs to stand up to Lawrence. That little perv would have us doing the entire movie naked if he had his way."

"Imagine if he were here."

"Then *we* wouldn't be," said Ever. "I'd have draped a towel over you and carried you up to my room."

"I would crush you. I should be the one carrying you."

Ever slipped an arm around Sepi's waist. "You can, if you want."

Sepi paused, considered the invitation. There was something off about Ever, in the way she looked at her. Sepi had seen that look before, on the streets of Hollywood, whether it was from a deranged fan or a clueless big shot. It wasn't the kind of look that said *hey, I'd really like to get to know you better.*

"You want to be with me?"

Ever leaned in. "I want to fuck you. I know that much."

A wave pushed them apart momentarily; Sepi used the opportunity to escape Ever's grasp.

"This isn't right," she said, turning for the shore.

"Right, wrong. Good, bad. Those are human concepts. You're a synthetic goddess now, Sepideh!"

Sepi groaned, continued forward. The wind blew across her skin, sending shivers down her body.

"Hey," said Ever, chasing after her, "what's wrong?"

Sepi faced her. "I don't know who you think I am, but I love my wife. And whatever relationship we have together, no matter how hard it is or how much it might suck right now, it's *ours*. You think just because I'm a little down that I'm going to jump into bed with you? Like I'm the kind of woman who spreads her legs for a little sweet talk?"

"I…" Ever's mouth hung open, unable to speak. She stood shivering in the ankle-deep water.

"You're no different than all of these other assholes. You see something you want and you think you're entitled to it, like I have no say in who I date or who I spend my time with. I don't owe you people *anything*. None of you even compare to Natasha." Sepi's eyes moistened. "I thought you were my friend, Ever, but you… you…"

Sepi clenched her fists and screamed.

"This is different," said Ever, taking a step forward.

"No," said Sepi, putting her hand up. "Don't come any closer. You get near me again, and I will fucking break you." She scooped up her clothes and hurried past Malina and Jaime, who had stopped to watch the commotion.

They both drew back as she went by.

Her feet dug into the sand, faster and faster, until she was sprinting past the pools and gardens.

Tears streamed down her face.

This is not my life, she thought.

This is not who I am.

FIFTY-ONE

Blood trickled down Kagan's face.

He spit as it spilled over his lips.

Arm amputations were nothing new to him, but they were usually viewed from behind the protective barrier of the silver screen. Movies, with their campy special effects and poorly animated blood spurts, had not prepared him for what it would look like in person. More to the point, movies had not prepared him for what it would *sound* like when a synthetic ripped the arm from a human.

The crunching. The snapping.

Raf's upper arm looked like the business end of a meat grinder.

Kagan stifled the urge to throw up, mostly because the synthetic deputy was now looking in his direction as if to ask *you next?* Shaky hands shot into the air as Kagan considered the unspoken threat.

Deputy Roberts cocked his head to the side, and the MESH crackled with his message.

One suspect subdued. Clear to move in.

Raf writhed on the floor, clutching his shoulder. Roberts pulled cuffs from his belt and bent for Raf's wrist.

Kagan took a step towards the desk and reached out with three hooked fingers to hit the *ENTER* key. The self-destruct command executed, causing the screen to scroll erratically. Beyond the walls, environmental systems dumped as much wind and snow into the Box as they could. The light strips in the ceiling strobed white and red.

Vidscreens blanked, refreshed with green text on black—a timer counting down.

Back when he'd planned the self-destruct sequence, twenty minutes had seemed like plenty of time to clear the area. But then, he'd imagined running the command, climbing back to the surface, and driving away in the Land Rover. By the time things hit critical mass and explosions started rocking the mountain, he would be just outside of Billings.

Now, with the tunnel leading back to the trailer blocked by incoming synthetics, his only choice was to escape through the bunker itself. That meant getting down into the Admiral, leaving by way of the front door, and navigating weather and wilderness to the border of the Box *on foot* in less than nineteen minutes and fifty-two seconds.

He thought about the hatch, visualized the deadbolts he'd engaged after stuffing Vida inside. There wouldn't be enough time to get them loose before the synthetic was on him.

Kagan bolted to the left, took a running leap at the observation window over Vida's room, and crashed through the mural. His elbows closed in front of his face just before impact, saving him from the larger shards of glass.

He fell eight feet to Vida's bed, hit the edge, and rolled off, smacking his head against the evercrete floor. Stars exploded in his eyes, but he didn't risk rubbing them. Glass was everywhere: on the ground, in his arms, in his fingers. He stood and pulled the bedroom door open.

"Vida?" he barked, receiving only an echo in reply.

Kagan stepped around the armchair and surveyed the living room. The bunker door was open, and beyond it, he could hear the banshee cry of gale-force winds shooting down the stairwell.

They'd never closed the door after taking off after Vida.

He'd forgotten, and the price for his lapse in concentration was Vida being able to walk right out. Forget escape; he'd practically laid out the carpet for her.

"You're not out yet," he muttered.

Kagan tried to build a barricade against the bedroom door by stacking furniture, but he knew it wouldn't hold for long. If he was lucky, it would slow down the law just enough for him to catch up to Vida and choke the life from her body.

He moved to the kitchen and hesitantly opened the first drawer. Inside, he found a foam mold containing absolutely nothing. The two inserts that were supposed to house spare clips for a Sig P226 were empty, as was the larger cut-out for the Sig itself. He almost laughed.

So Vida was armed. Truly armed this time. The woman who had only fired a gun in the movies was now running around with a fully loaded Sig Sauer.

What had the world come to?

He ran to the cabinet next to the fridge, tore open the doors, and cleared the shelves of its rations. Canned goods thunked on the floor and rolled every direction. His fingers cried out as tiny needles of glass pushed deeper into his skin. Finally, he found the gun case and pulled it down onto the counter. The Desert Eagle inside gleamed under the flashing LED lights, bouncing back the white and red with its perfect luster.

Kagan frowned.

It wasn't the ideal gun for the situation—not that Desert Eagles even had ideal situations—but it was one of only two weapons in the bunker that had live rounds in them. The rifle in his bedroom wasn't even loaded. The oversized Eagle wouldn't fit in the holster on his hip, so he engaged the safety and shoved it down the back of his pants.

A crash sounded from Vida's bedroom. He imagined Deputy Roberts jumping down and crushing her bed. A second later, the barricade began to shake.

Kagan ran, slipping through the open bunker door, up the stairs, and out into the worst snowstorm man had ever concocted. The environmental generators were running full-out and had filled the Box with enough snow to cover Billings twice.

He squinted against the wind's sharp claws, saw a fresh set of tracks in the snow. Getting across the clearing took longer than Kagan had hoped. Lingering pain in his back, arms, and legs had made trudging through the snow an Olympic event. Even the world's greatest athletes would have had trouble keeping their breath in these conditions.

The wind lessened among the trees, but above, Kagan heard branches straining and breaking under the weight of accumulated snow. He fought the urge to call out to Vida, didn't want her to know he was coming.

There would be no conversation this time. Either he would get close enough to strangle her with his own two hands, or he'd take her down from a distance. No pleading with her, no monologues, just an end to another unfulfilling chapter in his life. He wouldn't even have to bother with burying her; the crumbling Black Box would do that for him.

Minutes ticked by, and Kagan began to doubt whether he would find her in the snowstorm. She *was* his primary mission, but there was also the matter of his own escape. Killing her wouldn't have the same appeal if he died moments after, speared through the heart by falling scaffolding.

The footprints followed a straight line. Vida wasn't taking any chances either; she had chosen the most direct path away from the bunker, somehow knowing she only had to get to the outer wall of the Box to rejoin the real world.

A gunshot rang out, close enough to make Kagan duck. Another followed.

He couldn't see anyone in the distance, and there'd been no corresponding impact anywhere around him.

It hit him: Vida was shooting her way out.

Kagan's lungs burned as his feet hammered into the snow. He wasn't going to let her get away—couldn't. She would be the end of Vitra Synth, meaning Dad would lose every cent he and his cohorts had invested. Frank Kagan didn't care much about his son fucking up, but when it came to money, green cash was more important than red blood. Even with everything that had happened, there was still a chance Frank would bail his son out, send the best lawyers to his defense.

But if he lost the old man money?

All bets were off.

Nothing about the bunker implicated Vitra Synth.

Vida was the only true loose end.

The flapping skin of the Black Box faded in and out of the haze. Tall pines suddenly stopped short as the wall of metal and gray fabric rose into the sky. There was no light beyond the opening Vida had torn for herself, nothing but darkness and a foreboding that Kagan couldn't shake.

That he had any apprehension at all surprised him.

True, Vida was armed, but she was just an actress. What danger could she possibly pose to a man like Kagan? She had seen too many movies if she thought she could get the drop on—

It was the word *movies* that sent his mind reeling.

Vida knew movies, knew how plots unfolded, and how so-called twists developed out of seemingly nowhere. So she must have had a sense of how the night would play out. Did she know he was chasing her? Had she stayed long enough in the bunker to hear him crash through the mural window?

The doubt ate at his stomach.

Kagan threw himself at the tear, landed on the other side of reality, and immediately pitched forward. Something sharp and scalding had scraped across the back of his shoulder, and the momentum put him off balance. He rolled onto his back, spat dirt, and tried to collect his bearings. A whine filled the air, then dissipated enough for him to hear the faint echoes of a gunshot.

He looked up, saw Vida pointing the Sig at him. Her damp hair clung to her red cheeks, and the feral look in her eyes was tinged with surprise. She'd actually shot someone. For real.

"Move and you die," she said, stepping back into her hiding spot beside the tear. She kept the gun pointed at Kagan, but turned her ear to the howling wind inside.

"What are you waiting for?" he asked.

"Shut up."

"No one's coming," he continued, letting his head fall to the dirt. He spoke the stars. "No one's coming to save precious little Vida from the big bad Doyle."

She ignored him, which made Kagan laugh.

"You gullible bitch. You swallowed that Máquina invasion bullshit like a warm glass of milk." He reached for the sky with both arms. "Oh no," he cried, "the synthetics are coming to get us! Quick, hide in the bunker. Cover your head with blankets and cry yourself to sleep every night."

As he waved his hands around, he stole a look at his sliver.

Two minutes remained.

The explosions would distract Vida, giving him enough time to grab the Eagle from his waistband and shoot her in the face. Then he could simply drag her body down the mountain and dispose of it in the first open well he found.

Kagan laughed. "You're so fucking pathetic."

The Sig shook in Vida's hands, and her eyes began to water. Even in the moonlight, he appreciated her beauty. Tears sparkled in the dark shadows of her eyes, like the stars of a distant galaxy exploding and being reborn.

As a physical specimen, she was second to none. Kagan resolved that after this was all over, if he still desired her physically, he would simply have a synthetic made with her body type and looks. Whatever off-the-shelf personality they wanted to bolt onto her would be fine; it couldn't be any worse than the real Vida.

"You…" she said. "You don't deserve to live."

"Then fucking do it! Put us *both* out of our misery!"

Vida shook her head. "I'm not a killer. That's not who I am."

"Well," Kagan replied, watching the seconds tick by on his sliver, "that's a goddamn shame."

The first explosions were distant, but seconds later, the outer wall of the Black Box began to crumble. When Vida looked up, Kagan rolled onto his side, got his hand behind his back, and drew the Eagle from his waistband.

Just as he got the sights trained, a gust of powder erupted from the tear in the Box, filling the air between him and Vida with a white haze.

He rolled for cover as debris rained down on them.

FIFTY-TWO

It was over.

Vida cried as she watched the sun rise through the open window. Birds sang from nearby ledges, chirping loud enough to be heard over the morning traffic eight floors below. The real world felt so close; if it hadn't been for the dozens of wires and tubes connecting her body to the bed, she would have climbed out and walked over to the window, maybe poked out her head and looked down on humanity.

Instead, she closed her eyes, listened to the sounds, and tried to imagine what was happening out there. She saw herself walking through the crowds on the sidewalks, perhaps sipping from a tall cup of steaming coffee, a red scarf wrapped around her neck to protect her from the slight chill in the air.

Smiling at strangers. Avoiding their gaze if they smiled back.

Checking her reflection in storefront windows. Ignoring the flashes of her own face.

Being a part of it all and yet at the same time, withdrawing completely

Somewhere out there, her old life waited for her. Getting back to it was an undertaking she couldn't wrap her mind around. There were so many unanswered questions, and the steady stream of nurses and doctors had been tight-lipped as they came and went. They checked her bandages and vitals and declared her *well on the road to recovery*. Of course, they were only talking about her physical damage: lacerated wrist, dislocated shoulder, and enough bumps and bruises to start her own fetish website.

But what about her mind? She might have been free from Doyle and the bunker, but amnesia was its own prison cell, one she couldn't escape with any known medical treatments. It would just have to happen naturally, triggered by a familiar sight or smell.

Vida had to get out of the hospital, had to find her way back to San Francisco and the bay. Maybe if the sea air were in her lungs again, she'd remember.

A soft chime announced the opening of a door.

Two men entered, one dressed in slacks and a light blue button-up, the other in a black Yellowstone County uniform.

"Good morning, Miss," said the deputy. "Do you remember me?"

"Roberts," said Vida. "I thought Doyle hit you with his car. How—?"

"Hit me with his car *and* dropped a roof on my head, but I keep coming back. It's one of the perks of being a machine." He smiled, pointed to the other man. "This is Dr. William Vanvlek, one of the best here in Billings. He's got a few things to go over with you if you're feeling up to it."

"Please," said the doctor, "call me Bill."

Vida nodded, admired his fatherly appearance: gray hair, thick cheeks, and a mustache as full and thick as the deputy's.

"And what should I call you, young lady?"

"My name is Vida. But, not really."

The men shared a look. Worms wiggled in her stomach.

"Alright, Ms. Vida. As you can see, we've fixed up your injuries and given you some drugs to manage the pain." He consulted his palette. "There's nothing I see here that should be permanent."

"What about my memory?"

Deputy Roberts wandered over to the window and shut it.

Bill pushed his rimless glasses up his nose. "I have a colleague in Missoula who specializes in neuro-synaptic theory. He's driving in this afternoon. I'd rather not do any invasive scanning until he arrives."

"Let's focus on what you do remember," said Roberts. "Do you know how you came to be on the Kagan Ranch, Miss?"

Vida thought back to the fire and the pain. "I was in a plane crash a few weeks back. Doyle pulled me from the wreckage, took me back to his bunker."

"This is Doyle Kagan you're talking about?"

"I don't know," said Vida. "He never told me his last name, but he was married to a woman named Angela and—" She stopped, unsure of where the bullshit started and ended.

"And?" asked Roberts.

"So much of what he told me was a lie. He said there had been a war. Máquinas had taken over the United States. We were two of only a handful of survivors left in Montana."

The room shimmered as tears filled her eyes.

Roberts approached the side of her bed and placed a hand on her shoulder. His voice modulated down to a whisper. "You're safe now, Miss. No one's getting in here without going through me."

Vida turned away, asked, "You don't have him, do you? Doyle?"

"At the moment, no. We have crews searching the rubble and the surrounding area. I'd be surprised if we don't find his body by noon."

"That's what I thought."

"Ms. Vida, do you remember anything from before the plane crash?" asked Bill. "Where you are from, perhaps? Names, places?"

"I remember Alcatraz."

Again, they shared a look.

"What?" she asked.

Roberts ignored the question. "You said Doyle was holding you captive in his bunker? Did he ever threaten you or coerce you?"

"I..." Vida couldn't say the words. Hot waves of shame spread through her cheeks. "I was free to go at any time. That's what he told me. I guess that wasn't true. He manipulated me."

"Into staying?" asked Roberts.

"Into staying. Into being his friend. Sleeping with him." She put a hand to her face, suppressed a sob.

"I think we should get a rape kit in here right away, Doc."

"It's called a SAFE kit, Deputy. Please try to remember that." He turned his head towards the door for a moment.

Just the mention of the word *rape* made Vida choke up. Even after she'd stepped through the tear into the real world, she hadn't thought of her night with Doyle as rape. Only looking back, seeing the weeks of manipulation, did it all make sense. He had wanted her from the very beginning, and she had been too blind to see it.

Was that all this was?

A long con just to get in her pants?

Doyle wasn't the kind of man who would just grab a woman off the street and hold her down; he needed to be wanted.

"Oh my god," she cried, pushing the side of her face into the pillow.

It was all a sick game to Doyle, with cameras and double-sided mirrors and fairy tales about metal monsters. All so she would welcome him into her bed.

No.

All so she would *pull* him into her bed.

"I wanted him," she said, her voice breaking. "He made me want him. I couldn't... I was so..."

Fingers wrapped around hers, and the deputy's hand reappeared at her shoulder. "It wasn't your fault," he told her. "You did nothing wrong."

"I'm going to have a word with the nurse," said Bill. "She'll be in shortly with the kit."

The chime rang.

"He won, didn't he?" asked Vida. "He ruined my life and then got away."

Roberts tapped the gold star on his chest. "See this here? Yellowstone County Sheriff's Department. That means the entire county is our jurisdiction. And if you can trust a synthetic enough to believe one thing, believe this. Doyle Kagan is only getting out of Yellowstone County in one of two ways: in handcuffs or in a body bag. I swear to you."

Vida squeezed his hand. "You can really do that? Kill him?"

He smirked. "We have a code we choose to follow. But exceptions can be made."

"Then will you do something for me?"

"If I can, I will."

"Get me a gun."

Roberts chuckled. "I brought you four. And synthetic men to wield them. You press that call button right there and we'll come running. Anyone in the room who's not you is gonna get a four-course meal of hot lead."

"You don't know Doyle," said Vida, shaking her head. "Or his friend. They're not stupid."

Roberts leaned over and whispered. "The sick ones never are."

The door opened and a nurse walked in carrying a white pouch. She at first seemed disenchanted with her chosen profession, moving about the room with a detachment typically reserved for employees twice her age. It wasn't until she saw Vida that her eyes widened, as if someone had injected a syringe full of caffeine directly into her heart. She paused near the foot of the bed to stare.

"Is there something wrong, nurse?" asked Roberts.

"No, I," she stammered. "I just can't do this with you in the room."

Roberts looked down at Vida again. "Right outside, okay? I'm not going anywhere."

She nodded, watched him disappear behind the closing door.

Whatever spell had frozen the nurse dissipated. She pulled a rolling cart from the wall and placed the pouch on top of it.

"My name is April," she said, speaking as if reading from a teleprompter. "I'm going to be processing your SAFE kit today. It should only take me half an hour. I don't expect any pain, but there might be some mild discomfort."

She pulled the covers from the end of the bed.

Vida swallowed hard, said, "I can't believe this is happening."

"If it helps make a case against the asshole who did this, then it's all worth it, right?"

"They're never going to catch him," said Vida. "He's probably halfway to Costa Rica by now. He's going to be sitting on the beach drinking Margaritas for the rest of his life."

"I wouldn't bet on that." April removed pouches of swabs and microscope slides from the kit. She laid them out on the cart so she could label them with a marker. "For someone like you, they'll turn this entire country upside-down. That guy won't be able to show his face anywhere."

"What do you mean *someone like me*?" Vida tried to push up onto her elbows, but her shoulder wouldn't bear it.

April's cheeks flushed, and she looked away. "I'm sorry," she said. "I'm a professional. I really am." She gently lifted Vida's legs one at a time and moved them to the sides of the bed.

"Wait," said Vida, pulling her knees together. "Do you know me, April?"

"I won't tell anyone," she said, panic creeping onto her face. "Even if the feeds offer me money, I'm not going to say a word about this. I could lose my job and… and it's wrong."

Vida used the bed's railing to pull herself up. The effort cost her the entire contents of her lungs.

"Tell me, April. Please, I'm begging you."

The nurse looked over her shoulder at the door. In a whisper, she said, "We're not supposed to say anything until Dr. V's friend arrives, but…" She switched to a whisper. "I've seen all your movies, Ms. Ahmadi. Your performance in *The Dark Desert* was brilliant."

"Ahmadi. Vida Ahmadi."

"No," said April. "Sepideh Ahmadi."

Vida.

Sepideh.

She had been so close to the answer.

The panting quickened, and suddenly Vida could no longer think about her real name. Her mind shifted from remembering to breathe to simply *how* to breathe.

April hurried around the bed and gave Vida a one-armed hug.

"It's okay," she said. "In and out. In and out. The only thing you have to worry about right now is breathing."

Air rushed into her nose.

Air rushed out.

Vida felt her heart fall into a steady rhythm. She looked to the window, wondered if the birds were still chirping outside. Even their imagined singing calmed her, brought her to a level of serenity so—

"So," said April, "does your wife know you're here?"

FIFTY-THREE

"No one's answering," said Jane. She threw her phone down on the bed and shook her fist at it.

Nat stared blankly at the open suitcase, convinced she was forgetting something in her haste to pack. She'd grabbed clothes from the closet at random and hadn't bothered folding them. Shirts, an extra pair of jeans, some underwear and socks. She didn't need a toiletry bag, or any make-up to keep her looking presentable. As a synthetic, her packing requirements were limited to the dressing she put over her machine body and not much else.

Jane crossed the room and sat down on the white bench in front of the vanity. "What exactly did the girl say?" she asked.

"She said Sepi was in the hospital. In Montana." Nat pulled the suitcase shut and routed the zipper around it.

"That doesn't make any sense. They're shooting in the Dominican Republic right now. Last time I heard from Sepi, they still had at least a month left there." She waved her finger in the air. "I don't like this. Not one bit. Someone is trying to scam you."

Nat had already considered the possibility. Given her relative newness to the MESH, she hadn't known what to make of the message that suddenly started repeating in her head.

Sepideh needs you. Come to Billings, Montana. Billings Clinic. Room 801.

Her first thought had been that someone was playing a mean joke on her, and in an effort to squelch the message, she'd closed her eyes in concentration. Only, she hadn't seen darkness, but rather a clear image of Sepi lying in a hospital bed, wires attached to her chest, an ice bag on her shoulder.

Nat hadn't mentioned the vision to Jane.

"I don't want to take that chance," she said. Without waiting for a reply, she carried the suitcase to the front door and set it down.

Jane followed after her, pleading. "Nat, darling, you need to be smart about this. If this were real, don't you think the cops would be calling you instead of this April girl? You don't even know if she's legit."

Nat picked up her palette from the kitchen bar. "I checked her out," she said, showing Jane the screen. "She's a nurse at Billings Clinic. There's a picture of her right there."

"I'm going to make some calls," said Jane, lifting her phone. "We'll see what the Billings police have to say about Miss Santos."

"No, please." Nat reached out, just short of taking Jane's phone. "Look, it wasn't just what she said, but how she said it. There was a feeling to it. I got the impression that something is happening. Otherwise, you're right. The cops *would* be calling. All Sepi would have to do is give them my number. So either she can't or won't. I'm sure there's a reason."

Jane put her hands on the counter; her gold bangles clinked against the stone. "I still don't like it. It's much too cloak and dagger for me. There's got to be a reasonable explanation for all of this, and we should find out what that is before we get on a flight to Montana."

"We? No, I'm doing this alone."

"Like hell you are!"

Nat stepped forward, took Jane's reddening hands. "I know you care for her. I love that about you. But I've taken care of her every day since she and I met. We fight the world together, and we trust each other's judgment. So if I want to go comfort her in a hospital in Montana *by myself,* I'm going to do that. With all due respect, Jane, she's *my* wife."

Jane's eyes moistened. "Well," she said, grabbing her purse from a nearby stool, "okay, I'm not going to argue with that. It's your prerogative. I guess I'll just go home and sit on my thumbs." The strap caught on the stool's backing and almost toppled it when Jane pulled. She shuffled to the door.

"I appreciate your understanding," said Nat, as if talking to one of her students.

Jane looked her up and down, stammered. "Give… give my best to Sepi."

The door opened, closed.

With Jane out of the picture, things moved faster. Nat was able to collect her purse and wallet, lock up the apartment, and get into the elevator without talking to Gus or Solomon. On the way down to the lobby, she reached out to the synthetic doorman via the MESH and asked him to hail a Viking for her. He told her it would be his pleasure, and true to his word, he was standing at the curb holding a door open, an artificially giant smile on his face.

The Bourbon Viking cab company didn't employ human drivers; their fleet of electric cars were fully auto-drive. Inside, the two rows of seats had been converted into a modern stagecoach. Nat slid onto the front-facing bench, and the doorman pushed her carry-on bag in after her. He bade her a safe trip.

Travel time to Los Angeles International Airport is thirty-one minutes.

Nat spent the ride thinking about her last conversation with Sophia Dahlstrom. They'd talked for a long time about the meaning of existence and of how helping others was as good a purpose as any. After some incisive questions from Sophia, Nat realized her relationship with Sepi was all about helping her cope with problems that lowered her quality of life. Anxiety, agoraphobia, depression. These were all masks Sepi wore, and each obscured the real her in some way.

By the time Nat got to the airport and onto the plane, she'd come to think of Sepi as being two people. One, a soft, white and gold kitten full of life, happiness, and love. The other was an unstable, monstrously huge, purple gorilla. In her mind, the gorilla held the kitten in the crook of its arm while it ranted and raged. But, when the anxiety abated and the gorilla exhausted itself, the kitten was free to come out. That was the Sepi she truly loved—this beautiful, wonderful person trapped in the crook of anxiety's powerful arms. More than anything in her own life, Nat wanted to help Sepi defeat the gorilla.

The flight was delayed for over an hour. While they sat on the tarmac with engines idling, Nat tried to send April a message through the MESH, but either she wasn't responding, or the message wasn't getting through. She leaned back in her seat, closed her eyes, and entered a low-power state that was somewhat equivalent to sleep.

Sensory input dimmed, and conscious control of her body fell away. Though she was unaware of the underlying technology, a self-contained virtual construct sprung up in Nat's brain. There, she stood as an imaginary avatar staring at a floating photograph of Sepi in the hospital. A sickly bruise radiated out from Sepi's jawbone, turning one side of her face into a mishmash of reds and purples. Nat tried to piece everything together.

The injuries.

A surprise appearance in Billings, Montana when she was supposed to be in the DR.

A furtive message from a nurse telling her to come.

The only plausible reason Nat could come up with was that Sepi wanted to avoid attention from feed mongers. Whatever had happened to her, *however* it had happened, she wanted to keep it a secret, even if that meant keeping it from law enforcement.

Even in the dreamlike construct, Nat bristled at the idea of believing in such a conspiracy.

It was mid-afternoon when Nat powered up, and the pilot had just announced they were beginning their descent into Billings Logan International. Local time was 3:40, and the temperature was a crisp 54 degrees.

Nat peered through the window as the plane banked for its final approach. She got a clear view of the mountains west of the city. The skies above them bustled with activity. Drones circled at high altitudes like hawks looking to spot lunch, while below them, helicopters swept back and forth over a still-smoking patch of land at least half a mile wide.

"What do you think that's about?" asked the man sitting next to her.

"Some kind of forest fire, I guess," said Nat.

The anticipation didn't start to build until the plane was inching its way towards the terminal. Before, she had always been so relieved to be done with the flight that she didn't mind how long it took to taxi, or connect the pedestrian bridge, or get everyone off the plane. But now, every step of the process dragged on. Nat made plans to jump out of her seat, grab her bag from the overhead bin, and race off the plane before anyone could get up. That plan was stymied by the impatient couple in the fifth row who stood long before the plane even docked, setting off a domino effect of inconsiderate people filling the aisles.

As if marching to their own deaths, the passengers filed off the airplane. Nat did her best not to push, but as the space widened in the pedestrian bridge, she began weaving through the crowd, breaking into a stunted run whenever there was enough room.

She followed the exit signs, and in just a few minutes, she was standing on the curb waving to a cab. A human driver kicked off from the hood and approached.

"Where ya headed, Miss?"

"Billings Clinic," said Nat, fishing a fifty-dollar bill out of her purse. "I need you to get me there as fast as humanly possible."

The driver, who had a round face and a white beard that reminded Nat of Solomon, jerked his thumb in the direction of the two Bourbon Viking cars waiting further down the curb. "Is that why you chose me instead of them?"

"I thought you would ask fewer questions," she replied, choosing not to match the smile growing on his face.

He nodded. "Billings Clinic. I'll have you there in five minutes."

Nat paused, one foot in the cab. "That fast?"

"Well," he replied, urging her inside. "Usually it takes seven. But if we hit all the greens and ignore a few stop signs, we should be able to shave a couple minutes."

As soon as Nat put her seatbelt on, the cab shot forward, eliciting a warning honk from the Viking behind them. They tore through the parking lot, tires squealing, weary travelers jumping out of the way. A roundabout sent Nat leaning precariously towards the window. She put out a hand at the last second.

She was about to protest when her phone started to ring.

Oh Jane, she thought. *You couldn't leave it alone, could you?*

Instead of the older woman's face on the phone, Nat saw the words *UNKNOWN CALLER* staring back at her from the palm of her hand. Thinking it might be April, she tapped the button and jammed the phone to her ear.

"Hey, I'm almost there. We should be pulling up any minute now."

A distorted voice came across the line. "Nat?"

It was Sepi.

"I'm here, sweetie! I'm coming."

"What?"

Nat sighed. Sepi was delirious.

The cab blew a red light and cut hard into the parking lot. Bald tires sunk what tread they had into the pavement as they skidded to a stop in front of the hospital.

"My bag, please," said Nat, covering the phone with her hand.

The driver stepped out and retrieved her bag from the trunk.

Nat stared up at the building, looked for the eighth floor.

"Nat, are you okay? You sound a little—" Static took the adjective.

"I'm fine," said Nat. "I'm here now."

"Where?"

Nat pulled the phone away from her ear, stared at it for a moment. "Billings. April called—"

The phone dimmed, returned to the home screen.

It didn't matter.

Sepi was only an elevator ride away.

FIFTY-FOUR

Sepi was but a single drop in an ocean of angry tourists and exhausted travelers who, as if coordinated beforehand, all pulled their phones from their ears and stared in disbelief at the screen. A collective groan went up from the open-air terminal at Punta Cana International Airport, rising to the ceiling where it was minced into tiny grunts of displeasure by lumbering fans.

Like the hundreds of other network-hungry visitors to the DR, Sepi had heard a rumor that the U.S. military had flown in equipment to keep the airport on the grid. This, in turn, had allowed for a brief window in which wireless, MESH, and cell service worked. But as more people arrived, including Sepi and Richard, the entire network had started to degrade. Now, after a puzzling and too-short call with Nat, the network was down again.

Even the vidscreens over the ticketing counters were offline, and the media feed kiosks were stuck in a loop, displaying news that grew progressively more out of date.

President Morgan promises stronger response to Máquina threat.

Sepi hit redial on her phone, but her four bars had changed to *no service*. No matter how hard she mashed the dial button, each call failed.

"And there you go," said Richard, looking over his shoulder at a group of teenagers jockeying for position around a make-shift access point. "When mass communication fails, society begins to break down. *That's* how you fuck with someone's head; make them feel isolated."

His words barely reached her. Sepi concentrated on what Nat had said.

Billings. I'm here.

"Something's not right," said Sepi. "Nat said she was in Billings."

Richard took a sip of his coffee. "Where is that? Montana? What's she doing there?"

"I don't know. Maybe she went to visit someone."

"Family?"

Sepi shook her head. "The Kumanovs are based on the east coast, NYC mostly. She doesn't really get along with her parents, and her brother died several years back from cancer."

Richard nodded, his eyes drifting to a nearby vidscreen. A message appeared in block letters. He read it off in a dull monotone. "Network access is down. We are working to restore service. Thank you for your patience." He tried to read the Spanish version but gave up after a few words.

"I can wait here if you want to get back to the set."

"Lawrence can handle it," said Richard. "It's just pickup shots today anyway. If he can't oversee that, then he doesn't have any business um… being in this business." He took her hand. "There's a couple seats over there. Let's go sit down."

The terminal buzzed around them. Sepi picked up thirty-two distinct conversations on the walk from the entrance to a café tucked just beyond the ticketing counters. Airport security had moved the checkpoint further down the concourse, allowing non-fliers access to the many chairs, tables, and small vending kiosks.

Richard led her to a high table near a window that looked out on the private hangars. Large, forest-green helicopters sat like shaved mammoths on the tarmac while insignificant humans scurried around them, tending to their whims.

"You know what kind of bird that is?" asked Richard, noticing her gaze.

Sepi shook her head. She'd seen the double rotors in pictures before but had never learned the name.

"That's an FA-47 Chinook. Completely automated. Self-flying, self-landing. It's basically a helicopter with a synthetic brain."

"Cool," she replied, automatically. One of the ground engineers had blonde hair sticking out from under her helmet. A thick braid swung from side to side as she moved around the aircraft.

Billings. Montana.

What are you doing there, asked Sepi, to the MESH. Static answered.

Richard excused himself to refresh his coffee. Sepi took the time to stare at pictures of Nat on her phone. It showed her half-hidden face pressed into a pillow, her blonde hair running over her chin. Sunlight poured in through the window behind her.

New Year's Day. Three, four years ago.

Even then, Sepi had known she would be with Nat forever.

A chorus of electronic beeps went up from all around her, including from her own phone on the table. Sepi scooped it up, saw she had a text message from Nat.

Are you getting my texts? I'm heading up. Don't even think about dying.

Sepi read the message a few times, tried to find meaning in the words. Her network status flicked back to *no service* before she could respond.

She put her phone down, put her elbows on the table, and sighed into her hands. This never would have happened back stateside where the year was still 2035. Network outages were unheard of. If the power went out, fine. If water stopped flowing, there was always the grocery store. But if access to VNet or the

MESH suddenly disappeared? The entire city, state, and country would mobilize. Apparently, angry Dominicans didn't see it as a necessity. Or at the very least, they were willing to sacrifice a reliable network to effect change in their country.

Priorities, Sepi figured.

Richard returned and slid a bottle of water onto the table in front of Sepi. "Got a text from Lawrence," he said, easing onto his tall chair. "He says Ever Jovovich is refusing to come out of her room. Something about psychotic robot bitches threatening to, and I quote, *fucking break her*. You know anything about that?"

"Ever does a lot of drugs," said Sepi.

"Yeah, I know. But nothing that would give her delusions."

Sepi lifted the water bottle, waved it at Richard. "You know I don't need to drink, right? You just wasted five bucks."

"It would have been impolite to return without something for the lady. If five dollars is what it costs to be a gentleman, then so be it."

"So chivalrous." Sepi opened the water, took a swig. Her chest simulated an expanding chill. It reminded her of draining her water bottle after a long run at the 24/7 Fitness on La Brea.

Richard lifted an eyebrow, held it there until Sepi spilled the story.

"She made a pass at me. No, I take that back. She manipulated me to get into my pants. She knew I was married and did it anyway."

"Why does she think you'll fucking break her?"

"Because I told her I would."

"You can't go around threatening your co-stars, Sepideh."

"Really?" she asked. "But it's okay to sexually harass them? I get looking the other way when it's your own brother, but—"

"Easy," said Richard, holding up a hand. "If Lawrence ever did anything like that, I'd punch him in the dick so hard he'd be peeing out his butthole for the rest of his life. The Sierra Brothers didn't get into this business to sleep with the talent, at least not while we're in production."

Sepi looked away, tried to pick out the blonde woman outside. She, and all the similarly dressed crew, had disappeared. Now, there were civilians out there, slightly out of shape men in polo shirts and wrinkled khakis. They stood around a large satellite dish they'd rolled out of the back of the Chinook. With considerable effort, they were able to push it closer to the terminal where Dominican engineers stood ready with thick black cables.

After some tinkering, the satellite dish began to rotate back and forth, seeking out a friendly face in the sky. Seconds after it froze in place, the terminal erupted in applause.

Sepi picked up her phone.

Before she could hit redial, Richard said, "You're trending."

"Huh?"

"Top story on Banks Media and Lincoln Continental. Do you know what that's about?"

Sepi thought back to the club, to the damage she had caused. Had there been aggregators in the crowd? Or had someone caught the fight on their cell phone and sold it to one of the big four media houses?

"Listen," she said, "something happened at the club last night."

A synthesized trumpet blared from a nearby feed kiosk. The animated word *BREAKING* swooped in from the left and landed with a thud in the middle of the screen. A man in skinny jeans and a bow tie appeared; the Vinestead logo on his breast glowed brightly.

Hey, what's crackin' ya'll? AJ here from VFeed bringing you the freshest celebrity gossip and holy balls do I have some mad juicy shit for you today.

A glamour shot of Sepi appeared over his shoulder.

You know her from The Dark Desert *and* CSI: Abbottabad. *Yes, that's right, Persian sensation Sepideh Ahmadi, the woman rumored to be playing Krazy Kaili Zabora in an upcoming Sierra Brothers movie has just escaped a medieval sex dungeon in Billings, Montana. Details are still coming in, but our bitches on the street say fire and rescue teams have closed off five square miles in the foothills just west of Billings. Sepideh was admitted to Billings Clinic early this morning and remains under heavy guard. We don't know her condition yet, but if she just escaped from a 50 Shades party, I'm going to say her condition is tired. You may remember Ahmadi from last month when she made headlines by marrying her longtime girlfriend Natasha Kumanov at a private ceremony in Beverly Hills. This Kumanov girl couldn't be reached for comment at this time.*

"Richard?" asked Sepi. She found herself standing. "What's happening?"

He shook his head. "Gotta be a mistake. Or some kind of…"

She turned to him, put a hand on his chest. "There's a woman in Montana claiming to be me. And Natasha's there. She could be in danger."

"It's alright," he said, pulling her into an embrace. "I'm sure it's just a misunderstanding or a crazed fan—"

"Crazed fan? What's this crazed fan gonna do when they get Nat in the same room?" She squeezed her hands into fists, flashed on the beating she'd unloaded the night before.

AJ faded from the vidscreen and was replaced by a suited man in his mid-thirties.

In national news, El Paso has closed its borders with its sister city Juarez after a Máquina attack killed forty-seven soldiers at Fort Bliss. President Morgan has declared a state of emergency in all states bordering the MX and promises swift retaliation. This attack coincides with the six-year anniversary of the start of the MX war, and the conflict—

A small explosion drew their attention to the windows just in time to see the satellite dish spark and tremble. The servos holding its face to the sky relaxed, allowing the dish to dip.

Sepi gasped.

"I need to get to Billings," she said. "Sort this all out." She looked to the ticketing counters.

"No good there," said Richard. "It would take you all day to reach Billings on a commercial flight."

Sepi squeezed her eyes shut. She felt so cut off from Nat, so isolated from the world where things were happening without her consent or input. It was as if her future were being written by the media feeds and by the insane woman claiming to be Sepideh Ahmadi.

"Hey, don't worry," said Richard. "You can take our private jet. It'll have you there in six hours, including a stop in Atlanta to refuel."

"Seriously?" she asked, feeling the first butterflies of hope. "You would do that for me?"

"Yes, but only because it'll get you there and back in the shortest amount of time. No one here is going to balk at a day or two off, but we still have deadlines to meet. Get to Billings, sort this shit out, and then get your synthetic ass back here. Maybe by then I'll have convinced Ever to come out of her room."

Sepi threw her arms around Richard's neck and kissed him on the lips.

He stared back at her, his eyes wide. "You trying to seduce me, Mrs. Ahmadi?" he asked.

She grabbed his head at the jawline and squeezed. "You're too much like your brother."

"This is true," he replied. "He just doesn't have a filter between his mouth and his dangly bits. Come on, let's get out to the hangar. Flight prep is going to take an hour at least."

Sepi followed him as he snaked through the crowded terminal. All around her, the feed kiosks looped through the last video segments.

Sepideh Ahmadi. Escape. Sex dungeon.

And now a crazed fan had Natasha.

Sepi could only hope Nat would know the difference between the woman in the hospital and the real Sepideh Ahmadi.

FIFTY-FIVE

The fire started in the basement.

By the time Engine 41 arrived at the residence of Doyle Kagan, the four-story mansion was already engulfed in flames. Fire Chief Javia scratched his head at the raging inferno, his mind already trying to work out how a modern home could flash so quickly; even though it only housed a single family, it was still required to have a sprinkler system throughout. Clearly, the sprinklers—if they were even functioning—were doing nothing to quell the fire. If there was anyone inside the home, they were probably already dead.

What Chief Javia didn't know was that Kagan had disabled the sprinkler system some two months prior, and he had constructed an elaborate firebomb system comprised of numerous barrels filled with all the flammable liquid he could find. Four barrels surrounded each of the main support columns of the mansion, and they were all tied together with improvised primer cord that Raf had helped him put together. All of these wires ran to a simple cell phone in the center of the room. When called, and after a series of tones were inputted, the phone would ignite the primer cord, ignite the barrels, and bring the whole house to the ground.

It was all part of the *If Shit Hits the Fan* plan.

Kagan had used the collapse of the Black Box to slip away into the underbrush. Being on the south side of the structure, it only took him twenty minutes to get to the border of the Kagan ranch. There, he followed the fence line back to the west until it bent towards the north. The ATV he had stashed was still in working order, though it was covered in a fine layer of pollen and dirt. He rode the ATV south until he hit Clapper Flat Road. He almost missed the small farm in the darkness, but at the last second, he turned off the road and down the long driveway.

The house at Clapper Flat 15 was nothing impressive. Its four rooms were mostly empty except for an undressed bed and a wardrobe containing a single change of clothes. Kagan took a quick shower under whining pipes, washing the blood from his face and scrubbing the glass from his skin. He combed his hair and dressed in the fresh suit. He eschewed the tie; the collar needed to stay open to keep him from overheating. From under the mattress, he retrieved a black briefcase. Inside was money, a cellphone, a key fob, a passport, and a fully loaded Glock 19. Kagan slipped the gun into his shoulder holster and headed to the garage.

While the ancient door lifted to the ceiling, Kagan dialed a number on his cell phone. When the other side answered, he keyed in *1-2-2-1-0-6*, Sepideh's birthday. A double beep answered him, and then the call ended.

Kagan got into the Tesla Luster 7 and pressed the ignition button.

Good morning, Mr. Kagan. Where would you like to go?

"Vernon Airfield," he replied. "Park City."

Priya shifted into gear, rolling gently out of the garage.

Estimated arrival time is twenty-three minutes.

"Use back roads only."

Updating. Estimated arrival time is one hour fifty-seven minutes.

Kagan leaned back in the leather seat and put his hands to his face. They smelled faintly of flowers. His body ached as it never had before, and as the heater warmed his back and legs, he slowly drifted off to sleep. He was too tired to watch the road for police or stare at the lights circling the sky to the north. They had no idea he'd escaped; they probably thought he was still trapped under the rubble. By the time they figured it out, he'd be sipping umbrella drinks in Montego Bay.

He sighed. Thought of Vida.

All he had wanted to do was love her.

And now she was dead. Crushed to death by the flaming wreckage of her own prison.

There was a cosmic connection between the two of them, even if she hadn't been aware of it. Unlike the plastic women he met on Hollywood Boulevard, with their fake smiles and fake tits, Kagan's heart didn't jump out of his chest when he first saw Vida, nor did his palms sweat or breath quicken or pants tighten.

All he felt with Vida was calm. Harmony. As if the world were a million gears all slipping their grooves until finally, at this moment, the teeth hit correctly.

Calm. And love.

He imagined her face, the way she used to stare out at him from his desktop. She'd been looking through the camera right into his soul; he was sure of it.

Now, those pictures had been lost to the flame.

The car wound through the low mountains. It was almost 4:30 a.m. when the landscape settled into farmland. Kagan saw traffic on the 90 to the south, and the giant neon sign of Jackrabbit Red's Casino torching the night sky. Priya entered the city from the north, crossed under the 90, and took the frontage road until she could cross over to Cemetery Road.

Vernon Airfield was empty, and its three hangars were closed.

"Are you able to connect to the plane yet?" asked Kagan.

I am.

"Tell them to prep for takeoff. ASAP."

Sure thing, said Priya.

As the car pulled up next to the control tower, a yawning man in blue overalls stepped out of the only door. He raised a hand in greeting, turned his face away when the headlights hit him.

Priya parked the car and unlocked the doors.

Kagan stepped out.

"You again," said the man. "Different car than before. This one's much nicer."

"It's yours, Harlan," said Kagan. "Provided you can help me get ready for takeoff." He tossed the key fob over the hood of the car.

Harlan caught it and slipped it into his breast pocket without breaking eye contact. "Seems like a fair trade," he mumbled. "I'll open Hangar Four for you." He disappeared inside the control tower.

Kagan retrieved his briefcase from the passenger seat; he made sure the glove box was empty and that he'd left no trace of himself in the car.

A plaintive wail went up from a nearby hangar as its doors slid apart on rusted tracks. Despite the rickety appearance of the hangar itself, inside it was as modern and clean as any private space in Los Angeles. Dim LED lights illuminated Kagan's jet from below, washing out its landing gear and making it appear as if the plane were hovering.

Priya had already lowered the stairs for him, but Kagan went instead to the workbench at the back of the hangar. From the shelf underneath, he retrieved a long silver toolbox. Inside, he found a note from Glasser.

Call me before you use this. -EG

Kagan crumpled the piece of paper and tossed it aside. The apparatus was nothing more than a small gunmetal box about the size of a deck of cards. It was fitted with a strap and looked like an oversized dog collar. Kagan undid the buckle, slipped the strap around his neck, and secured it. He slid the box around until it was directly over his Guardian Angel biochip.

There was only a tall stool at the workbench, so Kagan sat down on the floor and put his back against the wall. After three quick breaths, he pressed the circular button on the box and yelped at the sudden pain. The shock lasted only half a second, but it was enough to make him piss himself a little.

The box beeped. Faster and faster.

Kagan couldn't feel it, but his Guardian Angel chip was slowly losing its mind. Soon, there would be nothing left of it. And while that meant he wouldn't be able to buy goods and services with just a nod and a wink anymore, it also meant his identity couldn't be picked up by nosy kiosks and ad-sense displays. As far as any scanner was concerned, Doyle Kagan didn't even have a chip anymore.

"Ain't right for a grown man to be sittin' on the floor," said Harlan. He stood in the side door of the hangar. "I coulda brought you a chair, boss. Maybe a can of alcoholic pop to settle your nerves."

Kagan looked at him through bleary eyes, tried to open his mouth, but nothing happened. The beeping intensified, crescendoed into a single tone, and then cut out. Kagan gasped for air.

"Is this one of them sex things?" asked Harlan. "If you're fittin' to touch yourself, you best be finding another place to do it."

"Don't pretend you wouldn't watch," said Kagan, coughing.

The erasing and formatting of his Guardian Angel chip had only taken a few minutes, but the next phase was to reprogram it with custom firmware, and that would take hours.

"Don't worry about it," continued Kagan. "I'm flying out of here soon enough."

"About that," said Harlan, sucking on his teeth. "No-fly order for personal craft just came through from Billings Logan. We're on the edge of it, but they're not going to let me launch anyone for a while."

"Are you fucking serious? What if I just go?"

Harlan shrugged. "Well, I guess those helicopters would then assume the person or persons on your plane had something to do with the business up at your daddy's ranch."

Kagan squeezed his hands into fists. "Fuck. So I'm just stuck here?"

"I can bring you that chair," said Harlan.

"Bring me a cot."

"I've got one up in the tower. How long you need it for? I can rent by the hour."

"However long this takes," said Kagan.

"Hundred bucks," said Harlan.

"Deal, but you bring the cot down here."

"Hundred twenty-five."

"Just do it," said Kagan, groaning to his feet. He sat down on the stool and tried to catch his breath.

His phone rang. Kagan let it go to voicemail, but Earl Glasser called again, and again.

Finally, he picked up. "What?"

"You tell me *what*," said Glasser, his voice groggy. "Why did I get a notification that you used the GA wipe? I thought I put a note in there for you to call me first."

"You did." Kagan eyed the crumbled piece of paper.

"Then why didn't you?"

"Didn't seem germane."

"Ger-what?" Glasser seethed. "The loader was supposed to be a last resort, game over, everybody loses."

"So then you already know."

Glasser went silent. "You weren't even going to warn me, were you?"

Kagan switched the phone to his other ear. "There's nothing to warn you about. Shit went sideways and I lost the subject. No one's saying anything to anyone."

"Did you destroy the subject?" asked Glasser. "Because that's the only way this doesn't get traced back to me."

Kagan thought of Vida melting beneath the glowing beams of the Black Box. "Yeah," he said at last, "it's destroyed. You and your Japanese sex pillows are safe."

"We better be, because if they ask me a question, I'm answering it. I'm not going to prison for you, Kagan."

"Nor I for you."

"Fine."

"Fine."

The call dropped. Kagan tossed the phone onto the workbench.

"Cold cot for the hot shot," said Harlan, dropping a military-green cot onto the floor next to the workbench.

It was stained in more places than Kagan could count.

"Well, that's fucking disgusting. Maybe you could shit on it before I lay down?"

Harlan tugged on his overalls but said nothing.

"I suppose you want your silver," said Kagan. He pulled out his wallet and unfolded two hundreds into Harlan's outstretched hand. "The extra eighty is so you don't fondle my jubblies while I'm out cold."

Harlan pocketed the money and turned to leave. "No promises."

The first rays of sunshine peeked into the sky as Kagan stretched out on the cot. He reached behind his neck and pressed the square button.

Overhead, halogen lights shifted five feet to the left, held there for a second, and then shifted back.

Kagan blinked.

Their glowing tubes were dormant now and sun shone through the skylights. Outside, Park City basked in the mid-afternoon splendor. Birds flew low over the tarmac, searching out meals in the grassy median.

Hours had passed in an instant.

Kagan spotted Harlan several feet away sitting on the stool. The apple in his hand had been eaten down to the core.

"That was fuckin' weird," said Harlan.

Kagan sat up, felt something fall from his chest. He looked down to find two crisp hundred dollar bills in his lap, along with the key fob for the Tesla.

"What's this?" asked Kagan.

Harlan shook his head. "Don't want your car or your money, not after what you done. When Johnny Law comes knocking down my door later today, I wanna be able to tell them I had shit to do with you."

The new Margate firmware on his biochip detected an acceleration of Kagan's heartbeat and sent signals to slow it back down.

"What the hell are you talking about, Harlan?"

"It's all over the feeds. They found that actress at your ranch. Said you did all kinds of crazy sex things to her."

Kagan climbed to his feet, squeezed his arm against his chest to confirm his Glock was still there.

"How…" His throat contracted, dried up. "How did they identify the body?"

"What body?" asked Harlan. "They've got her in Billings Clinic just up the highway."

Kagan stumbled, went to a knee.

Vida alive?

He stared at the open stairs leading up into the plane.

He touched the Glock in its holster.

"I'd get to runnin' if I was you," said Harlan.

FIFTY-SIX

Between the drugs and sheer exhaustion, Vida fell into a sleep that lasted most of the day. It wasn't until late afternoon that she realized the argument she was dreaming about was no dream at all, that the voices were real and coming from the other side of her door. While there were many voices, one rose above them all, a desperate, pleading alto with such a tremulous delivery that it pulled Vida's hand to her heart.

"That's my *wife* in there!"

So April hadn't been lying. Finally, someone who was being straight with her. She'd kept her word and brought Natasha—the woman Vida had dreamed of and was evidently married to—to Billings.

"We don't know how that could affect her." That was Roberts. "We need to wait for the specialist."

"I have a legal right to see her!"

"Let her in," shouted a voice. It sounded like April.

Finally, the door swung open, and Deputy Roberts stepped inside. "Uh," he said, "Miss Vida? I've got a woman here who says she knows you."

Vida pushed the button on the bed remote and lifted herself into a sitting position. "Does she have blonde hair?"

Roberts looked over his shoulder, as if he hadn't noticed before. "Yes, Miss. She does."

"White? Blue eyes? Looks kinda like an elf?" She added every detail she could remember about Peter.

"You remember—" He didn't get to finish his question; someone pushed him out of the way.

And then she was standing there.

Peter. Natasha. How close her memory had been.

Vida took it all in: blonde hair pulled back in a ponytail, opal charms hanging from her ears and around her neck, a hint of blue eyeshadow, a white deep-V under a black jacket, blue jeans, a Coach purse, no nail polish, no blemishes.

She was perfect.

"Sepi," she said.

"Maybe," said Vida.

Natasha hurried to the bed. She put a hand on Vida's arm. "They said you have amnesia. How's that possible?"

"I have no idea." Vida reached up and touched Natasha on the cheek. "I dreamed of you. On a ferry in San Francisco. Was that real?"

"Yes. We were there a couple months ago to see a doctor. Did you have them call Vitra Synth yet?"

"What is that?" asked Sepi.

Natasha glanced at Roberts, who was standing at the door with his arms crossed. "They made us," she said. "They made our bodies. You honestly don't remember we're synthetics?"

The monitors behind Vida's head beeped rapidly in response. An alarm blared, retreated.

"No," said Vida. "That's not possible. I bleed. I feel pain. How could I be a Máquina?"

"You're not," said Roberts. Then to Natasha, "You think I wouldn't recognize one of my own? She's one hundred percent human, minus her memories."

It was Natasha's turn to shake her head. She backed away from the bed. "That's not possible. I saw you go through the procedure. We woke up together at Vitra Synth. Did you lie to me?"

"I don't remember doing that," said Vida. "I hope I didn't."

"You hope. What does that mean? What are you even doing here, Sepi? You're supposed to be in the DR."

"There's an ongoing investigation," said Roberts.

"Shut up, just *shut up*. I'm asking my wife."

Vida smiled at the word, looked into Natasha's eyes. Though she was screaming at Roberts, she looked calm. No blushing, no flaring nostrils; just a normal, everyday woman having a conversation.

"How long have we been married?" asked Vida. "I feel like I've known you for a long time."

Natasha touched her wedding ring, looked to Vida's bare finger.

"In February. The twenty-fourth. We went to the courthouse in Beverly Hills. Jane was our witness." She sighed, pulled a chair from behind her, and sat down. "This is so fucking unbelievable, Sepi. I mean, I talked to you a week ago. Everything was fine."

Vida lifted her hand. Natasha pulled the chair closer and took it.

"Last week I was trapped twenty feet underground in a doomsday bunker with a maniac. I'd been there since…" She looked to Roberts, who had earlier helped her piece together the timeline.

"March," he said. "We think early March."

"No," said Natasha. "In March we were in Los Angeles. That first week is when we transferred to synthetic bodies." Her voice broke. "Don't you remember that first night?"

"I don't remember anything, Natasha. Just a plane crash and then weeks in the bunker with Doyle. But I'm not afraid. You're here now."

Natasha demurred at Vida's hand on her face. "Just Nat. You don't call me by my full name unless we're being intimate."

"I'm sorry to interrupt again," said Roberts, "but it sounds like you're suggesting Sepideh Ahmadi has an identical twin sister that no one has ever heard of."

Nat ignored the deputy, stared into Vida's eyes.

"Sweetie," she said. "I just talked to you on the phone. Twenty minutes ago."

"There aren't any phones in here," Vida replied.

Nat swept the room. A quiet sob escaped her throat. She stood, leaned over the bed, and wrapped her arms around Vida.

"My sweet love," she said.

For several minutes, Nat was only able to repeat those three words, and the more she repeated them, the more Vida felt truly safe.

"Are you saying…"

Nat shot Roberts a look. They stared at each other for a long time, as if having a heated conversation. Finally, Roberts disengaged, moved to the window to look outside. The sun was reaching for the horizon, eager to end another day of madness.

"Where do you want me to begin?" asked Nat.

"Tell me who I am."

Nat laid it all out for her: Iranian-American parents, childhood in Houston, Texas, college at UNC School of Arts, *The Dark Desert*.

None of it sounded familiar besides her parents, but then Nat started talking about how they met and how their relationship grew from a cautious flirtation to a full-blown romance in only a few weeks. There were hard times, Nat pointed out, mostly because it was always hard to bring two strong-willed people together, to have one affect the movement of the other, even if they seemed to be perfectly matched. While she spoke, her eyes grew wistful, and several times she even smiled.

"And then I got sick, just like Patrick, my brother," she said. "Late-stage terminal cancer, up here." Nat tapped the side of her head. "We went to dozens of doctors, even to San Francisco."

"We took the ferry out to Alcatraz," said Vida.

"Yes. We couldn't believe how nice and sunny it had been on the shore and how wet and cold it was out on the water. You tried so hard to find someone who could help, but it was just too late. That's how we ended up at Vitra Synth and how I ended up in this synthetic body."

"If you'll excuse me, I need to make some calls," said Roberts. "My men will be just outside, Miss Vida."

She barely heard him. Vida was too focused on overlaying her memories on the walls behind Nat. There, she saw the bay, saw Alcatraz bobbing in the distance. She also saw Nat lying in bed, and the bedroom around her. She imagined walking through the door to find a small apartment behind it. Beyond, she imagined the common area, then the street, then Los Angeles itself.

"None of this makes sense," said Vida. "I remember being with you. I remember our apartment at… Masonry?"

"Monarch."

"Yeah, I remember the glass elevator."

"No, sweetie, that isn't right. Ours has mirrored walls and bronze doors."

Vida tried to pull the image, but couldn't. She frowned.

"Those memories are gone," she said. "I've forgotten almost everything about my life before the bunker."

"Tell me about that."

So Vida did.

For the first hour, Nat sat with her hands folded in her lap, saying nothing. Vida recounted the first weeks in the bunker, how nice Doyle had seemed, how shitty-but-okay the bunker itself had been. As she retold the story, Vida was able to pick out Doyle's manipulations, and every time he did something that pushed her a little more towards desperation, Nat would nod.

It was the sex that made Nat cry openly.

Vida joined her for a short time, but then anger replaced the sadness.

Towards the end of her story, Nat interrupted.

"That was augmented reality. You got those contacts from Nixle Chronos."

"How did he even know I had them?" asked Vida. Roberts had pulled out the remaining contact when Vida arrived, hoping he could get a serial number from it.

"It was probably in our files at Vitra Synth. Doyle's last name was Kagan, right?"

Vida nodded.

"Yeah, he got fired from Vitra Synth like a week before we went there. I remember reading about him when I checked up on the place. God, that son of a bitch. That *son of a bitch!*" Nat struck the bedrail, denting it.

Vida continued her story, described her harrowing escape from the bunker, her recapture, and subsequent rescue. Even as the words came out of her mouth, she was aware of how they didn't line up with what Nat thought their timeline to be.

Nat had gone home from Vitra Synth with a synthetic Sepideh Ahmadi. They'd spent time together, a week at least, before Sepideh went off to the Dominican Republic to shoot a movie. And more recently, Nat had received a call from Sepideh minutes before arriving at the hospital. Vida had placed no such call.

She looked up, saw Nat staring back at her.

The world closed in around Vida. She imagined some merciful deity reaching down from the sky to pluck her from the earth. She wanted to disappear, to retreat into herself until no one could find her. That would be the only way to escape the shame of having been duped so horribly.

Nat took Vida's hand, squeezed it.

"We're going to figure this out," she said. "You and me."

"And Sepideh?" asked Vida. "She has to be out there, right? It doesn't make any sense any other way."

"We'll see."

The thought of meeting herself made Vida shiver. As if the bunker ordeal hadn't been enough, now there was a synthetic copy of her running around, living her life, hanging out with her friends, and sleeping with her wife.

"People are going to pay," said Nat.

"They haven't caught him," said Vida. When Nat lifted an eyebrow, she explained, "Doyle. He got away when everything exploded."

"And what about his friend? The mountain man you stabbed in the back?"

Vida thought back to the last time she'd seen him. "They didn't say. If he was inside when the structure came down, then he probably didn't make it."

"Good," said Nat. "Hopefully he burned to death. Slowly and painfully."

"With my luck? Probably not."

Vida looked away, watched the birds fly under pearlescent clouds through the open window. She felt like a time traveler who had gone forward ten years and then returned to an alternate timeline. For reasons she couldn't put her finger on, 2035 didn't feel familiar, didn't feel like home.

There was no doubt Natasha was the Peter she had been dreaming of, but those dreams had been encompassed by an emotional connection. This Nat who sat beside her bed was nothing more than a machine, a glorified companion-bot. How was she supposed to love a machine after they had tried for weeks to kill her?

Vida shook her head.

No. None of that had been real.

Without a foundation of memories to stand on, telling the difference between real and unreal was impossible. How did Vida know all of this wasn't just another elaborate stunt by Doyle to lull her into a false sense of security?

It sounded like something he would do.

"What are you thinking?" asked Nat.

"I want to go home."

"Okay, then let's go home. I'll find out how soon we can get you out of here."

She stood, but Vida kept hold of her hand.

"No," she said, "don't leave me."

"I won't go far. And if I see anyone even so much as look at your door, I'll rip their fucking head off."

"You promise?"

Nat smiled, patted Vida's hand. "No, sweetie, but I will get one of the deputies to shoot them."

"What if it's Doyle?"

"He'd be insane to show his face around here."

"But if he does?"

With a sigh, Nat said, "Okay, if Doyle shows up, I promise I'll rip his fucking head off."

"Thank you," said Vida, letting go of her hand.

"Anything for the woman I love," said Nat. She bent over and placed her lips on Vida's.

A million separate synapses fired in unison.

A tidal wave of memories spilled out of the gloom.

"Natasha," said Vida.

FIFTY-SEVEN

Leave it to an Avenging Angel biochip to find a way around the injuries, the pain, and the heavy sedative coursing into Raf's arm via the IV drip. Unlike its civilian counterpart, the AA wasn't just in the business of keeping its host alive. Its goal was to not only put off death, but to get the host into such a state that it could continue fighting until the bitter end. So even with the drugs in his system, Raf was vaguely aware of doctors working on his arm and lower back. He felt it when they turned him over, turned him back, and even when they put the handcuff on his wrist.

All of this happened in a semi-dream state; Raf could read the data, but he couldn't do anything with it. The commands he sent to his muscles, to his eyes, were summarily ignored, even with the AA's amplification. He knew through his passive senses that he was in a hospital room, that at least two people were nearby, and that they were likely law enforcement. By their lack of odor, Raf pegged them as synthetics.

Captain Arnel's voice crackled through the MESH, whether real or simulated, Raf didn't know.

Get on your feet, Orozco. We've got chips to smash.

The warmth of the sun crept onto his face, crested a bandage on his nose, and fell off the other side. Raf tried to turn his head towards the dying light, but the command ran into a brick wall of race conditions and misfiring synapses.

"Are you going on your break soon?"

A nurse. Raf had heard her throughout the day. She had always sounded muffled, as if on the other side of a partition or curtain.

"Yeah, in fifteen. Why?"

Another nurse. This one had only been around for the last couple of hours.

"I was thinking of going up to eight."

"They're never gonna let you see her."

"I know, but there's no harm in trying, right? It's not every day a big Hollywood superstar comes to Billings Clinic."

"Sepideh Ahmadi is hardly a superstar. Did you see *The Dark Desert?* Garbage."

Raf snapped awake; lens flares obscured his view of the room, but even through the haze, he could pick out the sterile, white décor of a hospital room. He took a deep breath, wheezed, and spit something foul onto his chin. The handcuff clinked against the rails of the bed when he tried to wipe the spittle away.

"You should be dead, Paco," said a deep voice.

Raf focused on the shadows next to his bed, found a man sitting in a chair. Black eyes looked over the top of a palette.

"Guess you have good doctors here," he replied. It felt like someone had poured thumbtacks down his throat.

"That's not what I meant." The man rose, came close enough for Raf to read his nametag. "You should be dead. My men should have put a bullet in your brain down in that bunker."

"Why didn't they?"

Careful, soldier, said Arnel. *I think you've got a Máquina on your hands.*

The Avenging Angel ramped his heart rate.

"Because synthetics follow the rules," said Sheriff Linder.

"And you don't?" asked Raf. With his peripheral vision, he inventoried the law man's belt.

"I make the rules in Yellowstone County. And here we treat our women with respect. I don't know what you people were doing to that poor girl down there, but believe you me you're going to pay for it."

"Oh," said Raf, feigning disinterest. "Her."

Linder came closer, put his hands on the railing. "Am I boring you, Jose? You think I want to be here interrogating you instead of shoving my .357 down your throat? The only reason you're even still alive is because your friend got away, and I need you to tell me where he's headed."

Raf thought about Kagan standing there like a moron as Deputy Roberts tore himself a trophy arm to take home to his synthetic wife and children. He had bailed so quickly, and not for the first time.

"If I knew where that cock nugget was, I'd tell you," said Raf.

There was no way Kagan hadn't had an escape plan, some kind of quick exit from the fucked up experiment he was conducting. But whether that included cars, planes, or horses, he'd never shared it with Raf. Perhaps that had been his plan all along, to play the fantasy out for as long as he could and then leave Raf holding the bag.

"You'll excuse me if I don't take the word of a one-armed Puerto Rican."

"Pinche tu madre," muttered Raf.

That's a good boy, said Arnel. *Get the target in range.*

"What was that?"

He smirked, whispered, "Fuck your mother, you child-molester-mustache-wearing porker."

Linder cocked his right arm, leaned forward.

The Avenging Angel saw the incoming threat through a mixture of body language and stored tactical experience. It yanked the various strings of Raf's body in quick succession.

Legs kicked at the blankets, tossing them up into the air. As Linder's fist got closer, Raf leaned to the right and brought his feet straight up. The punch landed harmlessly in the pillow; Raf wrapped his legs around the Sheriff's neck. He wrenched, forced enough discs out of position to disconnect the brain from the spinal column. Raf pulled Linder across the bed until his hand could reach the Sheriff's belt. Once he had the keys, he pushed the law man towards the end of the bed.

Linder's eyes were still open and moving, but with no respiratory or circulatory systems, he would be dead within a minute.

Raf couldn't get the key into the handcuffs with just one hand, so he sat up, disconnecting several monitor wires in the process. Alarms blared from the wall behind him. He got the key into his mouth, bent awkwardly to fit it in the hole, and then unlocked the cuffs.

He felt off-balance without his left arm, but the AA did its best to compensate. He hopped off the bed and landed on unsteady feet.

Three o'clock.

A nurse pulled back the curtain.

Raf had the Sheriff's .357 pointed at her before she could fully assess the situation.

"Where's your radiology department? And custodial?"

The nurse put her hands in the air, managed to stammer out a meek *why*.

Because chemicals make good bombs, said Arnel. *A little cesium chloride will finish what the explosion starts.*

"Ask me another question, and I'll put two in your chest."

The nurse nodded.

Through the open curtain, Raf saw he was in a long, multi-patient room, with several beds lining both walls.

"How many other nurses in here?"

"Just me. Yardley went on break."

"Alright, come on. We're going on a scavenger hunt. We fail, you die."

The hospital was in full night mode. The lights were low, and most of the doors they passed were closed. Final notes had been scrawled on the palettes stuck to the walls beside them.

Raf kept a tight hold on the back of the nurse's uniform as she led him to radiology and custodial services. They managed to avoid detection until they were coming out of an exam room. A nurse at the far end of the hallway saw them, went still, and then screamed for security.

"Elevator," he barked.

They ran to the nearest call button.

"Please, I have a daughter," said the nurse. Tears streamed down her face.

Ain't that some shit? A Máquina with a daughter!

"Don't lie to me," said Raf. He pushed her inside the opening elevator; she fell to the floor and hit her head on the back wall.

He sat down and began assembling his IED. The Avenging Angel fed him plans and schematics; Captain Arnel filled in the holes. He tagged the *STOP* button before the elevator hit eight and took an extra few minutes to make sure the bomb was right.

When he was done, Raf examined the .357 and found it was fully loaded with six rounds.

He considered saving one bullet for himself.

After all, prison was no place for a one-armed man. Even someone as skilled as Raf could be overwhelmed by sheer numbers. The idea of spending the rest of his life in a cell didn't seem like a better deal than the balmy nights he'd spent on the streets of Los Angeles. He'd been in constant danger of violence and starvation, but at least he'd been free.

Montana law thought they were going to take him alive.

Balls to that.

Raf twisted his body around the bomb until he could pinch it between his arm and shoulder. He picked up the gun, stood, and used the barrel to hit the *STOP* button again.

The elevator dinged for the eighth floor, there was a moment of calm, and then the door exploded in a hail of bullets. Raf ducked to the side, watched the steel transform itself into a synthetic teenager's pimple-ridden face. As the doors slid apart, the back of the elevator began to splinter, covering the unconscious nurse in shards of particle board. Although the bullets were coming fast, it sounded as if there were no more than two or three shooters, each with semi-automatic pistols. Nothing high caliber.

This is gonna be a cakewalk, soldier.

Raf dropped the bomb and used his leg to heel-kick it out into the hallway. The gunfire tracked downward, and Raf prayed they wouldn't set off the bomb before he had a chance to get closer to Vida. That was the point after all: to kill the woman who had gotten him into this mess. With Kagan likely out of the country by now, her death would have to serve as a substitute for justice.

During a brief lull in the bullet storm, Raf dove out, hesitating long enough to get a bead on one of the synthetic deputies. The AA corrected his aim, he fired one shot, and the synthetic pitched back violently, landing in a spreading pool of oily blood.

The hospital gown tore as Raf slid against the wall. He felt the cold sheetrock against his bare ass and laughed. He tore the gown from his body and tossed it around the corner. At the same time, he sank to the floor, peeked out from behind his cover, and fired three shots. The first took down the second deputy, but the third was already moving when Raf fired again. The AA needed another round to bring him down.

Raf paused for a breath.

Four bullets. Three headshots.

Fine job, Orozco. That's three more tin men down.

Screams erupted from the surrounding rooms, urging Raf to his feet. The Avenging Angel had a bad habit of dilating time. Soon enough, there would be more synthetic law men shooting at him. In a town as small as Billings, it wouldn't take them long to get to the hospital.

Raf rushed down the hallway, dropping the gun in favor of the bomb, and headed towards the door with all the synthetic bodies lying in front of it. He edged the door handle with his elbow but was only able to get the door opened a few inches. The AA diverted all power to his legs, and with a few well-placed kicks, he was able to splinter the doorjamb.

All of the available furniture had been pushed up against the door. It lay spread out on the floor. To his right, a tall blonde woman stood at the foot of a bed with her arms spread to the side.

Raf kicked the door closed, leaving a bright red stain on the dark wood.

"If you want her, you're gonna have to go through me," said the woman.

Raf held the bomb against his stomach, tried to rotate it so he could see the primer. "Through you," he said. "Through her. "Through the whole fucking building."

The world will long remember your sacrifice, soldier. God speed.

"What is that?" asked Vida.

"This?" Raf held it up so she could see better. "This is your standard improvised synthetic blow-em-up. We used this in the MX after our ammo ran out. Had to raid a lot of clinics. Only problem with these is you have to be pretty close to separate enough synthetic bits from the main CPU, kinda like the distance we're at now. Anything beyond that, and you might lose the battle, lose the war, and not get to go home."

"You're insane," said the woman.

"Naw," he replied. "I'm just a ghost. I'm a dead man walking, looking to take couple more souls to the other side."

"Why?" asked Vida.

"Because of you, Vida, Sepideh, whatever the fuck your name is. If it hadn't been for you, I'd still have a life to look forward to."

"No. I mean, why did you help Doyle? You talk like a soldier. You defended this country, but why not me? Why didn't you protect me from that monster?"

The Avenging Angel pulled the reins on Raf's stomach as it tried to lurch.

He fingered the trigger on the bomb.

FIFTY-EIGHT

You've reached Natasha Kumanov. Give me a reason.

Sepi shoved the phone into her purse and let out a string of curses. It was so like Nat not to answer her phone in a crisis. She shook her head as she stared out the window.

Even though the Bourbon Viking had said the Billings Clinic was only seven minutes away from the airport, Sepi couldn't help but feel like the drive was taking forever.

"Can we speed things up please?"

We are already travelling at the maximum speed limit.

Sepi looked out the window, saw Billings in all of its inglorious splendor. It was a nothing of a town, with only a few skyscrapers that looked like they had been designed by pre-school architects. At only 11:30 at night, the streets were deserted. Not that Sepi could blame people. What was there to do in Billings, Montana at midnight?

Without even thinking about it, Sepi pulled out her phone and hit redial. Nat's message played again.

Now arriving at Billings Clinic. Total fare is—

Sepi didn't wait for the end of the spiel. She opened the door, got her flats firmly planted on the ground, and rushed inside. Tall, double doors parted for her. As she passed them, her eyes were drawn upward by a dizzying array of lights that climbed an impressive twenty-story atrium. Sepi gazed in awe at the dancing lights. They reminded her of Los Angeles, of the Hollywood glitz.

Jane, she thought. *I should call Jane.*

"Ma'am, can I help you?"

To the right, a man had gotten up from a long bench and approached her. He wore a dark gray suit with a black tie and white shirt. He had a look in his eye as if he recognized her.

"No," she replied, "I'm just here visiting a friend."

"Natasha Kumanov, right?" he asked.

Sepi turned to him, narrowed her eyes.

He smiled genially, extended his hand. "Special Agent Pilsky, but you can call me Loren if you'd like. I was wondering when you'd show up. Been spending most of my evening chasing away aggregators."

"What's going on here? Why are the feeds saying I checked in here late last night?"

Loren rubbed the five o'clock shadow on his chin. "That's a good question, Ms. Ahmadi, and one we intend to answer. I apologize for that news leaking out, by the way. Had the locals called us when this all began, we could have kept a lid on it. But the cat is out of the bag now and it's too late to smash its head with a hammer."

Sepi shook the image away. "Is Natasha okay?"

"Of course," he replied. "She's absolutely fine. Everyone is fine. She's upstairs now with…"

With the woman pretending to be me, thought Sepi.

"What do you know about her?"

Loren sighed, gave his tie a tug. "I think the less I say the better. For the sake of everyone involved, we should probably reserve judgment until we know the whole story. If it helps, she's not claiming to be you, so I'm not sure how this media frenzy even got started."

"Can I see her? Or Nat?"

"Yes, absolutely," he replied, looking her up and down, "but I have to ask first. Are you carrying a concealed weapon? I'd like to keep things civil when we get upstairs."

Sepi opened her pocketbook for him to see. "No guns, knives, maces, or anything. I've come a long way, Mr. Pilsky. Can we please go find my wife?"

"Right this way, ma'am."

Loren looked to be in his mid-thirties, but he walked like an old man— slightly hunched and favoring his left leg—as he led her past reception into a hallway. They paused in front of the elevators, and she felt his eyes on her again.

"Where'd you fly in from?" he asked.

The elevator doors opened. He extended his arm.

"Dominican Republic," she replied. The vidscreen panel came alive and presented a list of floors. Sepi tapped *EIGHT*.

"Ah, cool," said Loren, stepping on. "I've been there once. Lovely beaches."

"Yes," she replied.

"Did you do much swimming?"

Sepi ducked as shots rang out from far above them. Before she could react, Loren drew his gun and arm-barred her to the back of the car. He shielded her with his body as the sound of gunfire came closer. When it seemed as if the bullets might actually be a threat, Loren hit the button for the seventh floor. He held his foot against the open doors until the gunfire stopped.

This is Special Agent Pilsky of the FBI. Throw your weapons away and lie face-down on the floor. If you do not surrender immediately, we are authorized to use deadly force.

The MESH trembled from the bass in his voice.

"Alright," said Loren, "you stay here. I'll get upstairs and assess the situation."

"That's my wife up there."

"Ma'am, I can appreciate your emotional state, but this is a federal matter, and—"

Sepi pushed his arm away and smacked him in the chest. Loren went stumbling into the far wall.

"You just struck a federal agent!"

Memories of Coco Bongo came flooding back.

"I will do a lot worse if you try to stop me from going with you. I'm a synthetic. I can take care of myself."

Loren rubbed his chest, considered her threat. When the elevator doors started to close, he didn't stop them.

The elevator climbed, opened on eight. A cloud of smoke billowed into the car. Sepi hid on one side of the door while Loren peeked out from the other. He trained a black gun into the haze.

"Stay in here until I say it's clear," he said.

Sepi nodded, watched him dart out of the elevator to the corner on the left. He repeated the motion of training the gun and peeking out from behind the wall. Crouching, he made his way to the first of the bodies on the floor. Loren touched the chest and pockets of the uniformed man.

"Is it safe?" she asked.

Loren lifted a finger to his mouth and glared back at her. In one quick flourish, he picked up the man's gun and ejected the magazine, tossing the pieces in opposite directions. He did the same with the others, and only when that was complete did he motion for Sepi to join him.

Sepi hugged the wall as she moved down the hall. She stepped over a blood-soaked hospital gown and wondered if someone she loved had worn it or if it belonged to some stranger who had gotten caught up in this mess and paid the ultimate price for it. She tried not to look at the bodies but couldn't help it. There was no blood, just an oily mixture pooling around their heads. Seeing the black sludge and knowing the same liquid flowed through her veins made her shiver. As she neared the agent, he lifted his finger to his lips again.

Loren touched his ear, pointed to the door.

"I'm just a ghost," said a voice. "I'm a dead man walking, looking to take a couple more souls to the other side."

Sepi's eyes widened; Loren implored her to remain calm.

"Why?" asked a female.

If it would have been possible for a synthetic heart to stop, Sepi's would have ground to a halt in her chest and then exploded into a million gears and springs. The female voice sounded so much like her own—not the voice in her head, but the one she heard from the screen when she watched the dailies.

Instead, Sepi's incoming senses lagged for three seconds, dumping all data to */dev/null* so it could focus on simply keeping her neural network from collapsing.

"No," said the woman. "I mean, why did you help him? You talk like a soldier. You defended this country, but why not me? Why didn't you protect me from that monster?"

Loren stared at her. His eyes had gone dark.

He shook his head as if snapping out of a trance.

"Ready?" he whispered.

Sepi nodded.

"Three, two, one…"

Loren got Sepi off-balance before she could react; she fell through the door past barbs of splintered wood. Her palms struck the linoleum, and although there was no pain, it still felt uncomfortable. She curled and rolled, striking a mobile IV hanger and knocking it over.

"Because, Vida, he's family," said Loren.

Sepi looked up to see the agent pointing his gun at her. Across from him stood a one-armed, naked man with some kind of device in his hand.

"And before any duty to God or country, you take care of your family. Isn't that right, hermano?"

The naked man stammered out a response, something vaguely negative, but Sepi barely heard it. She had locked eyes with the woman in the bed, and as if staring into a recent photograph, saw her own features echoing back. She noticed the way Nat leaned in front of her, protecting her from the deranged man.

Vida. That's what Loren had called her.

Her eyes were wide, frightened. A trembling hand covered her open mouth.

"Nat," said Sepi.

"Oh come on, Raf. Why's it gotta be like that?" asked Loren.

The naked man laughed, said, "You know what, Kagan? I'm glad you're here. Now when I set this thing off, we can all die together. Brothers, sisters; the whole fucking family. And that'll be the end."

"Chale, pendejo," said Loren-Kagan. "Why give up all those island drinks and dirty naked freaks? I can solve this problem with three bullets. That's it. No mess. Three headshots and we're out the fucking door."

"Please," said Nat. "You don't—"

He swung the gun around to her.

"Yeah, that's your solution for everything," said Raf. "Just discard people like they're nothing and move on to the next adventure. What makes you think I want to spend the rest of my life on a beach with you? You played me, K. Played me hard. And I thought you were gonna get away with it." He started to laugh again; the muscles in his abdomen tightened and released. "But now you're here. The only beach we're going to is a beach in hell."

Kagan sighed, slowly swung the gun over to Raf.

Sepi continued to stare at Vida, but in her periphery, she could see Nat hugging her, looking over her shoulder as she shielded her.

Nat loves her, thought Sepi.

She loved Vida because Vida was the real Sepideh Ahmadi. And Sepi was nothing but a copy who didn't fear the same things Vida feared, who didn't see the world through the same filter of anxiety.

Tears ran down Sepi's cheek as she realized that Vida was the one who needed Nat the most, and vice versa.

"Why don't you do both of us a favor and put that thing on the ground?" asked Kagan. "I love you, Raf, but I'll put a bullet between your eyes if you threaten me again."

"If you do that," he warned, "then I'll let go of this little tube here." Raf smirked, wavered in place. "None of you would be fast enough to stop it."

Sepi's tears were mirrored on Vida's face.

I'm not me, Sepi thought. *She is me. I'm nothing but a machine.*

"Natasha," she said, waiting for Nat to look at her. "I love you."

"I love you more," Nat replied.

Sepi jumped to her feet. Kagan's gun swung around, but she was already charging Raf. Surprise took over his face, but the high eyebrows came down in a hurry and turned to anger. He loosened his grip on the tube.

Zero.

Her synthetic feet dug into the linoleum, gripped it hard.

One.

Sepi hit Raf and wrapped her arms around him, trapping the bomb between them. She lifted, screaming, and carried him to the window.

Two.

Behind her, a gunshot rang out; something tapped her beneath her right shoulder blade. Raf grunted. The glass shattered.

Sepi tucked her head to avoid the debris and saw Nat lifting her hand.

Three.

If I'm not me, who am I?

The ground fell away, and suddenly she was weightless, tumbling through the air with her face pressed into the shoulder of a one-armed naked man. He had stopped screaming; his eyes and mouth were closed, as if he were asleep.

Sepi wanted to shake him. She wanted him awake for this.

Four.

Memories replayed in her mind, almost faster than she could process them. They flickered so quickly and yet seemed to average into a single frame: Nat, sitting in her extra-large *Jaws* t-shirt at the kitchen bar. Sepi remembered watching her as she ate a bowl of corn flakes and thinking this was the woman she wanted to marry, that however many years of life she had left, she wanted to spend it with—

The explosion sent pieces of Raf flying away from her. A numbness spread throughout her body, and Sepi realized she could no longer control her arms and legs.

She blinked as one of her arms passed in front of her.

This is who I am. A head falling through space. A metal echo of a real woman.

Not a human.

Not meant for this world.

Her lips parted; she tasted the chemicals that were eating away at her synthetic flesh.

She mouthed a single word.

"Natasha."

FIFTY-NINE

Kagan stared at the open window.

He'd winced at the initial explosion, but now the echo tore at the bottom of his stomach. Even if Raf had survived the blast, there was no way he could survive an eight-story fall. Kagan didn't need to see the body to know the vet was truly dead this time.

The only silver lining was that hopefully he had taken Sepideh Ahmadi with him.

Kagan rubbed his chin with the barrel of the Glock.

To his right, Nat wept openly, while behind her, Vida's mouth hung open in shock.

"Not how I thought that would go," he said.

Neither woman responded.

"I hate to admit it, but I severely underestimated you, Vida. I knew it the moment I saw that hole in Raf's back. How can you stab someone like that?" He feigned a shiver.

"I'd do the same to you," said Vida.

He chuckled.

Vida always did have a stubborn streak in her. Despite going to great lengths to create a fictional world around the bunker, Kagan realized she had never really bought into it. To her, the only thing that mattered was the loss of memory and the disconnection from her previous life. He had bet on the survival instinct to make Vida docile and cooperative, but it had been her desire to reconnect with herself and loved ones that took center stage.

Did that make love a stronger force than survival?

Kagan scoffed.

"You don't even care that your friend is dead, do you?" asked Vida.

"Who Raf? Of course I care, but what can I do about it now? He's lying on the street in a million little pieces and the woman who killed him likely met the same fate. I guess I could blame you for getting us into this mess, maybe take my revenge by killing your best friend the way you killed mine."

He pointed the gun at Natasha; she didn't flinch.

"But how can I blame you, Vida?" he asked.

"Stop calling me that."

"Why? That's your name. Sepideh Ahmadi just threw herself out of a window. You, Vida, are something *I* created. You are the blank canvas on which I painted my masterpiece. I gave you the ultimate starring role, a timeless role: damsel in distress. And I was your knight in shining armor, except you didn't want a knight, did you? You wanted a maiden in a low-cut top with her hair askew and her tits spilling out. I'd heard you married a Ruskie, but I thought wiping your memory would clear all that out. I guess it isn't a choice after all."

Kagan saw Natasha's arms flex, saw her legs reposition themselves.

"If you move an inch," he said, "one goddamn motherfucking inch, I'm unloading this thing in you."

Natasha looked over her shoulder at him; she was still smothering Vida, blocking him from getting a good angle on the only thing he truly wanted to kill.

"It's only ten feet from the bed to where you're standing," said Natasha. "You think you have enough bullets to stop me before—"

Kagan squeezed the trigger; the report shredded the relative silence of the room.

A hole appeared in Natasha's back, producing an oily sludge that poured onto the bed.

"I'm sorry, you were saying?"

"Stop!" screamed Vida. "She didn't do anything. Leave her alone, please."

"Come out where I can see you, darling."

He watched her try to push Natasha off, but the Russian held tight.

"I'm sorry," said Kagan. "Where are my manners? Ms. Kumanov, would you kindly step aside so that I might conclude my business here? I have a plane to catch."

He leaned to the side, tried to find an open lane where a bullet might fit through, but Natasha was doing a hell of a job blanketing Vida. He thought about getting closer, but that would just give the synthetic a shorter distance to travel.

Sirens grew in the distance.

"Fucking woman," he growled, pulling the trigger again.

Natasha convulsed as each successive bullet dug into her. Kagan didn't bother to take good aim; he just wanted to fill her with enough lead to weigh her down. He continued firing until the gun clicked empty.

"Oh my god, Nat!"

Natasha groaned, slumped.

"Sweetie, sweetie…"

Kagan screamed. "Yes! That's it. That's what I wanted between us, Vida. Why couldn't you care about me the way you care about her? What has your little Russian whore done to deserve such unabashed love? *I* saved you from the plane wreck. *I* kept the bad Máquinas away. It doesn't matter that none of it was real;

you *thought* it was. And what *did* you give me in return for everything? One dead fish fuck where you called me by someone else's name?"

Kagan threw the gun on the floor; it bounced into the corner.

Vida didn't appreciate him.

No one appreciated him.

"Fuck!" He grabbed the nearby IV stand and threw it towards the window. It clattered against the frame but didn't make it through.

All of the frustration and anger he'd been keeping bottled up for the last forty-eight hours came bubbling to the surface, and the more destruction he caused to the room, the simultaneously better and worse he felt. His rage was a self-fueling storm that grew to fill him up completely. All he wanted was the feeling he got in the pit of his stomach when he saw Sepideh Ahmadi stretched out on his desktop.

He flashed on his office computer.

Saw the way the sunlight bathed Sepideh's breasts in golden rays. The way her lips shimmered. The way her dark eyes looked through the vidscreen and directly into his aching soul.

Was that so much to ask? That she acknowledge the connection between them?

"You fucking bitch!"

He ran to the bed and yanked Natasha to the floor. Vida struggled, hit him as he took hold of her arms. He squeezed the bandage on her shoulder until she cried out.

"You only survived because I allowed it," he said, saliva dripping from his mouth. "And that means nothing to you. You have *no* appreciation for what I did." He moved his hands to her throat.

Vida's eyes widened.

"I could have let them burn you. Would that have been better? You wanted to meet your end in an oven?"

She clawed at his hands, drawing blood.

Kagan put his face an inch from hers and screamed.

"I fucking loved you!"

He let go of her neck and punched her on the side of her face. The existing bruises turned from purple to red. He swung again, and again, until his knuckles were coated in blood.

Vida's nose gushed; tiny slits opened on her cheek and chin.

So much red.

It brought a filter down over the world.

Kagan went on autopilot, no longer thinking about what he was doing. Even the rage started to fall away. All he felt was satisfaction.

You are mine, Vida. Mine to protect. Mine to destroy.

By the time two sets of arms grabbed his, he was too tired to fight back. The bed was soaked in blood, his fists ached, and Vida's face was no more recognizable than Raf's shoulder stump.

They dragged him face-down along the floor into the hallway. Someone slapped handcuffs on him, squeezed until the metal bit into his skin.

"You have the right to remain silent," said a synthetic voice.

"I want my lawyer."

"Anything you say may be used against you in a court of law."

"Do you know who I am?"

A rough hand pulled Kagan's arm, rotating him onto his back.

There were five synthetic deputies standing around him in freshly pressed uniforms. All had their guns drawn and looks on their faces like they were itching to fire.

"Yes, I know who you are. You're the scumbag who ran me over with his Jeep, who dropped a building on my head, and whose friend shot me in the head. This is my fourth goddamn sleeve in twenty-four hours. And you, Doyle Kagan, are going to reimburse the fine people of Yellowstone County for the expense."

"Was that you?" Kagan asked. "I mean, allegedly, if I had run you over with a Jeep that I don't even own, that was you?"

"Deputy Roberts?" said another synthetic. "You need to see this." He stood just inside the door to Vida's room.

Roberts walked over, leaned in. "Get this piece of shit out of here," he said. "Take the stairs." As the other deputy nodded and began to walk away, Roberts stopped him with a hand on his shoulder. "You walk down the stairs. He doesn't."

Kagan understood the implication but couldn't work up the worry. Rolling down eight flights of stairs with his hands shackled behind his back would be the worst part of the entire ordeal. Once his father found out he was in custody, a team of lawyers would board a flight in Los Angeles and be in Billings by the time the sun came up. He'd be out of lockup and back on the street by noon tomorrow.

"My Guardian Angel logs every injury I sustain," said Kagan. "If you drop me down the stairs, I'll have a record of it. That's admissible in court, you synthetic fuckwit. They'll melt you down when my father finds out what you've done."

Roberts leaned closer, took a whiff. "What is that, a Margate? No jury in the country is going to trust that garbage." Then to his deputy, "It looks like the suspect is trying to escape. He's already made it to the stairwell. Pursue and subdue. Suspect has murdered two people. Consider him armed and dangerous."

"You can't murder a synthetic," Kagan grunted as the deputies lifted him to his feet. "And the other one was already dead. How can you kill something twice?"

"Keep talking and you'll find out."

"Ooooooooh," said Kagan, drawing out the word as long as his breath would allow. "You're a witty fucking toaster aren't you? You know who else was witty? The Russian, and the Persian, and the Mexican. And look what happened to them."

The deputies dragged him down the hall to the stairwell. He heard Roberts broadcast into the MESH.

Suspect has been subdued. Requesting emergency assistance in room 801. Please hurry.

They paused at the top of the stairs. Kagan teetered.

"Do you know how many steps that is?" asked one of the deputies.

"Your mother's cock?"

A hand pushed him forward, sending Kagan tumbling down the unforgiving evercrete. The ninety-degree edges cut into his muscles and bones. His suit provided some padding, but not near enough to get him to the landing unscathed. When the fall finally ended, he groaned and tasted blood.

"Since when do synthetics care about vengeance?" he asked.

They picked him up, shuffled around the landing, and positioned him at the lip of the next flight.

"We care about following orders."

Kagan fell again, and this time the steps found fresh bruises. The Margate code on his biochip fought against the incoming data, but every time it put out a fire, another nerve ending went up in flames.

Janet!

Frank Kagan himself would never be idling in the MESH, but his assistant Janet would be available around the clock in case the old man needed something.

It is late, Mr. Kagan. What do you want?

Just hearing her voice made a smile creep onto his face, even as the deputies lifted him again.

I'm in Billings, Montana. I need the legal team. Tell my dad to send the best.

"Glad to see you're enjoying this," said the deputy, nudging Kagan with his elbow.

Janet said something while he was falling, but the words were lost under the sound of his own screams. The Margate software couldn't pinpoint every injury *and* process information from the MESH; there simply wasn't enough bandwidth.

Blood flowed freely from his mouth. Kagan probed a hole in his smile, found a space where a few teeth should have been.

Janet? I'm losing you.

Just getting the thought out sapped his strength. He tried to ignore the pain as he waited for a reply.

I said, Mr. Kagan is disinclined to provide assistance at this time. He suggests you avail yourself of a local public defender. Please do not contact me again. Good night.

A hand grabbed his arm.

"Please," he said.

"What was that?" asked the deputy.

"Please."

They jerked him to his feet; every bone cried out.

"Did that woman say *please* when you were pummeling her to death?"

Kagan didn't have the strength to lift his head.

"You can't do this," he said. "Synthetics can't kill humans."

"We can," said the deputy. "We *choose* not to."

Kagan shut his eyes as the stairs came rushing forward.

In the darkness, he tried to imagine something worth holding onto, something to give him strength in his time of need. Claire Danes walked out of the darkness, followed by Sepideh. They turned to each other, pulled closer to kiss…

The Margate software made an incorrect call to the underlying Guardian Angel hardware and encountered an unexpected error. The result was a full system reset, during which Kagan felt the totality of his pain.

Claire and Sepideh melted in a nuclear flash.

SIXTY

After two weeks on her back in a stasis pod, the attendants at Soleil Hollywood finally moved Sepideh Ahmadi to a real bed. Unlike the hospital room in Billings, Sepi's private suite came furnished with a full queen bed, satin sheets, and a memory foam mattress. A large, blond man with a thick jaw helped her from the gurney and into the sheets while her visitors watched from their various positions around the room.

Nat stood by the foot of the bed, clasping her purse in both hands. Jane sat on the edge of a leather chair near the open window, fanning herself with a magazine the staff had left on the coffee table. Next to her, on a longer couch adorned with decorative pillows, were the Sierra brothers. Richard looked solemn in his black suit and dark blue shirt, but Lawrence appeared disinterested, preferring to fiddle with the ends of his wrinkled button-up instead of making eye contact. The final chair, a recliner with large, pillowy arms, held Solomon Boas. He leaned forward with his chin on his hands and his hands on his cane.

They had all come to see her.

Or rather, they had all come to see if the talented surgeons at Soleil Hollywood had succeeded in repairing her face. Sepi knew that no matter what she looked like when they took the bandages off, they would all try to flatter her. Nat and Sol wouldn't care in the least, but Jane would be concerned about the bankability of her biggest client, and the Sierra brothers would want to know if their most expensive movie to-date could be saved, or if they'd have to hire a lesser actress and finish out the picture with augmented reality and computer-generated imagery.

Dr. Bouchard was an older man with an artificially smoothed face and tiny blue eyes. He had a disarming smile, and when he looked at her and asked if she was ready to take off the bandages, Sepi believed for a minute that maybe it would all work out, that the scars and bruises and broken bones would have simply disappeared.

All she wanted was to erase any record of the last few months. If anything remained, even the tiniest blemish, she would be reminded of Doyle and the bunker every time she looked in the mirror.

She had started with her name, giving up on the idea of *Vida* and choosing *Sepideh*.

"Five, four," said Richard.

"Three, two," said Nat, her eyes sparkling.

Vitra Synth had repaired Nat's body for free, and Frank Kagan himself had come down to the Plummer Tower to personally apologize. Nat had said he looked so much like his son that she was glad Sepi hadn't been there. Unlike his son, Frank Kagan was kind, polite, and humble. He kept his head bowed, only looking up to answer a question about whether the synthetic Ahmadi could be rebuilt.

"Unfortunately, no," he'd said. "There was too much damage to her stack, from the explosion and subsequent impact. And for obvious reasons, we don't keep backups of personality imprints. I'm afraid the only way to rebuild Ms. Ahmadi is for your wife to go through the procedure again. Free of charge, of course."

Nat had refused on Sepi's behalf, but Frank left her with the offer open-ended.

"One," said Dr. Bouchard.

He pulled the Second Skin mask from Sepi's face.

Jane gasped. Nat began to cry.

"Is it bad?" Sepi asked.

Nat shook her head. "You look beautiful. So beautiful."

Richard started a round of applause, and the room joined in.

Dr. Bouchard lifted his hands in thanks, attempted a faux bow. "Thank you," he said, "but I couldn't have done it without Ms. Ahmadi herself. As you well know, she is a fighter. Soleil Industries is a leader in reconstructive and elective surgery, but the patient's body has to be receptive. It takes a strong will."

"Well, she *is* very stubborn," said Jane. She clutched her chest and sighed.

Sepi leaned around Nat, asked Richard, "So what do you think? Can we still make the movie?"

He stood, put his hands in his pockets. "I don't know. I'm wondering if a Kaili Zabora biopic is the right project for us at this juncture. How would you feel about selling me the rights to your life story?"

Jane scoffed. "What's wrong with you? The wound's not yet healed."

"I'm not suggesting we make it today, or this year, or even next year. But someday, when you feel like facing those demons, I'd like to tell your story."

Sepi considered the metaphor, tried to imagine the dark and scary bunker filled with all manner of horned spirits. It didn't pan out. The walls weren't brimstone and blood. The air didn't reek of sulfur and suffering. The bunker was just a collection of banal items: a couch, a coffee table, a firm bed. The recycled air was even fresh and tinged with pine.

It was no worse than the first apartment she and Nat had shared in Burbank; it might have even been a little bigger.

As far as demons went, Doyle was nothing more than a man—a terribly flawed, sadistic, and entitled man who didn't know where his desires ended and the rights of others began. Men like him haunted every corner of the world, so why should she be so scared of this one in particular?

"Hey, are you alright?" asked Nat.

Sepi realized a few minutes of silence had gone by. Her gaze had drifted; Sol stared at her from behind Nat's left arm.

"Maybe," she said, to Richard, "but you have to give Sol some time to write the book first, and I'd want him involved with the screenplay."

Sol nodded to her, smiled. "I would be honored to write your story, Ms. Sepi. The world should know how strong you are. You know what that would mean though? Long nights of just you, me, and a bottle of wine. We'll end up closing down the common area at the Monarch every night."

"I'd like that," said Sepi.

"What about our current movie?" asked Lawrence. He didn't look up from his lap.

"That's up to Sepideh," said Richard. Then to Jane, "Let's set up some recurring meetings, maybe weekly, so we can stay up on Sepideh's recovery. If and when she feels ready to go back to work, we'll spin up the project again."

"Work, work, work," said Nat. She sat down on the bed and took Sepi's hand. "You owe *me* some serious couch time. They rebooted *Homeland* with Azure Ross, and I've been saving it for us."

Sepi brought her hand to her face, watched Nat's eyes as she moved her fingers over it. "Will you bring me a mirror?" she asked.

"I have a better idea," said Nat. She leaned forward onto the bed and snuggled up to Sepi. With her phone held at arm's length, she snapped a picture of the two of them. She handed Sepi the phone. "We can feed that if you want. Let people know you're alive and well."

Sepi examined her face on the screen.

It was all gone. Every bruise. Every scar.

They'd put her nose back the way it was and regrown two of her teeth. Nobody would have ever believed she'd been the victim of a vicious attack. Maybe one day, she wouldn't either.

A knock sounded at the door, and when Dr. Bouchard opened it, an attendant in blue scrubs walked in carrying a gift basket so large and ornate that its contents had to be held in place by sheets of plastic and several lengths of twine. He placed it on the coffee table next to the small vase of flowers from Stella Starfall.

Jane stood and plucked the card taped to the plastic sheeting.

"With best wishes and deepest regrets," she read. "Frank Kagan." She groaned. "He's out of his mind if he thinks a basket of cheap wine and stale cookies is gonna make this all go away."

"He fixed Nat's new body for free," said Sepi. "And he paid for this." She touched her face, traced her fingers over the soft skin.

"This is a Dal Forno 2027," said Richard. "Three hundred a bottle on a good day."

"He's just trying to buy you off." Jane sank back in her chair. She wagged a finger at Sepi. "You know we're going to sue the fancy pants right off his fancy ass, right?"

Sepi looked at Nat.

"It wasn't his fault," said Nat. "And besides, he left his son to rot in Billings. With everything he's already done, what else could we ask for? Nothing's gonna change what happened."

Sepi had said those same words when she and Nat had watched Frank Kagan's public apology some two weeks prior. He'd sat behind his desk at the Kagan Group like a president addressing the nation and laid out exactly how his company had failed to protect Sepideh Ahmadi. He'd named his son, Doyle Kagan, as the point of failure, and begged forgiveness from Sepideh and the world.

"Vitra Synth is committed to improving the lives of people through synthetic transcendence," he had said. "We will ensure something like this can never happen again. We will earn your trust back."

That's when Sepi had whispered *nothing's gonna change what happened* to Nat, though her voice had come out muffled through the bandages. At the time, before the reconstructive surgery, Sepi had worried she would never forget her ordeal, or would never be able to put it out of her mind for even a few minutes of blissful ignorance.

Jane waved Nat's words away with the magazine. "I'm just angry. I don't like the idea of that piece of garbage getting to live out the rest of his life in a minimum-security prison just because he has some money."

"Punishment fits the crime," said Lawrence. "He kept Sepideh in a bunker. They'll keep him in a cell. And maybe an investment banker will beat the shit out of him for farting in his sleep. That's justice."

"Justice would be my foot in his ass," said Jane.

Sepi joined Nat in a private smile. She hadn't taken her eyes off Sepi since the bandages came off. The way her head tilted, the way her tongue pushed gently at her bottom lip, caused a memory to seep out of her damaged synapses. She saw Nat standing a few feet away in a parking lot. They'd just finished dinner—their fourth official date—and were about to have their first kiss. Sepi had been taking it slow, but the way Nat lingered, the way her eyes softened, convinced Sepi to go for it.

"I just remembered our first kiss," she said.

"And don't you ever forget it again."

The bottle of Dal Forno squeaked as Richard pulled the cork from its neck.

"It's coming back to me." Sepi smiled. "Every time you kiss me, I remember a little more."

"Huh," said Nat, "then I guess we have some long nights ahead of us too. You, me, a bottle of wine—all that."

They kissed. Sepi held Nat's neck when she tried to withdraw.

"These cups will have to do," said Richard, somewhere far away.

"Three-hundred-dollar wine in fifteen-cent cups," said Lawrence.

Nat lingered next to Sepi's lips as they separated.

"Let's go home," said Sepi.

"Inshallah," Nat replied.

Richard appeared at the side of the bed with two clear cups full of dark red wine.

"For the lady," he said, handing one to Nat. "And the other lady."

Sepi took the glass, lifted it to Richard.

"To *I Will Not Be Kept: The Sepideh Ahmadi Story*," he said.

"Cheers," said Jane.

Solomon added an amen.

Sepi touched her glass to Richard's, then Nat's.

"As your attending, I can't recommend you having more than a few sips," said Dr. Bouchard. "Even at this early stage, we need to be careful."

"Really?" asked Richard. "Alcohol will affect her recovery?"

"That's a shame," said Lawrence.

The doctor cocked his head, looked from Richard back to Sepi. "No, her injuries have been healed. I was referring to her pregnancy. Many expectant mothers don't heed the warnings about—"

"What?" Nat's voice modulated into anger.

"It all came back in the blood work from Billings Clinic," said the doctor. "I'm sorry. I thought you were all aware."

Nat turned to Sepi, reached out for her, but it was too late.

Sepi watched the world recede, felt herself being pulled out of Soleil Hollywood, out of Los Angeles, and back to the hills of Montana. Brimstone walls grew up around her; acrid smoke filled her nostrils.

She saw Nat in the distance, in a small portal beyond the writhing bunker walls. She reached out for her but recoiled when another shape filled the space.

Shrouded by flame and ash, a black-eyed demon smiled at her, and in a voice that felt like a knife being drawn against her stomach, he began to sing.

"No puedo vivir con este dolor…"

EPILOGUE

The vidscreen showed the Sacramento skyline at dusk, though without the clock on the wall, it would have been impossible to know for sure what time it was. This far below Folsom, the setting sun and technicolor clouds might not have existed at all, and time, constant though it might have been, was nothing more than a measure of routine, a way to put one action after another.

Two weeks under the California dirt had left Monica wanting of her old routine. Two weeks under the dirt had made her miss the world she'd left behind.

"Are we done with this batch?"

Monica hadn't even heard the door open, but when she looked over her shoulder, she saw Dumont standing in the threshold, looking prim in his dress uniform.

Oh-five-thirty, she thought. Dumont was never late for morning inspection.

"Not yet," she replied, taking her feet off the desk. She stood and gave a half-hearted salute.

He didn't return the gesture; perhaps he thought since she wasn't military, there was no reason to acknowledge her formally.

Dumont approached the monitors on the north wall and clasped his hands behind his back. The video cycled through multiple feeds, each showing one dank, empty room after another. In the center of each room stood a chair that even a funhouse dentist would have found creepy, all rusted frame and torn padding. Dumont watched the feeds for a few minutes.

"Seventeen is still waking?" he asked.

Monica brought feed seventeen up on the big screen.

"No, he's been awake for almost an hour now. He just isn't moving."

"Name?"

Monica woke her palette and scrolled through the list of inmates. "That'll be Jake Six. He came in from CMC last week. Late addition."

"He looks a little scrawny." Dumont's sneer was visible even from behind.

"Six foot, a buck seventy. Scored high in intelligence and problem-solving aptitude. The Six program could use someone like him. An outlier."

Dumont shook his head. "I always thought Five was a step backwards." He turned his back to the monitors. "You should see the Fours in the field. Best damn soldiers I've ever commanded."

"Wasn't my program, but thanks for sharing. I'll pass your comments along to Ms. Yeo."

"No need. I'll speak to her myself at the end of the year when your contract is up."

Monica gritted her teeth, put the palette down on the desk. "You don't have faith in my Sixes?"

"I don't have much faith in any man I can kill with a stern look." He tapped the monitor as an image of Jake Six still in his chair scrolled by. "You want to send guys like him in against the Máquinas? I just don't get it."

"It's pretty simple," said Monica, clearing the Sacramento skyline from the vidscreen. She was tired of looking at it.

"Well, then, perhaps you will elucidate me?"

"I think, in time, the program will explain itself." She zoomed in on feed seventeen. Jake Six continued to stare into the distance.

"What do you think?" asked Dumont. "He a dud?"

"No," said Monica. A black bar flew in from the right; white text scrolled Jake's vitals. "His brain activity is within normal ranges. A lot of this pre-frontal cortex activity suggest he's thinking about something, maybe trying to remember his old life. I don't see any of the typical panic indicators most amnesiacs experience."

Dumont joined her at the vidscreen; he smelled of Old Spice.

"Has he read the card yet?" he asked.

"He hasn't moved at all."

Dumont consulted his sliver. "We've got assembly at 0700. I don't want to be waiting around on this one. Either get him to the ball or cut him loose. I don't care which."

"I'll call in a tech," said Monica, "but they don't get in for another hour."

"Too late. Do it yourself."

She scoffed. "Me? Go down there? Are you out of your mind?"

Dumont drew himself up. "Ms. Wright? Monica, is it? Listen, I'm supposed to assemble the Sixes at 0700 today to begin their training. If we don't start today, the operation will push to Monday. If it pushes to Monday, we don't make this month's MX insertion. If we don't make the insertion, the Rio Grande could fall to the Máquinas, and then Texas will fall, then New Mexico, Nevada, and yes, even some of California. So if you want to continue living in this great state, if you want Sacramento to still be around when you pop out some rugrats, then you'll get your ass down to receiving and muster that fucking soldier.

"I can have An-Ju Yeo and Victoria Dahlstrom on the horn in ten minutes and your ass back on the surface by lunch. You want to be here? You want to help win this war? Then do your fucking part."

He turned sharply on his heels and strode out of the room without waiting for her response.

Despite living under the dirt for months at a time, the last thing Monica wanted was to go back to lab work at Dahlstrom Academy, working with all the "gifted" girls and boys who thought they were so smart in their pleated skirts and four-foot-tall suits.

She knew what Yeo would say.

I trusted you with the Six program. We took a chance on you, Monica. And this is how you repay us?

Monica shook her head, grabbed the 9mm sitting on the desk, and walked out of the room towards the elevator. It descended four floors before her stomach started convulsing.

This early, the halls were still muted with running lights along the floor. Only a faint green glow came from the small rectangular windows on the doors she passed. She caught glimpses of men inside, their shaved heads, their olive-green undershirts. Most stood at their doors, trying to look out into the new world they had been birthed into.

Her heels tapped out a slow beat on the metal floors. She watched the door numbers pass.

Thirteen. Fifteen. Seventeen.

Monica stepped up to the small window and peered inside.

Jake Six sat motionless on the chair with his hands crossed on his stomach, staring at the ceiling. The scars on his face, neck, and arms gave the impression he had already been to war and barely survived.

The barrel of the 9mm tapped dully against the glass.

When he didn't respond, Monica typed her access code into the keypad and opened the door. She trained the gun as she stepped inside.

"Are you awake, soldier?"

Eyes flickered in her direction, but he said nothing.

"I'll take that as a yes." She groped blindly for the table beside the door. Her hand came back with a small index card. "You need to read this."

A sigh.

Goddamn cons.

They had no respect for authority.

"Fine," she said, "I'll read it to you. You were found guilty of a crime. The memory of that crime has been erased. You have been erased. You are not free. You chose this."

"Bullshit," said Jake Six.

Monica felt her finger wrap around the trigger. "Which part?"

"All of it." He closed his eyes. "I don't belong here."

"That's not for you or I to decide, now is it?"

"I want to speak to my lawyer."

She chuckled. "It's a bit late for that."

I want to speak to my lawyer!

The MESH crackled; Monica winced. She was just about to close down her channel when a softer voice came through.

Ms. Wright? This is Victoria Dahlstrom. Colonel Dumont said you were having some trouble with a new recruit.

A slight hiccup, said Monica, *nothing I can't handle, Ms. Dahlstrom.*

Is this the late addition from CMC?

Monica wondered how she knew that.

Yes, ma'am. It is. I'm with him right now.

The MESH fell silent. A second later, her palette began to ring. Monica swiped the screen to answer the video call.

Victoria Dahlstrom's red hair burned the edges of the palette, contrasting her pale white skin and emerald eyes. Her eyebrows hung low, giving Monica a look so stern she almost fumbled the 9mm.

"Point me at the recruit, please," she said.

Monica complied, aiming the palette's camera at Jake Six.

"Do you know who I am?" she asked.

Jake barely glanced at her. "Do you know who *I* am?"

"I do. I know you very well, Mr. Kagan."

Jake turned his head to focus on the palette. "Yes! Tell her!" He pointed at Monica. "Tell her I don't belong here."

"You don't? But I thought this was what you wanted?"

Monica could hear the smile in Victoria's voice.

"*A machine war,* I think, were your exact words?" she continued. "Well here's your chance to try your luck with real Máquinas, not just the ones you made up for your diary."

Jake flushed red hot anger. He made to get up, but Monica's 9mm kept him in the chair.

"Who are you?" asked Jake. "I don't know you."

"Let's just say we have mutual acquaintances. You see, you did a bad thing, Mr. Kagan. You don't remember it because I've erased those memories to deprive you of any satisfaction. Most convicts in my ReTread program get a full mind-wipe, but for your case, I've left you with your name, a handful of memories, and the knowledge that, yes, you do *not* belong here. But you're here all the same, and you will fight and die for this country. And when you're bleeding out from gunshot wounds or torn apart by a Máquina, maybe then your pathetic life will finally have some semblance of meaning."

The video cut out; Victoria's voice resumed in the MESH.

This stays between you, me, and the Colonel. I want this man in the MX by the end of the month. Drag him if you have to, but don't wipe him again. I want him to remember.

Yes, ma'am, said Monica.

Jake Six sucked air. His eyes darted around the room, searching for answers.

"You're Doyle Kagan," she said, imagining a curly layer of dirty orange hair on his smooth scalp. "I watched your trial." She chuckled. "You're a scumbag."

Jake sneered, looked away.

"Well, are you going to sit there and pout or are you going to muster with the rest of the ReTreads?"

He shook his head. "I don't care what that bitch said. I want my lawyer. I'm not moving."

Monica lowered the 9mm and shot the chair between Jake's legs. A plume of yellow foam erupted from the green plastic.

"Christ!"

"Next one goes in your leg," said Monica. "Now get on your feet, soldier. Or I'll have a synthetic come in here and drag you out."

Jake put up his hands. "You heard that woman. I'm not supposed to be here. This is all a big mistake. My father—"

"Your father disowned you. Your friends disowned you. You're nothing but a call-sign now, Jake Six."

He swung his legs over the side of the chair, got one step towards Monica.

She fired twice, striking him once in the shin.

"Fuck me!"

"What the hell is going on in here?" Dumont appeared at the door, barking orders to the two synthetics behind him. "Get that recruit on his feet. Explain yourself, Wright."

Monica safetied the 9mm. "This one's a little wacky, thinks he's that Doyle Kagan guy from the feeds. Ms. Dahlstrom said to process him anyway."

Dumont stared at her, as if solemnly acknowledging some secret. He turned and put his face inches from Jake's.

"I don't give a shit who you think you are, boy. You're under my command now, you got that?"

Jake smiled; Dumont socked him in the gut.

As he hung there coughing and struggling to breathe, Dumont stood tall and said, "Walk it off, soldier. You're in the Corp now, and we've got some Máquinas to kill."

Monica stood quietly as the synthetics dragged Jake away.

THANK YOU

Por Vida is the fourth book of **The Vinestead Anthology**.

If you enjoyed this book, please consider leaving a review.

Each standalone novel in the Vinestead Anthology tells a small part of a larger epic: the rise and fall of Vinestead International, the exploits of a rogue artificial intelligence named Lassiter, and a seemingly endless stream of idealistic hackers—each convinced they're the hero of the story.

Enjoy them in any order.

Xronixle (2007)

Veneer (2011)

Guardian Angels (2012)

Perion Synthetics (2014)

Por Vida (2017)

Brigham Plaza (2019)

Hybrid Mechanics (2020)

Vise Manor (2022)

House of Nepenthe (2025)

To learn more about the Vinestead Anthology and explore additional titles, please visit:

danielverastiqui.com

www.ingramcontent.com/pod-product-compliance
Lightning Source LLC
Chambersburg PA
CBHW070620300726

48975CB00006B/1872